STARS

TO

LIGHT

THE SKY

DENNIS R CROCKER

STARS TO LIGHT THE SKY

DENNIS R CROCKER

MILO LUI & OZZIE PUB

Milo Lui & Ozzie Pub

Copyright © 2023 by Dennis R Crocker

First edition published by Milo Lui & Ozzie Pub February 2023

This is a work of fiction. It deals with subject matter that may be difficult. The author asks if you need help to seek it out. There are many forms of help available. Names, characters, businesses, places, events, locales, and incidents are either the products of the author's imagination or used in a fictitious manner.

Copy edit by Penina Lopez

Cover and banner design by Vanessa Mendozzi

Audiobook narrated by Sierra Kline

ISBN: 9798987065709 (Hardcover); ISBN: 9798987065716 (Paperback);

ISBN: 9798987065723 (Ebook); ISBN: 9798987065730 (Audiobook)

Library of Congress Control Number: 2022919215

Printed in the United States of America

Milo Lui & Ozzie Pub

City of publication: Monmouth, Maine

https://dennisrcrocker.com

CHAPTER ONE

SILVER EARRINGS

T hick fog saturated the air on Daizon's 4:00 a.m. run. It clung to the mountain forest and rested on top of the road as he scratched loose bits of sand with each step. It was an eight-mile morning, four up and four down. He ran to stay in shape; he ran because it helped him zone out. Daizon closed his eyes and imagined the wet haze cleansing him. He pushed himself faster. Too many beers the night before had his head pounding, and leftover beer bile jetted into his mouth as he sprinted the last few hundred yards to the edge of his driveway.

After a quick purge in the woods, Daizon brushed his teeth, gargled his mint mouthwash, took a shower, and dressed in his army fatigues, minus the uniform shirt. No longer a part of the military, he wore jeans mostly, but for fishing and hunting, his fatigue cargo pants were both functional and comfortable. He drank his orange juice as a couple of eggs sizzled in one pan and half a dozen sausage links browned in another. Without thinking, he refilled Holly's food dish. He glanced around the empty house, closed his eyes, and shook his head.

Daizon placed his rinsed-off dish and silverware into his dishwasher and walked to the garage entryway. A few careful twists of his feet kept his mud-caked black army boots from spilling debris until he stepped into the garage. With a heavy boot brush, he scuffed the mostly dried mud from his boots.

He grabbed his dark olive military parka with its soft-shell lining from its hook. Then he retrieved his jungle hat, two trolling rods, a tackle box, and a fishing net. It was lighter outside than it had been during his run but still dark as he followed the trail from his house down the mountain to the lake.

Every footstep and noise seemed magnified in the morning's quiet. When he stepped onto his dock, Daizon's fifteen-foot deep-V aluminum fishing boat rocked and butted against the hard foam spacers that kept it from hitting the hard wood. Fog hovered above the lake at about the height of the boat. A loon hollered and splashed somewhere not too far away as Daizon set his gear inside the boat. It was a perfect morning for fishing, and Dave was missing out. Kyle probably would have come, but he didn't want to go there with him just yet.

Daizon smirked as he thought of sending Dave a picture of his first trout of the day. He couldn't imagine having to fly out to California as often as Dave did, but Dave seemed to thrive on it. He was a brain surgeon and had been called out the prior morning for an emergency. Dave was networking his way into opening a practice on the East Coast near Bar Harbor with one of his surgeon friends, but they hadn't finalized anything yet.

Daizon unlocked the case built into the rear of the boat for access to the battery packs and checked the power levels before hooking up the electric trolling motors and sitting in the captain's chair behind the steering wheel. The electric motors hummed to life and pushed the boat over the glasslike surface into the fog. Water splashed against the sides of the boat and rebounded outward behind him in V-wave formations. The barely audible hum of the motors and the whoosh of the water created a soothing sound Daizon enjoyed. This was his escape.

Two Mooselook wobblers—the Wonder Bread, which was white with speckled pink and blue spots, and the original copper—dangled from the trolling rods. Flicking the silver levers on the trolling reels, he let the first three colors, white, dark gray, and aqua blue, of the heavy line roll out beneath his thumb. The trout in early spring tended to be nearer the top of the lake. He kept a slight pressure on the line to keep it from unspooling into a knot. The tactile pressure of the line threading out left a smooth tickling sensation. The wobblers danced behind the boat and sank out of sight. Clicking the silver levers, Daizon tested the drag on each. They both clicked, and the ends of the rods curled and danced with the wobblers.

Opening another case built into the boat, Daizon grabbed a bottle of water from the cooler inside. He glanced up to where his Maine mountain getaway should have been, but he saw only patches of shadowed forest. The fog had risen enough for him to see the banks of the forested shoreline but not much else. He felt the morning sun trying to burn through the low cloud. A glance at his watch told him it was only six in the morning.

Tonya, his agent, had given him a script to read, *Prime Suspect*, but he couldn't bring himself to read it after burying his most loyal friend. He drank and watched several episodes of *Forged in Fire* instead. If he got the part, it would be his transition into more complex characters and Academy Award–type roles. He had finished shooting *A Dragon's Rage*, the second installment of *Into the Dragon's Den*, five months ago. He'd been a month into shooting when he caught Kyle with his girlfriend.

A couple of months after that, Tonya convinced him to sign up on Psyche and Eros, a dating site built for professionals who wanted to be discreet in their search for true love. After answering hundreds of questions and verifying all his information, he told Tonya to delete the account. Daizon shook his head and laughed. As much as he wanted to believe in true love, his experiences told him it was a lie, a fairy tale beyond his reach. He didn't blame the women he ended his relationships with—he knew he was the one with the issues. It felt good to pretend he was normal for a while, even if he knew how things would end.

A ripping bounce yanked the trolling rod tip with the Wonder Bread wobbler. Daizon tripped out of his thoughts, grabbed the rod, and felt the heaviness tugging at the other end. He slowed the motor, guided the boat, and reeled.

Flashes of silver and black spots twisted in the water. A short while later, Daizon had the net dipping into the water, and he scooped out a very respectable salmon. After removing the hook, Daizon snatched a quick selfie with his catch before letting it back into the water.

He increased back to trolling speed, reset his rod, and sent the photo to Dave. Then he remembered Dave was three hours behind, probably sleeping after surgery. The fog had risen past the treetops and started dissipating. Rays of sunlight burned through several areas and shone like multiple beams of heavenly light. Trying to decide whether he should taunt Dave with an accompanying text, Daizon squinted as light flashed into the corner of his eye.

Then his phone vibrated with a new text from Dave. *Nice salmon. Sorry I had to cancel. I thought you might stay home. I'm glad you went. Good luck!*

Light flashed into the corner of his eye again. He searched the shoreline, maybe a hundred yards away, inside a tucked-away cove for the source, but he didn't see anything other than several strands of tall grass on the gravel shore and a thick forest budding to life.

When he was about to turn away, a beam of light burst from above and flashed off something on the shoreline.

Curiosity getting the better of him, Daizon reeled in his fishing lines and headed toward shore for a better look. A loon hollered maybe forty feet away and startled Daizon. He smirked, shook his head, and turned his attention back to the flash. Daizon lifted the propellers from the water and let the boat bend short reeds of grass out of its way as it crunched onto the gravel shoreline.

Attached to the flash was a pale blue, fallen-angel type figure with long black hair. Daizon searched the shoreline for signs of anyone. Besides a few squirrels somewhere just out of sight scurrying around, the loons, and a few morning birds, everything seemed quiet.

Daizon stepped out of his boat and tugged it up on shore enough so it wouldn't float away. He scanned the area again. The only thing there was a ghostly, bruised, naked woman lying on small gravel stones several yards away from the shore. Her head was tilted at an awkward angle, with her long black hair splayed out away from her face, fanlike on the ground.

His mind flashed to another woman staring up at him with dead eyes, one he had killed. She had a strong nose and similar complexion, copper brown turned to a ghostly blue. Daizon shook away the image. Then her chest rose ever so slightly and fell. She was alive.

He acted. In the middle of nowhere, it would take a helicopter several minutes to get there. His bet was that she didn't have that long. Consequences be damned, he removed his jacket and draped it over her. He wanted to move her as little as possible, knowing he could do more damage than had already been done. Taking off his boots, he slid his stockings over her feet and put his boots back on. Inspecting her head, he saw blood pooling down over a rock she must have struck it on. He removed his T-shirt and carefully slid it behind her head, wrapping it as a makeshift bandage. He called emergency services. As he spoke with them, he gathered as much dry tinder as he could and sparked a smoky fire with his lighter. He didn't smoke, but he gripped the lighter and was thankful he always carried it with him. Luckily, there was no wind to speak of, so the smoke drifted straight up. It would help the helicopter find them and warm her at the same time.

Daizon finally remembered Dave was still up. He called him to tell him about the situation and what he had done. "Is there anything else I should do?"

Daizon checked her pulse and breathing. It had grown stronger, and she had already warmed some. He reported the information to Dave. With what seemed a smile on the other end of the line, Dave said, "You may have saved her life."

Inspecting the silver earring that wrapped around her ear, he noticed some etching. Leaning closer, Daizon saw the name "Amia," circled by an etched heart. "Keep fighting, Amia. Help is on the way." He gripped her hand and held it. "Keep fighting."

CHAPTER TWO

ALIVE

A wareness nudged her with the soft rustling of fabric. A steady-paced beep entered her dark but expanding world. The fresh scent of flowers and a slight pressure tickled her nose and throat. Metal scraped over metal, and the world beyond her heavy eyelids brightened. A smile grew as the soft light warmed her skin. The first thing she blinked into focus was a bouquet of pink, purple, red, and yellow with shafts of green and patches of white. The room was white except for a thick-bodied nurse in pink at the window. A few quick pulls on a string split the shades, and sunlight flooded the room with warmth she readily welcomed. A few blinks helped her eyes adjust to the new brightness. The nurse, fortyish, with dark brown eyes and brown hair cut to her shoulders, noticed her and smiled. She tried saying hello to the nurse, but it came out as a pained, grunting type noise.

An itch grew from a slight pressure inside her nose and throat. The back of her head pulsed and sent throbbing waves through her entire mind. A wrap circled her head, leaving her face uncovered. Her head felt like a warped balloon. She tried scratching the tickling itch at her nose, but the foreign appendages at her sides tingled with heaviness. It was all she could do to lift her hand to a hover. A black cuff buzzed to life and strangled her upper arm. Panic sped its assault on her mind. Hoses and lines attached to her body at various points, then strung out to machines and liquid-filled bags. Suddenly she felt them snaking inside her, the itch. Something gripped her calves, squeezed and released. Glancing down, she saw her legs under a blanket. They seemed as though they belonged to somebody else. Tears fell. Her mind raced to comprehend, to remember, to remember anything.

A gentle voice reached for her. It was the nurse in the pink. "It's okay. You're safe, Amia." The nurse smiled while repeating the soft words. "You're okay. You're safe."

Terror slipped back to a teetering edge.

Amia? She ran her name through her mind. It felt right, but she couldn't be sure. Maybe this woman could tell her more. Her name tag read, KELLIE.

Kellie reassured Amia with a squeeze of her hand. A few more assurances, and she was off to get the doctor.

The walls in her new world pressed inward in a warped sensation. Her window to the outside grew smaller as some force pushed it away. *Amia?* Her name sounded familiar but foreign. *I'm Amia?* The terror clawed its way back into her mind. *I'm Amia.* No matter how many times she sparked the flint to the kindling, nothing ignited.

After what seemed like an eternity of waiting, two doctors strode in with easy gaits. They both wore amiable smiles and had slicked-back hair. The shorter one had salt-and-pepper hair, while the other had black wavy locks. The shorter one stepped forward while the other observed and glanced at a uniformed officer standing at the door. *Why is an officer at the door?* Both men seemed somewhere in their late thirties, maybe early forties. The taller one had handsome features and tanned skin, while the shorter one, who took charge, had a thinner build, big ears, and seemed more approachable. He said, "Hello, Amia. My name is

Dr. Hempshire. My friends call me Dr. Hemp." His smile faded with her lack of a reaction. Approaching her, he motioned back with an open hand. "And this is my colleague Dr. Avendale. We've been discussing your case." Dr. Avendale smiled and nodded.

The two doctors exchanged a glance, almost as if Dr. Hemp was deferring to Dr. Avendale, but it was Dr. Hemp who stepped forward. He removed a penlight from his chest pocket and flashed the light into Amia's eyes. "Look straight ahead." He began the search for her mind. "Follow my finger with your eyes. Don't move your head."

As she blinked away the white spots corrupting her vision, she noticed Dr. Avendale studying her. He smiled as if to say she was going to be okay. Then he glanced around the room at the various bouquets of flowers. The slightest of smiles tugged at his lips. Her attention swung back to Dr. Hemp as he placed his hand near hers and said, "Squeeze my hand."

Amia tried lifting her heavy arm. Noticing her struggle, Dr. Hemp placed his fingers into her palm. He said, "It's okay. Try again." He smiled, but his brows told a different story as they furrowed ever so slightly toward Dr. Avendale. Amia felt his fingers against her palm, but coiling any type of grip around them was beyond her. She searched his body language for clues to his thoughts. He smiled, and they repeated the process on the other side. His posture relaxed as he probed her extremities. He said, "I want you to blink when you feel pressure. Okay?"

A fiery, needlelike tingle burned in her limbs, especially inside her legs. She blinked every time the pressure from the penlight overcame the fiery tingling sensation. He continued to her feet, running the pen up the soles of her feet, heel to toe. Her toes curled. Amia blinked at Dr. Hemp's smile. A tear curled over her cheek. Dr. Hemp smiled and strode to Amia's side. He placed a hand on her shoulder. She recoiled at his gentle touch, not sure why. He said, "I have some yes-no questions. Two blinks for yes and one blink for no. Do you know where you are?"

Amia looked around the room, outside the window, and back to Dr. Hemp. One blink.

He smiled. "You're at East Coast Harbor Medical Center in Bar Harbor, Maine. Do you understand why you are here?"

Amia glanced at what she could see of herself. Two blinks. Then, after a momentary pause, one blink. She could see why she was there, but what happened to her? Why did this happen to her? Why were her head and body throbbing? Why couldn't she remember?

Dr. Hemp said, "It's okay. You have some contusions and abrasions varying in severity. The head injury you sustained caused swelling and fluid to build pressure inside your head. We performed a craniectomy to relieve the pressure. Your MRI did not show any significant lesions at the point of insult. However, the impact caused swelling near your primary motor cortex and premotor cortex. People with similar insults experience similar motor control and memory issues, as well as difficulties with speech. The lack of significant lesions combined with sensations in your extremities provides me with a sense of encouragement as to your recovery." He glanced at Dr. Avendale, and they shared some kind of unspoken agreement. Dr. Hemp continued. "As with all traumatic brain injuries, there is the element of the unknown. You've been in a coma for four days. Right now you have a paralytic in your system that explains part of your inability to move. The paralytic was so you would not injure yourself while intubated. The next several weeks to two months will provide us with a better idea of what kind of recovery you should expect." He glanced at Dr. Avendale again and smiled as if convincing himself they were in some agreement. He said, "I have a friend who specializes in situations like yours. Her name is Dr. Karen Wolf. She wants to meet you." He cupped Amia's shoulder and offered a confident smile.

Thoughts reeled in Amia's mind as she returned the smile. A few short moments after they left the room, she succumbed to the pressure inside her head and the weight that tugged at her eyelids.

CHAPTER THREE

THE DRAGON

D aizon slid his thumb and middle finger down the tip of the nine-millimeter round and rolled it forward with his pointer finger. Lifting it slightly from the deck railing, he stood it up and repeated the rolling motion, lift and repeat. Her pale blue, beaten figure wouldn't leave his mind. Another memory he didn't want. He kept reminding himself that she was alive and not dead.

His modern-rustic home contoured as if part of the mountain, and stood as Daizon May's mountainside oasis. The home blended with the forest carpet that wrapped around it, overlooking a glassy blue pond below, his spoiled fishing escape. Shafts of light from the morning sun burned through the last remnants of dark, dissipating clouds as they drifted away. The scene flipped in the pond's mirror.

He knew the dark side of humanity, but she'd lain there like a fallen angel beneath his home, a reminder of a past he tried to forget. Detective Johnson did not believe his alibi, but he also knew the truth never set you free. Those were lies meant to trap people into believing they would be safe, that their souls could rest easy knowing they held no secrets, or some crap like that. Daizon learned long before entering the military how to hold a secret. Hoping for peace of mind was like pissing in the wind—you could do it, but the results might not be what you wanted. Still, he hoped the flowers brought Amia some of the beauty and freshness he knew she wouldn't feel for a long time.

Leaning against the railing of his deck, Daizon drank in his surroundings along with his morning coffee. He had too much time to think about his past. In the four days since he'd found Amia, all he could think of was the image of her lying there pale blue, beaten, bloody, and swollen on her way to the beyond. Her ghostly face would not stop playing in his mind. A part of him wished he had not seen the flash of the sun off her earrings. Her face and form brought back memories he did not want to relive. He worked hard at blocking them out. He had to function.

This was the first day since finding her, since saving her life, that there were no investigators or media personalities hounding him. Not yet. They came in their helicopters or moved down below like ants, searching for answers to the disturbance. Daizon wanted answers too.

Car tires spat as they gripped the dirty tar and climbed toward his retreat. Eventually, utility vehicles would be by to sweep off the winter sand, but out where he lived, his road was not on the priority list. On the table behind Daizon, by itself, lay his Beretta PX4 Storm.

Daizon's gripping presence went beyond his six-foot-tall rugged frame and his intense gray-green eyes that made him an easy fit for the Hollywood leading man type. Tonya, his agent, found him a few years ago, when he worked with the construction team building her summer home on the Maine coast. She found the juxtaposition of his easy nature and intense eyes captivating.

People will see what they want to see, his father would always say. *Create a persona of who you want to be and become that person.* Daizon became adept at reading people and situations. He gave Tonya what she wanted to see. His ability to adjust his personality to the people he interacted with magnified when Tonya had him attend a course on acting called the Method Actor. She provided Daizon with an opportunity to escape the life he was living and become somebody else. Darren Mason, the former Special Forces soldier turned construction worker, became Daizon May the actor.

Gazing out from his deck, Daizon saw the early strokes of greens, browns, reds, and whites reaching into hues of blue, gold, and black. It was life renewed from death.

Daizon laughed to himself and shook his head. *Hollywood's newest heartthrob. Yeah, right. People will see what they want.*

A full-figured Tonya sauntered around the side of his home and down the hill instead of using the deck walkway that wrapped around the side of the house. Sometimes he wondered why he'd put it there since nobody used it. Maybe it blended a little too well with the house? Fresh streaks of red ran the length of Tonya's shoulder-length blond hair. Always tanned, she wore her customary designer free-flowing white capris with a bright flowered blouse. She said, "Hey, gorgeous. This place is beautiful. I'm jealous."

Daizon's posture and body language puffed with an air of playful confidence. He said, "Sweetheart, don't forget I worked on your place. You're looking fit and fantastic. You've been working out. And fresh streaks? Bold—I like it."

Tonya lit up. Cradling her head with flared fingers, she tossed a hip and struck a playful pose. "Honey, I'm always fresh, fit, and fantastic." Tonya strutted up the first few deck stairs before assuming a natural gait. "As for the yoga, I'm not sure bending like that is worth it."

Daizon smirked. "Oh, I don't know, a little flexibility has its advantages."

Tonya raised an eyebrow and smirked back. "Honey, these old bones could show you a thing or two about the advantage of experience."

They hugged and swapped cheek pecks. It was her thing, and he went with it. Daizon glanced at the corner of his house. "You don't look a day past thirty and you know it. Where's Dave?"

"He's at the hospital, consulting with Dr. Hempshire. He wanted to come. He thinks you're going to make him into some expert hunter, fisherman, or some foolishness like that. Can you imagine Dave, a hunter?"

"He bagged you."

"Honey, I'm the huntress in our family." Tonya quickly recovered her smile after sighting the Beretta on the table.

"I'll put that away. I was going to show it off to Dave. Thought he'd get a kick out of some target practice. He says he wants to learn, but he never practices. I thought we could take advantage of the quiet before the circus comes. You can have a seat here, or we can go inside? Want some coffee? Or I can make tea?"

"I'll try some target practice if you're willing to teach an old girl some new tricks."

Daizon figured she was placating him, but she seemed earnest enough. He said, "I'll get the ammo if you get the coffee?"

⊰⊱

Black earmuffs on, Tonya stared down the pistol sight toward the four-inch black center spot on the target ten yards away. Hay bales and sand bags four rows deep and six high provided a shooting wall within a long, narrow clearing. Daizon turned Tonya's shoulders and tapped her feet to adjust her shooting posture. He said, "Elbows in for support—think triangles. Remember to breathe slow and steady. Fire at the natural pause in your breathing before inhaling or exhaling. I prefer to fire on the pause at the exhale, but the important thing to remember is to keep it consistent with whichever pause you choose. When you're ready, flip the safety off, find your target picture, breathe, and fire. You have three rounds in the magazine." Daizon secured his earmuffs and stepped back with a subtle, encouraging nod.

After a long pause, probably gaining her courage while holding a deadly weapon for the first time, Tonya fired. The recoil and action instantly generated a broad smile on her face. She swung toward him. "Oh my God. That was amaz—"

Daizon grasped Tonya's arm and steadied her posture with the other hand. He said, "Stay focused. Your safety is off. You have two more." Daizon smiled and nodded toward the pistol and target.

She quickly refocused her attention on the weapon in her hand, unable to contain the giddy smile pasted on her face. Readjusting her position, she focused on her breathing and fired the next two rounds. Two of her rounds found the outer edges of the two-foot square target that held the black circle in the center. One round hit about two inches from the black four-inch circle. This time, before she turned, she flipped the safety on. "I hit it. Did you see that? Oh my God."

Daizon cleared and secured the Beretta in his shoulder holster. He gathered the spent round casings and gave Tonya a grin. "You're a natural. Let's see how you did."

Practically bouncing, Tonya eyed the target in Daizon's hand. "Can I have it? I have to show Dave. He's been trying to convince me to buy a gun for protection when he's not around. I might surprise him."

Daizon slid out some used and new targets from between the hay bales and hung a new target. Tonya's eyes grew wide. Almost all the holes in the used targets were inside the four-inch black circle. More than that, she probably could have covered most of the groupings with a quarter. Daizon handed Tonya her evidence. A smile plastered her face as she held her accomplishment. Daizon grinned. "Dave better practice. You're already a better shot. He's going to be jealous."

Her devilish grin widened. "I know." She gestured at the used targets. "Did the military teach you to shoot like that?"

"I'm sure they helped. It's mostly about practice and repetition. Keep practicing what I taught you, and before long you'll see a lot of improvement."

Tonya eyed his easy smile. "Before I forget why I came, thoughts on the script I gave you? Guess who's on their short list for the lead?"

Daizon shook his head. He didn't like making excuses. "I'll read it this afternoon and let you know."

Tonya's excited expression faltered to a worried downcast.

Daizon asked, "What's wrong?"

"There's some pretty disturbing stuff that happens. He's not an altogether good guy, and I know how you prepare for roles. Plus, with the recent events, I want you to keep in mind that you can say no. You don't have to take this role."

Daizon forced his smile to reach his eyes. "Don't worry. I can say no if it ever gets to be too much. Let me read the screenplay. I have too much time to think out here. I could use a challenging project to keep my mind occupied."

"You just remember what I said. You don't have to take every project I offer. Besides, it had to be difficult finding that woman like that."

Daizon offered the reassuring smile he knew Tonya wanted to see. He wondered if Dave had let her know how Amia was doing. He wondered what she'd told the detective, but knew better than to ask, at least not directly. Shaking the thoughts away, he said, "I would have never seen her if it weren't for her earrings. The sun flashed off them while I was fishing. I didn't even call Dave until after I did everything I thought needed to be done. I told the detective how Dave and I were supposed to go fishing that morning, but he was a brain surgeon out in California and had been called into work the day before. I may have hinted to the detective that I was at your place and didn't come home until later on that night before."

Tonya shook her head. "Why would you do that?"

Daizon noticed her mind spinning. "I wasn't about to tell the detective somebody hit my cat with their car, that I buried her, and was at home drinking."

"Why not? It was more than Holly dying. It's the way you found her. They'll find out the truth and then ask why you lied. Jesus, Daizon, let me think. I told the detective about Dave being called back to work and you coming by our place that afternoon. I don't remember if I said anything about when you left."

She paused, opened her lips to speak, and changed her mind. It seemed Tonya had her own secrets to keep. Daizon smiled and motioned a wave, not wanting to get into a conversation about his cat, Holly. "I'm sure it won't amount to anything. After all, haven't you heard? I'm a hero. Has Dave said how she is?"

"He said your quick thinking and lucky timing saved her life. He said the surgery to relieve the pressure went well, but she wasn't out of the woods yet. Things could turn in a heartbeat, which is why Dr. Hempshire was consulting with him. He said there was an officer posted outside her room, and Detective Johnson was stopping by regularly to check on her. He also said you don't have to send her flowers every damn day. Her room smells and looks like a florist's."

Daizon grinned.

Tonya's subtle grin morphed into a devilish one. "You know, not everyone is like Brittney."

Thrown briefly by the sudden change of subject, Daizon adeptly regained his balance. "A pretty smile can hide sharp teeth."

Play scolding, Tonya slapped Daizon's shoulder. "Have you even signed into your Psyche and Eros account once since we set it up?"

He rolled his eyes and continued smirking. "I told you to delete it. Some people are not meant to find their true love. We're not as lucky as you and Dave. Besides, I don't want that kind of attention from the media."

"We can use the attention you're getting right now from the media. Like you said, everyone sees you as a hero. Besides, we chose Psyche and Eros because they specialize in verified professionals who would rather keep their love lives private."

Daizon's eyes narrowed. He studied Tonya's frustrated disposition. "What's going on?"

Tonya sighed. "There's nothing going on. This script is what you've been waiting for. It's your transition into the dramatic features with award potential." Tonya paused, obviously mulling something over in her head. Daizon had agreed with her when she originally brought it up, but he wasn't sure how much of this was his dream. He was really just kind of going along with it.

She continued. "The attention you're getting right now cuts both ways. They like the story line of you saving her life, but what happens when they tire of that story line? What happens when they ask why she was on the edge of your property in the first place? The only reason the media hasn't plastered her image all over the news yet is because of how badly she was beaten. Right now they're showing the images of her earrings with the engraved heart and her name inside. They're talking about how they led you to her so you could save her life. It would be great to build on that story line, but I also think we need to get you away from the media."

Daizon asked, "What did you do?"

Tonya lifted an eyebrow and measured Daizon, as if seeing through his facade. A bit of compassion seeped into her posture and voice. "I want you to see someone. I know you're going to want the role because it's what you do—it's who you are. This will be part of your preparation." Tonya retrieved a business card. "You're going to admit yourself into her care in a couple of weeks under your given name. I've already taken care of the financial side of it."

Daizon took the business card and read aloud, "Karen Wolf, PsyD, East Coast Wellness Center, the Whole Me?"

Tonya said, "Think of it as another acting class. It will keep you out of the public eye for two months, and you might even find it beneficial to your well-being."

"You want me to commit myself to a psychiatric hospital for two months? What the hell is the Whole Me?"

"It's a wellness program. You'll learn about mindfulness, self-compassion, and attend some counseling sessions. Dr. Wolf will expect your commitment to the program. You'll need to fill out some paperwork beforehand—questionnaires and stuff. It's a secure facility. There are no cell phones, and you'll be out of the media's reach."

There was more. There was always more. Daizon tried reading between the lines. He wouldn't mind getting out of the public eye. He liked keeping his private life private. Nobody needed to know his deepest secrets. Hell, he didn't want to know them. And Tonya wanted him to share those issues with a psychologist by the sounds of it. He asked, "Is it you who think I'm unstable or them?"

Tonya tilted her head as if to soften some imaginary blow. She reached out with a placating touch to his arm and lied. "Nobody thinks you're unstable."

"And if I don't commit myself to the psych program?"

Tonya sighed.

Daizon laughed and shuffled ideas through his mind. He wondered why somebody left Amia for dead on the edge of his property. He owned a lot of land, so it was possible whoever left her there simply thought it was a good secluded spot to commit their heinous activity. There was also the possibility they knew exactly what they were doing and were trying to frame Daizon. He'd known it when he'd first assessed the situation. The faint smell of bleach stuck with him even if the rain washed away most of it. That alone suggested the individual had at least a rudimentary will and forethought to clean up after himself.

Daizon had received his share of hate mail over the last couple of years. They were all pretty graphic, so no one stood out in their disdain of him. He should have told Detective Johnson the truth about Holly when he gave her his stack of hate mail. He wondered how much of his reason for lying had to do with not wanting to look weak as opposed to not wanting to look guilty. If it was somebody trying to frame him, he'd probably messed up their plans when he found Amia and saved her life.

Daizon wanted to know more about Amia. He wanted to know she would be okay. He couldn't learn anything stuck in a psyche program. *Fuck.* He did not want to talk with a psychologist, much less commit himself for two months. His closest ally thought he was unstable. The industry he escaped into thrived on media attention and image. They were all pretenders in some form or another. Nobody needed to know he agreed with the assessment that he probably needed psychiatric help. Daizon said, "I don't need it."

Staring at him for a few silent moments, Tonya said, "You're going to have a choice when you get there. You can open up to the doctor and begin healing those deep wounds, or you can waste the opportunity and simply learn to play another role."

Chapter Four

FOG

The pressure in Amia's head made her feel like a plant that had been hit by an asteroid. Her sense of time was distorted. The scent of fresh flowers elicited a smile. Her insides ached, while a tingling fire raged in her arms and legs. A wall of fog stood between her and her memories. She was sure if she could push through that wall, she would retrieve her life. Squeezing her eyelids tight, Amia pushed into the fog. The throbbing inside her head intensified. *Please*, she pleaded with herself, *I have to know.* She pressed onward. Pain washed over her and sleep took hold.

Several attempts to retrieve her memories had met with similar results. The fog was a barrier Amia could not overcome. Not yet. When she woke again, Amia tried something new. She opened her eyes to inspect the world surrounding her. The scent and sight of fresh flowers reminded her of walking through fields of them in her dreams. Sunlight bathed the room, and Amia welcomed the warmth once again.

Sitting straight-backed in a chair but angled to the window was a fortysomething woman with glasses down on her nose. She was reading a book, something about mindfulness and compassion. The cover of the book had dark meditation rocks in calm water under a blue sky. The woman wore blue dress slacks with a matching blouse. She managed her unruly brown hair, which dangled between her shoulder blades with a loose braid. Pinned to her blouse was a hospital badge with her picture and name, Dr. Karen Wolf, PsyD. She had the look of someone rolling ideas around in her head, sorting them into categories and adding notes. Then her eyes shifted to focus on Amia. She slid out a slight quirk of a smile.

Amia returned the smile. A gesture that both hurt and felt good at the same time. The good far outweighed the bad. Without a word, this woman's calm, assessing nature helped settle Amia's mind.

Dr. Wolf placed her pink, tethered bookmark into the crease of the book and set it on the small table beside her in what seemed like a series of choreographed events. Her quirk of a smile and penetrating eyes held Amia captive. She came to Amia's side and gently folded her hands over one another. "You have a powerful spirit, Amia. I've watched you fight over the last few days."

Amia's eyes darted about. *Dr. Hempshire was just here, right?* Light and dark mixed with such frequency, she couldn't think clearly.

Dr. Wolf continued. "Yes, you've been here for a little while now. It's natural for events and memories to blur together after a traumatic event. Dr. Hempshire firmly believes you will be up and about in no time. Maybe not running marathons right off, but healthy. He asked me to come and assess you myself, perhaps assist with your recovery. Do you remember that conversation?"

Realizing that conversation wasn't a dream, Amia squeezed her eyes together for two thankful blinks.

"Excellent. You remembered the blink system for answering questions. Do you remember where you are?"

Mind easing, Amia blinked twice.

"Do you remember Dr. Hempshire's nickname?"

Amia twitched a smirk and blinked twice.

"Yes, he thinks he's funny. He means well. If you're up to it, I'd like to work with you through a few assessments. Is that okay?"

Two blinks.

Dr. Wolf retrieved a black locking binder with a clip on the front that held a notebook. She also had a folder-sized touch-screen computer. Opening the binder, she withdrew several papers. Some papers had shapes, some had images of plants and animals, while other papers had math or word problems. While Dr. Wolf prepared, Amia noticed a dark-suited individual hovering outside her hospital room. Following Amia's gaze, Dr. Wolf maintained a steady presence as she spoke. "Detective Johnson has been checking in on you. She's in charge of your case."

Amia's eyes bounced around, not sure how to respond. *What case?*

Dr. Wolf said, "We'll be in a better position to answer Detective Johnson's questions after we finish with the assessments. Shall we begin?"

The threat of Detective Johnson's presence abated for the moment. Amia glanced at the lingering detective and blinked twice.

Several assessments later, matching objects with words, solving arithmetic problems with Dr. Wolf's creative help, motor function tests, and questions to assess her memory, Amia learned the basic thing missing was her identity and ability to move properly. Her personal memories seemed locked away in the fog particles orbiting her mind, kind of like when planets form out of billions of particles that eventually fuse. Or maybe it was more like when Theia struck the earth, and the moon formed out of the debris. She did not know. Amia wondered how she remembered Theia striking the earth. Those memories, that kind of knowledge, just seemed to be there. She brushed against the fog particles, no idea how her mind would re-form. Was her injury worse than they were telling her?

Dr. Wolf maintained her quirk of a smile. "I'm here. We will get through this. Would you like to continue? I think you should meet Detective Johnson."

Amia took a few breaths. Even with Dr. Wolf's calm presence, Amia's heart raced. Confusion reigned over questions she couldn't answer. Who was she? Why was she there? Maybe the detective could tell her more about what happened. Did she want to know? She had to know. Part of her wanted to scream, but she knew even this was beyond her at that moment. Amia found Dr. Wolf's steady presence. She projected a calm focus combined with an intelligent and empathetic nature. She blinked twice. She had to know.

Detective Johnson had sharp, chiseled feminine features. Short red hair flared like a fox's mane. She had the look of a warrior with her athletic build, quick assessing nature, and fluid gait. She stood several inches over Dr. Wolf, dressed in a dark suit with a silky pink blouse underneath. At her side, she carried a manila folder and notebook. Amia watched the detective's micro-expressions tighten as she assessed Amia's bruised and battered form. The detective tried masking her emotions by projecting a smile that didn't reach her eyes.

Detective Johnson cleared her throat. Anger seeped into her sympathetic words. "It's good to see you awake. I'm sure this is very difficult for you. I'm sorry. My name is Detective Johnson, and I have some questions for you. From what I understand, your ability to answer those questions right now is impaired. We'll do our best. Maybe my questions will help jolt some of those memories. Okay?"

Detective Johnson may have appeared like a fox, but a bulldog with a bone flashed into Amia's mind as she studied the detective.

Amia smirked at the random thought and remembered to blink twice.

Detective Johnson spoke with animated hands, facial expressions, and body movements, the idiosyncrasies tied deeply to the ebb and flow of her emotions and delivery. She said, "You were assaulted, and at some point, the back of your head struck a rock. I understand you suffered multiple contusions to your body and face, along with some minor chemical burns. It seems your assailant poured bleach over your body and the crime scene. Your blood tests suggest they slipped you some sort of drug cocktail. A few traces remained in your system by the time you arrived. We suspect whoever did this to you didn't expect you to live or be found as quickly as you were."

Detective Johnson swallowed some anger before she forced a comforting smile that obviously conflicted with her emotions. She said, "The rape kit came back negative. I have some pictures that may be difficult to view, but again, I want you to know that you are safe and we will do everything we can to find the individual responsible. Are you ready?"

No, she was not ready. Amia's head spun with the information. It floated about in her mind but couldn't find purchase. She could not find the memories and could not relate. Detective Johnson withdrew several photos. Amia inhaled a long breath and blinked twice.

Detective Johnson slid out the first photo. It was beyond an out-of-body experience for Amia, seeing the listless stranger covered with a camouflaged army jacket. Oversize black stockings covered her feet, and a folded up, bloodstained black shirt was wrapped around her head. Trying to identify with the person lying there like a corpse created a dissociative type of experience. Surely the person in that photo was not somebody still alive. This was supposed to be her?

Amia's eyes flicked from her prone form in the picture to the detective and back to the picture. It was surreal. The person lying there couldn't be her. How could any of it be true? Amia tried to remember, but her world up to that point was blank. She wondered for the hundredth time, *Is Amia even my name?* She glanced away, but not before a few tears sprang.

Amia found Dr. Wolf's steady, compassionate gaze. With a flick of her eyes, Dr. Wolf guided Amia back to the photos.

Detective Johnson flipped to an image of a serene mountain lake. The lake seemed like a glass mirror to the mountain forest surrounding it. It seemed so peaceful and devoid of threat. "Does this place seem familiar? Stir any memories?"

The place was beautiful, not some horrible thing of nightmares. Amia blinked once.

The next photo was a closeup of Amia's pale blue battered and swollen face. Perhaps it was not wanting to stare at her battered face, but the silver earrings held Amia's attention. They stirred an urge in Amia to reach for her ear. She didn't know why, but she had to know if they were still there. The log attached to her hand resisted her effort. Amia pressed.

Detective Johnson gave Dr. Wolf an expectant, encouraged glance. Dr. Wolf fetched a small white box from beside the fresh bouquet.

Amia finally reached her naked ear with clumsy fingers. It seemed wrong. Dr. Wolf opened the box and held it out to Amia. Her silver earrings lay on top of cotton. A warmth filled Amia at the sight of the engraved heart that circled her name. She didn't know why she was having the reaction. The earrings were a part of her she didn't realize was missing.

Detective Johnson cleared her throat and gave Amia a hopeful-expectant look. She asked, "Did we jar some memories?"

Amia's smile faded. She felt the undeniable warmth the earrings provided. She knew they were important to her, that they represented something beyond the actual object. They were more, so much more, but the words and memories associated with them still wouldn't come. Amia gripped the earrings, tears formed, and she blinked once.

"It's okay. It's obvious they jarred something by your reaction, even if you can't place it yet. Right now those are the only things we have to identify you with." Detective Johnson offered a consoling smile that had a bit of disappointment in it. "I want to show you one more image."

Dr. Wolf spoke up. "Detective Johnson, it's clear Amia cannot assist you at the moment." Amia had the look of a battered animal. "Could I speak with you outside for a moment?"

Detective Johnson overcame some inner struggle after observing Amia's current state. A reluctant smile formed. She said to Amia, "We'll talk again soon. I'll leave my card. I want you to know that I'm here for you if you remember anything or want to reach out. We'll find whoever did this to you." She glanced at Dr. Wolf and gave a subtle nod. "But for now your health is more important."

Amia knew she could press on. She was upset and confused, but she could endure. It was one more photo. Amia pressed one long blink to exacerbate her point. She had to see all the photos. She bounced her eyes between the folder and Detective Johnson.

Detective Johnson grinned her foxy smile, and Dr. Wolf nodded her assent.

The last image sparked something thrumming inside Amia. The bare-chested, handsome man before her had a chiseled body and intense, captivating hazel eyes. A pulling sensation had her reaching out as if to connect with him, but again, no memories came to her rescue. Then Amia noticed the background. It was the gravel beach and lake from the earlier pictures. He stood before an aluminum boat that had fishing rods hanging out on either side. He wore green camouflage army pants, black boots, and a dark green camouflaged jungle hat. Thinking back to the jacket, shirt, and stockings, she realized this must be the man who found her, the man who tended to her, and the reason she was alive. There was a depth about him, a familiarity like the fog that she couldn't quite grasp.

Detective Johnson was curious about Amia's reaction, and hope crept into her question. "Do you recognize him?"

Something tickled her mind as if the fog was trying to form a thought in her head but couldn't coalesce into anything substantial. It was like trying to retrieve a dream lost to consciousness. He had a haunted, deep thought type of expression, probably from finding her the way she was. Amia blinked once and darted her eyes between the photo and the detective, hoping she would see her question.

Thankfully, Detective Johnson noticed. "His name is Daizon May. If you didn't already piece it together, he's the one who found you on the edge of his property and performed the initial response that saved your life. He's an actor. He's also the one who's been sending all the flowers." Detective Johnson stood and aimed a frustrated tightening of her facial muscles at Dr. Wolf before returning a softer gaze to Amia. "Call if you remember anything. We will find the man who did this to you."

After the detective left her card on the table beside the flowers, she left the room with Dr. Wolf. The flagrant, colorful display had a new meaning. A few racing moments passed while she tried to make sense of her new reality before Dr. Wolf reentered the room.

Dr. Wolf said, "We'll keep in contact with Detective Johnson as we move forward. I believe we can work together and help you regain your sense of self. Would you like to work with me, Amia?"

Was this a question somebody would say no to? Amia blinked twice.

"We have a team of people at a facility on the coast. We tailor the Whole Me program for a group of eight to twelve people at a time for an eight-week period. It's geared toward people suffering from depression, anxiety, and other issues after traumatic events. We combine individual counseling with group activities based on mindfulness, and self-compassion. It starts in a little over two weeks. The work we do here with the physical therapists will continue there." Dr. Wolf paused.

She said, "Based on your reaction to Daizon May's photo, I think I already know the answer to my question, but I need to ask. He signed up for the program under an assumed name a few days ago. Is there even an ounce of you that has any kind of adverse internal reaction? I need to know so I can let him know he'll need to attend a different session."

An adverse reaction? The thrumming inside Amia was anything but adverse. He'd saved her life, and a glance at all the flowers told her he cared about her health. She wanted to see him, to meet him, to say thank you. She wanted to know him. Amia blinked once.

Dr. Wolf's smile grew. "If you change your mind and are no longer comfortable with the situation, let me know. You are my priority. Okay?"

Amia blinked twice.

Dr. Wolf said, "On a more immediate front, I have some good news. Dr. Hempshire informed me we're removing the tubes and wires."

This woman projected an infectious energy, and Amia dared to hope.

CHAPTER FIVE

EVIDENCE

T apping away at a workbench with Amia's laptop providing the only light, he signed into Psyche and Eros. She was alive with a security detail posted outside her door. Nobody was getting in without them noticing. Would they follow her when she left the hospital? He itched to know what she remembered. Scuttlebutt around the hospital inferred that they suspected temporary amnesia. She should have been dead, but Daizon had found her and saved her life. His original plan could still work now that he knew she was going to live. He would make a few modifications. The press calling Daizon a hero was a joke. Daizon kept sending her flowers. Would he visit her in the hospital?

He laughed, his new plans already set in motion.

How long before she recognized Daizon? How long before his miserable world eroded into what-ifs and whys he could not explain? It would be better if she recognized him and remembered her budding love match; then the evidence would speak for itself. It had to be believable.

Searching Amia's profile, he smirked at Daizon's profile picture among her matches. He clicked on her messages. Daizon wouldn't leave something like that behind. Clicking on all the boxes, he confirmed, *Delete All*. Several months' worth of work, gone.

Satisfied, he brought up Amia's account information and hit *Cancel Account*.

A warning message popped up saying, *We delete all account information for security reasons. Are you sure you want to cancel your account?*

Yes.

Before we delete your account, we would love to hear your feedback. Would you mind filling out a brief survey?

He clicked on the radio button that said, *Highly Satisfied*, and left the feedback section blank.

He slipped a thumb drive into the laptop and, in a few clicks, removed the Trojan software. A three-pound hammer was the tool needed for the next task. Frustration bled out with every swing. Pieces flew.

Gathering all the shards and chunks, he tossed them into a fifty-five-quart cooler. The pieces splashed over and mixed with the black and gray ashes that were the remains of her clothes and purse. With all the investigators and press at Daizon's, he would need to dump this stuff in a different lake. He wondered how long it would take them to find the other stuff he left for them. He poured lighter fluid on the remains and watched it burn.

He could have left the messages he made using the *It Wasn't Me* deep fake impersonation software, but again, Daizon would not leave something like that behind. While Daizon was gone, he would have to dump the rest of her trash.

CHAPTER SIX

PRIME SUSPECT

I nside his modern-rustic home with an open design, Daizon finished the last page of the script bound with a couple of gold braids. He tossed the story on the glossed over, three-inch-thick slice of a large oak-tree coffee table. The script landed beside a tray that held a three-tiered pyramid of Granny Smith apples and a bottle of water. The title of the script read, *Prime Suspect*, by David Young. Wearing a stoic debate mask, Daizon grabbed the water bottle, leaned back on his leather recliner, and relaxed his mind.

Becoming the character was about understanding their mind. It was not about what he wanted, thought, or believed. It was about what the character wanted, thought, and believed. What was their history? Why did they want what they wanted? What was their motivation? How did they go about their daily lives? It was kind of his own five Ws.

The main character was complex. He did wicked things but was not a wicked man. He experienced immense pain over an extended time frame and eventually snapped. Daizon imagined the assault triggering a change. The first thing to go would be innocence. Then, as bullies continued targeting him, he developed a hyperfocus. He didn't say anything for fear of further harassment and isolation.

Daizon walked to his glass doors that led out to the back deck. He stared into the blackness of night beyond the glare of light reflected at him. Relaxing his eyes, returning from the black, he found his dark reflection staring back. He knew he could be this man in the story, the one that snapped. His was a story he didn't want to remember.

Thinking of his conversation with Tonya, he realized other people were starting to see his wrongness as well. The same thing that attracted them to him held them at bay. His mask was slipping. He frightened them because of what he might become, by what he might be. Was his pain too obvious? *No.* They did not see it, at least not to its full extent. They worried in the general sense of the term. They couldn't know. Nobody knew. Hell, he didn't know why he hated himself so much. He'd gotten away. He'd done what he'd needed to do. That was what he always told himself.

A memory flashed in his mind of a shaky, triangular knife point an inch from his eye and a feeling of helplessness. Then a more recent memory flashed through his mind. Amia's battered angelic face, so similar to the dead one that always weighed on his mind.

Daizon's thoughts returned to the present and his dark reflection. The darkness hid his tears. He needed a new role. He was an actor. It was his job, not who he was. Did it matter? Those thoughts were best left with the reflection in the darkness. He wiped the moisture from his eyes. It was time for therapy.

Daizon's basement had a small bar, a pool table with leather pockets, and an open case with custom cue sticks lining a wall. A dartboard hid inside a walnut case, and a rubber mat covered the floor to create a gym area. A heavy jump rope hung over one peg, and a towel hung over another. He owned a curved treadmill, a stationary bike, a rowing machine, a bench press, dumbbells, a speed bag, and a Torso Man heavy bag.

Daizon's gloved fists worked the Torso Man with combinations to his abs, ribs, and head. He dodged, blocked, and weaved from imaginary punches and kicks. He kicked him in the head, drove a knee into his abs, punched his nose, and then let loose with a series of rapid combinations of punches to the ribs and head.

He fought as if it were an actual person, always maintaining a guard. Sweat soaked Daizon's gray workout clothes. Skin glistening, he smashed a powerful hook to the side of the head, then another and another, again and again.

Daizon noticed his supposed friend Kyle Flanagan leaning against the doorframe from the upstairs. Kyle watched with a confident nonchalance. He finished polishing his Granny Smith apple against his black designer long-sleeve and wide-collared shirt. He snapped into the apple, crunched, and chewed. "Looks like someone needs to get laid." He snapped another bite of the apple.

Daizon smashed a few more punches to the Torso Man's head. He took in the sharply dressed ruffian. Kyle considered himself a ladies' man. Just as well. The ladies seemed to see him the same way. There were no expectations of a long-term relationship with this man. Daizon said, "Help yourself to an apple."

"I already did—crisp and juicy, just the way I like it. You about done playing?"

"I told you I'm not going. I've got things to do, a role to plan for."

"*Prime Suspect*, yeah, I saw. I bet he did it, right?" Kyle continued to devour the apple.

"I'm not going." Daizon shook his head and drank from his water bottle.

"Come on. We can dick around here all night, or you can accept the fact you already know you're coming with me. A few beers, a few games of pool, some darts, and everybody's favorite—guess the natural blond."

Shaking his head, Daizon replied, "You're a dick."

"Everybody knows one and nobody wants to be one. How can that be? Nah, I just accept my role in society. It's why everybody loves me." Kyle grabbed a couple of beers from the fridge behind the bar, walking one to Daizon.

"I don't even like you," Daizon said as he took the beer.

Kyle slapped Daizon on the back. He had the look and size of a grizzly bear that shaved and was trying to make everyone believe he was a teddy bear. "Come on, you're going to hurt my feelings."

Daizon said, "If only that were possible."

Kyle raised his brows and pushed out a lip. "Is this the part where we kiss and make up? Or do we just go to the bedroom? Maybe a reach around? Tickle the touch-hole?" He swirled his finger around.

Daizon shook his head, the smirk on his face stretching into a smile. Kyle maintained his deadpan gaze. He raised an eyebrow, innocent and guilty at the same time somehow. Daizon knew that even though Kyle was joking, he would do the things he said if ever called on them. That carnal abruptness seemed to be what women loved about him. They saw his sense of humor, his confidence, and would think they knew what they were getting. Maybe they did know, and it was simply about seizing an opportunity to let loose of their inhibitions and experience the animal within themselves. They likely knew going into the experience there were no expectations of love. Maybe it was all about lust and anonymity? Daizon said, "You are the creature in the darkness that women seek to satisfy their curiosity."

Kyle's demeanor darkened. His dark blue eyes glazed with a hardening stare.

After several seconds of silence, Daizon sighed. "That was a low blow."

And like a switch, Kyle's demeanor lightened. "We both know I deserved it. I provide a service most men only dream about. I deal in base desire."

"You didn't have to service Brittney," Daizon challenged.

Kyle chugged his drink. "That was ages ago, and you're welcome." He tipped his bottle before drinking again.

Daizon squeezed his beer bottle. He wanted to hurl the thing at Kyle's head. Instead, wanting to make sense of the senseless, he dove into Kyle's perspective. In Kyle's eyes, Brittney would not have cheated on him if she were a faithful woman. In Kyle's warped reality, he really had done Daizon a favor. He'd let Daizon know trust would always be an issue with Brittney.

It was still a dick move, not something you did to a friend. Four years together as squad mates experiencing the darkness of men created a bond between them. They understood each other in ways nobody else could. Kyle was a constant reminder of a time Daizon wished he could forget.

Kyle broke the silence. "I know, I'm a dick. Can we get over it already? That goth chick you like is playing tonight. Just imagine the trouble you could get into with her. Come on."

Daizon shook his head.

CHAPTER SEVEN

LOW PLACES

Hundreds of locals and out-of-staters packed into Shady Jay's. Being between Bangor and Bar Harbor, the tavern was able to draw from both crowds regularly. Friday and Saturday nights had live bands, and this band, in particular, always packed the place. Shoulders and arms constantly bumped, with quick smiles and curious looks being the norm. After all, part of the allure was who you might bump into while you were at Shady Jay's. More and more famous people were frequenting the area. Daizon arrived dressed in jeans, a flannel shirt, and a Patriots ball cap. The outfit allowed him a kind of camouflage where he could blend. He noticed the flashes of recognition on people's faces, quickly followed by smiles and doubts that it could actually be him at Shady Jay's.

Born in Maine, Daizon had been introduced to cities and towns outside the state and country by the military. They were big, noisy, and had too many people. Maine was quiet and laid-back, away from the bustle. Shady Jay's appealed to locals and vacationers by providing the best entertainers in a welcoming environment, where people could forget about their worries and enjoy the atmosphere. Some locals enjoyed playing to the illusions out-of-staters had, such as being dim-witted and the rolling of *R*s or the occasional, *ayah*. Locals didn't always have to work hard at emphasizing these assumptions, as there were seeds of truth in the beliefs. It seemed like a harmless illusion mostly.

Daizon observed his surroundings while standing in line at the bar. The pub had three main sections, all semi-open to each other. The bar stood central to the live entertainment and dance floor, while the sports room stood slightly off to the side. Nick and Ellie worked separate sides of the bar, but they helped each other out when one would get overwhelmed. They wore their white bartender shirts buttoned to the neck. Gold nameplates with black lettering hung high on their chests. Both physically fit, Nick wore loose black slacks while Ellie had on a formfitting black skirt that ended just above her knees. She had curves in all the right places with hot girl-next-door looks. When Daizon glanced back up, Ellie wore a mischievous grin and winked. *Damn*, he thought. *Caught*.

Daizon smiled back and continued his assessment of the pub. It was probably close to capacity—several hundred people. Many of the private and less private booths surrounding the dance floor seemed to have women dressed to impress or imply it was time to party. Meanwhile, boyfriends drank and pretended not to notice as they scanned for rivals.

An amused grin formed as Daizon watched a frustrated muscular guy twitch his triceps and biceps while puffing himself like a rooster. He was with a group of similar friends, all puffing their plumage. Their girlfriends, dates, or wives cooed at them one moment, then flirted with friends and passersby the next moment. Some women would glance at their partners, trying to see what kind of reaction they could elicit, while others were oblivious and simply had a good time. Guys flirted as well. Singles stirred the pot already brewing.

Was this some sort of test men had to pass? It seemed some women wanted to be seen as a goddess for the night, while other women simply wanted to be seen or go unnoticed, as the case might have been. Maybe Daizon was misreading them all, and they just wanted to be left alone. Daizon realized he didn't have a clue. He found their games both befuddling and amusing. It was a game Daizon didn't like, but he was in Rome.

The inebriated band played both rock and country but mostly rock. The true talent of the band, Nitrous, the lead singer, was a bone-thin woman with long spiked black, purple, and yellow hair, one side shaved around her ear. She wore purple lipstick and white pasty makeup. She had an assortment of tattoos covering her legs and arms, with the thorny vine of a rose that wound up her chest and around her neck to a budding rose on the shaved side of her head. Her ear formed the base of the bud, and the rose petals burst out from there. She had multiple piercings through her ears, nose, and eyebrows. Even with everything else she had going on, including what seemed a disconnect from her current reality, the most captivating thing about her was her voice. Daizon imagined she could sing as the archangels came to earth to do God's will at the end of days. She had a rock opera kind of vibe.

Wearing a smirk, Kyle gained Daizon's attention. He had his arms around two curvaceous young women with long blond hair, twins. They both wore the same spaghetti-strap dresses, except one was red while the other was black. Kyle winked at Daizon as he walked them into the sports room. They smiled and waved.

Kyle's serpent tongue had Daizon shaking his head. How?

Waiting patiently for Daizon to turn, Ellie stood with her sassy smile and Daizon's Long Island iced tea. His focus returned to her and his place in line. She glanced and raised an eyebrow at Kyle and the twins. She said, "I heard you might be back on the market."

Daizon took in Ellie's dark brown eyes, the eyes of a good-natured, hardworking woman with a great sense of humor. "You deserve a lot better than me."

"As long as you know that up front, we have a chance." Ellie opened a beer bottle and set it beside the Long Island. "I'll send Becca with a round of Jose Cuervo."

Daizon placed a hundred on the counter and slid it to Ellie. He smiled as she stared at him with those seductive brown eyes. She knew how to make a living with men hitting on her all night. Daizon offered her a smile and walked away.

Ellie took a deep breath, adjusted herself, and grinned at the next man in line. "What can I do for you, handsome?"

Daizon woke on a king-size bed. He searched the strange surroundings, some hotel room. It was probably the place across the parking lot from Shady Jay's. He saw the spaghetti-strap black dress laid over the head of a kitchenette stool. A lace trail led to the bed—bra, thong, and long lace stockings. One stocking hung off the edge of the bed. Sleeping beside him was a beautiful young blond. He said to himself, *Don't do it. Don't do it.*

He glanced down. *Yes, blond.* He smiled and shamed himself at the same time. She was somewhere between twenty-three and twenty-eight. He knew to assume the younger when guessing the age of a woman. *God, what was her name? Cassie? Cassandra? Cass-something?*

She woke with a slight smile that grew toothy-delighted as she glanced down. "Oh, and a good morning to you, too. I guess it's time to slay the dragon again."

Daizon looked down. *Shit.* He gave her a flushed smile.

She pushed him over to his back and mounted him. As she ground against him, her ample features came to erect points. She kissed and bit, grinding for a while before reaching for a condom in the box on the nightstand.

"We don't have to—" Her pointer and middle fingers covered his mouth.

"Shh. Don't ruin the fantasy." With a predatory gaze, she watched his eyes as she slid and rolled on the prophylactic. She guided him with a slow, gyrating thrust of her hips. She slid her hands back and took his hands from her hips. When she interlaced her fingers through his and pinned his hands behind his head, he saw a flash on her finger. That was when he felt it, the sharpness of it, her engagement or wedding ring. She hadn't worn it the night before. He would have noticed. The diamond pricked his skin and scratched. The sharpness of it penetrated much deeper. He felt the wrongness that he was.

CHAPTER EIGHT

RECOVERY

A few more days had passed. Amia's throat throbbed and itched like she had never felt before. Then, remembering she could not remember her past, she laughed at herself. The pressure inside her chest reminded her it was probably better to keep her morbid self-amusement to a minimum. Determined to find relief, she pushed through the pain of using her arm and held ice cubes to her lips. She wanted to shove the things inside her mouth for some quick relief, but the nurse warned against it, saying she could choke. Amia wondered if that would be better. She thought of scratching her throat out with her nails, but breathed deep instead. Then she wondered if she'd made the right choice. Eventually the ice cubes provided enough relief for her to think of something else. She found her eyes moving about the room to the bouquets of flowers.

Working the oxygen out of her nose, she inhaled the soft, calming scents. *What is his name?* He saved her life, and she could not remember who the detective said he was. *What was the detective's name? Johnson, Detective Johnson. Yes.* Amia smiled to herself. *There was Dr. Wolf, Dr. Hempshire, Dr. Avendale, and Daizon, Daizon May.* Amia managed a giddy head bob at her success, which she instantly regretted as the pain once again reminded her of her situation. Then she caught movement out of the corner of her eye from outside the room.

The uniformed officer, a twentysomething woman with dark brown eyes and skin, peeked inside and nodded with a soft smile. Amia performed the smallest of smiles and nodded back. Seeing the officer brought the pictures the detective showed her to the forefront of her mind. The officer returned to her post, but Amia was imagining her own battered form moments away from death. Why would somebody leave her like that, much less do the things they did to her? Then the thought of Daizon's picture brought him into a quasi-dream, imagining his almost glowing, angelic form stood before her and offered her a smile. The beeps on the machines quickened and grabbed Amia's attention. She glanced at the flowers, bare walls, and her window to an outside foreign world. Her body felt more like a shell she was trying to grow into, like a crab or something alien. However, she was alive and aware.

Amia smiled at the thought of reentering the conscious world. The scents of various flowers had drifted into her dreams. She had imagined herself in a field of them while basking in the sun. Those dreams were preferable to the dark entity that clung to the shadows and observed.

Being truly cognizant of her surroundings, even if she did not know who she was, was progress. Her talks with the doctors earlier were like a blur in her past. It was as if somebody had pressed the fast-forward button on her personal remote and finally hit play again. A tingling fire roamed over her skin, especially her legs, and a constant high-pitched tone kept singing in her head like a damaged tuning fork. She reminded herself, *I'm alive.*

A knock at the door grabbed Amia's attention. Nurse Kellie seemed to float inside with the physical therapist carried along in her wake. The guard at her door switched shifts, and a new one arrived, but she could not make out the new, larger man who replaced the previous guard. She noticed he had been watching her but was turning away by the time she noticed him. He moved like the dark entity within her dreams.

She shook her head and said to herself, *I will not let fear and anxiety control me.* She inhaled deep and slow through the pain. Then, sensing the air fill her, she slowly breathed out. *I will get better.*

After a few days of physical therapy, her arms were no longer like logs and she could move her legs, not very well, but she could move them. A glance at her toned arms showed her she was somebody who exercised regularly. She wondered what activities she enjoyed. Was she outgoing or an introvert? Did she like puzzles? She grinned at the thought of her fit arms and legs being rather useless at the moment. Her arms were not completely useless, she decided as she scratched her nose and readied herself for her next therapy session.

Chapter Nine

EAST COAST WELLNESS

High on a cliffside overlook, small islands speckled the deep blue ocean below. The dark blue of the ocean extended what seemed like forever underneath a pale blue sky. Amia lost herself, staring out from her wheelchair. It took little to lose herself; she still didn't know who she was. Her one grounding influence, her silver earrings, said she was Amia. And now that they were back in her ears, she felt a warmth whenever she reached for them. Two weeks had passed since she'd woken from her coma, and she still did not know who she was.

The same questions, or different variations of them, ran through her mind daily. What kind of life had she lived? What kind of person was she? What did she care about, and who cared about her? What kind of work did she do? What did she like and dislike? Basically, who was she?

Physical and psychological therapy over the last couple of weeks allowed her some progression. Her movements were slow and arduous, but she could move all her extremities and had begun walking and talking again. She stroked the large white bandage that was still wrapped around the top of her head. The wrap was due to come off the next morning, and Amia wondered what she would find underneath.

Buried in a pile of warmed blankets, she pushed past the pain and stretched out her arms. She wanted to feel the touch of the chilled air and warm sun. The bruises on her arms were a faded brown and yellow. She wore matching bruises on her less-swollen face and legs.

The other clients of the Whole Me program arrived throughout the day. She wondered, *What will they see when they look at me?* Afraid and curious to meet them in equal parts, she was eager to learn their stories and why they were there. After all, they needed help, too.

She smiled at Penny, her attendant friend. Facial expressions seemed the best form of communication, since she still had a hard time forming her words correctly. The words she thought of in her mind did not always make it to her mouth as intended. Amia increased her proficiency over the last couple of weeks from making sounds and grunting noises in the beginning to her current ability to spit out syllables and sound in a way that neared normal speech. If she tried speaking while too excited or frustrated, sounds jumbled and became inarticulate noise.

Amia decided what she could do was show her gratitude to these gracious people helping her. She smiled, listened, and did as guided. Her battle was not with them but with the brain fog keeping her from functioning correctly.

A kindly middle-aged woman, Penny spoke often of her daughter, Rose, and her son, Timmy. Rose blessed her with a grandchild recently, little Emma, and Timmy was smoking too much of the weed ever since they made it legal.

Penny said, "Don't you get me wrong though, Amia. I love that boy of mine. He's a sweetheart. He's just mixed up with the wrong crowd. You know how it is. You try your best to show 'em the way of good, honest living, but you can't compete with their friends. They're gonna do what they want. Doesn't matter what you say or do. It's natural for 'em to rebel. They gotta find out for themselves. You know? Experience life on their own. That's just the way it is. You just have to accept it and do your best. That's what I do."

Amia smiled again at Penny. She did not know, but she also didn't think it mattered. Penny wanted somebody to talk with, to listen to her. Amia didn't mind. She actually rather enjoyed listening. Listening seemed natural. It was the least she could do for this woman, who was giving so much of herself.

"Are you warm enough, princess?" No sooner than she asked, Penny seemed to remember something and rushed out. "Amia. I know I'm supposed to use your name. I'm sorry." Penny checked the blankets, retucking them. Then, in her next breath, Penny continued. "Amia is a pretty name. Sounds Mexican. You have the look of a princess to me. You have that naturally tanned copper skin that's so beautiful. Never you mind those bumps and bruises. They'll go away soon. They're already fading pretty good. Everybody will see what I see. You'll see too."

Amia nodded at Penny. She didn't recognize the constantly morphing, battered image in the mirror when she looked. She didn't know what her normal was. The buzzing pressure in her head, which seemed to ally with her clouded mind, left only impressions of something more. The haze was like cloud formations, implying faint representations of something familiar.

Glancing around, Amia found there were several people either walking or being wheeled about. She not only wondered what their history was but yearned for that sense of pain and feeling from her own memories. She did not even have her memories to keep her company. It was like she was being exiled from her own body and was now living in somebody else's shell. This shell did not belong to her, which would explain why it would not function properly.

Then Amia remembered the photos Detective Johnson showed her. That battered body was the shell she took over. It did not feel like her. Was the pain of remembrance the pain she wanted to know? Amia's eyes glistened.

"I'm sorry. I've gone and upset you." Penny dabbed the tears from Amia's face with a soft cloth. "I just don't know when to keep my mouth shut sometimes." She cupped the side of Amia's face with the gentlest of touches. "How about we go for a walk before your physical therapy? A walk sounds nice, right?"

Amia nodded, unable to voice her apology. She wondered if she had always been so emotional, or if it was something new. Some inner voice answered, *It's okay to hurt*. It was a stray thought, but it made her smile.

Penny guided them toward a pebbled walking path on the right that veered off the main cement path. The main path was wide and led directly to the Whole Me entrance. The tributary walking path meandered along the edge of the property. It branched out from the main walking path and off in the distance.

Groundskeepers tended to shrubbery and freshly planted flowers that painted a colorful welcome to either side of the main pathway and parking lot entrance. Strategically placed plants, flowers, and shrubs covered the entire grounds as if by an artisan's touch.

East Coast Wellness Center had the look of a white tiered modern castle lined with dark glass. A massive dark-glassed dome covered the Whole Me entrance, cafeteria, and meditation area. Multiple walkways acted like small streams meandering throughout the lush castle grounds.

That was when Amia saw him dressed in a black suit and white-collared dress shirt. A couple of buttons at the top of the shirt remained unbuttoned, and he carried a black duffel bag at his side. He had an erect but relaxed posture to go with what she knew was a muscular form hidden beneath flowing attire. The surrounding people gave way to his presence as if it were a bubble. He seemed to infect those around him with smiles, long glances, and greetings.

He paused before the entryway and observed the grounds. His gaze slowly fell upon hers. They held eye contact for the briefest of moments that seemed to last forever but ended abruptly when Penny turned them off onto the smaller walking path.

"Da-z-n?" Amia was not sure if it came out right. *Daizon May. He's the man in the pictures. Without him, I wouldn't be alive.* There was a deeper recognition, but she could not place it. She wanted to thank him for saving her life, for all the flowers. It seemed knowing he would be there and him actually being there affected her in a giddy way she had not expected.

Amia closed her eyes to concentrate. She wanted to talk with him, to meet him. "Da-zn A—" *God, say it.* She had to see him. She tried to point toward him. Her arm was better but still slow. She knew she could move faster. She had to gain his attention before he went inside.

Penny paused her pushing of Amia's chair and leaned forward. "Oh my. What is it? Something has your attention. It's okay." Penny looked toward the entrance. She saw nothing out of the ordinary.

He was gone. Was it Amia's imagination? She tried telling Penny what she saw, what happened. "D-z-n M-ay, I saw" was roughly what came out. Other tries resulted in similar repetition. Amia's struggling arms fell with a sigh.

"It's okay." Penny tucked Amia's arms back inside the blankets. She petted her shoulder. "Nobody wants to be here, but you'll get better. You'll get better soon, and then you can go home." After another lingering glance toward the entrance and another pat on the shoulder, they continued on their stroll of the grounds.

Amia's heart fluttered, threatening to burst through her chest. Her malfunctioning lungs could not hold a breath. No, there were breaths. They were quick. Her body tingled with new zingy sensations beyond the ones she felt right along. Her body was trying to tell her something that her mind could not convey. Maybe her mind was sending her messages through her body since the normal means of conveyance were not working. Words entered her mind, *Neurons that fire together, wire together.* Where was that from? Everything blended inside her mind like some kind of unrecognizable smoothie.

Her fluttering heart slowed. She closed her eyes and thought, *Who am I?*

CHAPTER TEN

COMMITTED

D aizon paused before entering his voluntary caging at the East Coast Wellness Center. It was the Whole Me side of the facility, but that did not seem to make much of a difference. It was the thought of being there that gnawed at him. Hospital staff, in multiple shades of hospital garb, mingled with themselves and walked with patients.

Tonya voluntarily committed him for two months. The Whole Me program supposedly based their outline on the concepts of mindfulness and self-compassion with an added component of individual counseling. It was a kind of AA retreat for depressed people. The people there suffered from severe forms of anxiety, abuse, and ailments of the mind, that kind of thing. *That bitch.* Daizon laughed.

Turning his attention toward the main walkway and the oceanside view, he found, "Amia?" A bandage was wrapped around her head, and blankets smothered her in her wheelchair. She was being pushed by a talkative, grandmotherly figure. Her face had more of an oval shape now instead of oblong. She seemed to have a copper tone to her skin, while the healing bruises provided some different hues. It was her. Her bright blue eyes locked onto his. The depth behind those eyes drew him. Even in her current state, she shone like a star.

Granny turned them onto a walking path. He could not just go over and talk with her. Well, he could, but what would he say? The inner strength this woman must possess. The pain she must be enduring. Right then was not the time. He had to check into the program. The state she was in when he found her, she would not recognize him. Granny pushed her along the path.

Tonya must have known Amia was a puzzle that was irresistible to him. She could have told him. Daizon entered the facility.

⁂

After he passed a guarded entryway checkpoint, the interior opened with an air of floral vegetation. A massive waterfall wall ran a good twenty feet off at a diagonal, with cafeteria tables on either side. It seemed to serve as a barrier wall directing the flow of traffic to a reception area. The wall alternated between smooth and stepped-out rough boulders. Vines and flowering water plants weaved all about the wall and around the bottom of the pool area, which recycled the water in a churning flow. Vines and plants surrounded the whole of the great room, rising to the dome. The exotic display filled the mind with splashes of sound, color, and intrigue while the scents permeated the room. It was like entering a tropical retreat minus the tropical heat.

A couple dozen people sat at small dining and viewing tables that surrounded the water-wall feature. Staff mixed with patients. Some conversed, but what filled the room was the gentle splashing thrush and visually appealing nature of the wall and surroundings. It was an excellent distraction.

A glass room jetted off on the far side of the fountain. It was a circular area with white sand and large, smooth rocks. It was probably for sitting on or maybe meditating beside? A wood deck wrapped around the entire Zen Garden. Floor mats and pillows circled the room. Large unlit candles with some kind of triangular plate stood in front of each mat. It was hard to tell what else was in there from Daizon's current position.

Orderlies in white casually spread themselves throughout the area. Most of them stood on the edges, evading people's attention, while others mingled with smiles. It was a different type of evasion or infiltration, requiring a distinct set of skills. It was a subtle use of subterfuge. There was a fine line between orderly and security, and they were probably mixed. Glances revealed dozens of security cameras strategically placed.

Their eyes were on him. Daizon returned orderlies' attentions with a slight smile and a nod. He played the role of lamb. More eyes turned on him. He was the threat in the room, and they knew it. A wolf knows a wolf. He continued to the reception desk.

Sherri, as her nameplate told him, was a thickset young woman with large red glasses about two or three sizes too big. They fit her as soon as her smile and expression hinted at a playful-friendly personality. "How may I help you?"

"I'm Darren Mason, here to check into the Whole Me program."

Sherri stared, sizing him up with a pondering smile. She had one of those smiles that told you she knew more about the comings and goings inside this place than anyone else. "Well, let's get you situated, Mr. Mason."

"Thank you."

Sherri's fingers pressed adeptly at the keyboard. She glanced at her computer screen and placed a quick call before typing again. "Mr. Mason is here . . . Thank you, Daryll." It was a syrupy thank-you. "Daryll will be out in a moment to show you the way. You're welcome to a seat while you wait."

Daizon smiled. "Thanks. Have you worked here for a long time, Sherri?"

"Since we opened the Whole Me wing a few years ago." Her eyes grew with excitement. "You'll love this place. Dr. Wolf is amazing. She has to be the smartest person I know. And she's nice, too. She treats everyone around here with respect, and everybody loves her. You'll see. Daryll is going to bring you to meet her."

"That's good to know. Thank you. It seems they know what they're doing. They placed the perfect person out front to welcome and direct people."

Sherri beamed. "Thank you, Mr. Mason."

Daizon pondered a politically correct way on how to ask about the mentally unstable people held at the facility. "You have a lot of security hanging around. Should I keep an eye out for dangerous people?"

Sherri glanced at some orderlies watching Daizon and reassured him with a broadening, impish smile. "We'll take care of you while you're here. Don't you worry. Most people don't even notice the security." She finished with a wink.

A towering brick of a young man, Daryll, wearing a white orderlies' uniform, approached. The human Sasquatch smiled with interest toward Sherri. He made Kyle seem like a small man, and that was hard to do. He spoke in a low rumble. "Hey, sweetness." He leaned deep into Sherri's window.

Sherri's eyes flicked to Daizon. She was this man's sun, as he was her moon. "Daryll, this is Mr. Mason." She rolled her eyes at Daryll, doing that covert head jab thing that really was not covert, because Daryll did not pick up on the signals. Or did he?

Daryll smiled and winked at Sherri before turning to Daizon and rising to his full height. He said, "Hey, Mr. Mason. I'm Daryll." He held out his larger-than-life hand. It was the mouth of an anaconda. "Let's take you to Dr. Karen."

Daizon inserted his hand into the mouth of the anaconda and smiled. He said, "Damn, you're a big man." Its mouth clamped down. It was a grip that conveyed, *I'll crush you if you even think of getting out of line, but hey, I can be your friend if you stay in line.*

Daryll gave Sherri a raised-brow glance. She rolled her eyes and smiled with a flush. Daryll said, "I'm the baby in the family." An amused grin stretched over his face.

⚶

Daryll, still wearing his amused grin, nodded at Daizon before he stepped out of Dr. Karen Wolf's office. It was a cozy office with a plush couch and two chairs. She lined it with shelves upon shelves of books. Besides plenty of psychology books, there was a wide range of fiction and nonfiction. Were those erotica books mixed in there? The side wall had a massive bay window that offered an excellent view of the grounds and ocean. Daizon gazed out at that view for a long moment. Islands seemed to cling to the coast by an unseen thread. From this height, the ocean reached beyond sight to the horizon.

When his eyes finally came back to Dr. Wolf behind a desk, he found her watching him with a kindly, patient smile. This was a woman clearly confident in wearing her own skin. She said, "I'm glad you came, Darren. Or do you prefer Daizon?"

Daizon raised an eyebrow at the owl-eyed doctor. She was a petite, fit woman with long black hair in a frizzy braid. She wore large glasses low on her nose and stood maybe five foot three or four inches. She had a calm, see-through-you, curious and slightly mischievous demeanor.

She said, "Yes, I know who you are. My guess would be that most of the staff knows, but we'll pretend not to know if that's what you would like. Your presence here won't go beyond these walls."

Daizon smiled. "I'll have to have a talk with my manager. Darren was my given name." He left out the part about preferring Daizon.

"Tonya told me you needed my help. I agreed to give you an opportunity. I understand the need to keep your information private, and that's the way it will be. We expect the same courtesy for others in return."

Daizon nodded in agreement.

Dr. Wolf continued. "Let's talk about goals. Mine are simple. I'm here to help guide and retrain people in the way they view themselves and, to an extent, view other people. I don't cure people. I help them understand and deal with difficult emotions and hopefully provide them with some tools to help them experience life in a new light. I expect you to take part fully if you choose to stay. Otherwise, you are welcome to leave right now. I'll have been happy to have met you and wish you the best." She paused, comfortable in the silence as it stretched.

Daizon wondered how much this woman knew. Could she see through his mask? *I'm fine*, he thought. He said, "I'm here to learn."

"If you are here to learn, here is your first lesson. Everyone has issues. We often try to present our best self while hoping the worst remains hidden. I deal in the hidden, in the dark. Only together can we bring light into those dark places. It takes courage." Dr. Wolf grinned. It was a kindly wolfish grin. "Are you willing to go into those dark places with me, Daizon?"

Heart thumping, Daizon said, "I'll do my best."

"That's all I ask." Her wolfish grin slid into a soft smile. "Let's get you settled in. You will find a few books on mindfulness and self-compassion in your room. They will help augment the program and provide a base for some exercises and information we learn." She moved from behind her desk toward the door. "Daryll will take you to your room, where you will secure your belongings and find the mandatory attire for your stay. We posted a schedule in your room with the daily activities. We'll go over the full outline"—she glanced at her watch—"with the entire group in a couple of hours. Until then, after you settle into your room, you are free to roam the grounds." She opened the door. "Daryll, please escort Mr. Mason to his room and give him the basic tour."

"Yes, Dr. Karen."

"Thank you." Dr. Wolf swung her easy posture to Daizon and offered her hand. Daizon used his not-too-firm handshake. She cupped her other hand over his and then moved it to cup his elbow. This was the two-handed handshake used by politicians and salespeople to insist they were being sincere and you were their primary focus at that moment. They used it all the time to sell their souls. Besides the handshake, she was steady, confident, and relaxed. She was so real, it threw Daizon off as he worked on an angle of approach. She continued. "I think we'll have a chance to learn from each other, Darren. Thank you for coming."

Daizon smiled. "Thank you for allowing me into the program. I'm sure I have much to learn. I don't know how much I'll have to teach."

"I find there is always so much I don't know. Think of our relationship as more of a partnership that works best with shared perspectives and knowledge. In fact, I think you will find the more we share, the more beneficial our partnership becomes."

Daizon's mind churned with fear at the implication of what she wanted. He smiled.

Daizon closed the locker door inside his room. It was a cozy second-floor room with a large window. The window overlooked a mountain forest nestled up beside the ocean. A large walking path meandered and hugged the coastline as it threaded into the forest in the distance. A few smaller trails looped off into the thicker part of the forest before returning to the main trail. It was this main trail that hugged the coast and led back to the facility.

Amia's hypnotic, bright blue eyes stayed with him. *Why is she here? Tonya had to know she would be here. Right?* Daizon imagined what Amia had endured. Then he thought of not knowing who he was and not remembering anything that happened. She had a clean slate with the world before her. What he wouldn't give to have a clean slate. How far would he have to go back to change the things that happened to him or the things he had seen, done, and experienced? *If I didn't know, I wouldn't care. I would be free. Is that what it's like for her? Would she even care about forgetting the past? What if her past was beautiful before? She would want to remember. Not knowing, is that a blessing or a curse?* Beyond the bruises, bandages, and blankets, Daizon knew this woman was more than a survivor. He could see it in her eyes that she was an observer, a fighter, and astute by the depth in her gaze. This was a woman who sought knowledge and didn't shy away from a challenge. She would want to know about her past, no matter how much it hurt.

Then Daizon remembered Tonya telling him he could prepare for the role while he was there, or he could seek help. Daizon shook his head, not knowing what to think.

Knowing he was stalling, Daizon clipped his DARREN—THE WHOLE ME photo badge to the left breast pocket of his dark blue scrubs. With a sigh and a shake of his head, he continued fussing with a few micro-adjustments of his attire, using the mirror on the locker. *Why am I here?* Was it really for his mental health, the role, or was it to meet Amia? Did he really want anyone to know what happened to him? Would they really care? What if people found out he was there? His family, the press—they would have a field day ripping him apart. No, they would assume he was researching a new role. It was the truth, but not the whole truth. His fans considered him a man's man, the type of man women wanted to be with and men wanted to hang out with. Daizon knew people wanted the illusion he provided. Darren was just another character he needed to play while he was at the psychiatric facility. It was the last person he wanted to play. He couldn't imagine anything more frightening at that moment. Perhaps it was imagining people finding out he was so much less than what they believed or than what he believed he should be?

A slight movement in the mirror snapped Daizon from his inner turmoil of trying to decide whether staying was going to be worth the pain he knew was ahead. He grinned in the mirror at the bored-looking Daryll. *How could I almost forget about the behemoth? Now, that's a man with talent.* "How long have you and Sherri been seeing each other? Seems like a good girl?"

Eyes narrowed, Daryll replied, "Long enough."

Daizon raised an eyebrow. Still fidgeting, he kept studying Daryll through the reflection. "Come on, now. Is that 'Long enough, we don't have to try anymore'? Or, 'Long enough, she's a pain in my ass, but she's damn hot and I like her feisty nature'?"

Daryll eased out a lion's grin. "We don't discuss our personal lives here."

Scrunching his smirking face, Daizon cocked an eye. *Isn't that exactly what you do here?* He said, "So, she's a pain in your ass, but she's damn hot and you like her feisty nature. But you can't say that out loud because you think it would violate some unspoken oath. See, that wasn't so hard."

The big man said, "It's about respect."

"Tom-ato, to-mato. Relax a little. This is between you and me. What do you do for fun? Hobbies? You know, like wrestle bears or something like that?"

"I write poetry," Daryll deadpanned.

Daizon eyed Daryll for a long moment. He played along. "Good for you. I've heard it helps to get in touch with your emotions and stuff like that, right?"

Daryll rolled his eyes. With a sigh and a smirk, he assumed his relaxed posture of observation.

Daizon raised his brows at Daryll as he fumbled with his attire and name tag. "It takes work to achieve a look of nonchalance, you know?" Daizon continued his fuss. He took a deep breath and offered his reflection a reassuring nod. He would play the role of Darren Mason. Was that even possible? *God, that's the last role I want to play.* His next steps would be worse than standing naked and giving a speech. It would be like peeling off the nakedness to reveal the true flesh. He could see the look in Dr. Wolf's eyes. She wanted nothing less than to devour his true flesh. Would he let her? Did he want to heal the wounds nobody could see? Could they be healed? And then there was Amia, the way he found her on his property.

I could go right now and nobody would care, nobody would know. Daizon thought of Amia's pale blue form clinging to life at the edge of the pond below his home. He instantly contrasted that image with her bright blue eyes full of life. He wanted to run, to escape before the cage door closed and he was just another animal seeking freedom.

CHAPTER ELEVEN

STRANGERS

A lmost to the end of the parallel bars with Nancy, the physical therapist, on one side and Penny on the other, Amia focused on her left leg while holding firm on the right. Nancy told her it was like building new bridges, and once built, traffic would flow. It would travel slowly at first but would increase as her strength and reflexes returned to normal. Amia found her rehabilitation to be more like building an entire infrastructure. She built bridges, roads, walking paths, train tracks, subway systems, airports, and the means to travel said forms of transportation. And then there was the communication network. What she wouldn't give to mediate a working relationship between her mind and muscles, never mind her speech.

Meanwhile, she also thought of Daizon. Was it actually him? It had to be. Why else would his name be in her head? Did she know him? Did he know her? If they knew each other, he could help her remember. He would help her. But what if he didn't know her? If she knew him, how did she know him? Was he a friend? A lover? Amia smiled and flushed at the thought as butterflies filled her stomach. Or was the fluttering and twisting in her stomach from the mush of smoothies she ate for half her meals? What if he didn't know her at all? Amia brought her attention back to her task. She tightened her stomach, left butt cheek, and thigh. Pressing on a stiff right leg, she took the weight off the left, *Lift, let the knee bend, move, move.* She flashed a sweaty smile at her six inches of progression. In two weeks, she went from needing help to bend her arms and legs, especially her legs, to half-inch steps, to three-inch, and her current six-inch feats of wonder. She neared the end of the parallel bars.

Penny cheered, "Great job. You're amazing."

Nancy, the physical therapist who looked like a cute mouse but sang like a drill sergeant, said, "You're not done yet. You have more to give. Do you want it? Earn it. One more step. Let go of the fear. Focus on the process."

Amia smiled, half wanting to slap Nancy and half knowing if she did, she would fall. Amia repeated the motions as separate steps rather than as a fluid movement. Every step seemed a foreign task. Her thoughts returned to Daizon. *It was Daizon. Dr. Wolf said he would be here. But why? Does he have a girlfriend? A wife? He has the look of a dream.* He visited her dreams. She smiled at the thought of him approaching her with that dreamy, intense smile she just knew he had and him leaning in to kiss her with the softest of touches. Her blood heated.

Focus, she told herself as she flashed Penny and Nancy a glance. Then Amia wondered how much of the sweat was from exertion and how much was from her imagined encounter. She grinned at the thought. If he knew her, he would have actually visited her at the hospital instead of just sending flowers. He would have gone to her as she strolled with Penny. Amia remembered Dr. Wolf had told her he had signed up for the program before her, so he would not have known she would be there. Then she wondered if finding her half-dead made him sign up for the program.

He was a handsome man with a certain intensity about him that spoke of depth, danger, and passion. Their eyes met for only an instant, but she was sure of the intensity. She could see he cared about her wellness, but not once did he visit her at the hospital. Why? Was it as simple as him finding her and being concerned about her well-being?

⚶

With Amia's workout done, she washed up, and then Penny wheeled her past the water wall to the edge of the meditation room and through the double glass door entryway. The meditation room was like a slightly tinted glass bubble cut in half, like a fantastic snow globe. Smooth stones and boulders of various sizes sat on the well-groomed white sand. A twelve-foot-wide white hardwood floor circled the Zen Garden. Exercise mats and meditation cushions were spread evenly around on the hardwood floor with a single unlit cylinder candle in front of each spot. A few extra-long wooden matches and a candle-snuffing tool lay beside each of the candles. A black triangular base on the other side of the candles held first names written in white. Penny rolled Amia past words and phrases attached to the wall on plaques: *courage, hope, trust, perspective is a version of the truth.* The words and phrases surrounded, but also blended with, the room. *Probably so they would not be a distraction,* Amia thought.

Dr. Wolf sat at the far end, her seemingly ever-patient self. Amia observed three men and seven women, not including herself, Dr. Wolf, or Penny. The group circled around to their names and stood with nervous nods and smiles. Finding their names seemed to ease some of the stress, as their postures relaxed ever so slightly. They climbed over their mats and sat on their meditation cushions.

Two empty mats lay in the last two spots, which would complete the circle. The nameplate to the left read DARREN, and the one on the right read AMIA. Penny wheeled Amia to the position behind her spot. She tensed at the thought of climbing out of her chair in front of all these strangers. A glance around confirmed their eyes on her. Nervousness mixed with curiosity, and she was the show. Would she stumble out of the gate? She gripped the rails of her wheelchair, not sure what they expected of her. She wanted to be like everybody else and assume her position on the floor, but she also didn't want to leave the safety of her chair.

Penny whispered over Amia's shoulder. "I can help you onto the pillow?"

Amia hesitated. That was when he walked in, past a large usher who remained at the door. He strode in with what seemed an easy, unassuming nature. His gentle smile contrasted with a rugged form. He scanned the room. Her thumping heart wanted out of her chest. Heat washed over her in a rolling flash and found a home churning inside her stomach like some kind of hot twister. Her smile stretched out to meet his when his gaze fell on her. His eyes held an intensity that spoke of deep thought and empathy. They searched her for deeper understanding.

Daizon, she thought. As he approached, Amia absently reached for her silver earring. She rubbed the earring between her fingers. His smile grew as he got closer. Amia's chest heaved with small breaths and rapid heartbeats. His eyes held hers as he positioned himself in front of her and leaned down with a hand out.

"Hi. I'm Darren. It's nice to meet you, Amia."

As gracefully as she could, Amia moved her hand to his. Her fine motor skills were coming back, but—God.

He noticed and reached out further to meet her effort with a warm grip. His smile split a rift in her mind. The buzzing sensation in her head burst. Something unlocked inside her, allowing her to speak her first fluid word, "Hi." It was such a small thing. Her smile grew and clamped. A happy tear threatened her composure. She let go of his hand and pressed her fingers to her lips.

Darren leaned back with a not-sure-of-what-he-did-wrong look of concern on his face. Penny leaned over Amia while cupping both of her shoulders in her hands. "Sweetie?"

Amia's face lit with emotions, joy being the primary one. Darren relaxed his posture and gave a warm smile in return. Darren—his name was Darren, not Daizon? She dimmed for a moment but quickly regained her focus and tried building on the momentum. "Hi, Darren. Sorry." Her speech was slow and broken but clear. Amia rolled her eyes up and pointed to her head. "My mind"—she rolled her eyes down and rolled her tongue out with a silly face—"and mouth, they haven't been working together." Her smile grew again. "I'm happy."

Daizon said, "That's good. Well, not that they were not working together, but now they are, I mean. Yeah. Sorry. I noticed you eyeing that pillow. Would you like a hand?"

Unsure, she debated internally. Would she risk being the entertainment? Amia gripped the chair and smiled her assent.

Darren retrieved the pillow and placed it in Amia's lap. Her tension melted away at the unexpected gesture. She could not help but laugh.

He said, "I mean really, you look like you already have a comfy spot. Best seat in the room by the looks. I should probably take mine. I think the doctor has it out for me. She thinks I want to be the center of attention or something like that. I don't know. If I must." Daizon glanced at Dr. Wolf and continued. "Oh yeah, she's definitely watching me. We'll talk later. It was nice to meet you, Amia."

Amia watched him wave small flashes of hello to the entire group, who were now all staring at him. He adjusted his butt onto his cushion. He leaned this way and that, pushing and pulling at the cushion. Then he adjusted his sitting position, first with his legs out, next with one leg out and one bent up, and finally with both knees up and leaning over them with his arms. He winked at her before feigning a childlike I'm-innocent-it-wasn't-me look toward Dr. Wolf.

A glance around the room showed amused eyes focused on him while he focused on Dr. Wolf, seemingly oblivious. Amia laughed silently to herself and brought her attention to Dr. Wolf.

Apparently, everyone else had the same idea and switched their attention to Dr. Wolf as well. There was a lighter air in the room. Tension had eased not only from herself, but she could see it eased in others as well. She glanced at Darren for a moment and thought she caught him peeking at her from the corner of his eyes, but he kept them focused on Dr. Wolf.

Dr. Wolf fixed everyone except Darren with a steady smile. With him, she smirked. She had everyone's attention. "Thank you all for coming. Giving up eight weeks to focus on how you view yourself is not a simple decision. We all have bills to pay and lives to live. I'm sure some of you are doubting why you came. Some of you are thinking to yourselves, 'I'm not really worth it, but I'm tired of hating myself. I want to feel better about myself, and maybe there's a chance this strange woman knows something that can help change my life.' Maybe?"

After a brief pause, she continued. "We have an ability to fool everybody, even ourselves, into thinking everything is okay. After all, life is messy. Who cares if I don't feel good about myself? If I don't like myself, why should anyone else? Or, we obsess over all our inferior qualities and always imagine we can be better. If I could only do this better or that. I bet if I had that thing, my life would be a lot better. He's got it so good. Or, she's so smart and pretty. How many of you have had some of these thoughts?"

Subtle nods of agreement, nervous smiles, and laughs spilled from the room. All hands were raised.

Dr. Wolf said, "It's okay to have those thoughts. We're human. We naturally compare ourselves and our lives with others around us and the way they live their lives. We want to fit in and be part of the community." Dr. Wolf paused and gathered everyone's eyes. "We should make one thing clear from the start. I cannot make you better. I'm not a miracle worker. I'm not selling magic pills or a process that will cure all your ailments for the rest of your life. Poof." She gestured an imaginary explosion with her wiggling fingers and smiled.

Laughs bounced around the room.

"We created the Whole Me program around the idea of coming to accept ourselves for who we are, good and bad, and approaching life with another lens. Not only the way we see ourselves but the way we see others as well. We do this in a combination of ways. There will be individual counseling sessions, blended with group and individual activities, along with mindfulness and compassion training. These things will help build our new foundation. We will gear specifics within those foundations for each one of you, because each one of us is similar but different. It's okay to be similar and different." Dr. Wolf stared around the room at each slightly terrified person.

The man directly to Dr. Wolf's left, Conner, had strings of shiny hair combed over the egg-shaped balding crest on the top of his head. A wiry man in his late twenties or early thirties, he had quick eyes that shifted with his seemingly hyper-nervous thoughts. He smiled at Dr. Wolf and quickly cast his eyes down. Then his eyes darted to others as if trying to determine whether they were watching him.

Amia recognized the anxious feelings he exhibited. Some of them anyway. She did not have any memory of her past. Everything to her was new but sometimes familiar without knowing why. She knew what certain things were but did not know why or how she knew them. She was there because Dr. Wolf, Dr. Hemp, and Dr. Avendale concluded the environment and process used in the Whole Me program might help her situation. While she recovered, she would be safe.

Dr. Wolf told her during one session at the hospital, "It must be scary not knowing who you are or anything about what happened to you. It's okay to be scared." She spoke of how the program benefited people with repressed or violent memories. Dr. Wolf thought the program might work similarly for her.

What if it doesn't work? What if I'm destined to live out the rest of my life without knowing who I am, my dreams, my family? Her family must miss her. Instinctively, Amia reached for her silver earring with her left hand. The warmth she felt from that small piece of jewelry somehow assured her she was loved. Would she ever remember?

She glanced over to see Darren steal a glance at her. He smiled as she caught him, and she warmed at the thought of him wanting to steal a glance. Then she wondered what he saw. A large white bandage wrapped around her head. Yellow and brown bruises faded, refusing to go away. Her left hand slid from her earring and brushed the side of her face. Did he really see her, or was he just kind and curious? Then she wondered why he was going by Darren and not Daizon. Her current state of mind made it difficult to wrap her mind around him using a different name. Was it him?

Dr. Wolf regained her voice. "The step each of you took in coming here was a difficult one. The next steps will be more difficult because they will require you to open yourself to your greatest fears, the ones that always seem to stand in the way of you reaching your destination. Let me give you a basic outline of the program. As you already know, the program lasts eight weeks. Week one is an introduction to mindfulness and compassion through group and individual activities. We will also begin our one-on-one counseling sessions. We'll meet for group sessions and activities a few times a day. Our beginning sessions will be short and will lengthen over the weeks as we progress. There will be personal time and time to reflect on what you have learned. Weeks two through eight will build on previous progress at an individual and group level. We invite family and friends to visit during the last couple of weeks as we prepare for life outside this environment. As with the rest of the program, we will schedule these visits according to the individual needs. Simple, right?"

Nervous laughs filled the room.

"You will find words and phrases hung on the walls of the room for when you want to find some inspiration, courage, reminders, or simply to pacify some curiosity. Let's start with mindfulness. At its very essence, mindfulness is about being aware in the moment. Think of your connection with the earth. Notice where you feel that pressure physically. Perhaps it's in your buttocks, trying to find a comfortable position on your seat." Dr. Wolf paused, staring at Darren with a smile as he situated himself again.

His head popped up, and he glanced around the room. Smiling faces stared at him. "Sorry, I think I got it. Yup, that's better." He waved a nothing-to-see-here kind of wave and stared ahead at Dr. Wolf as if he were not the center of attention.

Dr. Wolf circled her focus around the room, making eye contact as she spoke. "Perhaps for others, they feel their feet pressing against the floor. Or the way their skin presses against the material covering their foot as it presses against another material and then against the floor. Can you feel the air around your foot? A coolness that somehow swirls around it even though it's covered with shoes and stockings. Now, wiggle your toes and notice the sensations. Can you feel each toe as it presses against the restricting force? Can you feel each toe moving in space? How about the muscles, tendons, and bones as you flex?"

The group seemed enthralled with the grounding exercise. Then, without thinking, Amia brought in a slow breath through her nose. She felt the coolness of the air as it passed through her nostrils and windpipe and entered her lungs. They expanded with the breath, pushing out her diaphragm and filling her body with energy.

Dr. Wolf's voice drifted into Amia's thoughts. "This is part of one of our grounding exercises. It's your connection to the world that you will always fall back on throughout our sessions and beyond. We'll go through multiple exercises, and after we have gone through them, you will choose the ones that work best for you. You might even make slight alterations to make them your own. Another grounding exercise that seems to work is mindful breathing. Focus on your breath as it enters your nose. Notice the sensations as air enters and flows over your skin. Feel it as it rushes down and into your lungs. Notice every sensation you feel as the breath enters your chest and fills your body. What do you feel?"

Amia's breath caught. *I've done this before.* Excitement interrupted her thought process, and she dug for answers only to find her original clue. She knew what she was doing was called mindful breathing and that it was a grounding exercise. But as always, she did not know how or why she knew.

Dr. Wolf's voice came back into awareness. "We normally think of compassion as having sympathy for and a deep awareness of suffering in others. It motivates us to attain or use knowledge so we may ease that suffering in others. Think about it. We see a baby crying and we want to comfort her. Does she need a diaper change? Is she hungry? Does she have gas? We search for clues and attend to her needs."

Dr. Wolf assessed her audience. "Here's another example. A neighbor moves frantically about their vehicle. We inquire about their distress and learn they left the lights on all night and now their car won't start and they're going to be late for work. We tell them we have jumper cables and offer to jump-start their car, which we hope might jump-start their day and help ease their suffering. In either case, we expect nothing in return. We do it because we see them in distress, gain a general awareness of their suffering, and provide help if we have the requisite knowledge and are able. Our reward that we were not seeking comes from knowing that we helped ease their stress and anguish. We helped ease their suffering so they could continue with their day without that stress and anguish. In a selfish sense, it makes us feel better to help them feel better. What we will do here in the Whole Me program is learn to direct that compassion toward ourselves when we need it, self-compassion."

She took in all the transfixed, contemplating faces. "Before we practice the grounding exercises that are fundamental to the process, let's go around the room for introductions. A first name and hello are fine. If you would like to share a little more, that's okay too. Remember, it's only what you are comfortable sharing. I'll start."

Anxiety crept into Amia at the thought of having to introduce herself. She'd barely opened the communication network a few minutes earlier. Was it still open? Did it still work? A look at the others in the room told her she wasn't the only one with the fear of speaking to the group.

Dr. Wolf began the introductions. "My name is Karen. You all know me as Dr. Wolf. Hello and thank you for having the courage to come. It takes courage coming into the wolf's den when you know you could be what's next for supper. I'll promise not to devour you if you promise to be respectful of my pups and the process. I'm a protective mother, and just so you know, I consider all of you my pups in this process. Intruders will be dealt with swiftly." She offered a smirking glare around the room and gained some laughs.

She inhaled as if preparing herself for a heavy lift. "My call to counseling began with trying to understand why my mother committed suicide when I was eight years old. She was always there for me. She gave me kisses and hugs and let me know she loved me more than anything in this world. But, as I came to find out, she did not love herself."

Dr. Wolf received nods of understanding. "It broke my dad for a long time. My sister and I didn't understand either. We were a happy family. Why would she do this to us if she loved us? My father brought us to individual and family counseling, and living slowly got easier. We found a new normal. Through my pursuit of why, I began to find my way and realized I wanted to help others by becoming a counselor. Then I learned about mindfulness and the concept of self-compassion. I understood that my mother could love me and hate herself at the same time. I learned what happened with my mother wasn't my fault. There was nothing I could have done to stop her, not then. I knew what I was learning could help others in similar situations. Part of my learning and insight came through the study of evolutionary psychology with influences in neuropsychology and other psychologies. Add in the heavy influence of mindfulness and self-compassion, and eventually we opened this facility. That's why I'm here and part of what drives me."

Dr. Wolf said, "Okay, I've gone on long enough." She turned to Conner, the wiry, balding man with the nervous ticks. She asked him, "Would you start us off, Conner?"

Conner looked like he wanted to say no, like he wanted to be anywhere but first, or even in the room. He fidgeted with a quick down cast of his eyes. Finally, after some thought, he spoke with a twitchy, treble voice. He probably wanted to get it over with. "Hi. I'm Conner." He paused, looking like he was trying to decide whether he wanted to say more. Then he shifted his eyes to the dark-haired woman beside him. He held her eyes for only a moment before turning his gaze down and away. It was his way of passing the introduction baton.

"Hi. My name is Rachael." Rachael spoke with a clear, matter-of-fact, almost aggressive tone. She had short hair, large breasts, and a four-leaf clover tattoo on the side of her neck. She wore the same pastel pink scrubs as the rest of the women in the group. "I'm here because my girlfriend said she thought I needed help and unless I got it, she was leaving." Rachael inhaled deeply and breathed an exaggerated breath, seemingly to vent some anger. "I know she means well. And maybe I need some help. I don't know. I'm here." She cast her eyes to the tiny woman beside her and passed the baton.

"Hi. I'm Maxie. It's nice to meet you." With a few quick turns of her head, Maxie flashed quick little smiles at everyone. Her light brown hair fell just beyond her shoulders. She had long lashes, a tiny nose, and eyes that darted a few times at the group before passing the baton to the slightly orange-tanned, platinum-blond bombshell beside her.

"Hello. I'm Caitlyn." Caitlyn had a fit physique with ample personality. Not as ample as Rachael, but she held her own. She had the look of a lingerie model covering up between shoots. The glance she gave Darren said she would not mind showing him what was underneath. Amia glanced down and shimmied a little before shaking her head and smiling inwardly at her reaction. Caitlyn continued her introduction, glancing at the group while lingering on Darren. "I'm sure getting to know each of you over the next eight weeks will be a pleasure."

Judy assumed the baton passed to her when Caitlyn stopped speaking and looked beyond her to Darren. In her midthirties,

Judy had thick, short, wavy hair. She had the look of a professional, someone who had knowledge and experience in her field. She pursed her lips at being ignored by Caitlyn. "I'm Judy. Hello. It's nice to meet you," and then she swung her focus for a moment on Caitlyn before returning to the rest of the group. "All of you." She nodded at Darren.

Darren took the baton. His gracious smile seemed to connect with everyone, especially a few of the women, Amia included. He held a confident posture, but there was some hesitation before he spoke. His fist clenched and unclenched a few times before he relaxed and observed the group. He was probably trying to think of what to say as he studied the group. It was as if he were on a different level than everyone else in the room, except perhaps Dr. Wolf. They were like two dragons among lambs in the way they seemed to observe their surroundings.

He spoke with an orator's presence. "My name is Darren. I hope to be as courageous as every one of you as we embark on this journey together. I hope we all find the knowledge and whatever else it is we're seeking. It's nice to meet you, and I look forward to getting to know you." Darren's intense eyes fell on Amia as he finished.

Amia wanted to melt into those eyes. It was as if infinity were stretching out to include her in the secrets of the world. Or perhaps the secrets of his heart. The room was quiet. *Ooh, he finished talking*. Amia blushed as he continued to smile at her and brought her attention back to the group with a flick of his eyes.

What was it she was supposed to say again? Oh yeah. "Amia. Hi." She beamed at the group as if she had just delivered the Gettysburg Address. She found the eyes of the man to her right with the messy blond mop on the top of his head. She passed the introduction baton without fumbling it.

Travis seemed a cross between a surfer and a farmer. He could be both. Amia could imagine him chewing on a long strand of hay grass at the beach with a small harem around him. There was a simplicity to him that had a certain allure. He seemed kind of like a wounded puppy you wanted to help nurture back to health.

Travis took the baton. His eyes swayed around the group, as if making sure he was safe. He had a slow drawl. "A-yeah, I'm Travis." His eyes crept over to Maxie. When they found she was watching him, he flashed a quick smile and cast his eyes away. "Oh, and hi."

After a quick glance from Travis, Faith accepted the baton. She had the build of a blueberry and the personality to match. She had a big, toothy smile to go with her round cheeks. She spoke near a helium-level pitch. "Hey, y'all, I'm Faith. You know, like in Jesus. I miss my babies already." She paused in deeper thought. "Anyway, I guess I'm a lot like Dr. Wolf's mama. I love my babies and that's why I'm here." Faith wiped a few tears that managed their way out as she projected a bright smile.

Next with the baton was Bill. Bill had a darkness about him. His dark stubble haircut highlighted a scar that ran from the side of his forehead to two-thirds the way around his head to the back of his neck. The mask drawn over his face seemed that of a man who had never known love or perhaps lost it in a tragic accident. Bill's expression seemed abnormally hard, angry, and, Amia noticed, sad at the same time. His voice had a deep resonance as he kept his introduction simple. "Bill." His dark eyes locked on to Darren's with a sense of angst before brightening as he shifted them to the red-haired woman beside him, Monica.

Freckles roamed about the entirety of Monica's skin as flowers on a field of white silk. She seemed to ease Bill's anxiety with her soft smile and nod as she accepted the baton. Her bright red hair had thick waves that ran to the middle of her back. She crunched up, ball-like, lifted her hand in front of her chest, and offered a tiny wave and a sliver of a smile. "Hi. I'm Monica." Her teeth flashed a bit more, and she bit her lip. She passed the baton.

Tarah, the last woman to take the baton, had the side of her head shaved, with a giant rose tattoo that used her ear to form the center bud of her rose. The other two-thirds were a blast of colored long hair slicked to a point at her shoulder. She was thin with pale skin. Tattoos and piercings covered her body. She spoke with a velvet rasp and had enchanting eyes that kept finding their way to Darren even as they bounced around the room. "My name is Tarah. Some of you might know me by my stage name, Nitrous. I'm not sure if this Whole Me program will help or not, but I'm here, and Lord knows I have issues. I salute thee and wish thee well on this journey into the light." She flashed a studying glance at Darren and then the rest of the group.

Darren nodded ever so slightly and returned her smirk with one of his own. He also seemed uncomfortable again as he readjusted his position. Darren had a few long glances at Conner as well. He saved his longest glances for Amia and Dr. Wolf.

Dr. Wolf observed the interactions of everyone with a slight hint of amusement in her eyes. It was like she already knew everyone there and held their secrets in her mind. She also seemed open to new revelations, maybe even looked forward to them. Her eyes and posture held a sense of nonjudgment, peace, strength, and warmth as well. She would be the rock they would seek shelter in and share their secrets with. This was a person who would not betray their trust.

Dr. Wolf took this weight on and gifted them a serene smile as she spoke. "Thank you all for sharing. Let's begin our grounding practice. If you find your focus wandering, that's okay; it's normal. Simply observe when your focus wanders and gently nudge your focus back to what we're working on. There is what we call an opening and closing of emotions. If you feel overwhelmed or like an exercise might overwhelm you, allow yourself to close off for the moment. In our individual sessions, we will delve deeper into the uncomfortable without the attention of everyone in the group. These group sessions should feel like a safe place but also a place where we push our level of comfort so we can expand our perceptions. Everyone's pace and focus will be their own. There is no one right answer to how this works. Find what works best for you. We will start with a simple gesture. Place a hand over your heart and repeat after me. May I feel compassion for myself and others."

The circle of strangers raised hesitant hands and eyes as they began their journey.

CHAPTER TWELVE

CLUES

Detective Johnson knocked on Daizon May's front door for the third time. She carried a manila folder with a few of the fan letters he provided to the police in her hand. She had more questions for the actor. The first question was why he had never brought those letters to the attention of the police before now. It seemed convenient and made little sense. These people he had letters from hated him—that much was obvious—but one of them dragging Amia to the edge of his property and leaving her for dead. Why? What would they hope to gain? How did Mr. May saving Amia's life change things? Maybe him finding her and saving her life was the plan?

She looped around to the back of his home. The lawn must have been built up because it did not quite match the slope of the rest of the mountain. There was a horseshoe pit tucked away inside a rectangular nook cut out of the surrounding forest. The whole area including the house seemed sculpted with the mountain in mind. It was a quiet stillness surrounded by wild beauty, and he was absent. She noticed the lake below. Glancing up at his deck, she imagined the view from up there. Climbing the stairs, she satisfied her curiosity. It was a multi-million-dollar vista. Detective Johnson focused more on the area where he found Amia. It was a long way away, but from her current vantage point, it did not seem so far. She wondered how the noise would have carried from down there. She could not exactly see the spot where it happened. There were too many trees surrounding the lake. But the sound would have carried. Then she remembered it had rained that night. The rain may have helped wash the bleach from Amia, but Detective Johnson shook her head. She realized it would have muffled the sound as well.

Then she remembered Mr. May saying he had gotten home late that night. If a boat had been crossing the water, he might have heard the motor. If there was a vehicle pulled over on the side of the road, Mr. May would have seen it and wondered why it was there on the edge of his property. He would have called the police. They had been going on the assumption a boat was used to get Amia to that specific location, but the marina was on the other side of the lake and was easy to miss, tucked away as it was. Mr. May owned private access.

She thought back to when she showed the image of Mr. May to Amia. Amia had seemed attracted to him, clueless to who he was. She did not seem threatened by the image. "Dammit." Detective Johnson had more questions than answers. So far, the only sure thing she had was that Mr. May had found Amia, saved her life, and he was evasive.

Nothing came back with fingerprints or DNA to tell them who Amia actually was. The only DNA found on Amia was all over her in the form of the clothing Mr. May had covered her with, clothes he used to help save her life. If he had not given her first aid, warmed her, or found her, Amia would have died. Could he have left her there the night before and then gone back the next day, expecting her to be dead, but finding her alive, decided he could look like a hero instead of a murderer? The theory was a stretch but not unrealistic. If it were so, he would want to make sure she never regained her memory.

Returning to her unmarked cruiser, a black Mustang, Detective Johnson drove slowly down the mountain, away from Mr. May's. The woods were thick on either side of the road. At the bottom of the mountain was a corner and a small turnaround area for big trucks. She pulled into the area and parked.

Exiting her Mustang, she walked around the edges of the turnaround area. Nothing stood out as far as an obvious trail. There was a small game trail, but that was all the detective found. She glanced back up the mountain.

CHAPTER THIRTEEN
PLEASANT DREAMS

A mia felt the white sand of the Zen Garden sift through her toes and prickle her feet. Daizon wrapped around her mostly bare form from behind as they sat on the edge of the wood with their toes digging into the white sand. Candles burned around the room, providing a soft, bouncing light. Scooping sand into his hands, Daizon sprinkled grains over her shoulders, arms, neck, and legs. Each grain sparked as brilliant lightning to and from her flesh. They ignited tingling sensations and left an afterglow as they bounced and rolled over other parts of her.

He moved the flow down her arms to the tips of her fingers, then her legs. His arms wrapped around her, and she leaned her head back. He nibbled at the flesh of her neck and stroked the tip of his tongue to her ear, and he nibbled some more.

She hungered for his lips as they inched to meet hers. He slid his hands up her arms and into her hands. He stroked the tips of his fingers over her legs with the gentlest of touches, which made them twitch with anticipation. He set them afire with a different kind of blaze. Electricity sparked through her entire being.

Then she heard *beep-beep-beep*. The sound did not match the setting within the room. She glanced around at the flickering candles, and showers of lightning flashing through her entire flesh. It was as if Daizon had electrified her with his healing touch, and she wanted more.

Beep-beep-beep.

※

Amia woke, heart pounding and drenched in sweat. She glanced around her room. *Beep-beep-beep.* She slapped at the snooze button before falling back on her pillow. She could still sense the sparks from her dream tingling through her body, her arms. Her eyes popped open. She quickly glanced at the alarm clock and back at her hand and arm. Excitement grew.

She flexed her arms, touched the tip of her nose with her fingertips. Turning her hands over, she opened her palms and touched her fingers to their respective thumbs. Then she flexed her toes, lifted and stretched out her legs. She stretched one leg at a time, then both of them at the same time. Twisting her body, Amia swung her tingling legs off the bed. They felt alive for the first time since she woke from the trauma. She did not have to think about each movement. It was as if she'd regained access codes to information that was lost. Dr. Hemp told her it was possible she would see tremendous leaps, followed by minor ones, or some combination back and forth, until she found her new normal. Amia's wheelchair sat beside the bed. Smile growing, she leaned forward and pushed up. She would stand on her own today.

A tentative step led to another, then another, and before she knew it, she was across the room. She went back and forth a few times. What she was doing would not be confused with graceful. Her steps were probably more like the steps of a toddler, but to her, they were like the first awkward steps on the moon. Another glance at the wheelchair and she laughed. Tears welled in her eyes. She felt like a turbine at Niagara Falls spiking energy for the first time, brimming with potential.

She searched her room for what to do next with her newfound powers. The shower stood as if waiting for her beyond the bathroom door. Amia rolled her eyes up and she felt the wrap around her head with her hand. Her face lit. It was due to come off. Dr. Hemp would be there soon.

In front of her bathroom mirror, Amia let her fingers brush over the fading bruises and the wrap as she viewed herself. This person in front of her was still a stranger. She had bright blue eyes, inviting and warm. Amia said to the stranger, "*Stelle per illuminare il cielo.*" Her fingers glanced over her silver earrings. She smiled at the warmth of the words as she translated them to English. "Stars to light the sky."

It was a memory, a figment, but it elicited an overwhelming sense of warmth. The intention of the words seemed clear to her. She was loved. It also meant the fog was clearing. Amia inspected further. The bruises and swelling continued their retreat, her natural copper tone becoming more obvious. She ran splayed fingers with the slightest of touches over her skin. She ran them from her forehead, around her eyes to brush her high pronounced cheeks, strong nose, gentle smiling lips, and a slightly rounded chin. Her head had an oval, almost round shape, only hinting at the previous balloon-like warp. She had dark eyebrows with long, dark lashes.

With her eyes on the wrap circling her head, she felt for the end. A knock at the main door stopped her. Seconds later, Penny was at the open bathroom door, grasping for words. Amia still had a hand on her wrap. They smiled at each other before Penny said, "Amia, wait."

Penny rushed into the bathroom with the wheelchair. "Princess, please sit before you fall."

Amia sat and saw a weight lift from Penny's expression. Amia spoke clearer than the day before. "I'm okay, Penny. I'm better than okay." Smiling widely, Amia stretched out her arms and legs.

"I see," Penny said, finally relaxing into a similar excitement to Amia. "That's wonderful, but walking around, and"—Penny glanced at the wrap on Amia's head—"the doctor or nurse needs to take that off." Penny placed a hand over Amia's forearm and said, "I'll go get them." Pausing before she left, Penny turned back to Amia. "You'll wait?"

Amia nodded and rolled herself into the main part of her room. A few minutes later, a nurse entered her room with Penny. Then, several minutes after that, Dr. Avendale arrived, slightly ahead of Dr. Hemp's scheduled visit. Dr. Avendale had a slick, confident way about him. He smiled graciously as he said, "Dr. Hempshire asked me if I could step in for him this morning. It looks like he missed out on a leap in your progress. Do you remember me from the hospital?"

Amia smiled at the tall doctor. "Yes, I remember."

"Has your memory taken the same leap this morning?"

Amia searched her mind. That fog was still there, blocking her from her memories. She shook her head. "No."

He said, "It's okay. Let's focus on the gift you gained today, your motor skills. Shall we test them?"

They went through a series of tests similar to what she had done when testing them herself that morning but more advanced. She walked with one foot in front of the other, held her hands out, palms up, and touched her pointer fingers to her nose. Amia squatted and stood while Penny and the nurse stood to either side of her to make sure she did not fall. Amia was not graceful, but Dr. Avendale seemed satisfied with the results. It was difficult to assume his emotions because he kept a poker face the whole time. He seemed to do calculations in his head as he observed results. He asked, "Would you like to take off the wrap and have a look?"

Would she? Was that something he really had to ask? She nodded. With deft, gloved hands, he unrolled the wrap covering her head. Amia felt the cool rush of air with the wrap removed. Behind her, Dr. Avendale removed a pad and tossed it onto a tray with the wrap. They had replaced the pad and wrap each day. The pads always seemed to come away with less and less residue as the days passed. The pad he tossed on the tray was fairly clean. He pressed and prodded before circling to her front. He said, "Dr. Hempshire is an excellent surgeon. You're healing well. I'd like to take a picture to show him your progress, if you wouldn't mind?"

Amia nodded her approval. He removed his gloves, retrieved his phone, and took the photo.

He asked, "Would you like to see?"

She thought they had already been over the fact she wanted to see. "Yes."

Dr. Avendale pointed out the circular area where they had originally drilled and how they had fit back in the piece they drilled out. He talked, but Amia did not really hear everything he said as she reached her hand back to touch the spot on the back of her head. He glanced at Penny and the nurse. "Would you assist Amia into the bathroom so she can see for herself in the mirror?"

Penny held a smaller mirror at a slight angle behind and above Amia's head. With steady breaths and inquisitive eyes, Amia stared at the mystery that was beneath the wrap. Short black stubble covered her head. She stroked the soft, slightly prickly hair covering her scalp. Reaching back, she felt for the scars, that place on the back of her head where the pressure urged her fingers to investigate. There was a circular indent with a line maybe an inch in either direction up and down from the indentation. She felt at the raised edges.

She continued the exploration of her stubble-covered head. The area around the wound was tender and itched with a tingling sensation. At least now it was merely an irritation instead of the mind-numbing migraines. Staring at the stranger in the mirror, she said, "I look forward to getting to know you, Amia. Don't be afraid. We'll get through this." Her grin grew wider as she thought of Daizon and her dream. She asked, "Anything you'd like to share?"

The stranger in the mirror smiled, expectant and curious. Then Amia remembered Penny and the nurse. Amusement danced in their eyes.

CHAPTER FOURTEEN

PERCEPTIONS

D aizon lay in his bed looking up at the ceiling but gazing inward. Amia was foremost in his mind, but seeing Tarah was unexpected. Then there was Conner. The sight of Conner put Daizon on edge. A knife point flashed in Daizon's imagination, hovering just above his eye. Daizon had to look away from Conner at the session before his mask faltered. Nobody could see his weakness. An urge to rip Conner in half raged through Daizon, even though he knew Conner could not be the man he recognized. He was too young. His anger eased at the sight of Amia. She scanned the others with a genuine curiosity. She smiled when she caught him observing her.

Daizon got up from his bed and started doing push-ups, crunches, and lunges. He flipped through his observations from the session. Tarah struck a chord in him with her music. She sang from a place where the angels watched over the world. He knew now, as he suspected before, that she had an intimate relationship with the darkness of man. Would she tell the others who he was? She may not have recognized him from Shady Jay's. Many of them appeared to know, or at least it seemed they had a general sense of who he was without being able to place where they knew him from.

Bill had the look of a serial killer plotting his next move. With the looks Daizon got from Bill, he was probably next on Bill's hit list. Daizon laughed at the thought. *He's probably a nice guy once you get to know him. Maybe a bit of an alcoholic, abrasive, and rude, but a nice guy under the facade.*

Caitlyn was probably the least shy of the group. Her confidence seemed tethered to her body image, and the entire act was part of her mask.

Travis seemed like a guy repeatedly kicked in the stomach who had somehow forced himself to come to this place. Or maybe he was tired of getting kicked in the stomach and was getting ready to stand on his own. He'd definitely suffered some kind of loss.

This group, who mostly held their heads down, had some spunk as well. Life beat them down, so the lights were dim, but there was fight in them. They wanted to get better. Did he want to get better? Was it possible? What would it feel like?

Amia drove his thoughts. Her cold blue form, barely clinging to life, flashed before his eyes as he placed his jacket over her. She was amazing, facing her fears with a genuine smile. Her bright eyes searched him—she searched inside him and did not find him offensive. *Well, not yet.* What was she like before? The strength in her posture and the warm comfort in her penetrating gaze were an innate thing. She was a woman of depth, empathy, and passion. This was a woman who sought perspective instead of assuming.

Could I be assuming too much? He was sure of a few things. Amia had a strong will to survive, captivating eyes, and a genuine smile. She appreciated being alive, showed gratitude, and was a fighter.

After finishing up some side straddle hops, Daizon sat on the edge of his bed and thought of the bullet he often slid in his fingers. His fingers moved to mimic the slide, rolling end over end and tapping the top of the bullet. There was always a tap at the end. His thumb, middle, and pointer finger pressed lightly with the soft mimicking motion of rolling the bullet. He tapped his pointer finger to his thumb and middle, the tip of the imaginary bullet.

He could end the fight. It would be messy. He had access to drugs, but what if he failed at the attempt? He could slit his wrists and enter a warm bath. The thought of it made him clench his fists. No, none of that was appealing to him. He could drive to some secluded spot and run exhaust fumes into his car. Any of these actions would suck for the people who eventually found him. The thought of hurting them was part of the fuel that kept him from pulling that trigger on any of the ideas.

Daizon's Dark Self spoke inside his mind. *You worthless idiot. You can't kill yourself because you're worried about hurting the people who would find you? Liar. You're a coward. Be honest. Do you really think you'll ever be loved for who you are? What if they find out? Think of the ridicule and the sad, pitying looks. Is a pity party what you want? Do you want them looking down on you? No. Suck it up and move on. Love is for fools and better people than you.*

His Dark Self, that critical voice, had been with him since childhood, grown stronger over the years. His Dark Self used fear and twisted reason to create logic in the chaos. Daizon knew his Dark Self was full of crap, but silencing that side of himself was getting harder as the years passed.

The right woman was out there for him. She could love him for who he was, not the image he projected. Would it be fair to the woman if he didn't love himself already? Could he truly love anyone if he didn't love himself? How could he know what he wanted if he didn't trust himself with his own future? It wouldn't be fair to that person. His many failed relationships attested to his lack of self-worth and provided insight. These other women did not even know the worst of him. They cheated on him, or he ended things when they asked questions for which they didn't want to hear the answers. Like they wanted him to go into depth about his past and his feelings, as if that would change things for the better. They wanted to judge him. What was the point? He would save them the trouble. It was him. He was the problem.

Daizon thought about Amia, how her bright blue eyes searched his soul. Her gaze was so warm and non-judging. She was beautiful in the truest sense of the word. Could a woman like that love a monster? No, she deserved a lot better than him, but still. Daizon smiled as tears formed and slid from the corners of his eyes. He was not worth being loved. He could help her get better. Heck, love? He didn't even know her. Talk about getting way ahead into fantasyland. He knew better than to delve too quickly into dreams that were traps. The idea of helping her get better had potential. Daizon nodded at the thought.

And then there was Dr. Wolf. An owl was not an accurate first assessment. She was more like a dragon in a human form. She had a presence about her, like ancient wisdom, patience, and strength flowed inside her. Daizon knew to cross her would be dangerous. She knew people better than they knew themselves. When would she confront them with the knowledge? Probably when she believed they were ready to hear it out. Yes, that would be how she worked. She would constantly soak everything in and reformulate the variables and facts to both understand and help that person understand at their own pace.

It was like some kind of advanced theoretical mathematics built for the inner workings of the mind. A smile pulled at Daizon's lips. Maybe she could help him? What would it require? He could crack open his skull and let her peek inside his mind. That would be easier than pulling out the defective pieces of himself and trying to sort through the mess himself.

A knock grabbed his attention. He opened the door to a slicked-out Dave. Daizon glanced at a different security guy and an otherwise empty hallway. "Come in. What the hell are you doing here?"

Dave stepped inside after a handshake. "I wanted to check on you while I was here. Tonya told me after the fact that she suggested you commit yourself to the program. Finding Amia the way you did had to have been hard. She also told me Kyle was thinking about signing on to the security team here to watch over you. Have you seen him?"

Daizon sighed. "It sounds like something he would do. I'm fine. I'm just assessing some things. Besides, not only do I get to research a role, but I'm curious to learn about Amia."

Dave grinned and cocked his head. "You like her?"

Heat rushed through Daizon's veins and warmed the back of his neck. "I think she's fascinating, but I don't know her."

"Be careful." Dave paused and switched topics, probably not wanting to get into client-doctor information. "What do you think of the program so far?"

Daizon's earlier ruminations came back. "It's early. We'll see."

Dave studied him. He set his hand lightly on Daizon's shoulder and said, "Give it a chance."

Not sure how to respond, Daizon nodded.

CHAPTER FIFTEEN

GOALS

A tray filled with scrambled eggs, bacon, sausage, home fries, and grilled biscuit in hand, Daizon searched the tables for Amia. Daryll left his side and took an observing position with one of his security buddies. Daizon half expected to see Kyle among them, but he was not. Most everyone in the program sat in a small cluster at the tables beside the water wall.

Dr. Wolf wanted everyone to sit together in small groups and get to know one another. She said it was important they understood they were not alone while they were there. Part of the healing process required connection.

Tarah sat with Rachael and Faith. Conner sat with Bill and Judy. Travis was with Maxie and Monica. Apparently, that left Caitlyn and Amia to sit with him, except neither one was there.

Daizon smiled at the group and positioned himself at a table with the water wall directly at his back. He'd learned from Daryll the previous day that this dining area was mainly for the participants of the Whole Me program, their families, and staff. It was situational for the guests who lived in the other wings. Daizon observed an older woman, one of those other guests enjoying her current situation. She was easy to spot in her purple and yellow attire. She had the look of a kindly grandmother type tickled to be out eating with her own little group by the water wall. They chatted like squirrels conniving with one another about the mischief they could get into as they smiled and sent a few waves his way. Amused, he waved back.

Caitlyn sauntered past the tables with her eyes set on Daizon. Her smile was slim and seductive. She grazed her fingers over his shoulder upon arrival. She said, "Lucky us. Looks like we have a table to ourselves."

As Daizon was about to answer, he saw Amia, wearing a pink safety helmet, carefully walking toward them. Daizon's smile grew wide. "I think we're lucky enough to have three." Daizon quickly got up to pull out the chair for Amia to the side of him and across from Caitlyn. Penny escorted Amia, carrying her plate. Penny set Amia's plate of scrambled eggs, a link of sausage, and a couple of home fries down on the table. She pointed to the side. "I'll be over there when you're ready, sweetie."

Amia's eyes were already smiling when she said, "Thank you, Penny."

Daizon said, "You're walking—that's great. And do I hear a bit more fluency in your speech as well?" Daizon caught her infectious smile. Underneath the large vents of her protective pink helmet, the wrap was gone. As she sat, he saw the thin line of a scar and the reddish remains of where she must have struck her head. From what he could see, a thick carpet of shiny black stubble covered her head, including her scar and the reddish remains of the procedure.

He took his seat, eyes moving between her eyes and head. "And you have your wrap off. That must feel good?"

Amia ran her fingers over the helmet. Her smile quivered a bit as her fingers reached into the vent holes.

Daizon said in a reassuring tone, "Don't worry, I could barely see anything back there. Your hair is growing in quick. I'm sure in another week or two, nobody will remember." He cringed at his word choice. "I mean, nobody will notice. You look great."

Amia relaxed and laughed, reaching out and comforting him with a touch. Her speech was smoother, but still off. It had a bit of a Southern inflection, not Deep South, but definitely not from Maine or the New England area. She said, "Thank you. I know you're being kind."

Caitlyn added her voice. "It looks like it must have hurt something awful."

"The migraines don't come as often." Amia fumbled with her fingers. "It felt so good to take a shower this morning. When I woke up, my body tingled all over and wanted to move. I had a dream and"—she blushed as she glanced at Daizon—"it was a pleasant dream. Anyway, I just knew I could function on my own with that tingling sensation pulsing through me."

Caitlyn instigated. "A tingling sensation after a dream. That sounds like a pretty intense dream."

Amia's blush grew.

Daizon spoke up. "I've had dreams like that where you wake and for a moment you feel you're still in the dream."

Caitlyn rolled her eyes before blinking them at Daizon. "Please tell us about your tingling sensations after a dream. I'm sure we'd both love to hear."

Amia sank back in her chair.

Daizon smiled easily, at least outwardly. "The last dream I woke from where something like that happened, I woke paralyzed. I could see my bedroom furniture and the open bedroom door. Outside the door was a rattling noise, but I couldn't move. My mind woke but forgot to tell my body. It was like everything seized up inside me, and the only things that could move were my eyes. My heart rate increased as I searched the room. I heard something or someone moving quietly across the hardwood floor.

There were little creaks of pressure on the wood, barely audible scuffs. It approached my open bedroom door, and although I didn't see it enter, I felt its presence. Holly, my cat, leaped onto my bed and scared the bejesus out of me. She smiled devilishly at me and banged her head against mine a few times before curling up at my feet. Then the buzzing, rattling noise I heard earlier released its newest batch of ice cubes."

Amia released an easy laugh. "Aw."

Caitlyn flashed her teeth. "Bad dreams?"

They were nightmares that haunted him since childhood. After years of wetting the bed, afraid to get up at night, eventually, he learned to change things in his dreams and fly, but he had to realize it was a dream first. It was like his conscious and unconscious minds would play out conversations and place him as an unwilling participant playing a terrifying role. When the unconscious mind would realize he was aware he was dreaming, it would change the imagery and situation to seduce him into believing in the new reality. His nightmares increased after his military service ended.

Daizon shook off the thoughts. Tapping into his nightmares at the moment was not something he wanted to do. He smiled at Caitlyn. "Just dreams."

"Dreams are the gateway to the mind." Amia seemed puzzled after she spoke. Daizon and Caitlyn focused on her, anticipating more. Amia shrugged. "I don't know where that came from. It just came out." She inhaled as if to say more, explain more, but stopped herself and glanced at her food instead.

Amia took a baby-size bite of eggs, and joy burst into her expression. Bliss grew with tiny bites of sausage and home fries.

Watching her, it was as if she'd found a small piece of heaven in her brief escape from trying to explain herself. He added ketchup in a thin coating over his fries and eggs before digging in.

Caitlyn squashed her face at the atrocity while Amia watched with curious interest.

Amia wondered how the other group members would receive her when she plotted her slow and steady course into the dining area, with Penny trailing beside her. The others in the group had split themselves up into smaller groups of three. She was the last to arrive and tried to maintain her concentration as all their eyes seemed to be on her again. *Yes*, she thought, *the wheelchair lady has regained her ability to walk.* The cost of being able to walk was a shiny new pink helmet. *It's a minor miracle, and now you all can go about your daily routine.* She smiled at them and inwardly at herself. Nothing about this was routine.

Luck was on her side. Darren and Caitlyn were the only twosome, so there was an empty spot there for her. Her face warmed at the sight of Darren's smile and those intense, keen eyes. The gentle splash and churn of water from the wall turned into a humming flow. As she approached the table with everybody watching, her other thoughts were simple: *Don't trip. One foot in front of the other. Easy does it.* Darren must have seen the small terror in her expression because he stood and pulled out her chair.

Her muscles eased as she sat, and Penny placed her food on the table. Amia wondered if she was clumsy by nature, or if this was a temporary thing. She contrasted her movements with Darren's fluid ones, which seemed agile and precise, proprioceptive. He had a natural ease, comfort, and control over his body. He performed with the skill of someone mastered in the art of movement. He was surely a master of seduction. Was she being seduced? Amia blushed at the thought that was based more on her dream than reality.

She brought her attention to Caitlyn across the table. She was model beautiful, with syrupy eyes, long flowing hair, and a superior feminine physique. Caitlyn's smile did not reach her eyes. Amia remembered they were in a program that treated depression, anxiety, PTSD, and those sorts of ailments.

After the conversation with Darren and Caitlyn and the way Darren eased her mind yet again, it was hard not to stare at him in awe. The ease with which he manipulated topics fascinated Amia. She had to wonder if he was aware the dream she had was about him and the way he made her feel. Darren acknowledged her crash helmet but acted like it was nothing out of the ordinary. He simply accepted it as something that was.

The dumbfounded expression on Caitlyn's face probably pleased Amia more than it should have. It was obvious after their brief interaction that Caitlyn had her own imaginings with Darren. She was beautiful and probably used to getting her way. Caitlyn did not even try to hide her perusals up and down Darren or Amia. She let her eyes linger on the new helmet.

Darren plunged his fork into his ketchup-drizzled eggs and home fries. He ate with a sense of enthusiasm. She could see his mind working as he produced a subtle grin behind his chewing. There were many thoughts he was not sharing behind that grin. His mask differed from the rest of theirs. A quick observation of the rest of the participants in the program highlighted his greater awareness and open disposition. He was receptive to new information. There was also sadness in most of their expressions, whereas he held his much deeper. The person he was projecting should not be here. He projected confidence, happiness, and security in his disposition. There was much truth in that projection, but it was not the whole truth.

Amia smiled at Darren in fascination. She wondered what he was hiding under that facade. She had a feeling she could spend time with him and help him find peace with who he was.

Where had that thought come from? Somehow Amia knew it was true. She knew she could help him, that she possessed the knowledge and ability if only she could access those parts of her mind.

After she chewed and swallowed another tiny bite of her eggs, without realizing it, she stared at Darren. The image of him from the picture where he was shirtless near his boat flashed into her mind. Without thinking, she said, "You saved my life."

Caitlyn choked a little on her bite of omelet. Her eyes danced between Amia's steady stare at Darren and Darren's lack of ability to find his tongue.

Amia knew she'd caught Darren—no, Daizon—off guard. Keeping his name straight in her head was a task beyond her at that moment. She also knew, however, that it was not her secret to divulge. She could see the spinning in his mind from the slight drop of his jaw and his inability to form a response. Amia touched his hand. "Thank you."

Daizon could not find the words to reply. She'd been unconscious when he'd found her, right? He played the memory back inside his mind. She'd lain there, pale blue, twisted, bruised, and she was barely breathing, but she was not conscious. Tears threatened to breach his eyes as the image flashed through his mind. Nobody deserved that torture and then to be discarded there like some leftover piece of refuse. He came back to the moment and realized curious eyes were on him. He started blinking his eye and worked at it with a finger, as if dislodging some debris. Using his shirt, he dabbed at the imagined invader. He still did not know how to respond, and he was out of time.

Caitlyn spoke up. "There's a twist I didn't expect. You two know each other? You saved her life?"

Turning her gaze from Daizon, Amia said, "I can't explain it. It was a flash in my mind from some pictures the detective showed me."

Daizon took a deep breath; his mask cracked a bit with the recognition in Amia's eyes. He said, "I'm glad you are alive. What you've been through has to be hard."

Caitlyn interjected, "You mean it's true? You saved her life? Oh my God. No wonder you two have this connection." Caitlyn quirked a smile and drank her cranberry juice. Her self-confidence seemed to flood back into her expression as she readjusted her attributes. Her worldview made sense again.

Amia stared at him as if he were some knight in shining armor. Daizon knew he could never live up to that high of an expectation. Still, her gratitude was simple and sincere. She was glad to be alive, and he'd found her. Maybe he could be a knight for her. He could be her protector and hero. He rolled his eyes at the fantastical thought. Not only did he not want to take advantage of the complete trust she seemed to have in him, but he kind of wanted to punch himself. He also realized what they had to talk about was not for everybody. Finally, his expression eased into something that agreed with his inner critic. He said, "I think we may have a few things to talk about in private."

Amia nodded in agreement after he pointed out all the curious eyes on them.

CHAPTER SIXTEEN

KNOWLEDGE AND SECRETS

A mia and Daizon found their way to the ocean overlook. A cool morning breeze attempted to chill the heated air between the two of them. Amia wondered how much of that heat was real or imagined. She fretted after the staff made it clear the only way she could go outside was in a wheelchair. Penny chaperoned from a short distance away. A much more imposing figure, Daryll, chaperoned Daizon.

The ocean surf crashed below, as if attempting to flush out their thoughts. It was satisfyingly different seeing Daizon have trouble finding his voice. He obviously thought a lot about the impact of his words, or maybe he was fishing for the right ones. It was odd, because he always seemed so sure of himself. She knew she made him feel uncomfortable at breakfast with her thanks and recognition. He was not hunting for praise. Amia wondered at the same time what he was actually thinking or hiding. She said, "I wasn't trying to scare you away or make you uncomfortable." She paused, and he let her build on her momentum. "I know your name is Daizon May and that you saved my life. Detective Johnson showed me a picture with your jacket over me, your shirt around my head, and your socks over my feet. God, I can only imagine coming across a sight like I must have been and then having the wherewithal to know what to do."

Amia gathered her thoughts. With her speech better but still broken, she had to slow herself down so he would understand her. He seemed able and patient, so she spoke again. "I still can't remember anything about what happened to me. Everything is mixed in my mind, and it seems what I'm able to grasp doesn't really give me a clue to who I am. I have my earrings."

Amia rubbed them between her fingers. "There's a sense of warmth when I touch them. It's as if this feeling of being loved comes over me, and I get warm inside when I think about them or touch them. They're how I know my name is Amia. At least I hope that's my name. I'm becoming a little fond of it. I might find it embarrassing if I discover later on that my name is something different, like Kate. Can you imagine?"

⤜

Amazed at her disarming nature and the way she didn't hide behind her frailty, Daizon could not help but want to open up to her. She used her trauma as if some sort of springboard to a deeper well of strength. They laughed. Daizon said, "I think Amia is an excellent name. It fits you. It was your earrings that got my attention. They flashed with the sun while I was fishing. I couldn't figure out where the flash was coming from, but it kept catching my eye. I thought you were dead. You were so blue, but then I saw your chest rise and fall. You were breathing, fighting for your life. I guess my first aid training kicked in, and I figured the least I could do was try to get you warm while we waited for help. I called Dave. You know him as Dr. Avendale. He was out in California when I found you, but he helped me the rest of the way until the paramedics arrived in the helicopter."

⹀

Amia noticed his downcast eyes. "Dr. Avendale never told me he helped you. Even so, from what you said, I owe most of my thanks to you. Thank you for the flowers as well. They brightened my room and filled it with pleasant scents. I think even the nurses wanted to see what flower arrangements would arrive as each new day began. The first few days, I smelled them and incorporated them into my dreams more than saw them. It was almost like being out in a field filled with flowers, only I had a bunch of plastic tubes inside me. Most of the time, I was unconscious. I don't know everything that went on in those first few days. My dreams were repetitive, as if I were flying through this cloud, trying to escape from this dark entity. I think the scent of the flowers must have infiltrated some dreams because sometimes the fog would lift and I imagined myself in these fields of flowers that seemed to go on forever."

Amia took a breath. "It was sometime later when I met Dr. Wolf, Dr. Avendale, and Detective Johnson. Detective Johnson showed me the pictures from the scene, and it was the first time I saw what happened to me. It was like an out-of-body experience. It still is. That woman in the photos couldn't be me. After seeing the jacket draped over me, the shirt wrapped around my head, and the socks on my feet, I knew they were yours because of the photo of you beside your boat. You were standing there without them, and you had a concerned expression on your face. You seemed familiar to me when she showed me the photo, but—I didn't recognize you. Detective Johnson told me your name. After the detective left, Dr. Wolf told me you had already signed up to come here. I have to admit, when I saw you here the day you arrived, I had that same feeling of knowing you but couldn't place it. Your name tag and introduction threw me. I had almost forgotten that your real name was Daizon. It's confusing for me to keep your name straight in my head. It was all I could do to not blurt it out."

After some contemplation, Daizon seemed to come to some conclusions. He took a deep breath and said, "I am Daizon May, but I'm also Darren Mason, or at least I was. I'm an actor, and Daizon May is my stage name. It sounded better than Darren Mason. I think the reason a lot of the people here look at me the way they do is because they recognize who I am. Sometimes, to hide who I am, I go by my given name. It's usually when I'm researching a role."

Daizon paused, and Amia asked, "Am I research? Do you know me?"

He fumbled a bit before finding her eyes. His smile was genuine. He said, "The first time I met you was when I found you beside the lake. I'm partly here for research. My manager signed me up for the program while you were still in a coma. I didn't know you would be here. The role I'm supposed to be researching is about a man suffering from amnesia, and he might have done some horrible things to his family. I'm supposed to figure out what makes a man like that become who he is, the why of his specific story. Then, of course, there is Tonya, my manager. She believes I may need some help with my emotional well-being."

Amia raised an eyebrow.

Daizon said, "I might. I don't know. I probably do. It's not like I really want to talk about all that with someone I—" Daizon's faced flushed for a moment as he cut off the sentence midthought. He tried again. "I haven't had much luck with relationships. My last girlfriend was sleeping with my best friend, Kyle, while I was working on my last project. I don't have the girlfriend anymore but somehow kept Kyle. I'm not sure I should call him my best friend after what he did. I'm not sure he was my best friend even before that. We have a complicated relationship." Daizon glanced around as if expecting to see him. "Anyway, Tonya thinks I'm depressed or something like that. She made it sound like I needed to come here to help me secure the role. I don't think she knew you would be here when she signed me up. Or maybe she knew and thought it might be a good way to keep me here. As you can see, I'm still here."

Amia knew he was editing his story, but the basics were there, and he seemed sincere. Even with the edited version, it was a lot of information. Plus, there was an implication hidden in his roundabout way of describing why he was still there. The insinuation sizzled in her mind. He wanted to get to know her.

He also said he was there for more than her. Dozens of questions formed in her mind. The one that slipped out was "Why didn't you visit me in the hospital if you wanted to get to know me?"

He studied her. Was this too direct a question? It felt right.

Daizon said, "Selfishly, reporters were already calling me a hero, and I didn't want that kind of attention. I thought if I sent flowers every day, maybe you would know somebody cared. I wanted to know you, to get to know you, and know if you were well. The last time I saw you—when I found you . . . that's an image I can't get out of my head." His lips quivered a bit, twitching as he seemed to try unsuccessfully to hold back the memories. "You looked like a fallen angel when I found you. All I could think was, Who could do that? I thought of the inner strength you must possess, and you wanted to live. It didn't matter what happened to you—you wanted to live. I think I've tried leaning on that image of your will to live more than anything else. My guilt and worries, my problems felt insignificant."

Their eyes met for a long moment. Searching his eyes was like being caught in an infinite well, and the only escape was to drink them in. There was such passion, insight, clarity, pain, love, and confusion. He was a tempest of emotions held at bay with willpower to rival anything she possessed.

His smile widened as he searched her eyes. He said, "The light, that spark in your eyes, is mesmerizing. They're like blue stars. I have a feeling you will find what you are searching for, because looking into those eyes, I know you won't stop until you do. I have the feeling that if your memory never comes back, you will make the best out of that situation as well. It's who you are. That's what I see and who I want to get to know. I hope you will let me."

Amia asked herself, *Is this like inviting a vampire into your home? Please, come inside and make yourself comfortable. Can I offer you a nibble?* She imagined stretching out her neck in invitation. Amia flushed at the random thought. It was his eyes and way of speaking that had her transfixed, as if she were in some altered state of mind.

A devilish smirk twitched on her lips. She could not tell how much of that warm tingling sensation throughout her body was because of him or the natural process of her body healing. *Bite me, heal me with your touch,* she thought. *Where did that come from?*

She did not have a baseline to compare him against, but she somehow knew he was special. Her memories were what she wanted. She wanted to share them with him. Without judgment, he would listen. He would listen because he wanted to know all her intricacies. He was earnest in his search for answers. She grabbed his hand, squeezed, and looked out over the ocean.

CHAPTER SEVENTEEN

WANTS AND INTROSPECTION

A few hours after her conversation with Daizon, Amia floated into her scheduled session with Dr. Wolf. Actually, Penny pushed her inside and left the room, but Amia barely noticed. She was first for the morning sessions after their group session. The group continued on their earlier progress from the previous day. Amia understood they were learning to communicate with their bodies and minds in a kindly, curious, nonjudgmental manner. It was like training the brain to listen and focus on the inner workings in relation to outside forces. Dr. Wolf had reiterated the goal was not to change anything; they were simply learning to be observant.

Anytime attention wavered, they were to notice what grabbed their attention and gently guide their focus back to their breathing and body mapping. If emotions overwhelmed them, it was okay to close off and gather themselves. When they felt comfortable again, they could continue with the exercise.

Thinking of the body mapping, Amia remembered her dream and flushed with heat. Daizon's glances during the session did not help. She imagined the slow glide of his hands over her skin, curling around her body with a feathery touch. Every inch he touched produced arcs of hungry electricity sparking through her.

Dr. Wolf sat across from Amia in her office with her ever-patient demeanor. She wore a subtle grin. Her voice crafted a knock at Amia's musings. "It must have been exhilarating waking up this morning having so much of your motor control back? Graduating to your protective cap and I'm sure being without your wheelchair soon has to be exciting?"

It took Amia a moment to stir from her musings. She answered, a little too excited, "Oh God, yes."

Dr. Wolf's eyes widened with her curious expression.

Amia blushed. "Sorry. Yes, it was like a rush of energy. My arms and legs felt different, almost like this was what they were supposed to feel like. They felt like mine, a part of me I was missing. I just knew I could walk. Dr. Avendale told me the swelling in that area of my motor cortex must have reduced significantly, allowing that area of my brain to function properly. All I know is that it healed enough for me to move about on my own. It was like neurons lit again, connected, and fired in familiar combinations. Things started working. And then . . . " Amia ran her fingers over her pink helmet. She felt the soft plastic. "I know I have a long way to go, but I showered by myself this morning. It felt so invigorating to let the hot water wash over me. I feel clean."

"Sometimes it's the smallest of things that makes us happy. It's a big jump in your progress. Are there any thoughts you would like to share?"

Amia rolled her eyes up and pointed at the pink helmet. "As if the pink helmet wasn't enough, they wouldn't let me go outside, or even here, without the wheelchair. I can't tell you how good it feels to express the words and complex thoughts in my head as intended." Amia grew more animated with her hands and facial expressions. "Yesterday, I knew what we were doing was a grounding exercise before you told us it was. And then this morning talking to myself in the mirror, I said, '*Stelle per illuminare il cielo.*' It's Italian and means, stars to light the sky. And I felt a warmth fill my body." Tears fell down Amia's cheek. "I don't know why I'm crying. It felt good and I—it was as if I knew somebody loved me and cared about me."

Wearing a sympathetic smile, Dr. Wolf brought Amia a box of tissues. "I'm sure you have a ton of confusing emotions right now. It's okay and natural to be overwhelmed. You've been through a lot and are doing amazing. Remember what we talked about before?"

Amia nodded. "I'll want to relax my way into it rather than pushing myself too hard."

"It's natural for you to want to push, claw, and climb your way to retrieving your memories. It's an excellent fighting spirit, which benefits you. I think you're finding out that in those relaxed states you're able to allow the process to take its natural healing course. You're doing great. More memories could flood your mind today, or perhaps trickle in. Then tomorrow the flow might be altogether different. Next week you might experience a gush of memories, or you might see a plateau. Next month might be a different story. There are no set rules for memory. We work with what each day—each moment—brings. These are encouraging signs of progress that you're showing." Dr. Wolf smirked. "Now, would you like to tell me about your trip outside?"

Surprised Dr. Wolf knew, Amia mirrored the grin. "Oh, where should I start? His eyes have so much depth. It's like he sees right through me and everyone here, to the people we really are. I think he sees people similar to the way you see people, but there's also an intensity. He's intuitive and kind. Yesterday, he took the attention off me and put it on himself. It was so selfless. And then this morning at breakfast, I slipped by sharing part of my dream. Caitlyn tried to flesh out some of the more intimate details

I'd already overshared, and again he took the attention off me by telling a story about waking paralyzed. It was a cute scary story that ended with his cat leaping onto his bed and showering him with affection. I think he showed his vulnerability as a way of making me comfortable. He acted like everything was normal. I couldn't help but smile."

"It would seem he is very intuitive," Dr. Wolf replied. "What happened next?"

"I recognized him from the pictures Detective Johnson showed us. Without a thought, I blurted out, 'You saved me,' and 'Thank you.' He looked like a trapped animal, except he smiled and didn't know what to say. Finally, he suggested we should probably talk in private. That's when we went outside. Only I had to use the wheelchair." Amia sighed. "And Penny and Daryll were with us, a short distance away. We talked about how he found me and my memories. I told him Detective Johnson had shown me the photos, and that's how I knew who he was. He told me why he was here." Amia could not hold the smile pushing at her cheeks. "At first I wondered what he could see in me. I don't even know who I am. Besides, we both know it can't go anywhere."

Dr. Wolf seemed to sort connections out in her mind. "Does it have to go anywhere? Could you be reading more into it because of what happened to you and his role in saving your life? Why not explore the relationship without the pressure of it having to be something more than a friendship?"

Amia smiled. "I'm trying not to read more than what's there. That would be unfair to both of us. I know you told me he would be here, but him going by a different name confused me. He told me why he used a different name and why he was here. He said the main reason was so he could prepare for a role, but that his manager might have thought he needed therapy. We talked about him finding me and saving my life. He said he saw a strength in me and a will to live that fascinated him. He wanted to know more about the person I am. He wants to help me find out who I am." Amia paused, not wanting to betray his confidence. "I think he is here for you, too. I think more than he wants to admit."

Dr. Wolf's eyes bounced around, as if clicking thoughts into place. She said, "Intuition is one of our strongest tools. Often, it's one way our unconscious mind communicates with us. The mindful-compassionate training we are doing will help facilitate an understanding of those feelings. Remember to be open and curious, but also sympathetic and understanding with yourself. You've been through a lot. It's okay to hurt and be kind to yourself. If your memories and emotions overwhelm you, remember to ground yourself with either the breathing or your connection with the earth. Perspective and understanding will come in time. I think for now, keep listening to your intuition and asking questions like you are. Learn to listen to your intuition with a healthy sense of fact negotiation. I'm surprised he told you who he actually is and why he's here. It's a pleasant surprise, mind you."

"I don't think he wanted to lie to me. He seemed earnest. He told me going by Darren gave him a certain amount of anonymity. Is he so popular as an actor? I see the way everyone here looks at him."

Dr. Wolf laughed. "I'm going to do you a favor and let you get to know him for who he is rather than what he's known for. I think that's fair to both of you. We should go back to something you said earlier. You mentioned a sense of familiarity with what we were doing in our sessions. Could you explain that further?"

Amia said, "You began guiding us in the breathing exercise, and I went ahead of you, doing the steps on my own, and knew what we were doing before you told us. It was the same thing when we did the body mapping exercise. I knew exactly what we were doing before you told us. Why would I know that?"

"That's a good question. There are a few reasons I can think of. Let's see if we can narrow it down. I want you to say the first few words and ideas that come into your mind as I describe a few concepts. We'll go back and forth, okay?"

Amia leaned forward, ready to listen.

After some thought Dr. Wolf began. "A response to repeated stimuli. A loud bang heard once may startle, but heard in a more repetitive manner over time produces less reaction. A baby may wake at the sound of the first bang, but if there is consistency in repetition, the baby may sleep. A process in the—" Dr. Wolf noticed Amia pinching her lips and paused.

After a moment, Amia said, "Habituation and the central nervous system. Arousal responses and potential dangers—one of the oldest forms of learning?"

Dr. Wolf smiled and gestured her hand in a slow rolling motion for Amia to keep sharing her thoughts. Amia's confidence grew. "Other types of learning are respondent, operant, social, and relational. Then there's learning through language, psychopathology, *The ABCs of Human Behavior*, Ramnerö and Törneke." Amia smiled. "I'm a psychologist?"

A pleased expression on her face, Dr. Wolf tossed her head and shrugged. "Maybe. We can contact Detective Johnson and have her check on that for us. Does a name come to mind when I say self-compassion?"

"Neff, Gilbert, *The Compassionate Mind*, I don't think they're together. And Tirch?"

Dr. Wolf said, "No, they're not together, although they mention each other. They all talk about compassion and self-compassion in use with mindfulness. Maybe you began using meditation exercises that included these techniques. These realizations could lead us toward a psychology background, or maybe you learned the information for another reason. Let's not completely settle on one thing until we know for sure, okay?"

Beaming, Amia nodded.

Dr. Wolf asked, "What do you think the crucial point of a conversation is?"

After hesitating, Amia said, "To communicate our ideas, thoughts, and feelings, our knowledge?"

Amia thought. There had to be millions of reasons. She said, "Everyone benefits, and there are lots of reasons. It's how we learn and get to know each other."

Seemingly placing information together in her mind, Dr. Wolf said, "Very good. Much of a counselor's work has to do with asking questions, listening, and asking more questions. Through conversation and shared experience, we learn to understand one another. Questions and conversations build understanding between ourselves and others."

Amia asked, "How do you know what questions to ask?"

"You don't. And that's the beauty of the whole thing. Understanding doesn't come from knowing. It comes from being open and curious to the unknown. Think of it this way: I've never had amnesia. I've read about it and worked with clients that had it, but can I know what you are thinking and feeling without asking questions and listening?"

Amia thought for a moment. "I guess you could use your knowledge and experiences to guide your questions, but you wouldn't know what I was thinking or feeling without asking and listening. What about me? I don't have access to my experiences. How do I know what questions to ask?"

Dr. Wolf spread an impish grin. "I would say start with the one on the tip of your tongue, but that might get you in trouble in certain situations. We use some deductive reasoning depending on the situation, and every situation is different. Right now this will be difficult for you because, as far as you can tell, your experiences beyond a couple of weeks ago either exist beyond your reach or they never happened. Memories like to attach themselves to emotions. It's a way for our minds to catalog knowledge gained through experiences, including relationships."

"You're saying I might not have the specific memory, but the emotions attached to those memories are still alive and well?"

"I'm saying those emotions are there even if we can't recognize them. Think of the feeling you get when you see and rub your earrings. When you're having a conversation, don't force a memory association. Rather, let your mind wander with a guided sense of purpose. Focus on how your emotions affect your body. Those sensations will help guide your questions. If you sense emotions overwhelming you, remember to be compassionate toward yourself and use one of the grounding methods to shift your perspective to observing the moment for what it is, no more or less."

Amia closed her eyes and let her mind wander. Her thoughts and hands went to her earrings. There was a similarity in the way Daizon and the earrings made her feel, a sensation of being loved. She knew her earrings represented love in its purest form. A sense of emptiness overcame her. Tears fell in waves, and she didn't know why. She shook her head, opened her eyes, and accepted a tissue from Dr. Wolf.

Dr. Wolf cupped Amia's hand and gave her a soft smile. "I recognized your reaction to the earrings at the hospital. It's obvious they are a trigger for both comfort and now it would seem deeper emotions. I think you might find some emotions, as you just experienced, are difficult to handle. Be careful of that trigger but not afraid. This is a safe place for you to recover those intense emotions. If you experience them when you are out of this office, I want you to remind yourself that whatever happened was in the past. I want you to remember that you are safe, and if you need to talk with me, I will make myself available. Let's work on some recognition tests for a little while."

Chapter Eighteen

SEEDS

Detective Johnson closed her eyes and shook her head as she spoke into the phone. She forced a smile, hoping it would bleed into her voice. "I'm sorry. It's a difficult photo to look at, but unfortunately it is our most recent. If you could compare it to your current or just graduated students, say in the last two to three years, we would appreciate it. If you have any reports of missing students, please contact me." A buzz vibrated her hand through the phone. "I realize they're on summer break. And it is horrible what happened to her. Thank you for your help." She ended the call and read the text. "Finally." Detective Johnson grabbed her dark blazer, shuffled past some uniformed officers, and sped to the dirt boat launch.

She climbed into the seventeen-foot aluminum boat with Officer Jess Cline. Officer Cline had an eager expression as Detective Johnson settled into the boat. The electric hum of the small motor made a quiet impression on the detective. It must have been one of those lakes in Maine that didn't allow gas powered motors. Officer Cline said, "We found them maybe fifteen and twenty-five yards from the shore. Forensics got here a few minutes before you." She pointed to a boat vanishing into a distant cove.

"Thank you, Officer Cline." Detective Johnson scanned her surroundings. Calm water provided an excellent mirror except for the small wakes from the boats as they spread out in small, curling waves. Woods and mountains surrounded the lake. The only house she saw up in the distance was Daizon May's. She turned to Officer Cline. "Have you seen Mr. May around? Do you know him?"

Officer Cline shook her head with a grinning, almost blushing, no. "I've seen him before at the grocery store and getting gas. He's always polite and smiles, but he keeps to himself mostly. Everybody around here has been talking about how he saved that girl's life."

Detective Johnson could see from Officer Cline's expression she wanted to say more. She said, "I'm surprised he's not doing more interviews to cash in on his heroics. I guess it makes more sense with you saying he's always been more private. You said he mostly keeps to himself. Do you know who visits?"

"Kyle—I can't remember his last name. Real big guy. I think they were in the military together or something like that. He usually stops by when Daizon is in town. Other than him, a blond woman, Tonya, I think, and her husband come out sometimes. She's always dressed in bright flowing clothes and is really friendly. Her husband, he has the look of money—you know, really nice hair, nice clothes, nice car, and he's kind of stiff."

Nodding, Detective Johnson said, "That would be his manager and her husband, Dr. Avendale." She motioned to their surroundings. "Have you ever seen anyone else out here that seemed out of place?"

After a quick thought, Officer Cline shrugged. "We have some hunters and anglers sometimes that the game wardens will escort off the property. Most of the anglers know to use the landing we used. Some of them will say they didn't see the posted signs on Daizon's property. I don't think he's ever pressed charges on anyone. He might have some press or fans come out hoping to glimpse him every once in a while. Like I said, he's pretty private. He's had a couple of girlfriends. I think he was even engaged to the last one, or almost engaged, but something happened. She cheated on him or he cheated on her. I don't know—that's just what I heard. But they broke things off like six, maybe nine months ago or something like that."

The boat turned into the cove, and Daizon May's house slowly slid out of view. Detective Johnson's attention swung to the forensics team and what looked like a travel bag and a rag with a bulge. The boat ground onto shore, and she showed her badge.

After what seemed like a couple dozen photographs by the forensics team, Detective Johnson got a peek. The travel bag had a woman's clothes and accessories inside. The rag was actually a tied-up shirt with a small rock and what seemed like a phone smashed into hundreds of tiny pieces of plastic and electrical parts.

CHAPTER NINETEEN

SPATIAL AWARENESS

A habit Daizon honed over the years was making himself aware of his surroundings, assessing potential threats. His meeting and conversation with Amia a few days prior challenged that awareness. A smirk kept assaulting his face. He had to focus. *Assess your surroundings, Daizon.* His mind was all over the place. He thought a short walk on the main trail, which meandered along the coastline, might help.

Two female joggers in the distance headed toward him. The women wore bright clothes. Lanyards around their necks held either whistles, pepper spray, or maybe loud horns. Whatever it was on the ends of the lanyards jostled in front of their bright pink and purple sweatshirts. Behind Daizon, probably stewing about the jaunt, was Daryll. Most people would have considered Daryll the greatest threat out on the trail system and overlooked Daizon. Daizon figured Daryll was around him all the time as protection. He thought about asking Daryll if Kyle had joined their protection team or had asked about joining it, so he could voice his opposition. He kept quiet and vigilant instead. The hospital was probably worried about bad press if something actually happened to him. Daizon worried about threats to Amia.

Dark shadows and corners around the hospital grounds provided excellent cover for any would-be attacker. Some threats might be obvious, while others would barely register on the radar. A quick loss of focus would give these predators all the time and space they needed. These predators hunted children and women mostly, occasionally, men. They were animals out for a fix. Their depraved needs were never satisfied for long, so they always hunted. These were the people like Conner. They could hide using their wiry builds and diminutive demeanors as a type of camouflage. It was a camouflage that kept people from asking questions and seeing their dangerous truth. It was their mask. Daizon wondered if this was the type of person who'd attacked Amia.

Some monsters had very little going on in the nervous tick department. They were completely comfortable with the animal they were. They were the hardest to see. Daizon wondered again, Was that the type of person who had attacked Amia?

Searching the shadows, Daizon imagined whoever attacked Amia and left her on his property to die would want to know if she'd regained her memory. They would want to keep her quiet. Daizon thought of the letters he gave to the detective. Could one of those people be responsible? A wronged ex? Did they hate him enough to attack Amia? Daizon thought of his past relationships. Women could be dangerous, but Daizon knew his failures with women were self-induced. Besides, those past girlfriends were better off without him in their lives. Amia would be better off without knowing him. Daizon took a breath before going too far down that rabbit hole. They were not a couple. He could be her friend.

What Daizon was learning from the mindfulness books and exercises seemed second nature as far as mapping his body and being aware of his environment. Daizon realized he listened to his heightened senses already. He used those senses to augment his assessments of situations. At a primal level, he understood the basic relationship between his senses and the way they played with his emotions.

The centered breathing exercise seemed a method to calm and focus the mind. Showing compassion for others seemed natural. Showing compassion for himself was anything but natural. He realized the pain in his gut, the tight sensation grasping his chest, was fear. It was a fear of never being enough for somebody like Amia. He feared never being good enough for himself. Self-hatred would cripple him if he let those dark thoughts go on for too long. His pain was his and deserved. He did not matter. He thought about the self-hatred, why he hated himself so much. The face so similar to Amia's flashed in his mind. Daizon focused on steady breaths. He'd hated himself long before then. There was a forgotten darkness beyond his reach.

He wondered what he would tell Dr. Wolf. He was the last of the group to see her for individual sessions. Why was he there? What did he want?

Sensing something off in the environment. He heard a light tread. With a few slow breaths, he readied a smile. The person jogging up behind him was probably on a mission to challenge him with her own special attributes.

Light on her feet, Caitlyn swished and swayed in her scrubs. She grinned, flashed her eyelashes a few times, and sized Daizon up as if for a meal. Caitlyn reminded him of Brittney, his last girlfriend. She had beauty and intelligence but, given the opportunity, would rip his heart out and chew on it like jerky in front of him as he faded into oblivion. Caitlyn slowed her jog to match Daizon's walk. She said, "I thought you might be an outdoorsman, that rough athletic type. I bet you like to fish and hunt?"

Daizon attempted to avoid the trap. Was that possible? He said, "I fish more than I hunt. What do you like to do?"

Caitlyn assessed him in a deliberate manner with roaming eyes. "I enjoy exploring interesting, sometimes dangerous terrain. I bet you know your way around those places?"

"I wouldn't want to find myself somewhere I don't belong."

Before increasing her speed and swaying her hips in an exaggerated motion, Caitlyn said, "A little danger enhances the experience." She jogged ahead.

Daizon thought, if nothing else, she knew what she wanted and went after it. He wished it was not him right there and then, but he also knew wishes didn't matter.

Daryll seemed to find the encounter amusing, as he was smiling, which Daizon found odd. If this was another time and place, Daizon probably would have taken Caitlyn up on her offer. She was a beautiful woman, obviously attracted to him and wanting more. But Amia had a strength and power that was inviting rather than repulsing. Her bright blue eyes felt as though they could see through him. Talking with her, he felt her vulnerability and earnestness did not warrant any lies. He would be honest with her. In her current condition, he did not want to confuse her or lead her on. Could he do that?

Lies were powerful weapons that could keep you safe, and they could also get you in trouble. He could see her mind coming into focus, re-forming from the ashes like a phoenix. That was the type of strength she possessed. He knew if he lied to her, she would never trust him.

He was a walking lie. It was what he did for a living, to survive. There were ways around lies. Telling the truth did not always mean telling the whole truth. Smiles in their varied forms disguised unpleasant truths. He had known enough fake smiles and used them himself. They were a way of helping others feel better, to feel more comfortable. Smiles signified a sense of happiness and approachability. They told people, *I'm okay*. Smiling kept a person from being isolated from the group. Smiling kept away questions of mental health.

There were people who walked around hiding behind angry faces instead of smiles. Bill was one of these types. Anger lurked beneath the surface, ready at a moment's notice to guard against the next slight. Daizon actually did not mind these types of people as much because they were usually easier to read. He knew instantly where he stood in their eyes. The look in Bill's eyes told Daizon he would not receive an invitation to join Bill's bowling team. Bill was one of those guys who would hide his anger behind a warped sense of humor. He probably went to church, shook hands with all the faithful, and then drank all day while working on various projects around his house.

The thought brought Daizon to Dr. Wolf. She believed she could help these people with their different ailments and issues. She was a master manipulator who could see into people and make them believe in some truth beyond what they could see. Was it hope? Did she use people's hope as a rope to help pull them out of whatever funk they were in? She knew how the mind worked and understood where she could poke and prod. How would she poke and prod him? He would find out soon enough. He had to head back for his appointment.

As Daizon turned around, the two twentysomething women joggers in bright colors flashed Daizon their best smiles as they gave him and Daryll a wide berth. Then they drifted closer with that wondering look, as if they recognized him. He had seen the looks often when he dressed down to go out. Some people would continue on their way, glancing as these two did. He waved hello. Others would stop and ask, *Are you Daizon May? It's so cool to meet you. I loved you in* Into the Dragon's Den. *I thought she was going to kill you.* Naomi Jackson was the *she* they referred to. Naomi played the head of a female group of assassins and he was their target. He was the Dragon, a former black-ops guy who specialized in killing dangerous people around the world. The tag line was *He thought they were falling in love, and she thought love would make him blind. They were both wrong.*

That was the role that had Tonya worried about his health. Daizon slipped into the role like a second skin. He became the Dragon for the duration of the project and while promoting it. People hesitated around him, not sure how much of what he did was an act. Moviegoers loved it. He was what the people wanted. Only they did not want him—they wanted the Dragon. He was a character that glimmered with intelligence and insight while also being capable and dangerous. His new character was a different monster with similar characteristics.

Then Daizon saw a monster he knew all too well, Kyle. In jeans and a designer shirt open to expose his abdomen and chest, he was out of place. Grinning, he sized up Daryll and Daizon. He said, "If it isn't Tom and freaking Jerry. I heard you were here, but I didn't believe it. What the hell is up?"

"What's up? I think that's a better question for you. What are you doing here?"

Kyle shook his head with a smirk. "I'm your freaking friend, asshole. I'm checking to see how you're doing."

Daizon glanced around at the woods surrounding them. "You just figured you'd walk out here in the middle of nowhere and think you'd find me? I heard you were trying to get on the staff here. How the hell did you know I was here?"

Kyle held his hands up. "Hey, slow down." Kyle roved his eyes up and down Daryll. "They're thinking about adding me to their team temporarily, to help watch over you. Come on. Did you think

I wouldn't know? Are you here because of that chick you—found? She remember anything yet?"

Daizon shook his head. "What the hell was that pause supposed to insinuate? You need to go, man. I'm fine. I appreciate you wanting to be here for me, but I need to do this without you here."

Kyle stood for a long, silent moment, digesting the words with the same effect as a punch to the gut. "Don't forget, I'm your friend. Maybe I'll talk to that blond bombshell that went jogging past us. She seemed more cordial." Probably not getting the rise he was searching for, Kyle said, "I could talk with the chick you found? Put in a good word for you?"

Daryll stepped forward and puffed himself out. "You need to leave, sir. I'm asking you nicely to not speak with our guests. We will not be needing your services."

Holding his hands out again, Kyle laughed. "Easy, big fella. I come in peace."

Daryll stared down at Kyle without a hint of amusement.

Kyle raised his brows and grinned at Daizon. "Be safe."

"Thanks for coming. I'll be out in a couple of months. I'll see you then."

Kyle studied him for a long moment with a blank expression before he strolled off.

CHAPTER TWENTY

LOVERS AND FRIENDS

Nancy stood with an appreciative gaze as she worked Amia through some range of motion exercises on the lawn in front of the building. Amia's wheelchair was absent from the scene. Nancy said, "I didn't think you would be this far along for at least another week or two. It's a good sign. And look at your hair. My God, it's coming in so thick. I can't believe you're moving so well." As a reward, Nancy worked Amia twice as hard with planks, lunges, and jumping jacks. They worked on fine motor skills. Nancy had Amia hold her hands out to the side, then touch different parts of her body with her fingertips. Amia touched her fingers and thumbs in distinct patterns, pinkie to pointer finger, and then reversed. Every time Amia wanted to stop with the strength exercises, Nancy would say, "Two more." Only two more ended up being four or five more.

Amia was a sweaty mess and tired by the time they were ready for a walk. Seeing Daizon coming back from a walk, she stopped and waved. Daizon greeted them with a smile and took in their appearance. He said, "It looks like you're working hard. Good for you."

"I am. It feels good."

"Keep it up. Don't overdo it." He smiled at Nancy and raised an eyebrow as he said, "Hi, Nancy. You know she won't quit."

Nancy brushed off Daizon's concern with an affable posture. "She's one of the most determined clients I've ever had. She'll be okay."

He turned his attention back to Amia. He was about to say something, but Nancy's I-know-what-the-hell-I'm-doing posture seemed to sway him. He stopped himself and smiled instead. He said, "Have fun. Don't push Nancy too hard."

Amia laughed. "I'm exhausted. I don't think I could if I wanted, but I'm going to try."

A few moments after Daizon left, Caitlyn returned from a jog and waved. Wearing a feral grin and staring at Daizon's back, Caitlyn said, "That was an invigorating run, excellent views. Have a delightful walk."

The grin and tone stirred a heat inside Amia that made her fingers, lips, and toes curl. The word that came to mind and slid out under her breath after Caitlyn left was, "trollop." She covered her mouth with her hand, knowing the word was wrong, but it felt right at the same time. It was a confusing sensation.

Amia had hoped nobody heard, but Nancy pressed her lips together, disappointment written large all over her expression. "I didn't see you as the fiery type. Try to remember that she is here for her own issues and not to judge her too harshly."

Amia released a tension she didn't realize she was carrying. "I'm sorry. I don't even know her. I'm not sure why I said what I did. It was like I knew her, or somebody like her, I think."

Nancy said, "Honey, we all know somebody like that. Come on, I think that was just the right way to get us started. You can tell me about Darren. Yes, I saw the way you two looked at each other. Never mind her. I think even the birds are jealous of you right now. Listen to them sing."

Heat flushed over Amia. Not sure what to say, she smiled wider than she already was. It felt right to smile like that. They laughed and began their walk.

Amia rolled a question around her mind. Why would Caitlyn be jealous? Or anybody else for that matter? Amia barely knew Daizon, and they knew each other even less. She wanted to know him better, and they had some electricity between them. *I'm not imagining it, right?* There was something so familiar about the situation in the way Caitlyn stared and acted. It was like a festering itch beyond the reach of her mind.

Amia smiled at Nancy as they walked at a pace that quickly increased, not really knowing what to say. She knew she was an adult, but she felt like a child masquerading in an adult body. How old was she? She had smooth skin, not black or white, it was like a copper sunset. A copper sunset? Amia smiled at the afternoon sun and the beautiful blue sky. She must have heard that description somewhere in her past. Frustration crept into her mind again, as the fog kept thwarting her attempts to access her memories.

Nancy studied her with a smile and said, "Let's increase the pace. You're doing great."

Amia thought about what Daizon had said to Nancy and smiled. He was right; she would not quit. Amia laughed and sped up. She thought about Daizon and their conversations. Amia said, "Darren and I are friends. He wants to help me get better." She pointed out her helmet and general appearance. She knew the black stubble and scars under her helmet would not be pretty, never mind her broken mind. He seemed to see something deeper inside her and when he told her how he felt, she believed him but maybe not completely. He was trying to make her feel better, more secure with herself. He was a caring person, and he saved her life. She beamed at the thought. He wanted to be a friend.

Nancy replied, "I think he might feel more strongly than you think. He seemed genuinely concerned for your safety."

A puzzled expression on Amia's face urged Nancy to continue. "He thought I was overworking you. He wanted to protect you from me pushing you too hard, too fast, or maybe you from pushing yourself too hard. I'd say he was trying to be protective without being overbearing. It's an excellent quality, as long as he knows his place. I'd say you are lucky to have him as a—friend." Nancy drew out the word *friend*. "All that said, he doesn't know what he's talking about."

They laughed.

Nancy increased the pace of their walk again. She said, "What I'm doing is assessing your ability to be on your own physically. If I let up on how hard we push, that's not doing either of us any good. How does a little autonomy sound? How much do you want it?"

Amia ate the cheese offered to her like a mouse being led through a maze. The walk was more like a grueling half marathon. She glanced at the shadows in the woods beside the trail as if some instinct said she was being watched. Then she shook it out of her mind.

Her autonomy would be another step toward being seen as normal. She imagined herself interacting with everyone without them noticing her deficiencies. Did it really matter what other people saw? To some extent it was about fitting in, but at what point did trying to fit in become detrimental to her self-image? Amia might gain back her memories and physical attributes, but she would never be the same. She would be something new. Something more? She would only be less if she let doubt fester in her mind. Nobody had that power over her, to make her feel less. Not Caitlyn. Not whoever put her in her current situation.

Happy and tired upon their arrival back at the facility, Amia collapsed to her rear and lay back on the lawn. She wore an exhausted smile and wondered where her self-insights came from. Was she a psychologist or a psychiatrist? Could she be a researcher or a teacher? Amia could not answer those questions at the moment. What she knew was that she needed another shower. Sweat soaked her clothes, and the pink helmet probably needed a wash as well. She wondered how much relief the vent holes in the helmet actually provided.

CHAPTER TWENTY-ONE

TWO DRAGONS

Daizon decided Dr. Wolf's office had an open den feel to it. It was inviting, with large windows and an expansive view of the ocean. It almost had the feel of being on a ship at sea. Knowledge was at your fingertips, and insight was the allure. Most of the books she owned, if not all, provided insight into the workings of the mind. The office provided solace after wading through the rigors of the world. It was the offer of sanctuary. Dr. Wolf's comfortable patience for Daizon was a bit unsettling. Seeing Kyle disturbed him as well. Applying to the security team to watch over him? He wondered if that was his idea or Tonya's?

Still, seeing Amia had glued a stupid smile to his face. She was tenacious and innocent at the same time. He wondered how much of what he saw in her was her actual personality. He knew she was not in any kind of condition for a relationship beyond friendship. Was he? *Hell no.* It was foolish to even think along those terms. He smirked and scolded himself at the same time. Helping her feel more comfortable with herself was his primary goal. It felt good to think of someone else besides himself. Who was he kidding? It was always easier to think of somebody else, but Amia was special.

Daizon knew his focus should be on the session itself and not on Amia. Dr. Wolf would ask questions he did not want to answer.

Answering questions about himself would be a price he would have to pay to help Amia. He had a pretty good idea about the doctor. Dr. Wolf was a dragon, maybe not like him, but this was her lair and he was her guest. Her insight grew from the way she asked questions and listened. She listened before and after asking questions. She seemed to care about each client she met.

Did he dare grab the rope she dangled and climb? What was it he wanted most? He pondered as he took his seat across from her. She was comfortable in the silence and did not press. She simply waited and observed. Dr. Wolf mirrored his smirk. Finally, she asked, "Would you like to tell me what's on your mind?"

Did he dare? "A couple of things." Was he ready to commit to this process? Would he ever be ready? He thought of Amia and smiled again. He thought of the bullet sliding through his fingers and tapping on the deck rail. He thought of the nightmares that were with him since childhood. No matter what he did, it was never good enough. He thought of failed attempts with pills. He thought of the multiple times a day of wanting the pain to end. As much as he wanted to be normal, he was broken. He was an up-and-coming movie star living a lie.

He paused. Could he put his trust in this woman? Everything he told her was supposedly confidential, but would it be? He let out a long breath. "I'm not sure exactly what my manager told you . . . why I'm here."

"Tonya told me you needed to do research for a role. Her and her husband's donation to the program paid for Amia and will allow several others who might not have the money to attend. I have to admit, I'm surprised you told Amia who you actually are. That took a lot of courage. I'm glad you were honest with her."

"It seemed the right thing to do. She's confused enough." Daizon took a few breaths, searching for the courage she seemed to think he had. "The role I'm researching, that's part of the reason

I'm here. I'm glad to see Amia is improving every day. I wasn't sure that would be the case when I found her." Daizon paused. He took a sip of his water and another. Dr. Wolf barely moved, displaying control and resolve. This dragon had a warmth and approachability to her. She was steady and trustworthy. Finding her eyes, Daizon thought of Amia and pushed out the other thought weighing on him. "I don't want to hate myself anymore. I'm tired." Admitting those words out loud felt like lifting a massive weight. It also felt as though he had ripped his chest open so Dr. Wolf could get a better view of the offering.

Dr. Wolf leaned down to capture his moist eyes. His posture had dropped with the ripping open of his chest. She said, "You're in the right place." Her voice was smooth and comforting, like hot chocolate after a chilly day of ice fishing.

The admission released tears from some unknown spring. The saddest of frowns replaced his confident mask. This was not exactly how Daizon had pictured this session going. What had he just done? He'd admitted to being broken. His heart was raw and out on display. She could slice him through with a word. She could end his life as he knew it. With his displayed and battered heart, his rotting heart as a target, he was ready for that final twinge. The pain would end. Maybe his life was over? Maybe she could help? So many maybes. It took a few moments for him to regain his composure.

Dr. Wolf handed Daizon some tissues before she dabbed wetness from her own eyes. She was steady and sure, but even dragons cry. She asked, "I'm guessing this is the first time you've opened up to anyone?"

Daizon nodded.

"It takes a lot of courage to open yourself up. The pain you're describing doesn't happen overnight. I'm guessing you've been hurting for a long time?"

Daizon nodded again. "For as long as I can remember." Dr. Wolf remained silent, so Daizon fumbled for words. "I don't know how long." Daizon paused. "Will this go on my permanent medical record? Will everyone know that I'm not what I pretend to be, that I'm broken?"

"Your records are private. The only way people outside this room will know is if you decide to share your story with them. That will be up to you. I'm going to share a little secret with you. Everybody is a little broken. It's okay. Feeling broken is normal. I've seen you show compassion for others. You took the attention away from Amia and helped her feel comfortable by taking that burden of attention onto yourself. You could have remained quiet and less noticed."

"I gave her a pillow." He remembered seeing Amia's terrified expression as she was obviously contemplating her move, but she did not need his help. She would have gotten out of that chair, smiled through the pain, and sat on the pillow. Amia was stronger than him. He said, "I gave her another option she may not have considered."

"Exactly. Compassion and mindfulness are not only about showing kindness and respect. They're about empathy and understanding. There are options to reduce the suffering. Sometimes those options come in the form of a pillow."

"It was just a pillow," Daizon replied.

Dr. Wolf smiled. "When was the last time you offered yourself a pillow?"

Daizon stared at Dr. Wolf for a long moment before gazing inward. Did having hope, even if it was only a small voice inside you, count? Was it that voice that made him reach out to Dr. Wolf? He'd worked hard to achieve his goals, but achieving them always felt hollow. The army had helped him become a killer. He was good at it, too good. Kyle was better. Kyle did not let the nightmares take control. Or maybe he did, and that was why he acted the way he did?

Daizon shook his head, not wanting to travel down that path. He used a pillow to smother all the thoughts that went down dark paths, like the thin, balding man from the cemetery. The dancing knife point flashed in his mind, along with the balding man's sadistic grin. Daizon pushed the image away.

Tonya showed him compassion. She helped him develop a raw talent after seeing some potential. She spent a lot of time helping him. Daizon used that help to strengthen his mask. He smiled, thinking of the white porcelain masks used to represent the art of acting. He realized he had formed his first mask way before those classes. Dr. Wolf came back into focus. Daizon said, "I've worn a mask my whole life. That was my pillow."

Dr. Wolf's eyes and posture remained solid as she spoke. "Let's find you something softer."

Daizon laughed. "I wish it were that easy."

"I didn't say it was going to be easy. This will be the most difficult thing you've ever done. We will not buy a new pillow. We will do some research, take some measurements, and design something that works specifically for you. Then, after we design it, we need to make alterations. After we're done with alterations, you're going to want to fluff that pillow up. You're going to take that pillow apart and rework it over the years for needed adjustments. You're going to smile and maybe not look forward to making alterations, but you'll know that you have the skills. You'll seek help on a continuing basis if you need help. That's what self-compassion and mindfulness mean to me. Perhaps it will mean something different to you, and that's okay. We're all slightly different."

Daizon remembered sewing a stuffed white husky for his mother in home economics one semester in middle school. He remembered the joy on her face when he gave her that stuffed dog. It was a white fluff of a husky with a curled-up tail and a crooked red tongue hanging out. Daizon sewed it on crooked because it added character, and he was a happy dog. Sewing his life back together sounded a bit more daunting than sewing that dog together. Would his tongue stick out in the same crooked way when they finished? Was it possible? Could he really hope?

Daizon thought of the stuffing inside the dog that nobody would see. That was what Dr. Wolf wanted. She would want to see the stuffing inside him that nobody but him had ever seen or felt. That was how this process would work. It was the only way it could work. *Is that how it works? No, there has to be more.* He would have to be more involved. Daizon asked, "Is this where I lie on the couch and tell you all about the bad things that happened to me?"

Dr. Wolf eased a crooked grin as she glanced at the couch. "If you would like to lie down, you can. If you are more comfortable sitting, that's okay too. We can go on walks. What we want to do in this process is explore what makes you, you. We do that through conversations and interactions. We see more substantial results when you're comfortable talking and we build trust between us. That doesn't happen in a day, but gradually."

She retrieved a black binder from her desk and returned to her seat. It had a clasp on the outside with a notepad and pen attached. Pressing a release lever on the side, she split the hard shell apart to reveal the folder inside. She studied and flipped through a few pages. "I'm guessing there were a lot of omissions in the personal history section of the questionnaire I asked you to fill out?"

A crooked grin answered her question.

She returned the crooked grin. "I'll let you fill it out again after our session." Dr. Wolf paused, seeming to search his soul. The way she studied him was as if she were differentiating from the lies in the paperwork and the truth. She was figuring out what was what for herself.

He realized she was studying his mask, searching the flaws in the porcelain to get at the stuffing. Perhaps he was the lamb for her afternoon meal. Dragons needed to eat. He remained quiet. His heart on display was not enough. She needed more. His feeble heart thumped.

She closed the binder, and the locking mechanism clicked. "How about we do this instead? Could you tell me your process for Method acting? How do you become the character?"

It was like getting a kiss while bracing for a punch, or maybe it was the other way around, because he staggered. Dr. Wolf smiled. Her strike had the desired effect. Daizon thought about his process, his process of becoming somebody else. Everyone knew the basics of Method acting, right? What could he tell her that she did not already know? "For me, it's about understanding motive and personal history. It's not about me—it's about them. The hardest part of the process is becoming a blank slate receptive to the information without bias. You can't really become a blank slate or rid yourself of bias completely, because it's always going to be your interpretation of how that character perceives the world. You gather as much information as possible and come as close as possible. Does that make sense?"

"It does. Please, continue."

"I guess it all starts with the screenplay. It helps when the writer infers enough about the basic outline of the character traits, mannerisms, backstory, and personality. Not to mention, motives. A lot of time it's through understanding their history and thought process so you can better understand their motives. The writers usually leave a lot of room for interpretation from producers, directors, and actors. It's a kind of creative collective. We all work together to produce the final product. It's not the same as reading a book and having access to all the character's inner thoughts. If a book is available, I will usually try to read it."

Dr. Wolf seemed intrigued, so Daizon continued. "Anyway, after reading the screenplay and book, if there is one, I'll begin researching the histories of people in similar situations or careers. I have to observe and interpret, trying not to inject too much of myself into the understanding. It's about how the character understands and sees things, not me. And slowly, I try wearing some of those interpretations like a tailored suit. If the fabric doesn't fit, or doesn't look right, it's not believable."

Dr. Wolf said, "You make it sound similar to what I do when I'm trying to understand and get to know somebody. I understand what you're saying with the believability part. I've seen you act, and what you do is difficult. It's one thing to know what someone feels and thinks; it's another to internalize it and synthesize it into an accurate portrayal. Your intuitive observation skills are exceptional, but it's more than that. I'm willing to bet you're constantly learning, researching, and internalizing new information into the knowledge, which helps you better understand situations and surroundings."

"It's part of the process. There are better actors than me." He wondered where she was going. He could feign more confidence than he had, but that would probably be counterproductive. If this was part of what he needed to do to get better, if that was possible, he would try. What was the worst that could happen—another failure and more self-hate? He forced himself to breathe slow and deep.

Dr. Wolf continued her study of Daizon. It was almost in the way a sculptor must look at a raw piece of material. Perhaps she was used to working with clay and he was a chunk of marble. What did she see? She said, "I'm going to give you a couple of assignments, Daizon. The first, redo the paperwork, filling in the omissions. The second, I want you to build a character for some exercises we're going to do later in the program."

Not sure where she was going, Daizon asked, "Is this a character for the entire group or just us?"

Eyes lighting with a twist of her grin, Dr. Wolf answered, "I wouldn't put you in front of the group like that. Everyone will eventually do a version of this, but I believe you already have the skills to build this character for yourself. I want you to start by imagining the most compassionate people you know and figure out the skills and qualities that make them the figures you want to draw from. We'll go over some of those qualities with the group as well, later. You will learn more about these qualities from the books supplied to your room. I want to remind you this is not about being perfect or building the perfect compassionate being. Are you with me?"

"Compassionate but not perfect," he replied. A tingling heat trickled into his awareness.

"Then I want you to look in the mirror at your reflection. Staring at your reflection, I want you to think of the image as just another character you're going to fill with these compassionate skills and qualities. Can you do that?"

This was like affirmations. Daizon wondered what the motivation for this compassionate character was. What would drive them to be who they were? Was this like creating some kind of alternate personality? If so, what exercises would they do? He gave a slight smile to Dr. Wolf, not sure where this was going. "I can do that. It's an incomplete profile. I need more information. I need to understand the motivations and personal history."

She gave an easy, comforting smile. Her eyes held a touch of sadness and warmth. There was also a sense of strength and insight in her stare. Her smile broadened as she must have sensed Daizon gaining an understanding of what she wanted. "For now, that's your assignment."

Daizon nodded in agreement and sipped from his water. He knew where the motivations and personal history would come from. *One step at a time. She doesn't want me to get too far ahead.* Dr. Wolf's demeanor eased and tensed. Daizon asked, "Is there something else?"

Her internal debate softened. After a moment, she said, "No. Not now. For now, I think you have enough."

She slipped the thought out of her expression and replaced it with acceptance. Whatever the thought was, he would never know.

CHAPTER TWENTY-TWO

ACTIVITIES AND DREAMS

A small tingling sensation, similar to what Amia felt before regaining her motor skills, began at the start of the newest day and lasted through dinnertime, when they were treated to a cookout. Amia smiled inwardly at the tingling sensations that flowed inside her like ocean tides, powerful and soothing. The group milled about the lawn as staff, led by Dr. Wolf, wheeled out an extensive set of wooden mallets, colored balls, hoops, and stakes.

Dr. Wolf said, "I thought we might try a few games of croquet today. How many of you know the rules?"

Amia glanced around. Four hands went up: Bill, Travis, Maxie, and Rachael. Dr. Wolf exclaimed, "Excellent! If you four wouldn't mind helping set up the game—don't worry about getting the distances exact. Remember, this is not a competition but a bit of fun." Dr. Wolf turned to the others. "While they're setting up the game, we'll watch, learn, and cheer them on. After they finish, we'll have another group take their place. Sound good?" She accepted the nods and smiling faces. "Wonderful!"

Amia stood with Daizon and Tarah on either side. They watched as Travis and Maxie paired up with nervous ease, and Bill and Rachael jostled over who was going to lead. The group laughed at the interactions. Rachael won the opportunity to go first after they smacked balls to see who got closest to the wooden stake a short distance away.

Daizon scanned the grounds and everybody there with hawkish eyes. Amia poked him with an elbow. She asked, "Is everything okay?"

Somewhere deep in thought, Daizon smiled and shook, as if to free himself from an unseen grip. "I was thinking, that's all."

Amia deadpanned a grin and said, "If you're thinking of running, I'm game." She glanced around. "I don't think the big guy would catch us."

Daizon glanced at Daryll, who was watching them with a curious eye. Amia's grin cracked into a wide smile. Daizon relaxed and said, "Daryll is faster than you think. He kept up with me, for a while at least, on my run the other morning." He studied her legs and grinned. "You think you're ready for a run?"

Heat washed over Amia. She tilted her head and narrowed a playful gaze at him. "They gave me a crash helmet in case I'm not. Seriously though, I feel like I could go jogging with you in the morning if you wouldn't mind some company?"

Daizon grinned. He glanced at Daryll and then over at Dr. Wolf. He said, "If it's okay with Dr. Wolf, I would love the company. We can walk if we need to. I know it's only been a few days since you got the okay to be free of your wheelchair." He scanned Amia again. "Are any of these activities helping to bring back your memories? You seem like you're on the verge of something, like you're seeing and understanding more, like things are clicking into place."

He was so observant. Things were clicking into place. It was a good way to explain how the buzzing felt. Excitement in her voice, she glanced at Dr. Wolf and said, "We think there's a good chance I might be a psychologist, a counselor, or psychology student. I understand a lot of the concepts behind what we are doing before Dr. Wolf gives us the actual reasoning." Amia cupped Daizon's shoulder without thinking. She leaned into him and lowered her voice. "I felt a tingling inside me days before my motor functions came back. I feel the same way now. My head and body are thrumming with energy."

The way Daizon smiled at her little win, at her excitement over her progress, tickled her insides. Then she noticed his deep, discerning eyes and lips that bent in subtle curves. Flames flared inside her, and she could not help but lean forward. An overwhelming pulling sensation guided her closer to him. Then Caitlyn squeezed between them with a hand on each of their backs.

She flashed a smile at both of them and said, "I hope I'm not interrupting anything important. I'm sorry." Amia could see Caitlyn was not sorry as she pressed her breast into Daizon and shimmied slightly. Caitlyn stared up at Daizon with a pouty expression. "I wanted to call first dibs on you as my croquet partner." She glanced at Conner and expressed worried eyes between them. Conner, almost as if sensing them talking about him, glanced over and turned his head down.

Amia pressed her lips together, hoping to not let her first thoughts slip out. She took in a breath and gave her best placating smile. Daizon started, "I don't think—" before Amia broke in, "It's fine." Amia pulled out of Caitlyn's light embrace. "I'll see if Conner would like to be my partner." Amia winked at Daizon before leaving him with Caitlyn and approaching Conner.

She knew she had made the right decision when he perked up at the sight of her. Then she briefly wondered about her decision after the four of them began their match. Caitlyn took every chance she got to place her hands and body parts against Daizon. Daizon smiled and was friendly with Caitlyn, but he kept his brief touches to Amia's arm or waist.

One thing Amia was sure of was some type of tension between Conner and Daizon. It emanated from Daizon as he kept a constant eye on Conner. There was no overt hostility, and he whispered to Amia at one point, "I think what you did was selfless." Amia wondered what the tension was between them. Even with the tension, Daizon treated Conner with politeness and respect, shaking his hand and congratulating him with an occasional, "Nice shot." It was this quirk in Daizon's personality that made Amia smile. Daizon was not only kind to her, but he was kind to everyone, even somebody that obviously made him uncomfortable.

Amia lay in bed later that night as experiences tickled at old memories and opened up new possibilities. Amia sought the warmth of her earrings. Was it odd that two pieces of silver metal could create such a reaction in a person? She realized quickly it was not the metal but the associations that flooded her mind, even if she could not identify all of them.

She wondered what she did for fun. What activities brought her joy? There were too few clues at the moment. Eventually, they would add up. She stared up from her bed, knowing more than the day before and a lot more from her initial awakening in the hospital. The tingling sensations would ignite her mind, and her memories would come back to her. She was alive, and she started feeling alive.

Then her crime scene photos flashed through her mind again. She was a pale blue ghost covered by Daizon's camouflage jacket. He tended to her needs while he must have waited in the cold without them until the paramedics arrived. What it must have been like to not only find somebody half-dead and naked but then knowing what to do. He told Nancy she was a fighter. What did that mean? What did he see in her? She thought of Caitlyn rubbing up against him. Then she wondered more about who she was. She was told her memories would come easier if she was open to them and did not force them. Amia relaxed further. She wondered how things would change when she got her memory back. She wondered if she already had a boyfriend and a family worrying about her. She would tell them she was well. She reached for her earrings, and tears swelled in her eyes.

Before she knew it, she fell asleep.

～

Amia dreamed she was in a large apartment among a crowd of college-aged men and women. They drank, danced, and passed around drugs without a care. Some smoked marijuana and others played games. Sometimes they did both. They played video games, darts, and drinking games. Many of them wore multicolored glowing tubes around various parts of their bodies as they did these things. An overwhelming sense of anxiety and fear flooded Amia. There was a sense of familiarity and wrongness.

Looking for someone, she declined offers of pills and other drugs but accepted glowing hoops to place around her head and neck from a blond underclassman. The underclassman's white T-shirt had a unicorn under a rainbow while standing on its hind legs and drinking two beers.

Amia thought to herself, *That's an odd detail*. She wondered
where he was. Then she wondered who "he" was. Amia flowed
with the dream. There were so many people, and she did not want
to be there. The atmosphere turned her off. They stared at her. A
curly-haired man sat on a couch with two women. The three of
them shared a joint and intimate company. Amia asked, "What are
you doing?"

He smiled and waved her over, as if everything were normal. She
found herself beside him, not sure how she got there. She swatted
his hand off her butt. He laughed again and returned his attention
to the long-legged brunette and winter-tanned blond. He was not
who she was looking for, but she still found herself upset with his
actions.

She searched the apartment again. Eyes from everywhere
kept turning their attention on her. Whispers went unheard as
thumping music played, but there was also absolute silence. How
was that possible? She realized she could not hear the music or
the whispers but knew they were there. Hushed mumbles passed
between them as they glanced at her and laughed, smiled, and
rolled their eyes. Amia asked, "Where is he? Have you seen him?"
Pointing fingers and stares answered her. They all aimed at the
hallway.

The dream hallway stretched unnaturally toward a red door at
the end. Anxiety pressed on her mind, and in an instant, she stood
before the red door. Beyond the door was her answer. In a matter
of a blink, the door somehow grew to massive proportions. The
whole hallway grew. She stood as a grown woman but seemed a
child before an enormous doorknob. A small child's voice inside
her pleaded, *Don't go in*. Amia felt for the child inside her, but she
had to know. It did not matter how small she was or how much
it would hurt, she had to know. Pressing against the massive door

with all her weight and strength, she nudged it open a crack, a bit more, and finally enough for her to squeeze through.

She stepped into what seemed a palace bedroom with grand accoutrements. The open door behind her was no longer abnormally massive. Amia was again in proportion to her environment. A king-size mahogany canopy bed stood against the wall several steps away. Sheer white privacy sheets allowed her to see and hear everything within. On her back, moaning atop the bed with sheets pulled into her mouth, was Caitlyn. Amia thought, *Caitlyn?* Amia stood at the end of the bed. The sheets clung to Caitlyn's form as she gyrated her hips. *It's not him*, Amia told herself. *It's not him*. Between Caitlyn's thighs was someone very caring and attentive to her needs. This was wrong, so wrong. Caitlyn smiled at Amia with her feline sensibilities. A sense of betrayal heated Amia at the core. Her eyes would not pull away from the horror playing out before them.

Back arching, Caitlyn moaned. He had his head between her thighs while his hands performed other tasks. Amia thought, *One hand allows access to the queen inside her palace while the other reaches out to stroke her ego.* Frozen, Amia watched as Caitlyn gripped his head with both hands. Her back arched again at the spasms, but he did not stop. He never stopped at the first spasms. His aim was to please, and he knew how.

Amia wanted to scream. She wanted to beat the both of them. She wanted to crawl away and cry. Something in the angry middle came out in her voice. "So, this is what you meant when you said we'd grab a bite to eat at Jennifer's." Nausea overtook Amia.

Waking from the nightmare, heart pounding and stomach twisting, Amia wiped at her tears. Her eyes flew about the room as she oriented herself. A soft light spilled across the floor, out from the bathroom. She found her shadowed reflection gazing back at her in her window. Amia let the surrounding air enter her once again in a controlled manner. "It's okay. I'm okay. It was a dream. He wouldn't." Another breath and she said, "Jennifer?" A few more glances confirmed this was not a party palace. Then another name entered her head. "Baxter?"

CHAPTER TWENTY-THREE

CHILLED AIR

A mia arrived earlier than everyone else for breakfast. She had things to do, and she was going to get them done. She finished before Daizon and Caitlyn arrived. Her eyes kept popping up as she inhaled her breakfast. Each time she glanced up, her stomach tensed and twisted. The tingling pressure inside her head grew. She did not have time for these emotions. The dreams were not real; she knew they were not. Amia glanced around. Neither Daizon nor Caitlyn had done anything wrong. Amia was at the Whole Me program to get better. She was not there for Daizon or anyone else. She needed to get better. They were not boyfriend–girlfriend. They barely knew each other.

After breakfast, Amia found a spot on the lawn surrounded by freshly planted flowers and a wide view of the ocean. Stretching out her body, Amia thought of the salt water and allowed the scents to fill her. Grounding came naturally as she moved on to loosening her body in small circles while practicing compassionate-mindful breathing. As she exhaled, she imagined letting the heat escape from her body. She tensed and relaxed different parts of her body, imagining the tense energy returning to the earth, air, and cosmos for recycling. She imagined the anxious, angry energy passing through tendons, muscles, fat, and skin, then breathing in fresh energy. The scent of earth, ocean, and an assortment of floral inspirations surrounded her.

Shifting her weight back and forth and flexing various parts of her body, Amia imagined the healing nature of salt water and positive energy flowing through her. She was pouring? *Tai chi*, she thought. Her focus eased back to her body-mapping exercise. Amia sensed tense energy knotted in her thighs and legs. She imagined the healing, positive energy replacing the tense and toxic energy. She moved back and forth like a wave surging and retreating with the pull of the tide. Her legs regained a loose sense of active readiness. She imagined that positive healing energy flowing to other extremities and felt the same sense of loose readiness. Encouraged, Amia guided the chi energy up her spine and connective tissue to her cranium and mind.

There was a rightness to what she was doing. It was who she was, a part of her, someone composed and secure. She did not know who she was—her personality or her memories—but she was sure this was a missing part. It was like slipping into a pair of old slippers molded to a just-right hugging sensation. She stepped into them with an easy gait. Time slipped as she progressed through slow, circular movements. Her legs, feet, arms, and hands moved by practiced rote, they directed the chi energy.

"Can you teach me?" Tarah asked with her raspy-smooth voice as she approached in her scrubs.

The plain clothing seemed at odds with the tattooed woman's sense of dramatic flair. Amia said, "I don't really know what I'm doing." She realized immediately that what she said was not the complete truth. She had practiced for several years, since she entered college. Amia smiled as more tai chi insights entered her mind. "It's Tarah, right?"

Tarah glanced at her badge and smirked.

Amia relaxed.

Tarah held out her hand, and they shook. Tarah said, "Trust me, I've watched people do this kind of stuff before. The way you left the dining room and the way you are now. I watched the tension wash away from you as you progressed through the exercises. I want some of that. You make everything seem fluid and inviting. It's tai chi, right?"

"It is. I didn't know I knew it until I just started doing it. You're welcome to join me, but if you really want to learn, we need to work on some basics first."

A friendship sparked. With relaxed thought, Amia guided Tarah into a stance and posture. She said, "These initial stances, movements, and concepts are very similar to the grounding awareness exercises Dr. Wolf started teaching us. We begin by allowing ourselves to relax into the present moment and notice sensations. Imagine there's this energy all around us and inside us. We call this energy chi. We can tap into it and wash ourselves in it. Imagine chi as a healing, positive type of energy we take in to help purify the negative used-up energy that weighs on us."

Amia watched her new friend smile as she followed direction without hesitation. "Now imagine breathing in that energy like in our mindfulness exercises. As you breathe the positive healing energy in, imagine yourself directing it to each part of your body. Sometimes it helps to rock back and forth, side to side and in circular movements. Doing this, you can feel how each leg and foot feels as your weight shifts. Imagine the tense, negative energy letting go of its hold on you and flowing into the earth and cosmos to be recycled. The fresh energy you take in as you shift around and move in circular movements flows into those vacated areas and fills you with warmth and rejuvenates you. What we are doing is the basis of a concept called pouring. We're gently guiding the energy to parts of our body. Some parts require more attention than others."

"Like this?" Tarah asked.

Amia smiled and gestured with her own posture to correct Tarah's. She pointed to the region below the stomach and above the pelvic area. "Imagine the breath entering slowly and guide it to your core first. The core is central to posture and balance of movement." Amia laughed. "That's right. How does it feel?"

Tarah said, "It feels like I'm doing breathing exercises to prepare for vocal gymnastics."

"I remember, you sing, right?"

"I do. The band I've been in since high school performs at bars doing everything from alternative rock, to country, to classic rock. We do a lot of covers. One of my inspirations growing up was Evanescence and Amy Lee. She's incredible."

Amia wanted to know more. "It sounds like you're unsure of what you're doing and want to remember why you fell in love with music. If you don't mind me asking, is that why you're here?"

"I don't mind at all. I think that's a big part of why I'm here. Somewhere along the way, it became more about drugs and partying instead of the music. I want more than that in my life. I want to perform my own music." Tarah laughed. "What about this stuff?" She motioned and mimicked what they were doing. "Any idea how long you've been doing it?"

Amia said, "I think when I started college, but I can't tell you how long ago that was. I don't know how old I am. My best guess right now is that I'm somewhere in my midtwenties." She shrugged. "More is coming back to me, but nothing seems to be in any kind of order. I didn't know I knew this until a few minutes ago."

Tarah said, "Well, I think your recovery is amazing, and I love your attitude. Could you show me something like the movements you were doing before I interrupted you?"

Returning the smile and laugh, Amia quickly found her relaxed state. With a guided nudge to her mind, she let the chi flow into and through her. She guided the energy through her body in a balancing of the core. She stood straight and relaxed in a moment of complete stillness. Then her arms, legs, feet, and hands flowed as a flower opening to the sun. She continued, and one elegant movement simply blended into another until she paused at the finishing movement and returned to her central stance.

Tarah clapped. "Holy freaking beautiful. Can you teach me more?"

Amia broke down each movement into tiny elements. Tarah mimicked the individual pieces of movements. They laughed and interacted with a relaxed playfulness. Tarah finished one of the complete moves in a decent facsimile to Amia.

Cheers came from Faith, Travis, and Maxie. Faith seemed especially impressed. She smiled with her entire presence, like the winner of tickets to a secret viewing of a not yet produced play. She said, "Y'all were butterflies in a gentle breeze. Oh, my. Do you think it would be all right if we joined? Could you teach us, too?"

An unsure, sorry expression flared in Tarah, obviously worried for her new friend. With a gracious smile, Amia let Tarah know everything was fine. It was better than fine. They welcomed the other three to their growing little group. Amia led without thinking. She just did.

CHAPTER TWENTY-FOUR

THE MINDFUL COMPASSIONATE MAN

D r. Wolf accepted Daizon's revised paperwork and sat quietly across from him in her office. Her eyes and mind seemed to assimilate the information with practiced ease. She gathered her notebook. Then her absolute attention landed on Daizon. She glanced at his paperwork and wore a consoling smile. It was an appreciative smile that also held his history.

Daizon said, "It's like you're holding a dull knife and working out the best way to perform the surgery."

"I think I understand the fear, but please, elaborate?"

"The paperwork doesn't really tell you anything about me, not in depth. It skirts around family history and tries to get a general sense of why I'm here. From our conversations, you already have a general idea of why I'm here. All I've done is hand you a dull knife when what you need is a scalpel. Unfortunately for me, the only way to sharpen that knife I just gave you is by grinding away at my protective material."

A devilish smirk danced on Dr. Wolf's face. It set him at ease and off balance at the same time. She said, "Well, that's not exactly how I would describe what we are going to do, but in a roundabout way, you are partially correct. It's important to remember that you are the one driving this change. We will proceed at your pace. Everyone in this program proceeds at their own pace. We will work together during our sessions, but the driving force of any change will be at your own impetus. You will do the work with guidance as required. It's up to you how we proceed."

Daizon laughed. "Let me get the sharpening stone and prepare my heart for the offering table."

"Maybe later. Let's hold off on the sacrifices for the moment. How did it go with the rest of the homework? Has the reading been helpful?"

"I'm creating a Mindful Compassionate Me character. I figured after the reading that's where you were going by having me do that work in front of the mirror. He's incomplete but working on achieving a sense of balance. He's kind, confident, has good awareness, and is comfortable enough in his own skin to ask for help."

"Very astute. You'll develop him further as we go." Ideas ran through her mind as if she were assembling pieces of Frankenstein's monster. She asked, "Have you ever kept a journal?"

"A journal? No, I don't think I ever saw the benefit of keeping one."

"I write in one every day. It was called a diary when I was young, but now that I've grown up, it's a journal. Don't you love how changing a word can change how we view something?"

"I guess."

She said, "Our early circumstances often set the stage for our development. We rely on our parents, relatives, friends, teachers, and local community interactions. We view ourselves based on skewed early influences. It takes a lot of directed effort to overcome those early biases and skewed perspectives."

Daizon imagined his home life growing up. His parents were far from perfect, but they loved him. He loved them even though he had wished for something different, some more guidance along the way, maybe? Everything that happened to him was his own fault. He was responsible, nobody else.

Daizon remembered a book Dr. Wolf had him read. It talked about how human brains evolved. It talked about old-brain and new-brain ways of interpreting and interacting with the world. The old brain was some reptilian thing representing base needs and desires, all the primal stuff that helped us survive in a harsh world with countless threats. They believed the new brain developed later, involving things like thinking, interpretation, and imagination. The author talked about the old brain hijacking the new brain and how our mind could get stuck in these harmful loops of rumination. Daizon found it an interesting read, offering an interesting perspective on how we view ourselves and the world.

Daizon said, "It's not our fault for the way we think. It's a combination of genetics, experiences, and learning. We don't have complete control over how our old brain instinctively reacts, but with the training of our new brain, we can temper our reactions with understanding. We can understand why we act the way we do in certain situations."

Nodding, Dr. Wolf said, "I see you've read. Sometimes with our experiences, the hardest person to forgive is ourselves. We compare ourselves to others and feel inadequate, like we're not measuring up. It doesn't matter if it's a fair measurement or even an accurate one. It's a matter of perspective. If you haven't already figured it out, I want you to give your Mindful Compassionate Me figure the ability to be open to forgiveness and the openness to consider alternative viewpoints."

Daizon nodded his agreement. She was right. He had already figured out where she was trying to lead him.

Dr. Wolf offered him a consoling smile. "I want you to start a journal. Include as far back as you can remember into your childhood. You can start with your situation now and then go backward if you like, or begin from when you were a toddler making your first memories. I want you to think of events, both good and otherwise, that have formed you into the person you are today. Keep asking yourself questions in a curious, nonjudgmental way. I want you to bring your Mindful Compassionate figure with you for support. He doesn't have to know what to do. He doesn't have to be perfect. I want you to remember that he's there, watching over you, and has already experienced these events. He has experienced the events and come out the other end as the mindful, compassionate figure he is."

Daizon walked over and looked out of Dr. Wolf's window. He could have been looking into oblivion for all he saw. He nodded his agreement.

She said, "Many people find this process difficult but rewarding. We usually find answers to questions we didn't know we had. I want you to go into this with an open mind. Don't force anything. Observe and write your observations into your journal. This usually works best if you are fully open to the experience, raw emotions, and memories, as they were."

"You want me to not only write my entire life story but to relive it. All of it?"

"I want you to write about the events in your history you think are pertinent to why you are the way you are. Dig with curious intent. Ask yourself why, what, when, where, how, and who questions. How did those experiences make you feel? It's like writing a memoir nobody will ever see, not even me if that's your wish. It's of the utmost importance that we learn why you see the world and yourself the way you do. I'll be here if you need me or become overwhelmed, okay?"

Engrossed in numbness, Daizon nodded.

CHAPTER TWENTY-FIVE

FORBIDDEN FRUIT

Daizon found a three-person boulder to sit on just off one of the walking paths. While benches lined and faced the walkway, large boulders lay between the benches, allowing people to view the grounds in the opposite direction. Forty yards away on the lawn, Amia led Tarah, Travis, Faith, and Maxie in tai chi. He could not help but smirk watching Amia teach them, adjusting their stances, observing, and illustrating. Daizon wondered how much of what she was doing was reflexive versus remembered knowledge. Had her memory come back? Was she avoiding him on purpose? She seemed very much in her element, teaching them basic moves. He scanned the surrounding area for anything out of place, half expecting to see Kyle.

Caitlyn had rather enjoyed having him all to herself at the breakfast table. She was not a bad person. She seemed to Daizon as one of those people who hid extreme vulnerability behind rough edges, so the world would not consume her. *I know I hide plenty.* Caitlyn was exactly the type of person Daizon usually ended up with, probably because he could see past the rough edges to the soft interior. Maybe he ended up with that type of woman because he knew it would always be about them and he could hide in the background. Maybe he ended up with that type of woman because that's what he knew. Maybe he feared anything more.

In another situation, outside the facility, Daizon probably would have taken Caitlyn out and seen where things went. They would have probably gone to the bedroom and various other places, but they would have both hidden from each other emotionally. Communication and trust would suffer until eventually she would seek comfort and validation in the arms of other men. He would simply move on to the next acting project, escaping his reality.

Watching Amia move, he could see she was in a relaxed state, which allowed her to move with more precision and fluidity. Her mechanics had a practiced flow. She was healing at a fantastic rate. Amia expressed an excellent ability to transfer the knowledge she had to the others.

The way she interacted and guided the others not only spoke of comfort in her knowledge but a willingness to help them achieve their goals. Helping them seemed to be her focus. She was enjoying herself, and the group laughed and smiled as they worked. He wondered whether she was the type of person who had a hard time seeing herself in the same way she viewed other people, whether she was like him.

Amia glanced a few times in his direction without trying to make it seem like she noticed him. The fact she glanced multiple times told him she did. If she was avoiding him, there had to be a reason.

Daizon ran through their conversations and thought they were in a good place. She wanted to jog with him. He knew they were both attracted to each other, even if they could not—should not—act on those impulses. Neither of them was ready for a relationship. He remembered Amia's blue, almost dead form.

Another woman flashed before his eyes, a dead one. Her face and long hair were so similar to Amia's.

It was easier to forgive other people for what they might have done, or the way they acted, because he could put himself in their heads and imagine how they might see the world. This was probably the point Dr. Wolf was trying to get across. It seemed the point of the program. They were to be less rigid and more forgiving of themselves. A deeper understanding of why he was the way he was would help him achieve these goals. Could he ever forgive himself? He was compassionate toward others, but could he turn that compassion toward himself? Then he thought of finding Amia. She was on the edge of his property when he found her. His DNA would be all over her from saving her life. He remembered the faint smell of bleach. Amia had to know it wasn't him. What did she remember?

Daizon's shadow watched him with a raised brow. Daryll probably thought he was not all together in the head. He could be right. "Daryll"—Daizon patted the rock beside him—"let's have a conversation."

Daryll had the look of a predator who had suddenly become prey.

Daizon prodded, "Come on, look around. Nobody is coming after me out here. Rest your bones for a bit. Tell me how it's going with Sherri. I'm just kidding. I mean, if you want to, you can. Just sit, man. You make me nervous standing over me like that."

Daryll slapped Daizon on the back with his massive paw and sat on the rock. They both watched Amia and the others doing their thing on the grass for a while, saying nothing to each other. Daryll finally said, "Dreams and reality rarely meet. Sometimes keeping the two straight can be difficult. You have to know who you are before you can dream a new reality."

Daizon cocked an eye at Daryll. He thought, *A Buddhist monk disguised as a bear? Or was it the other way around?* Daizon said after some deliberation, "You're not just another pretty face. I thought there was more to you." He tapped the side of the big man's leg.

Daryll turned his head and lifted his chin, giving Daizon a strong-jawed pose seen on Greco-Roman statues. He said, "The looks help." Then he cracked a grin. They shared a laugh that broke an imaginary wall between them. "Sherri has her mom and pop up visiting from Alabama. Her pop was a drill sergeant, just retired, but her mama runs the family. They're like two Chihuahuas yippin' and yakkin' at each other one moment and then the next they're cuddling and cozy. Damnedest thing you ever saw. I told Sherri not to get any ideas because I ain't no damn Chihuahua. I'm a whole other breed. Ya know? Somebody's bound to get hurt if I get all riled up like that, and have you seen me? It ain't gonna be me that gets hurt. Well, wouldn't you know, they thought that was the funniest thing they ever heard. Her pops said he'd light my ass on fire nine ways to Sunday if I ever harmed his baby girl. He laughed, popped me on the shoulder, and said, 'Welcome to the family.' I was so confused. I thought I was on some episode of Animal Planet or something."

Laughing, Daizon said, "You probably had to reassess your whole situation, imagining what you got yourself into."

"I got myself into a whole bunch of crazy, all right," Daryll replied, beaming.

"Good for you, Daryll. We all need a little crazy in our lives."

Caitlyn exited the building at that moment and sauntered past. She tucked a cupping-type little wave in front of her chest, then continued waving her other assets as she walked past Amia and the others. She headed out for her morning jog.

Daryll said, "A little crazy."

"I hear you." Daizon's eyes found Amia's at that moment. Then her eyes swung to Caitlyn and back to Daryll before returning to her group. Daizon thought, *A little crazy.* And then he smirked.

Daryll did not miss a beat as he said, "Animal Planet, right?"

They laughed some more.

⤜

Amia and the others had finished up their exercises and were talking when she noticed Caitlyn exit the building. Caitlyn exaggerated her sway and cupped a cute little wave at Daizon, who smiled in return. Then, with a big smile aimed at Amia and the others, she swayed past and began her jog. A glance back at Daizon found his eyes on her and not on Caitlyn. He must have known she would want to see his reaction.

Then she reminded herself it was just a dream, and it was not him or Caitlyn. She was getting frustrated over something that was not real. They'd done nothing wrong. A thought came. *I'm using relational framing and augmenting parts of my past to reason the present. It was an association based on experience. I used avoidance as a coping mechanism, and when that didn't work, I came outside and coped by exercising.* She smiled at her diagnosis. She was gaining tidbits of insight.

Another glance found Daizon and his escort laughing together. They'd seemed at odds before. She wondered what had happened between them. A smile stretched her cheeks as she realized Daizon had not cheated on her. Then she chided herself. *We're not even in a relationship.*

Tarah edged beside Amia and leaned into her with a gentle bump. Tarah said, "The gods sculpted him, right?"

Her smile and dreamy eyes probably gave her away. She brought her attention back to Tarah and asked, "Darren?"

Tarah's eyes opened wide, and she tilted her head down. "You know his name isn't Darren, right?"

Amia flashed a questioning glance.

Tarah explained, "His name is Daizon May. He's an actor. He's actually kind of a big deal, an up-and-coming hot young actor. He must not want people to know he's here going through some issues or something. I don't know. With him it might actually make him more famous. He has a reputation—"

Amia stared back with a wondering blankness. He'd told her he was an actor, but hearing it from Tarah somehow reminded her of what he did for a living. He always came across as so unassuming. "What kind of reputation?"

Tarah softened her eyes and said, "Sorry, I guess maybe you don't know. Anyway, he seems like a nice guy and he likes you a lot. And he saved your life?"

Unable to keep the smile from her face, Amia said, "He wants to help me get better, that's all."

Tarah laughed. "He might want to help you get better, but that's not all."

Heat flooded Amia, and a different type of tingle danced around in her nerves.

A sweaty mess and working to catch her breath, Faith said, "Thank you, sweetie. I didn't know exercise like this could be so much fun. A few weeks of this and my baby ain't gonna know what hit him. The little babes ain't gonna recognize their mama." Tears broke through her laughter.

Amia said, "We'll work together and have some fun along the way, Faith. We have to remember why we're here. We can do it." What she said should have sounded weird from somebody suffering from amnesia, but it was like she knew maybe not the right words but the right tone and message her thoughts should convey. The advice came out as natural as instructing the tai chi basics.

Faith wrapped Amia in a tight, sweaty embrace before realizing what she was doing. She pulled away and petted Amia's arms ever so gently. She glanced at where the bruises had almost faded completely. "Are you okay, sweetie? I didn't hurt you. Oh, and I'm all sweaty too."

Smiling, Amia said, "I'm fine. It felt good. Thank you." She glanced at Daizon, wanting to know more about him and his reputation.

CHAPTER TWENTY-SIX

PROGRESS

D etective Johnson exited the doughnut shop with her refilled red thermal mug. It was eleven in the morning; the sun was out, and this was her second refill of the day. Waiting sucked. Forensics always took so damn long. Out of all the threatening letters Daizon had received, three people stood out from the rest as possible suspects. Detective Johnson dismissed them one by one. One turned out to be a guy in a wheelchair from Michigan. The second was a twenty-six-year-old drug addict from Texas. She was a mother of three with a record of fraud. The last woman was a supposed model who lived in New York City. She had sent Daizon illicit photos in acrobatic poses and got upset when Daizon refused to play along with her demands. Detective Johnson rather enjoyed crushing their hopes of an attempted extortion scheme. Her phone rang out with the *Cops* theme song as her ringtone.

Setting her mug on the top of her unmarked cruiser, Detective Johnson glanced at the caller ID: FORENSICS. "Tell me you found something I can use."

They'd pieced together a serial number for the phone. "Amia Viardo?" Detective Johnson's smile grew as she listened. They had retrieved call and text records, school and personal. "I'm getting into my car now to access the file. You are outstanding."

Detective Johnson set her mug in the center console cup holder, flipped open her laptop, and brought up the file. An unknown California number was the only number texted the day before Daizon found Amia. The next number was from Massachusetts. The *Cops* ringtone sounded out again. She answered without checking the caller ID. "I'm looking at the file now. Is there more?"

There was dead air for a moment on the other end. An unfamiliar woman's voice asked, "Is this Detective Johnson?"

"You've reached Detective Johnson."

Before Detective Johnson could get another word out, the woman asked a dozen questions about Amia. The detective shook her head, trying to keep up. She cut in, "Did you say your name was Beth? . . . Yes. You're Amia's roommate? . . . It's not your fault. Slow down. Amia is safe. Did Amia tell you why she was in Maine? Who she was with? Was she seeing anyone?"

CHAPTER TWENTY-SEVEN
KNOTS

I nspecting the angler's knot with an approving nod, Dr. Wolf congratulated Amia. "Well done. Now tell me, what are your thoughts after this exercise?"

Amia sat back and thought. What was the point? Was it about perspective and learning? They had discussed her teaching tai chi to the others in the program, her dream, and passing the information along to Detective Johnson. Amia guessed, "We learn in different ways. Building associations helps us understand the unknown?" Amia knew she'd ended the statement as a question.

Instead of answering, Dr. Wolf nodded thoughtfully.

The silence encouraged Amia to continue. "Associations are important. It was easier to complete the knot after receiving both verbal and visual cues." Amia thought for a quiet moment. Maybe the lesson was less about the knot and more about the exercise. Amia smiled at Dr. Wolf as a realization settled out of the mist inside her head. "You reframed my fears with knot tying." Her tone lifted with her smile. "You used R-F-T on me."

Smirking, Dr. Wolf cocked her head. "Did I? I don't remember using any theory. Does it matter? Did the point get across? Was there another point being made at the same time? What do you think?"

Amia thought of the feelings she had shared about Daizon. She replied, "I believe it was an open-ended question intended to stir thought and make multiple points. It was as much about the experience as the task." Amia delighted in the realizations. One of those realizations being that her memory was returning. It might not be as quickly as she would like, but it was returning, and it filled her with energy. Her hand gestures quickened. "The experience of interaction is as vital to improving well-being as is the actual knowledge of how to improve. Some might even say that the experience of positive interaction and group inclusion might influence well-being more so than being totally adept at a task."

Amia scanned the room with what seemed fresh eyes. It was a comfortable space that displayed professionalism and openness. Dr. Wolf designed it that way to instill ease and nurture conversation with clients. The books projected an image of Dr. Wolf being well read in a wide variety of subjects. Her economy of movement and mannerisms conveyed someone deeply aware of the human condition and her ability to communicate in multiple ways. At that moment, Amia was the center of this woman's attention. Amia said, "I think you are very good at what you do. I'm lucky that I'm here with you at this place. I think I would enjoy teaching the group what I know of tai chi, even if I'm not exactly a master of the art. In the time we have, it will be the basics. Not everyone will want to join the group."

Dr. Wolf said, "I'm the lucky one, Amia. Thank you for the kind words. As for the group, we'll offer access as an open invitation. Would you prefer teaching before our morning mindfulness and compassion session, or perhaps later in the day?"

Thinking of how the activity helped clear her mind and relax her body, Amia said, "I like the idea of the exercises in the morning. I think it would be a good warm-up to our morning mindfulness and compassion activities."

Amia's mind went to Daizon. He did not seem angry at her for avoiding him. If anything, he seemed concerned. The way he invited Daryll to sit beside him and the two of them laughing. Daizon charmed Daryll. He treated Daryll with respect, as an equal. It was clear after speaking with Tarah that everyone knew who he really was, but he did not act above anybody.

Daizon was a solitary figure with a massive heart and understanding of people. He was happy to let the topics of conversation develop around other people and their interests. He actually seemed to prefer the interactions that way. He was the type of person more selective in who he offered his focus to, but it did not make him any less caring or giving to others he did not know. Amia decided he must carry a heavy burden. He carried it well, and most people probably wouldn't notice.

Amia addressed her concerns to Dr. Wolf. "I think my actions this morning hurt Daizon. He didn't deserve to be treated the way I treated him. I ignored him, gave him dirty looks, or made believe he wasn't even in my world. He saved my life. Why would I do that? Do I tell him I had a dream?"

Dr. Wolf said, "You can explain to him what happened if you like. I think you will find he is understanding. He saved your life. That, combined with the tendency to feel closer to people within these types of groups, serves as a good reason to be wary of beginning a relationship in a place like this. Outside of here, you will both have separate lives, friends, and family."

Amia smiled. "I know. We've already discussed this, and I understand."

Dr. Wolf grinned. "If it were only that easy. Hormones will always be in the air. It's part of our nature. Ignoring them doesn't help to understand them. We need to remember our primary focus for being here. Can you tell me what your primary focus of being here is?"

Amia thought partly aloud, "I don't know who I am. That would be a good start. I mean, I know my name." Amia thought about Daizon. *Love might not be a bad secondary focus. Or was that lust?* Amia smirked. And the smirk broadened into a smile.

Dr. Wolf asked, "Anything you would like to share?"

Amia settled herself. "My primary goal here is to find out who I am, my past, and how to move forward into my future. Another thought came to me after your question. I believe it was advice given to me in my past. 'Sometimes love finds you; most often it's when you're not searching for it.'"

Dr. Wolf cracked a half smile.

Amia spoke up. "I'm not saying I'm in love. I barely know Daizon. And I understand your warnings about relationships at places like this. I'm not sure why I feel the way I do about him. I know he saved my life, but honestly, I don't think that's why I am so attracted to him. I don't know. He makes me feel good about myself, but I was so quick to jealousy and anger at perceived threats that may or may not be real. It was almost like I was trying to push him away before he could hurt me, and I don't want to be like that. But what if that's who I am?"

Amia had too many questions without answers. Her dream being a warning from experiences made the most sense. She was not crazy. As the thought passed through her mind, she smiled at Dr. Wolf, who observed her go through her imaginings.

CHAPTER TWENTY-EIGHT

A WALK

The evening mindfulness and compassion session ended. As everyone filtered out with a few conversations here and there, Amia caught Daizon's attention with a smile and a tiny wave to meet outside the room.

Perhaps what he did not expect was for her to hold out a hand and gesture to the outside. Amia enjoyed the surprised look on his face, maybe a bit too much. She asked, "Would you like to go for a walk?"

He studied her with a tentative smile of his own. She decided avoiding him was not the answer to an incomplete question but felt her courage waning. Tarah had made it known that not only was he an actor, but he was very popular. The way people reacted to him made more sense. Amia decided even without being an actor, Daizon had a powerful presence. What did that knowledge mean for her and a potential relationship with him? It was a friendship, Amia reminded herself. They didn't need to make it anything more than what it was. They could be friends. Why did her mind go to thoughts of a relationship with him? Was she like this normally? She was a grown woman. Surely she had more self-control. From what she was learning about herself, she was not the type of person who led with her emotions. Facts and actions would guide her. She was a logical person. Right?

Was it as simple as him saving my life? Is it base desire? Amia had so many questions, but the only way to find the answers was to face her fears and wade into the uncomfortable unknown of why Daizon made her react like a love-crazed teen.

Again, she wondered if all her memories would return. She wondered if she would remain in a constant state of déjà vu. Relaxing into a process where she did not have control over the results required trust in Dr. Wolf. She had to trust herself with Daizon. Amia's thoughts were all over the place.

Mercifully, Daizon tilted his head to the side and dipped it slightly to find Amia's eyes, which she had cast downward. Perhaps they drifted with the thought of him saying no. He was a handsome man crafted in some godly forge, and she was wearing a pink crash helmet. His smile lifted her before his words verified. He gripped her offered hand and said, "I would."

They walked the meandering paths onto the darkening grass behind the building. Amia hovered her fingers over budding flowers as they walked and talked. She removed her shoes so she could feel the short reeds of grass slip between her toes and under her feet. They provided hundreds of little tickling sensations. Walking beside Daizon was like floating along with no pressure to perform or be anything other than what she was.

Amia knew if Daizon wanted to scale her walls and invade her private thoughts, he could, but he did not. He accepted what she gave and remained content, even pleased with her offerings. Thinking about it, Amia realized she could not tell him her actual secrets. They hid from her as well. Except. And before she knew it, the words were out of her mouth. "You had your head between Caitlyn's thighs." Amia wanted to find a hole.

Both of Daizon's eyebrows slid up as he parodied a not-so-innocent sense of amusement. He asked with a smirk, "I did?"

Amia felt a flush shade her whole body. "I know it wasn't you." She inhaled a quick breath to gain her thoughts. "I had a dream, only it was a memory, I think, and instead of the original people that were supposed to be part of the memory, you and Caitlyn replaced them. Caitlyn was very thankful for your presence—very." Part playful, part terrified, Amia darted her eyes from the ground to Daizon.

He grinned but did not laugh, so Amia explained the rest. "The person attending the queen was my ex-boyfriend, Baxter, and Caitlyn was actually an ex-friend, Jennifer. Obviously, Jennifer was closer to Baxter than I knew before that night."

Amia narrowed her eyes at Daizon. She said, "I've seen the way she looks at you. Stop smiling. I know I don't have a right to be upset with you, that we're not together, but I am. Or I was." Unsuccessfully holding back a laugh, Amia said, "You should be sorry for what you did." Amia had a hard time maintaining any kind of poker face as she burst into a full laugh.

Daizon's smile pushed through his cheeks and lit his eyes. He held back, probably understanding the greater depth of the meaning behind the dream. Deciding to play along, he asked, "Attending the queen?"

Amia turned a shade that must have blended well with the red flowers surrounding them.

Assuming the answer in his head, he said, "Should we tell Caitlyn?"

Amia playfully swatted his shoulder. "No."

They laughed, and Daizon added, "I don't think she's used to hearing no."

Amia reenacted a bit of the dream. "I think it was, oh God, don't stop, don't stop."

Daizon followed the laughter by revisiting some of his own past. "I told you I caught Kyle sleeping with my last girlfriend. I've had other girlfriends cheat as well. I can unfortunately relate to your story and know how much something like that hurts. I'm sorry."

Amia said, "The thing is, it hurts, and it doesn't. It's frustrating because I know he was my boyfriend and she was my friend, but beyond the dream imagery, I can't remember anything else about them. How do you get angry at someone you don't know? Maybe that's why my unconscious brought you and Caitlyn into the dream, so I could get mad at somebody? You were proxies. Does that make sense?"

Thoughts deepened his eyes to something more serious. Daizon said, "Do you think you were trying to protect yourself from me?"

Amia fell into his deep, probing eyes. They seemed to have enhanced abilities. She trusted him more each time they interacted. She'd trusted him from the beginning. Amia wondered why that felt strange, like it was a mythical concept. How could she both trust and fear him at the same time?

Not receiving an audible answer, Daizon shared more about himself. "I think I have a tendency to keep people at a comfortable distance. I'm not good at being emotionally available. It explains why my girlfriends always cheat. They want more, and they're not getting it from me. The good times never last. Tonya, my manager, believed I simply attached myself to the wrong type of women. She tried setting me up on this dating site, and I answered way too many questions before telling her to delete the thing. She saved the account in case I changed my mind." Frustrated, Daizon shook his head. "I've been single for a little while now. I've dated and gone out, but I'm pretty sure my relationship issues have more to do with me than anybody else. I wouldn't wish that on anyone. I don't know, there might be something to this place and Dr. Wolf."

He stared at her with a smile that seemed to convey to Amia that she was part of what made this place the right place to achieve his goal. What was his goal? He had said before that part of his goal was to help her if he could.

Daizon said, "I think my point is, I might understand some of what you're feeling. I can't imagine having to relive that moment here and then not being able to remember the rest. You had the wherewithal to not assume everything was as it was. I think it's fascinating how you can compartmentalize the different aspects of what happened and form a coherent realization."

Amia warmed at his praise. Everything he said rang of truth. She said, "I'm not sure I deserve your praise, but thank you. I want you to know I appreciate your communicating with me the way you do. You are very patient and unassuming; it makes it easy to talk with you."

A long blink allowed dream imagery into her mind. "My dream was so surreal. I was there but also somehow watching from some detached lens that altered the reality of the situation." Those thoughts triggered the images of her battered, pale blue form, evidence of deeds she would rather not think of. She was told they had happened to her. How would those dreams compare to finding a boyfriend cheating on her? It would be a whole new level of worse. Fear seeding her mind, she said, "I don't know if I want to remember everything that happened to me."

Daizon reached an open hand for her, and Amia caught movement from her peripheral vision. Daryll was a reminder they were not alone. She flinched back from Daizon's open hand. Her eyes focused on Daryll long enough so Daizon would hopefully understand part of what made her jumpy. Her muscles relaxed with a laugh, and she squeezed Daizon's hand.

An easy, consoling smile played on Daizon's expression. Without entering further into Amia's personal space, he glanced at Daryll and said, "It shouldn't be as easy as it is to forget he's there." Daizon offered the massive man an amiable smile and nod in acknowledgment of his presence. Another illustration of respect for the man who watched over him.

Amia offered her own tentative wave and smile to Daryll. Daryll nodded and smiled in return before eschewing the both of them to ignore him. Apparently, he preferred less attention.

Daizon was like an angel sent to comfort her in her time of need. He did not ask for anything. All his actions illustrated his desire to help her feel safe and get well. There might be more to it from the beginning, but ultimately she knew Daizon was there for her. She wondered how saving her life played with his mind. What were his expectations? Did he have any? Was he content with friendship, or did he want what she wanted?

Romantic and platonic inclinations played with her mind. What could she offer him? They walked the grounds. Amia said, "With what happened to you, just the things you've told me, thank you for sharing. You don't trust very easily, and the women you date seem to reinforce your beliefs. I think you're right to trust Dr. Wolf. I think she can help you."

Again the beauty and depth in his eyes induced a hypnotic, pulling sensation. The way he saw the world was different. They told of a traveler who went to dark places nobody wanted to go. Yet he somehow carried himself with a belief everyone was deserving of respect. He held a great sadness at bay.

Daizon said, "It's not their fault. I don't blame them. Well, maybe a little, but—" They walked in silence for several steps. "It's like I said before. I didn't make myself emotionally available.

I've always protected myself. Communicating those innermost feelings is not my strong suit."

Amia could see the pain he was experiencing. He had not, in fact, protected himself. Daizon was a dreamer whose dream was slowly dying inside. He wanted love, to be loved for who he was, but he did not like who he was. He would seem fine to everybody who thought they knew him, but inside he was in deep pain. This side he showed her, this utter vulnerability. He did not let people into this part of his life. He let her in, not all the way, but it was an open door.

Was he testing her? Did he want to see her reaction? Was this his way of reaching out? It was like he reached out these feelers to figure out if he would allow her deeper access. She wanted to hug him, thankful for the invitation. She reached out her arms and asked, "May I?"

He opened, and she felt herself being swept into a dream. The dream broadened as she felt the hardness of his entire body. He covered up this whole time, but she could feel his tight, muscular frame beneath the loose-fitting clothing. He smelled earthy and clean. His face and neck had a hint of late-day stubble. Opening her eyes, she saw Daryll wearing a warning smirk. He raised his brows at her. Smile plastered on her face, she pulled away from Daizon. She felt lighter, as if some invisible weight lifted. She gathered herself, tingles and all.

Noticing her gaze again, Daizon smiled. "Daryll could intimidate bears if he wanted." Daizon grinned conspiratorially toward Daryll as he whispered in Amia's ear, "He writes poetry too."

Amia smiled at Daryll.

Daryll shook his head. "Don't believe a word he says. He's full of shit."

"He said you were a teddy bear and I shouldn't worry."

With a broad smile, Daryll flexed his behemoth frame. "He lies." Daryll winked.

Daizon said, "You're welcome to walk with us."

Scrunching his face at the crazy talk, Daryll eschewed them again, like he was taking two pets for a walk. "You two go about your business, and I'll go about mine. I'm a lazy cloud drifting along all happy, as far as you two are concerned."

Continuing their walk, Amia said, "You told me you were an actor. From what I learned, talking with the others is that you've downplayed how popular you are. It makes more sense why Daryll is always around. You seem more than capable. It doesn't appear you need him. Is there more that I'm not getting?"

"I don't think so," Daizon replied. "Sometimes in certain locations, the powers that be insist I have somebody." Daizon shrugged. "I think Daryll is here out of an overabundance of caution by the facility. I'd imagine they wouldn't want any adverse publicity if something happened to me. He's a good guy, just a rough exterior. I don't think he liked me very much at first. As far as how popular I am, or my reputation. My father told me something a long time ago, probably the best advice he ever gave me. 'People see what they want to see.' They see the image I project on the big screen or on their televisions. That's who I am to them. When I'm out and about like this, people might recognize me, but they don't see me. They see the guy who played the Dragon."

He motioned to the dozens of people milling about the grounds, doing simple activities, or sitting on benches watching the ocean. "Or, in a place like this, they might recognize me as the actor and imagine what life must be like for me based on their own assumptions. I give them a show and they appreciate the facade. If I don't provide the image they expect to see, they might think they recognize me, but they can't be sure."

His reasoning struck a chord inside Amia. At the moment, it was as if she was playing the role of herself rather than being herself. The chord resonated deeper to her core. She said, "I don't have any preconceived notions about you, other than you saving my life. But I don't remember any of those events. I only remember being told afterward and seeing the photos."

Before her was the man in the photos. The moment felt surreal. She was with the man who'd saved her life. Everything about this place, what happened, him, and the way she knew she was feeling toward him. It was all surreal, and she did not want the feeling to end.

At some point, she would wake from this dream and find out she was an ordinary person living an ordinary life. She could make the best of her time in this altered reality. She could be happy in this dream for a long time. Amia thought it was a pleasant dream as she gazed into his eyes. She hoped when she woke, he would still be there and they would create new dreams. For all she hoped, she sensed fragments of her mind were re-forming, and soon she would remember who she was. It was what she wanted most, yet she feared being fully awake.

Daizon said, "Watching you this morning with the others, you seemed very adept at teaching tai chi."

Brought out of her thoughts, Amia said, "I didn't know what I was doing at first. My mind seemed to relax on its own, and recognition followed. I hope they enjoyed the activity. It felt good interacting with them. When I told Dr. Wolf, she asked me if I'd like to teach the class regularly, an open invitation to join. I agreed, and now I'm equal parts terrified and excited."

Placing his palms together in front of Amia, Daizon gave her a martial arts' bow. He said, "I'll look forward to learning, Master Amia."

With a playful grin, Amia said, "I expect obedience." She winked. Then, realizing what she had said and done, she flushed and changed the subject. "Do you remember how I told you we thought I might be a psychology student or recently graduated or something? I'm remembering more. My memory is coming back. When I do stuff like tai chi or mindfulness exercises, it's as if my mind relaxes and things happen naturally. When I was teaching them, I wasn't thinking about what I was doing. I just knew."

His delicious, off-balance grin widened. "That's good news, right?"

Biting her lip, Amia said, "It is." They walked, and he waited patiently as she fumbled around for context. "I think I'm afraid of what I'm going to remember."

Taking a moment to assess her fear, Daizon motioned again to the grounds. He said, "If terrible memories return, I think you're at the right place. You're safe here. You have new friends here who will help you welcome old friends back into your life. I'd even be willing to bet Caitlyn would love to see you get better. As to the memories that I think you're referring to, Dr. Wolf seems incredibly insightful. You already know I'm willing to listen anytime. I could even teach you some self-defense using what you already know of tai chi. Watching you earlier, I'm confident you would pick up the new techniques fairly quickly."

He glanced at Daryll and back to her. "I think Dr. Wolf was right. We want the best for others, and when we see them achieve, we live vicariously through them for that moment and feel some of the happiness they feel. I think it's because we all feel pain and have similar experiences and can relate in some small way. When you feel happiness and joy, we will too. I think it's why we enjoy watching movies or reading books. Sometimes we want to see people overcome obstacles we can relate to and know that it's possible. It provides us with hope. Or maybe the movie or book is totally unrealistic. In those cases, movies provide us an escape from our realities and troubles for a little while."

His endearing expression melted Amia. He said, "You are the protagonist in your own life. No matter what anyone else may want or feel, this is your adventure, your story. What happens in your story is driven by your wants and desires, your fears and failures. The obstacles in your way, how you overcome them and create your own path in your own story, that's up to you. Personally, I think you are doing great. It's okay to struggle—we all do."

Amia wiped her eyes. She didn't know what to say. It was all she could do not to stumble as she stared at him in a dumbfounded, thankful way. They walked for a while before sitting at one of the cliffside benches. She wondered who the psychologist was supposed to be in their relationship.

A warm red sky held wispy semi-translucent clouds that stretched to the horizon. Seagulls squawked, and a gentle breeze brushed her skin. Daizon sat an arm's length away and leaned toward her. He let her close the final distance between them. It was as if she were a wild animal and he was leaving her space to let her know it was her choice and she was in control of the situation.

CHAPTER TWENTY-NINE

SHADOWS

Dreaming, Amia stretched out her arms and smiled as the dew from the dazzling white clouds engulfed her. Long, black silk strands of her hair streamed behind her in the wind. Her lilac-colored cashmere dress clung to her every curve and snapped in the wind behind. There was a sense of pride and pleasure in the way the material held her. Cool water droplets beaded on her arms and face. She was comfortable and secure until a dark presence formed a shadow beyond the white of the cloud. A white-tipped black wing reached into the cloud and struck her with its claws. Her dress ripped and peeled away from her. She held it to her. Her skin faded from copper to a pale blue.

The shadow circled her cloud. He was coming for her. A dark angel with white-tipped black wings stretched out before her. His face was a blurred white mask with black eye sockets. He grinned and reached for her with a gentleness that belied his intentions.

⤜

"No," Amia cried, waking from the nightmare. She curled into a ball. Sweat covered her body. Sheets clung to her in a messy tangle. She held them to her and rocked. Her right hand locked on to her left, and she pulled her knees to her chest. "I'm trying to rationalize what happened to me. It's okay. I'm safe. Nightmares are normal after trauma. Some memories will be difficult. I'm okay. I'm okay."

Amia drew a slow breath and breathed out. She closed her watery eyes and felt the breath as it filled her with life. Amia scanned the small, empty room. "I'm safe and in a good place, where people care. I'm in my room. It was only a dream. I'm alive and well." She dabbed at her tears with her sheet.

Amia thought about her long silky black hair in the dream and felt her month plus of growth. Her fingers lightly walked to the back of her head. Gently probing, she felt the slight rises of seams healing. She felt the tender spot that was becoming less tender every day.

Daizon's words from earlier filled her. "I'm the protagonist in this story," she proclaimed. Amia lightened and felt her strength return. A sense of determination washed over her.

The dark shadow hovered at the back of her mind, as if accepting the challenge. The presence slowly faded. Amia wiped again at tears and set her jaw.

⋘

While following Amia's tai chi lesson at the back of the group, Daizon observed how the facility bathed in the morning light. Dew misted off the dark solar glass of the dome, leaving a warm sheen. Gleaming tiles evoked a sense of renewed vigor. The vastness of the ocean seemed a cozy neighbor. Seagulls squawked and circled. They landed and walked about, asking for treats.

There were many kinds of birds, colorful and plain, large and small. Some kept their distance, while others introduced themselves readily. Some sang and others were silent.

Strong crustacean scents blended with floral, while the surf rolled and thumped on the beach below out of sight. Circling the building were the mountains and millions of trees, adding depth to the picturesque site. The whole environment had a calm and inviting nuance.

Groundskeepers tended thousands of flowers, both native and introduced. The atmosphere welcomed travelers who came here to confront their demons. They would leave here as a person, coming into their own balance with the world around them. At least they would have received a good push toward achieving this goal.

Daizon watched how Amia thrived in the environment as she hosted her group's morning exercise. She taught them introductory tai chi exercises. She taught them a new way to search for balance within themselves and the world they lived in. There was always another way to think and be part of the greater world. Maybe this was part of her lesson, too. She was growing as she taught.

The grounds provided a sense of security while they learned to withstand the challenges before them, current and future. Armed with knowledge and techniques, they would gain self-confidence for when they left this place.

Amid all the calm, Daizon also noticed Amia sneaking occasional peeks at the shadows. They were quick glances, breaks in her otherwise stellar in-the-moment presence. During those peeks, her smile would fractionally turn into something else. Amia hid the feelings well. Her eyes kept locking on to his, a smile forming every time they did.

Amia circled the group, inspecting their technique. She offered guidance, explaining and providing examples of how to perform certain movements. She guided Daizon's waist with a delicate touch that sent lightning through his insides. Grinning with playful eyes, she whispered in his ear, "You seem tight." She guided the other side of his hip with the same delicate touch and whispered into the back of his other ear, "Relax. Feel the energy from all around us and imagine drawing it in through your breaths, through your feet, hands, and skin. You can't force it. You accept it, use it, and guide it."

After charging him with enough electricity to set him sparking, she grinned impishly and swayed her hips for the first few steps. Then she assumed her normal gait as she made her way back to the front of the group. She had him so off-balance, all he could do was grin.

Daizon was a bit surprised when Caitlyn joined the group that morning. She and Monica were the newest additions. Caitlyn seemed to have taken Monica under her wing over the past few days. It was as though Monica brought out some kind of protective instinct in Caitlyn.

At the front of the group, Amia said, "Thank you. This was fun. We'll do this again tomorrow for those who want to join. For those who would like to stay, Daizon has volunteered to show us how we might use some of these tai chi movements in self-defense."

Any conversations quieted, and they all swung their attention to Daizon. Amia's joyful expression faltered, as she must have realized what she had done. Daizon breathed and smiled. "Oh, come on, you all knew who I was." He made his way up to Amia and offered her a smile and wink to let her know everything was okay. Then he smirked and said, "Amia's going to help me with illustrations."

Amia smiled up at him, eyes pleading with him to forgive her. Her stomach and chest twisted inside. Then, sliding out a mischievous grin, he winked at her and whispered in her ear, "You seem tight." He stepped back and raised his voice for the group. "I'm going to tell you right now that if you are in a position that you need to protect yourself, don't worry about fighting fair. What I'm about to teach you is more about survival. The strength you gain from this knowledge will be in knowing you can protect yourself momentarily from an attack. I say momentarily because, given time, most of you would be overpowered. Every situation will be different, but the essentials remain the same. Act quickly when opportunity presents itself, and escape."

He kneeled before Amia and gazed up at her with his intense eyes. Then he touched her as he spoke. "The toes, ankles, and knees provide excellent targets to slow somebody down." His fingers slid behind her knees, sending shivers up her spine. Her body heated, and she flushed with a smile.

He stood. "I'm not sure exactly how it is with a woman, but with a man, if you hit his groin with as much force as you can muster with a knee, foot, fist, or elbow, it will take him a few moments to gather himself."

Daizon rose to his full height and pointed. "The joints above are also potential targets, but they would not be my first recommendation. A strike to the neck, nose, kidney, or small of the back might work, but they are harder targets to hit. Remember, your primary goal is to escape the immediate danger."

Reading the group, Daizon winked at Amia and called over to the side, "Daryll, can I use you for a minute?" Daryll sighed but played along. Daizon punched a lightning-quick, small upward movement with his fist at crotch height. He stopped the punch a couple of inches away from Daryll before he could react. Daizon smiled at Daryll's glare. He tapped him on the side of the leg. "Thanks."

Daryll said, "Don't make me hurt you." He prepared for Daizon's next move.

Daizon made three movements to Daryll's knees, neck, and ankles. Daryll's actions to block the movements were like a shadow to moves already made. Daryll rolled his shoulders like he had seen a ghost. Daizon held up his hands in a placating manner. "It's a demonstration, big fella. We're friends, remember?" Daizon smiled and offered his hand to Daryll. Everyone clapped when Daryll gripped Daizon's hand. His grip tightened, and he whispered something in Daizon's ear. Daizon smiled and clapped Daryll on the back. "I know, you're not a Chihuahua."

Some tension lifted from the group, and Daizon said, "Let's see how some of these moves would apply to tai chi." Arm in front of him, he circled it slightly toward the outside of his body. "This is obviously a deflecting maneuver. Amia, would you make believe you are punching me so we can show what I'm talking about?"

Agreeing, Amia threw a slow punch toward Daizon's stomach. He circled to the inside of her punch with his hand and arm, gently guiding it away from him. He had her throw punches and kicks from different angles and heights. Using his hands and legs, he showed how to deflect and avoid the punches and kicks with similar circular movements and small steps.

They partnered up, and as the group practiced the movements, Amia took her turn, guiding Daizon's slow punches away from her. Daizon had them keep the movements slow, saying, "It's better to get the technique down before moving any faster. Plus, I think Dr. Wolf would have words with me if somebody got hurt. Keep it fun."

Amia noticed over the days and weeks, the group stood taller, smiled more, and they allowed themselves to cry more and not feel ashamed about their feelings. Caitlyn seemed to enjoy Daizon's extra lessons. To his credit, Daizon treated Caitlyn with the same respect he showed everybody else. His patience seemed limitless when people asked for help. He encouraged, reillustrated, and showed different ways of achieving a similar result.

The nightmares continued, and Amia glanced more often at the recessed shadows. They were each encouraged to choose activities to do with others and by themselves. If they did an activity by themselves, Dr. Wolf encouraged them to share what they had been working on and how those activities made them feel at the moment.

Tarah would hum and write, sometimes sing in a beautiful whisper. Travis had two left feet and loved to dance. His ability, or lack thereof, encouraged others to join him. Maxie had the rhythm and grace of a professional dancer. The two of them were a sight. Faith somehow got them all access to the kitchen and taught them cooking skills. Both chefs and several of the kitchen crew joined in after tasting her dry rub ribs and peach cobbler. Bill told fishing and hunting stories. Judy, Rachael, and Conner were the artists of the group. Judy sculpted. Rachael avoided a brush and found enjoyment in immersing herself in the paint. Conner sketched everyone doing various activities. Monica skirted around the edges. Caitlyn actually had a gentle way about her with Monica. Caitlyn took Monica aside and taught her ways to model herself. Monica's posture and presence seemed to strengthen and open to more smiles and invited more conversation. The longer Caitlyn was around Monica, the more her abrasiveness seemed to soften.

The longer they were there, the more it seemed Daizon avoided Conner, but he also stayed mindful of him. Bill and Daizon bonded over fishing stories. Bill was a former marine and Amia suspected they might have had some connection on that front as well. Bill was behind the wheel after a few drinks in an accident that killed his wife and almost killed him. He wished it had for several years before somehow finding his way to the Whole Me program.

Amia led her small group onto the lush green lawn, surrounded by a colorful array of blooming flowers. Others joined the group occasionally, but tai chi was not for everyone. Each individual was free to find their own way to practice mindfulness and self-compassion. As the weeks blended, the presence in the shadows grew.

⤜⤐

On this day, several weeks into the program, Amia had an extra bounce in her step. Her pink crash helmet was off. She wasn't going to let the shadows darken her day. Daizon walked with her to the beach. "I've noticed you seem jittery. Are you okay? Have you remembered any more about what happened?"

Amia let off some nervous energy with a laugh. He was perceptive. His steady presence helped her feel safe.

He squeezed her hand. "It's okay if you don't want to share. I've tried not to prod too much, but if I can help? I hope you understand by now that I won't judge you."

Amia's mood lifted at his sincerity. She squeezed his hand, took a breath, and gazed into his eyes. "I've been having more nightmares. Dr. Wolf believes it's my primal mind making sense of my trauma by distorting emotions and hidden memories. I told you about that buzzing sensation in my mind, like I'm going to remember everything at any moment. But then at other moments, it's more like walking on a sandy beach and feeling the sand squirm under my feet."

Knowing her deepest fears were figments of a powerful imagination and a warped sense of reality did not stop Amia from glancing over her shoulder or reacting to movements in her peripheral vision. She smiled through her anxiety.

The path opened at the beach about forty yards away. Daizon grinned and pointed with his eyes. "Think you're ready for a race?"

Amia smirked and took off running. She laughed as he caught up to her, winked, and then passed. When she crashed into him at the end of the trail, he caught her. "You almost had me that time."

Daryll labored along the trail behind them. They glanced at each other and laughed. Amia said, "Sorry, Daryll."

They both knew the Whole Me program was not the place to give in to their base desires. She also knew the more she was around him, the more those base desires grew.

When they arrived at the ocean, other members of the group played Frisbee and swam at the beach below the facility. The staff provided the women with one-piece swimsuits grandmothers would wear, while the men got knee-length swim shorts.

Over the weeks, Amia's hair thickened and grew. The rough ridges she felt in the back of her head now felt subtle and hidden. The best part was not having to wear her pink helmet any longer. Daizon's way of looking at her changed only in the sense of a growing warmth. She felt normal, or closer to normal. Her smile seemed easier. Daizon noticed the latter part, how she felt better about herself. When he caught her in the freezing-cold water of the ocean, she told him, "You're the most observant and insightful man I've ever met."

He laughed, and she frowned. He raised his eyebrows, glanced about the beach and up toward the facility. He opened his eyes a touch and waited, as if she were missing something. She took a few moments before understanding dawned. Splashing him, she said, "It shouldn't matter that I only know four men." She tried to keep a straight expression. They both laughed as she splashed him again.

The freezing ocean water meant quick trips into the water, followed by periods of drying. The sun kissed them with warmth. Back on the shore, when they were alone, Amia noticed Daizon seeming to lose himself in his thoughts. There were brief sullen moments where she saw his pained micro-expressions. She said, "You can talk about the stuff that muddies your mind if you like. I want to listen and be here for you, like you listen to me."

He wore a deep, contemplating expression, touched with a soft smile. He was not lying about his difficulty communicating. She sensed he had shared more with her than he had shared in any of his previous relationships. He smirked. "You make my mind muddy, in a good way."

Amia pecked Daizon's cheek, and then her lips hovered at the delicious taste of him. She fought the urge to go after his lips. Somewhere along the way they had stepped over that friendship line. She wondered who could have hurt this kind man, who never asked for anything. He just kept giving.

Daizon cupped and kissed Amia's hand. Shivers traveled up her arm. She had a sudden urge to bite him, just a nibble at his neck, but caught herself and closed her teeth.

He grinned with a hungry look of his own.

⚜

On the way back from the beach, Daizon said, "I'm sorry. You asked me where I go sometimes. You know I've been working with Dr. Wolf on the project I told you about. I was just remembering instances with my uncle and mother's family." He paused, measured Amia, and continued with his story. "I remembered my mother's family telling gay jokes when I was a kid. My uncle is gay, and he probably told as many as everyone else, if not more. It was confusing. It seemed there was something wrong with being gay, but my uncle seemed happy. I liked him and wondered at the time what I was missing." Daizon shook the thoughts from his head and smiled. "I was also thinking about when I found you." He studied the surrounding trees. "Did you know I found you on the edge of my property?"

Amia shook her head. "I knew you saved my life."

"We don't have to talk about this if you don't want."

"It's okay." Amia tensed, but she smiled. "Maybe it will help. I can't just avoid the topic forever."

Daizon grasped her hand and squeezed. Feeling her relax, he said. "You know how I found you? Well, that along with where I found you make me wonder why there. I'm pretty sure most of the DNA they found at the scene, besides yours, was probably mine from when I made the split-second decision to save your life. And before you think it, know that I wouldn't hesitate to save your life every time. Anyway, I keep thinking there's more to the story. And then on top of that, Dr. Wolf has me delving into parts of my mind I've tried to bury away. So, if I seem a bit off, that's kind of what's going on in my head."

Saying what was actually on his mind, Daizon couldn't remember the last time he felt more vulnerable. Probably in one of Dr. Wolf's sessions. He saw Amia searching her mind for clues about how to respond. He wanted to push her into remembering everything, but he also wanted to shield her from ever remembering something so horrible.

A tear slipped from the corner of Amia's eye. Her lips quivered, and she smiled as she embraced him. Before he could think of resisting, she pressed her lips to his and hugged him harder. His desire grew from the want in her lips. He had to quash that desire for her. He would not take advantage of her. She covered her wide smile as Daryll cleared his throat. They separated, and it was as if by sharing his emotions and thoughts with Amia, her feelings for him amplified. She seemed to think more of him and not less.

Amia seemed as though she might apologize for the kiss, but then she developed a hungry expression instead, one that said she was anything but sorry. She said, "Thank you for sharing."

He felt vulnerable and happy in a way he had never felt. His cheeks lifted.

Amia reached her hand to his and said, "I don't know exactly how to explain it, but the energy bubble thrumming inside me, I think when it pops, I'll be me again, whoever that is. I think we'll have answers soon." She smirked. "I don't know. Maybe I'm just constipated."

Daizon laughed. "I guess you'll find relief either way. It's a win, win."

Amia gripped his hand and squeezed. "Thank you."

Daizon wanted her to see the best of him. That is what he did in relationships. *Give them what they want to see,* he had said. He took that advice to a whole new extreme. That's how he hid from the pain. What he did not realize was that sharing that side of himself would be as cathartic for him as it was for Amia. She wanted to see those shades of him. She wanted to know his worst attributes as much as she wanted to know his best. The more he learned about her general nature, the more he felt himself falling for her. His hunger only grew with each taste she gave him.

⋹⋺

The next day, while teaching tai chi, Amia felt a sense of progress working with the group. She was learning who she was, even if she did not have her complete memories. She decided how she treated people, the things she did and learned, made her who she was. The other things, the dark angel lurking in the shadows, they did not define her. What she did and how she treated people mattered. She did not have to act on all her thoughts. Thoughts could deceive her. She could reason through problems and situations and act accordingly.

Amia knew she would not always be in control or know what to do or how to feel in certain situations. She would have to learn to be okay with not always being in control. She could feel lost and scared one moment and then the next feel found and fearless. It was part of experiencing life, good and bad moments. She knew she was not there yet—she was not whole—but she felt her progress, and that made her smile despite the worsening nightmares.

Amia smiled at Daizon, who seemed lost in some deep thoughts. He followed her tai chi instruction from the back of the group. His expression seemed stuck in a terrible memory or contemplation. His eyes were wet. She wanted to comfort him, to go to him but knew he would not want the group's attention, as she did not during that first group session several weeks back. Her own eyes teared up, and she turned from the group. She continued the exercises while facing away from them. She would not betray his trust. Her chest ached, seeing him in such pain. By the time she composed herself and turned around, he had gone. She glanced over the grounds but could not see him.

She forced a smile at the group and let her hands fall at the last motion. "Good job. You all are doing excellent. I think that's good for today."

The group slowly disbanded. Amia flashed a smile at them as they left. She held her pointer finger up to signal an approaching Tarah that she would be a moment. Amia increased her pace to intercept Dr. Wolf, who was making her way toward the building. Dr. Wolf paused for Amia, probably noticing Amia's feet slapping against the walkway. Then Amia noticed their reflection in the entryway windows.

Dr. Wolf said, "I saw," as Amia reached her. She used a calm voice. "I will speak with him in a moment. He'll be fine. You did an excellent job up there today, as usual. I think this is everyone's favorite part of the day." Dr. Wolf motioned to all the smiles and pockets of conversation. Then she said, "I have some good news. Detective Johnson verified your information. She is coming to our scheduled meeting in about two hours, if that's okay?"

Stunned, Amia nodded her agreement. A moment passed, and she realized she was still nodding.

Dr. Wolf held the inside of Amia's forearm with one hand and patted her shoulder with the other. She said, "It's okay."

Tarah walked up as Dr. Wolf walked away. "What's going on?"

CHAPTER THIRTY

REPRESSED MEMORIES

Rushing to his bathroom sink, Daizon splashed water onto his face. His chest heaved and his head throbbed. His eyes lost their ability to hold tears inside. He squeezed them shut, but the work over the last four weeks of dredging up his past had tangled memories and emotions assaulting him. His strength felt childlike all over again. How many of them had witnessed his weakness? He was in the back of the group. He might have slipped away unnoticed. Amia saw. He shook his head. *This can't be real.* Another wave of thoughts and emotions flooded his mind and told him it was all too real. This was his brokenness. He collapsed to the floor and cried.

A knock on the door shook him from his distorted time lapse. He glanced at his wet palms after smudging his face. He couldn't bring himself to answer the door. A few more knocks. He wanted to be alone. Then he heard the lock disengage on the door, and it swung open. Light footsteps, heels clicking across the tiled floor. How long was he on the floor? He couldn't have been there long, but this was his eternal hell, where he would forever burn.

Soft tones came to him from the doorway. Dr. Wolf stood there with a soft, steady disposition. She asked again, "May I come in?"

Daizon laughed. Laughing was all he could think to do. It was not her fault. She had not done this to him. He knew he was the one to blame. He was responsible. It did not matter that he was a child when these things happened. He should have known better. He knew better. They ruined him, but it was all his own fault.

Dr. Wolf spoke up from beside him. When did she sit down? Why was she there? "I'm here if you need me."

Her voice and offer were an arm's length of a rope dangling in front of him. He did not know what else to do, so he grabbed hold. He said, "It's my fault."

"What is your fault, Daizon?"

"I'm ruined inside. They laughed. God, they laughed, and they won't stop laughing. Even when I get away, they're laughing." Daizon inhaled a deep breath. "I need to run faster. I need to get away."

A steady voice, the voice of somebody calm and in control, broke through to him. "Daizon, I want you to stay in the moment, but I want you to know you're safe."

Daizon turned to her. "I know where I am. I just can't get the images out of my head. Give me a minute and I'll be fine."

Dr. Wolf smiled. "It would be nice if healing worked that way. I think you know by now that it doesn't. The only way through is to accept the pain and the emotions and try to understand them. I want you to do something for me, okay? I want you to think about the Compassionate Mindful Self character that you created. Can you do that?"

His breathing slowed, and he said, "Yeah."

"What would he say to you right now?"

Daizon's breath slowed further as he thought. "He'd tell me it's okay. That it's not my fault. They can't hurt me anymore."

Nodding in agreement, Dr. Wolf said, "Now, I want you to go back to the beginning and tell me what happened. Remember, your Compassionate Mindful Self figure has already experienced all of this, and he will be there for you after."

Daizon breathed deeply and steadied himself as he slipped into his memory and narrated.

> I was like five, maybe six, and was flying my paper airplane at my grandmother's. I was by myself outside the old farmhouse near a thin tree line that separated my grandparents' property from their neighbors'. You could see through if you were up close. Grammy was inside with Grampa while I played. The neighbor boys were twelve and sixteen, maybe older, and they were laughing. They saw me flying my airplane through the trees and asked if I wanted to see something cool. I looked back at my Grammy's house, at the big window in the kitchen where Grammy would make doughnuts sometimes. I knew I wasn't supposed to leave the yard. Grammy and Grandpa told me not to leave the yard. Grammy said, 'You don't have any business with those older boys. The only thing those older boys can show you is how to get into trouble.' But they were there, and they didn't seem like trouble. They were smiling and friendly.

I crawled and climbed through the tree line, and they led me to the back of their place. It was all dusty in their backyard with car parts and other scattered junk, like old tires, a broken dishwasher, and they had clotheslines full of drying clothes and white sheets. They pointed to a tree house in the distance. It was in the woods and this long grass, taller than all of us, stood in a bog that separated us from the land out back.

I looked back at Grammy's house and could barely see it. It was like a shadow beyond the tree line. One of them, the younger one, he started clucking like a chicken. The older brother was a lot bigger. He was quieter and told his brother to stop. 'Do you want to see it?'

I glared at the younger brother and said, 'I ain't no chicken.' I was big and could run fast. I was strong, too.

My dad, aunts, and uncles joked about gays. They joked with my uncle, who was gay. I liked my uncle. He was nice, and he was funny. I didn't really understand.

The neighbor boys led me to a trail they had built with planks to cross the long grass bog. Dragonflies and bees hummed around the brown cattails at the tops of some of the bog grass. You couldn't see anything beyond the grass when you were in it. I couldn't see Grammy's house or even the tree line anymore. Before they led me through, they said I couldn't tell anybody about this place. They made me promise before we continued.

When we couldn't see Grammy's house anymore, I got kind of scared because their smiles didn't look right. They looked mean. They whispered to each other, and I could see the tree house now. It had these gray-black boards with big nails holding them between three trees that twisted together. The boards leading up to the tree house seemed really far apart, and they didn't look safe to climb.

That's when the younger one said, 'We're gonna teach you a lesson, fag.' And he punched me in the gut so hard, my wind left me, and I fell to the ground, choking for air. I started crying, and I couldn't breathe. They laughed more. The older brother grabbed the back of my neck like a dog, and he yanked me to my knees. He faced me away from him toward his younger brother. The younger brother said, 'I have a lollipop.'

I was crying, and I was mad, and scared, and I didn't know what to do. The only thing I could think to do was bite, so I did. I bit down as hard as I could, and he screamed. He rolled to the ground in a ball. His older brother flung me to the side, laughing, and went to his brother. I ran faster than I ever ran. The older brother laughed harder as I ran, and the younger one joined in. The younger one yelled, 'Fag! Gay fuck!' And then they laughed harder, and their laughs chased me.

I didn't want to be a fag or gay. If I told my Grammy and Grampa what they did, I knew I would get in trouble for going over there when I was told not to go. I wasn't supposed to go with them. If I told them, if I told anyone, they would know I was a fag. I didn't know what that meant, but if I admitted to what happened, then I would be one.

That's why those boys laughed so hard. They taught me a lesson. They taught me I was worthless. But if I didn't say anything, then it could be like it didn't happen. Nobody would know.

Later, I didn't want to go outside at my Grammy's. When Grampa told you to go outside, you listened or else. He spanked me when I refused. He ripped my pants down and spanked my bare bottom harder when I told him again, 'No.'

Grampa said, 'You're going to listen to me, dammit.' He spanked me so hard I couldn't sit.

I went outside, and I hid behind the house. I told my mom and dad that I didn't want to go there anymore. They asked me why, and I said I was big now and could stay home. They didn't listen. Dad said I had to go, and I had better listen if I knew what was good for me.

I learned to stay quiet. I listened. I learned to be wary of people. People lied. I couldn't tell anybody what happened.

Dr. Wolf wiped her eyes. She said, "I want you to imagine your five-year-old self at your grandmother's with nobody around except your Compassionate Mindful Self. Imagine the time shortly after what happened and what your Compassionate Mindful Self would say to you. What would he say? What would your five-year-old self say to him? Imagine how that conversation would go."

⤙

Daizon was his five-year-old self. He was scared and staring at the tree line separating the properties. Daizon also imagined himself as the Compassionate Mindful Self character he had worked on over the last month. His compassionate self knew and had experienced the things that had happened. He understood the pain and conflict his five-year-old self felt.

His compassionate self reached out and held his younger self. He said, "What happened to us was wrong. It wasn't our fault. To think of being five years old and being responsible for something like that, no. We did nothing wrong."

Five-year-old Daizon said, "I don't want to be gay. I want to be normal."

Compassionate Mindful Daizon smiled. "What happened doesn't make us gay. Even if we were gay, that would be okay, too, but we're not. We're attracted to women."

Five-year-old Daizon scrunched a questioning face.

Compassionate Mindful Daizon realized he was talking over his younger self's head. He smiled again. "How we acted after what happened was normal. It was normal to feel ashamed. They were older boys who should have known better than to do what they did to us. They were boys, too, though. When you're taught hate for people that differ from you when you are young, that's what you know. It's how you see the world. All they knew was that Uncle Jerry differed from them. Their hatred got the better of them when they tricked us into going to the tree house and attacked us. But we are okay. It takes a long time and a lot more things happen in our lives, but eventually we meet some people that help us understand what happened to us was not our fault. Unfortunately, we have to relive these moments of pain in order to get better. I know it hurts. I'm sorry we have to go through this again."

Five-year-old Daizon teared up. His posture straightened. He said, "I can be strong, like you." He hugged Compassionate Mindful Daizon as hard as his tiny arms could squeeze.

Compassionate Mindful Daizon returned the hug and held his younger self to his heart. He said, "It's okay to be weak, too. We don't always have to be strong. From now on, we're going to have each other. We don't have to be afraid. We don't have to be ashamed. We don't have to be strong or weak. We can just be ourselves."

⋘

Back in his room with Dr. Wolf, it took Daizon a few moments to recover as he let the tears fall. He let them fall and did not hide them. These tears were a welcome release. He felt vulnerable and strong at the same time. The euphoric sensation seemed similar to sharing a part of himself with Amia. It was like recapturing a piece of himself that had been missing. It was also like letting go of a boulder he'd been carrying for a long time. He laughed.

He looked at Dr. Wolf with a stupid, relieved smile, and she returned the gesture. She let him feel the moment. He was physically and emotionally spent. He said, "Thank you."

"You're welcome. I think you know you did all the hard work to get here. It took a lot of courage. That event changed your life and the way you viewed the world. You didn't feel you could talk to anyone about what happened, so you bottled it up and internalized it. You made it into your fault. Unfortunately, you're not alone. Many individuals who experience trauma the way you did have similar reactions. They internalize the shame and they hate themselves."

"That's why you gave me those books on depression, mindfulness, compassion, and the other one, *It's Not Your Fault*. You wanted me to understand and see the situation from a different perspective that had knowledge of the things I had been through. You wanted me to understand why I was the way I was. That blade, my Compassionate Mindful Self figure, you were having me forge him for this moment."

"We practice our mindfulness and compassion exercises and reinforce them with knowledge and other skill sets. We geared your writing in a journal toward pinpointing where certain beliefs come from. There are usually triggers in these exercises. We're constantly becoming more aware. The reason we delve so deeply here in this environment, as I think you can imagine, is because it's a safe place to be vulnerable and build trust. All of you are doing the hard work. I'm a guide."

Shaking his head, Daizon said, "I think I understand." He motioned with a sweep of his hands to the wider picture of the room and facility. "This makes sense."

Dr. Wolf nodded. "I have our class session and an appointment coming up. If you want to rest for a little while and skip our morning session, it's okay. When you're ready to go back out there, I'm sure your friends would like to see you and know you're okay. And before you worry about who saw you leave and your state when you did, remember there's nothing to be embarrassed about. I'm proud of you. I hope you are as well. Ask your compassionate self what he thinks. Take your time and visit the others when you're ready."

"Thank you, Dr. Wolf." Daizon walked the doctor to the door, and they exchanged smiles before she left.

Daizon thought about his journal and back to the man with a knife at the graveyard. That man had held a power over him for too long. Daizon smiled. He knew what his next challenge would be. He thought of his Compassionate Mindful Self, lay back on his bed, and walked into a memory.

CHAPTER THIRTY-ONE

MEET AMIA

The Whole Me entrance beckoned Amia. Knowing Dr. Wolf was capable didn't stop Amia from wanting to be there for Daizon. A beam of late-morning light shone on Amia and Tarah. Shadows scrunched and distorted into specks of darkness. They spoke on the grass near the entryway.

Tarah reminded Amia with a wave and a smile that she was there. She let out a concerned, nervous laugh. "You still haven't told me what's going on. Are you okay?"

Amia shook her head. "I'll be okay."

Tarah cocked her head with a you-know-I-don't-believe-that-crap kind of look. Tarah had become a good friend at the Whole Me program. Amia thought of the pained expression that had washed over Daizon so thoroughly. "Daizon left before we finished the morning exercise. It's not like him, and Dr. Wolf went to check on him."

Tarah said, "If Dr. Wolf is with him, he's going to be fine. Besides, he could have eaten something that didn't sit well or something like that. That would make me want to leave in a hurry. I mean, I love having these hot wings at Shady Jay's Tavern. They make the best wings by far out of all the places I've performed. I could have been too inebriated to have an accurate recollection, but I'm pretty sure they have the best wings. The only issue is the next day, they burn just as much going out as they did going down. Every bit worth it, though."

They laughed. Shady Jay's rang familiar in Amia's mind, but she couldn't place it.

Tarah said, "You should come see me play with my band. Well, I might be solo after my stay here. Wait until you see me all painted up, dressed in black, with all my piercings and black accents. I spike my hair, almost like an extension of my rose tattoo. You can barely see it now with all this new hair growth." She laughed. "You might want to pretend you don't know me. I can cause quite the reaction dressed like that."

A broad smile stretched Amia's face. "I wouldn't dream of pretending not to know you." Amia looked around and leaned into Tarah. "You can't tell Daizon that I told you, but he told me you are one of his favorite performers. He said when you sing, he imagines the heavens opening up and the archangels descending upon earth to wage war on the evil that preys on humankind. I would say he thinks you are superb at what you do."

Eyes lit, Tarah smiled. "I thought I might have seen him at Shady Jay's a couple of times, but the lights shine on the stage and I tended to self-medicate. That's kind of why I'm here. I wanted to snuff out the problem at the root, you know?"

Amia nodded. She might not have known exactly what Tarah was feeling, but she understood the eternal war with darker forces. She didn't need her full memory for that type of understanding.

Tarah said, "The weekend we get out of here, I'm supposed to play at Shady Jay's again. It's a Friday-night gig. If you could come, I'd love to see you there. Maybe a few of the others might want to come as well. Or maybe just Daizon and you?" Tarah stared at Amia with a smirk.

Amia grinned. "It sounds like a fun time. I'm sure the more of us that can go, the better. I bet they would all love to see you perform. To be honest, I don't know how Daizon feels about me. I mean, whether he feels the same way about me that I do about him. He's so smart and observant, but in some things, he's oblivious and unsure. I think the main issue is that he doesn't want to take advantage of me in my current situation. It's complicated."

With a consoling smile, Tarah said, "I'll admit it's complicated, and he probably doesn't want to take advantage of you. But the way I see it, I think that man would dig a hole through that rock cliff to the depths of hell if it meant he could be with you."

"Maybe instead of digging, he should climb a ladder to a cloud, because that's where he's going to find me."

Tarah said, "Men are so oblivious. It's like they didn't learn a thing about mind-reading. I think that should be an essential course for men."

Laughing felt good. Shady Jay's kept buzzing around in Amia's head like a hungry mosquito. Soon his buddies showed up, and the little devils bit and nipped at her as she replayed the name in her mind.

⚓

The time came to meet with Detective Johnson and Dr. Wolf. Inside Dr. Wolf's office, Detective Johnson was mostly as Amia remembered her. She had sharp feminine features with short red hair styled back in a flair. Her athletic build, assessing nature, and effortless movement suggested an intense training routine. She thought of Daizon and a few of his early-morning workouts. His unyielding work ethic bordered between intense and something godlike. Amia wondered if Detective Johnson had military training like Daizon. Her posture gave off a military vibe.

Daizon had told her the military helped him hone his work ethic. Amia's eyes fell to the detective's black athletic shoes, which did not quite go with the high-sheen dark suit and white blouse.

Detective Johnson sat beside Amia on the couch while Dr. Wolf completed the triangle by sitting in front of them in her chair. Detective Johnson swung her foot in the air, legs crossed, modeling the shoes that gained Amia's attention. With a conspirator's voice, she said, "The heel came apart on my dress shoes weeks ago. I'm enjoying running around in these. Nobody's said anything. I'll squeeze it out as long as I can."

Dr. Wolf scanned the manila folder the detective gave her, which allowed the detective time with Amia. Besides her hair being short and the less visible wounds on the back of her head, it would have been hard to notice any defect with Amia physically. Detective Johnson said, "You look fantastic. If I didn't know what happened to you, I wouldn't believe it. How are you feeling?"

"I'm well," Amia replied. "I'm remembering more of who I am every day. It hasn't quite snapped into place, but it feels like it could happen at any moment. Right now it's more like I'm seeing my life and knowing things happened instead of having lived the events. It's weird. I feel the emotions paired with those events, but they seem disjointed and confusing." Amia smiled absently. "I'm teaching the class tai chi, and Daizon is teaching some of us self-defense."

Snapping her head up, Detective Johnson had the look of a bird who heard a noise. She swung her head to the doctor, who had her nose in the file, and then back to Amia.

Amia felt right to smile the way she did. She enjoyed the way he made her feel. Glancing at Dr. Wolf, she wanted to ask how he was doing, but a glance at the stewing Detective Johnson swayed her from asking.

With a glance up from her glasses to the detective, Dr. Wolf kept reading the file. She said, "Yes, Detective Johnson, Daizon is researching a role and taking advantage of the program."

"Here, with Amia? The same man I'm investigating? What were you thinking, letting him in here with Amia?"

Investigating Daizon? He saved my life. Amia aimed her confusion at Dr. Wolf as well.

In her calm manner, Dr. Wolf held up an open palm and one finger for them to wait a moment while she finished reading the file. Amia smirked as she watched the detective simmer. Dr. Wolf closed the folder and turned to the detective. "He couldn't be too high on your list of suspects if you didn't realize he was here until now. It's been over a month since the program started—seven weeks since the incident. Do you really think he would have worked so hard to save Amia's life the next day if he left her for dead the previous night?"

"It happens," Detective Johnson stated succinctly. She lost some of her surety, but what she lacked there she made up for with tenacity. "It doesn't matter what I think. The fact is, I don't know. Do you know, Doctor?"

"I know Amia has not been in any danger from Daizon—at least not the kind of danger you're thinking of." She smiled at Amia.

Amia understood the part about her feelings toward Daizon, but the rest? Then she remembered Daizon telling her how he thought saving her the way he did might implicate him. She shook her head and was about to state her support for Daizon when Dr. Wolf added. "In fact, I don't believe Amia would be this far along without his help. Not once have I seen him exert any sort of pressure on her. I believe he feels responsible for her safety, probably from finding her the way he did on his property. Beyond that, he has rights to his privacy. Now, before we talk about what we know, Amia, this is for you." Dr. Wolf handed Amia the folder.

In her hands, the folder summed up Amia's past in a few pages. Is that all she was? She ran her fingers over the folder with reverence, or was that fear? She opened it and read.

Name: Amia Aelise Viardo

Age: 24

Address: 16 Birch Way, Raleigh, Massachusetts

Occupation: Student

Education: Completed Master's Degree, enrolled first-year Doctoral Studies in Clinical Psychology, Raleigh, Massachusetts, School of Psychology

Amia's eyes danced over those first few observations. Amia Viardo played over and over in her mind. She said it again and again, like ringing a doorbell to her own home. Amia was not home, but the door was open and all her stuff decorated the interior.

She walked through the doorway and called out, *Amia Aelise Viardo*, to her imagination. She gazed around at the dry facts decorating her home. She lived and went to school in Raleigh, Massachusetts. She was on her way to becoming a clinical psychologist. Pictures of indistinct silhouettes hung on the walls.

Family: None

Emergency Contact: None

That had to be wrong. She was only twenty-four; she had to have family and friends. Amia felt for the warmth of her earrings. It was in that touch. Somebody loved her. She was sure of it. She reached for a silhouette on the wall. It was a woman being embraced by a younger woman, in front of a high school, wearing a graduation cap? Amia ran her fingers over the engravings on the bottom of the frame. It read, *Stelle per illuminare il cielo*. Amia's fingers slid over her silver earrings again. She thought, *Stars to light the sky.*

Amia read further through the file. She had a tenant, Beth Dixon. She'd grown up in Crystal Springs, North Carolina. She attended primary, middle, and high school there. She read more facts she couldn't relate to. Every time it was like ringing a bell that made no sound; it simply vibrated. Or maybe it was more like hollering to some version of herself she hoped would answer back. The house became a cacophony of jumbled echoes and the only realization: Amia wasn't available at the moment. Try again later.

Bringing Amia back to the moment, Dr. Wolf said, "Detective Johnson, Amia's roommate, Beth, you told me you spoke with her."

"I did. Ms. Dixon lives with Amia during the school year. She said Amia was in Maine on vacation. Ms. Dixon also said Amia was looking forward to her work-study with Dr. Rorke. The work-study was supposed to start five weeks ago, the second week in June."

Detective Johnson forced a smile at Amia and turned to Dr. Wolf. She said, "Ms. Dixon is on her way to Maine. I tried telling her I didn't know when Amia would be allowed visitors, but she didn't seem to care. She told me she was coming up to see her friend. I'm going to talk with her more when she arrives." She turned to Amia. "Ms. Dixon seems like a good friend to have."

The mention of Ms. Dixon, Beth, settled the noise enough in Amia's mind for a wide grin to form. Without thinking, she said, "Beth is a tad impulsive but the best kind of tenacious." Amia noticed the detective and Dr. Wolf staring at her. Then what she was thinking, what she knew, became mist in her mind. She clung to the memory she knew for the truth. The memory felt right in her mind, and it was solid, even if it was only for a moment.

Dr. Wolf said, "Normally we wait until the last couple of weeks before we invite family and guests. However, considering the circumstances, I'm sure we can make an allowance. I spoke with Beth before our meeting. She left several messages this morning while we were doing our exercises. I think both of you are correct in your assessments. Beth seems a good friend to have, the best kind of tenacious."

Dr. Wolf glanced at her watch. "Beth is arriving this afternoon at the Bangor Airport. She's staying at Matilda's Seaside Way Inn here in East Coast Harbor. Our appointment is at four o'clock. I told Beth you might want to attend the meeting, Detective Johnson. I also asked her why she thought Amia might be in Maine. She said Amia let her know she was staying at Matilda's but did not elaborate on her vacation. The only thing Beth could think of was that she'd convinced Amia to create a dating profile a few months before the end of the school year. Amia might have met somebody through the site and didn't tell her. She said Amia had a hard time with getting back into the dating scene after she caught her boyfriend cheating on her."

Dr. Wolf and Amia shared a knowing look. Then Dr. Wolf added, "Beth said Amia didn't trust the idea of internet dating. She knew Amia signed up only to pacify her. As far as Beth knew, Amia's primary focus was on earning her doctorate. The dating site was called Psyche and Eros." Dr. Wolf paused, conflicted. "Beth told me they had a laugh when the site matched Amia with Daizon May as her top match."

Amia's head spun with new information. Amia asked, "Psyche and Eros?" The name rang in her mind, and a memory materialized. "They match you after you answer hundreds of personality and preference questions for different scenarios. There were eight slightly different answers to each question, and you were to choose the one that was most like you. They based compatibility matches on personality, likes and dislikes, and what you were looking for out of a relationship." Amia paused and shook her head. "I don't know how I know that, but I do. My laptop. Did you bring my laptop?"

Detective Johnson shook her head. "We didn't find a laptop with your belongings. We searched your hotel room and your returned rental vehicle. It was not with your possessions we found in the lake below Mr. May's, either. We found your phone in hundreds of pieces and some of your clothes in the lake." She glared at Dr. Wolf but spoke in a sweet voice. "Tell me, Doctor, why is Mr. May not a threat?"

A strange realization dawned on Amia, and she locked eyes with Dr. Wolf. "Daryll isn't protecting Daizon. He's here to protect me from Daizon." The room circled Amia as thoughts clicked into place, forcing other gears to tumble. She was falling for him, and he could be the one who—

Dr. Wolf interrupted the thought. "While I don't believe Daizon is the person who did those horrible things to you, it would be irresponsible of me not to allow for the possibility. Besides his saving your life, I've interviewed him multiple times now and have seen nothing to suggest he would have done those things to you. The type of person who would have done those things has a certain rage toward women that I don't believe Daizon possesses. Again, I won't betray my oath to his privacy. I believe he is the type of person who would risk his well-being to save and protect you. Amia, I can see from your reaction that you may no longer feel safe with him at the facility. I understand. I'll let him know he will no longer be a part of this program."

"No," Amia blurted out. The thought of losing him tightened her stomach and chest. He had confided to her about finding her. Confused thoughts played out in Amia's head. The Daizon she knew would not do those things to her. He was kind, patient, and never forceful. He made her feel comfortable. He was also an accomplished actor. Was he playing a role? *No.* Even Dr. Wolf did not believe he was capable of those things. He was not that dark presence that haunted her nightmares and lurked in the shadows.

He'd saved her life. Psyche and Eros, did she contact Daizon? Did he contact her? Amia said, "I need to talk with Daizon."

Detective Johnson said, "He's a professional liar. He has both of you fooled. Dr. Wolf, you can't let this continue. I won't allow it. I'll arrest him if that's what needs to happen. I'll have your license, Doctor. This is too much."

"Detective Johnson, before you make idle threats and unsubstantiated accusations, realize we all want what is best for Amia. You want to jump straight to this accusatory tone, like you know everything. I've been doing this job for over twenty years. I have working relationships with federal, state, and local officials. You should know I am very well respected for my work and opinions, not because I am always right but because I don't jump to conclusions and like to see problems from multiple perspectives. Multiple angles allow me to gain a better understanding of the truth. So, before you accuse me of ignorance or incompetence, I ask that you please verify the account information for both Amia and Daizon on the Psyche and Eros site. We should make sure it was not somebody else using his name or whatever the situation may be. There are many questions I can think of, Detective. I'm sure you can find out if they were actually in contact with one another. Am I asking too much, Detective Johnson?"

Pinching her lips and grinding her teeth, Detective Johnson replied, "I may have overstated my position, but I'm sure you can understand my frustration. I said his alibi checked out, but now I'm not sure." She stood. "I'll start working on verifying our new information and will be back later today to speak with Beth. I don't think he should be here, but that's only my opinion. Thank you for your time, Doctor. You can keep the file. Amia, I am glad to see you feeling better. I didn't mean to upset you. I think you should be aware."

Amia didn't quite know what to say.

Dr. Wolf said, "Thank you, Detective. We know your intentions are well meaning."

Once Detective Johnson left the room, Dr. Wolf told Amia, "I'm not sure Daizon is ready at this moment for the conversation you want to have with him. I'm not sure you're ready. Would you like to share some of your thoughts and emotions with me?"

Amia did. She had a million questions and feelings jumbled in her mind. Was she falling in love with the man who had left her for dead? Was that a question she should ask? Amia thought of the trust she'd built with Daizon. If she could only remember everything. The dry facts in the file stimulated something inside her, but those facts seemed to highlight what was missing rather than what was there. She clawed at the memories. *What happened to my parents and my Nonna? Is Beth the only person in my life?* She asked Dr. Wolf, "Am I a fool?"

Dr. Wolf smiled. "Do you believe you are a fool?"

"I don't know. I might be."

"Being foolish and exploring potent feelings . . . I'd say we are all fools if that were the guide. It's not foolish to want love."

CHAPTER THIRTY-TWO

PAIN AND COURAGE

P hysically, Daizon was still in his room, lying on top of his bedcovers. Mentally, he was in another place. One lifelong weight lifted. He wanted to put his newfound ability and strength to his next childhood trauma.

He remembered small things, like his parents continually forcing him to return to his grandmother's. He remembered the sense of isolation. He went from always wanting to explore the outdoors and investigating shadows to not wanting to explore the underside of his bed after the lights were out. He saw shadows within shadows.

Daizon supposed this was when his acting career truly began. He didn't think he was a good actor back then. Surely everybody could see through his lies and realize he was only pretending to be normal. The undamaged kids ran around, oblivious to the dangers he knew were out there. If he hid the pain and acted oblivious, maybe they would see him as normal. Looking back on himself, he was a child, becoming hyper-aware. Acting oblivious led to being oblivious.

In the memory Daizon was ten. The main road in town led past the mill where his mother worked. Various small shops lined either side of the road. His favorite was a place that had sweet and sour candies on the lower shelves in big jars. They even had a bigger display of shelled peanuts inside a wooden keg. This day, Young Daizon, ten, stood in front of the post office, as he made a habit of doing after he got out of school. The candy shop owner always had an eye out for quick little hands. With his change, Young Daizon had purchased some of the stuff that would spoil his dinner. Several years had passed since the earlier event, and he had blocked the memory of it. He was building courage and exploring. His self-confidence was growing again.

A wiry-figured balding man, late twenties or early thirties, walked from where the mill workers left work and nodded at Young Daizon. Daizon could not remember exactly what the man said, but he remembered the man asking questions about what he was doing there. The man talked about how he worked with his mother sometimes. He mentioned the names of some of his mother's friends. He liked the shop where Young Daizon purchased his candy. The man mentioned the cemetery in town just up the street.

Young Daizon hadn't known it was there. When the man asked if he wanted to see some of the cool stones inside the cemetery, Young Daizon hesitated. He wanted to see the place. His mother would not be out of work for another thirty minutes. Many people walked around on either side of the street. The thin man smiled and presented himself as harmless. Still, Young Daizon said, "I don't think I can. My mom's getting out of work soon."

Balding Man glanced at his watch and said, "We have plenty of time." He pointed down the street. "It's only a little way away. You'll be back in no time." He pointed to a spot where the road curved.

⁓

Back in his bed, Daizon's mind swirled. How easily this man had deceived him. Then and over the years, Daizon often thought back to how he'd let himself be tricked when he knew better. Shame often washed over Daizon when he thought of how much of a coward he was for not speaking up. He knew the Balding Man would do it again to some other kid and that kid might not get away. This last part especially stuck with Daizon. He gathered his courage and went back into the memory, knowing his compassionate figure would be with him.

⁓

Young Daizon followed the wiry Balding Man to the cemetery. He could not see where the mill was anymore, and nobody walked near them. People clung to the town and shops. Balding Man pointed out the stones ahead and to the people not so nearby. Young Daizon recognized the road to the beach almost across the street from where they were. He gained some courage and followed the Balding Man into the cemetery.

Car noises became a murmur in the background as they walked farther into the cemetery. Buildings seemed small as they traveled down a hill. Balding Man's expression grew meaner, and he formed the slightest of smirks. Young Daizon realized he had made a mistake. "I'm going to go back."

Balding Man said, "Come on, don't be a pussy." He pointed to a large stone. "You've got to see this."

They were in the heart of the town but somehow had traveled to the middle of nowhere. Nobody would hear him if he called for help. The smirk on Balding Man's face grew, as he had positioned himself between Young Daizon and his escape route. He unfolded a lock-blade hunting knife.

The next thing Young Daizon knew, he was looking up from the ground after trying to make an escape. The slightly curved triangular tip of the knife blade danced in front of his eyeball, ready to plunge. He was helpless, pinned by the slimy man. The animal's eyes said he would plunge the knife if Young Daizon moved.

Young Daizon was not sure what scared him more, the knife tip hovering less than an inch from his eye or thoughts of how the pedophile wanted to violate him. So easily fooled. He was smarter than that.

Balding Man said, "I'll shove this into your eyeball quicker than you can blink if you even think of trying something." Mind squirming for a way out, Young Daizon relaxed his body, making believe he would submit.

The Balding Man's eyes danced with excitement as he slid back from the way he had straddled Young Daizon and pinned him to the ground. He propped himself up so he could undo his belt, button, and zipper. Saliva formed at the edge of his mouth as he pulled his knife hand back to assist with his task. When he rose several inches to pull them down, Young Daizon tightened every muscle he had and drove his knee into Balding Man's crotch.

Young Daizon pushed and rolled out as the pedophile collapsed to the side. He ran. He ran until people in the town stared at him. Then he slowed so as not to be noticed. Helplessness and embarrassment overwhelmed him. Some people smiled, but they all stared with twisting heads. They could not know what happened. He wanted to be normal, so he pretended to be normal. He smiled back at them as he slowed to a walk. Heat and nervous energy flooded his young self.

They smiled back at him, but what were they hiding? What were their intentions? Did they see how worthless he was? Young Daizon kept smiling, nodding, and he waved little greetings. *Give them space. Don't let them get close. Let them see a normal boy.*

⤚

New imaginings brought Young Daizon and Compassionate Mindful Daizon to the local beach. Daizon grew up swimming at this beach often, from swimming lessons to swimming laps. He knew people would never accept him into their friend groups, but they would grow to respect his athletic ability. They would even pretend to be his friends.

Compassionate Mindful Daizon sat beside Young Daizon on one of the boulders that lined the point overlooking the beach. The lush green park area had a walkway looping around the point of land that jetted into the lake. In front of them, ice-blue lake water swayed back and forth. Watching the dark blue water where he swam and fished helped calm Young Daizon. Tall blades of grass sprouted from the shallows where fish swam and hid. Wind pushed the blades this way and then the other. Dragonflies buzzed and perched on the grass.

Young Daizon balled his fist and said, "I want to kill him. He didn't even see me as a person. He fooled me with his lies. I thought I was being careful and was safe. I thought I knew what I was doing. He seemed harmless and friendly. Why couldn't I see?"

"You're a ten-year-old boy who's seen and knows too much already. You don't and can't expect to know everything already. You want to trust and believe the best in people. People like him are predators with skills honed for their prey. Wanting to kill him after what he did is a natural emotion. It's okay to be angry, upset, and confused. What happened and your reactions don't make you any less of a person."

"I can't trust anyone. I have to work harder at seeing people, what they want, what they really want. I won't let them lie to me or hurt me ever again."

"Yes, you will work hard and become hyper-aware. Your muscles will grow, and so will your mind. Hate and mistrust are heavy burdens. Living in fear isn't an easy way to live. No matter how far we bury our want to believe the best in people, we still see their potential for good. Especially if we see somebody hurting, we want to help them feel better. Help them believe in themselves. We don't want them to feel like we do. We let them know how we see them if we think it might help."

"I see how all the other normal kids talk to each other in their groups. I don't belong. I can't even talk to them. The way they look at me, they know I'm different and don't belong. They look at me and laugh. They don't want me around. They'll fear me."

"Look at me now, at the person you've become. Do you fear me?"

"No. But you are strong, fit, and smart."

"There are people stronger, fitter, and more intelligent. Being feared doesn't lead to happiness. It leads to loneliness and paranoia. Is that something you want?"

"I want to be normal and not afraid. I can't let anybody see me the way I am."

"You are hurt and in pain. Unfortunately, when this happened to us, we don't feel we can trust anyone enough to talk with. We assume we know what everyone will think of us. We keep them all at a distance. Teachers and people in authority, we don't trust them either. It all goes back to the experience with the neighbor boys and how we felt after. It was as if nobody noticed we were suffering. We felt if we showed even the slightest bit of weakness, our world would implode. We believed everyone would think less of us."

"They will," Young Daizon implored.

Compassionate Mindful Daizon locked eyes with his younger self, transferring a sense of calm and knowing. "That worthless feeling we have turns into self-hatred. The trouble with not telling anyone, with not being able to trust anyone, is that our anger ends up being turned inward. We become even more isolated and lonely. The self-hatred becomes stronger. Before long, we can never be good enough. We feel like we are less than everybody else, no matter what we accomplish. It's a wicked circle of lies and twisted truths that feeds on itself. Before long, it's hard to tell the difference between lies and truth. With an outlook like that, we don't trust anybody, including ourself. Holding on to that fear and anger, keeping people at a distance and having a hard time trusting, those are all normal reactions to the traumatic events like the one we just suffered and the one with the neighbor boys. We don't have to feel ashamed for the rest of our lives. We made mistakes, but we're not responsible for others' actions. Bad things happen and we don't always have control."

Young Daizon's eyes watered and his lips quivered. Tears fell, and he sniffed at the drips leaking from his nose. Compassionate Mindful Daizon held his younger self tight. He said, "It's okay to hurt and feel the pain. We need to let the hurt and pain out instead of holding on to it and letting it fester inside us."

Daizon exited the mindful compassion exercise and smiled through the tears drenching his face. It was a good cry, long overdue.

Once composed, Daizon filled a cup with water and drank. He knew those were the years when he put his father's advice into practice. Daizon developed his mask and pretended to be normal. He smiled, showed confidence, laughed, joked, and took part heavily in sports. Pretending became easier over the years, as buried memories became skewed emotions he could partition off from everyday life.

Daizon remembered how his teen years brought on new challenges and complications—girls. They seemed to know more. What it was they actually knew more of, he could not say. They were always whispering among themselves in their cliques of two, three, or maybe a couple more. They developed into young women, and trying to figure them out was hopeless. His best assessment at the time was that they expected him to read their minds. He would pick up cues they would send, a tight smile that pushed up the cheek, a dreamy gaze, a quick glance with a giggle, an absent-minded twirl of the hair with a finger. There were other signals, a quick disgusted lift of the chin, a flop of the hair that might whip you in the face, narrowing eyes that somehow looked down on you even though you were taller. The young women did not know what they wanted. At that point in time they seemed more interested in playing with his mind, pretending they knew what they wanted. He knew he was not a prize, but he wanted to feel like one.

Eventually, when Daizon joined the military, he learned he had talents in the things warriors do. The talents romanticized in war and espionage movies were not so romantic. He was a blade, bloody and sharp. Saving Kyle had its own cost. Daizon paid that cost in silence.

Instead of reenlisting, he would pursue other dreams. That was the story he told and was all anybody needed to know. Kyle knew Daizon better than anyone else, getting glimpses behind one of Daizon's many masks and perhaps viewing Daizon's true self and capabilities. Kyle was thankful, but Daizon also knew Kyle hated the feeling of owing his life. Daizon cheated Kyle out of repaying the act by not reenlisting. It didn't matter how many times Daizon told Kyle he didn't owe him anything or to forget it ever happened. Kyle could not forget any more than Daizon could. Daizon knew the question Kyle would always ask. Why? The image of the dead woman who looked so much like Amia flashed in his mind.

A knock on the door brought Daizon out of his mindful contemplations. "Hold on. I'll be right there." Daizon splashed his face with soap and cold water in the bathroom. A few pats from the towel had him presentable. Detective Johnson stood on the other side of the door with a twitchy hand on her pistol. She stood with an athletic stance and a tight-faced expression. Daryll stood to the side of the door, his narrowed eyes bouncing between the two of them.

She said, "I know you lied and I know what you did. I can only imagine the sick reasons you're here. Hero complex maybe? I'm not fooled. They can believe what they want. I've seen killers and rapists. There's always something off about them, and there's something off about you, Mr. May. Or should I say, Mr. Mason?"

Daizon offered a smile to Daryll and brought his attention back to the detective. "I don't know what you think you know, but you're welcome to come inside and talk."

Daryll swiveled his eyes back and forth between Daizon and
Detective Johnson. He seemed unsure of the situation. Daizon
told him, "I'll be fine."

Craning her neck, Detective Johnson sized up the large man. She
smirked, and her aggressive posture eased. She winked at Daryll
and entered the room as Daizon held the door and stepped out
of the way. Daizon closed the door behind them and watched
as she perused the room. Apparently satisfied with some inner
judgment, she brought her attention back to Daizon, who now
stood between her and the exit. She tensed. Daizon glanced at the
door behind him, shook his head, grinned, and stepped to the side.
Her tension eased.

"It's obvious you've learned a little about my background,
Detective. You don't need to fear me. I saved Amia's life. Do you
really think somebody with my background would leave her for
dead only to have conscience issues the next day? Do you think
anyone would have found her?"

Observing him, Detective Johnson remained silent.

Shaking his head, Daizon said, "I'm not sure what your bias is
toward me, but you are misguided if you believe I had anything to
do with what happened to Amia."

A grin formed on the detective's face. "Everybody makes
mistakes. Sometimes alibis check out at first only to dissolve under
further scrutiny. Tell me, how's your dating life? I've heard the
internet dating scene is a great place to meet people. Some sites
match you based on hundreds of questions, while others simply
post pictures like a highlight reel. Swipe left or right? Which do
you prefer?"

"What the hell are you talking about?"

"It's a simple question."

Daizon shook his head. "My manager convinced me to fill out
one where I had to answer hundreds of questions once, but I never

used it. I told her to delete it. She said she would hold it for me in case I changed my mind. My last girlfriend cheated on me, and I wasn't too eager to get back out there. One thing she liked to do was accuse me of things she did."

"So, she was intelligent. Were you having an affair with your manager?"

Daizon laughed. Then, reading her steadfast expression, said, "You're serious?"

Annoyed, the detective nodded.

"If Tonya was having an affair, it wasn't with me. She and Dave have a good marriage. She likes to flirt, but it's just playful stuff. Dave's a good guy."

Detective Johnson asked, "Do you remember the name of the dating site?"

"I don't know, Psyche and Eros, Eros and Psyche, something like that. Like I said, I told Tonya to delete it, but she held on to it in case I changed my mind." Then, remembering his conversation with her before he agreed to enter the program, he said, "I can call her if you'd like and ask? I'll have to use your phone. I don't have access to mine right now."

Seeming less sure of herself, Detective Johnson studied him. She said, "I'd prefer to speak with Mrs. Avendale in person. I have more questions for her." Contemplating or calculating thoughts in her head, Detective Johnson glanced at the door and said, "You're very smooth. I can see how you fooled everyone. Let me be straight with you. Even if you're not lying, you shouldn't be here. Why the doctor allowed you into the program is beyond me. I guess that leads me to my last questions, for now. How did you get into the program? And why are you here?"

Daizon thought about the exercises he had gone through moments before and throughout the late morning. He thought about all the mindfulness and compassion exercises. He thought of all the reading. Those things helped him see himself differently. A smile instantly stretched his face at the thought of Amia. The smile slid at the thought of him hurting her by being there. Was the detective right? Maybe he shouldn't be there? What the hell was he doing? He said, "Tonya got me into the program so I could prepare for an upcoming role about a man with amnesia. I didn't know Amia would be here when I signed up. She wasn't in the program at that point. She was so pale when I found her, I thought she was dead. I admired her strength and will to live. If there was some way I could help her recover? That's what I wanted to do. She was barely clinging to life when I found her."

A memory flashed into Daizon's mind. Men, women, and children lay dead and dying. It was a remote mountain village near a Middle Eastern border, a terrorist hideout. Their team had arrived too late. The terrorist group had already killed many of the townspeople. There was a commotion, and a woman in a wrecked building gave a muffled wail. Wary of a trap, Daizon crept to investigate. Kyle lay on top of her, holding tight to her throat. Daizon yelled at him, "What the hell are you doing?"

When Kyle turned to him, things changed in an instant. The woman retrieved a pistol from the floor and swung it toward Kyle.

Her head snapped from the bullet Daizon fired out of instinct and years of training. He was a killer, and he was good at it. She had long black hair, light brown skin, and looked barely into her midtwenties. Blood and brain matter spattered behind her head, where it had snapped backward. Blood spattered on Kyle as well.

Daizon went to help her. He pressed his hand to the hand-sized hole in the back of her head. Pieces of her head, skull fragments, and brain matter mushed between his fingers. Her dead brown eyes stared up at him.

⚜

Detective Johnson returned Daizon to the moment. "If you want to help her, you'll leave. It's that simple. I have other people to interview. Excuse me."

The door clicked shut behind her. Euphoria lost, Daizon found his way back to his bed and sat. That dead woman's image flashed in his mind and then blended with Amia's smiling image as he cradled the mushy remains of the back of her head.

Knowing the other woman was a confirmed terrorist did not ease his mind. Daizon shook his head to block out the wrongness of what he'd done, what he'd believed Kyle was about to do before knowing all the facts. Daizon knew it was this kind of stress that broke men, kept them from blending into the civilized world. Their job was to keep civilians safe, and the toll was high.

Daizon's heart raced at the thought of leaving Amia. Would leaving be the right thing to do? The euphoria he felt being around Amia, it was the first time he remembered feeling whole, human, and not hating himself. Those exercises had an incredible effect on his self-perception.

Daizon shook his head and set his jaw. He would not lose the ground he gained because of the detective's accusations. He could not. The image of the dead woman and Amia blended again in his mind.

Chapter Thirty-Three

GAIN AND LOSS
(PT. 1)

Amia exited Dr. Wolf's office when Daizon approached. She greeted him with a warm smile before her eyes slipped to Daryll, his constant shadow. Her smile faltered repeatedly. Dr. Wolf came to the door. Amia glanced over her shoulder at Dr. Wolf as if seeking some assurance before addressing him.

It was clear to Daizon the detective had spoken with Amia and Dr. Wolf. Amia's eyes had a pleading gaze, like she wanted to believe him, but the seeds the detective planted had taken root. Amia seemed to shake the thoughts from her head and smiled at him again. She said, "I was just about to find you and see if you would like to go for a walk."

"Yeah, that sounds good. Could you give me a few minutes with Dr. Wolf?"

"I'll meet you where we do our morning exercises."

Daizon smiled and nodded. "I'll be there in a few minutes."

Having stepped inside Dr. Wolf's office, he stood still while she studied him. Dr. Wolf asked, "How are you feeling?"

"I was feeling the best I remember ever feeling. I did the Compassionate Mindful Self exercise a couple more times. It was like winning some emotional marathon. Then a knock rattled my door. It seems Detective Johnson isn't too pleased I'm here. I got the distinct impression I'm her primary suspect." Daizon glanced at the door. "And by the way Amia looked at me just now, I'd say the detective had a talk with you and Amia as well. It's pretty obvious I need to leave. I'm sorry if I caused you any issues with the detective or Amia. I'll apologize to Amia in a few minutes. I doubt she'll actually want to go on a walk."

Squeezing his hands and flexing his fingers a few times, Daizon attempted to dispel the angry, sad energy. "I didn't do those things to Amia, and the thought of her thinking I did—that hurts more than I can really express at this moment. I'm sorry. I wanted to help and learn. I didn't expect—" Daizon fumbled with his hands, searching for the right words. His emotions were all over the place. He hadn't expected to have such powerful feelings for Amia. He hadn't expected the program to work. The way it helped him see himself, to fight the self-hatred, felt precious. He would not let the detective take everything from him.

"You've come a long way in a short time, Daizon. I believe you have exceptional instincts and insights that helped you progress at a rapid pace. You can understand your perspective is only one version of the truth. Few people ever get to that point. Not in the way you do. The exercise you did usually takes months of training, not only in perspective but in learning about mindfulness and self-compassion. The rest of the participants in the program are just now learning the steps you've already traveled. Some are farther along than others, as I think you already understand."

Numbness prickled inside Daizon's head. He nodded his agreement.

"I don't believe you did those things to Amia and told the detective as much. For what she said to you, I'm sorry. You must have hundreds of emotions raging right now."

Daizon was not sure what to say.

"It would be easy for the progress you've made to be shattered after what you just experienced. Your conversation with Amia may add to your difficulties. I implore you to remember what you've learned here. Please take the books I've given you and reread them. Keep practicing the exercises in mindfulness and compassion."

Dr. Wolf stepped up to Daizon and placed a gentle hand on his shoulder. "Amia is confused at the moment. The situation is not her fault or your fault. It's the way it unfolded. The only thing I ask of you during your conversation with Amia is to be mindful and compassionate to both of you."

She went to her desk and retrieved a business card. "If you need a friendly ear or kind words, please realize I'm still here for you. You'll need to practice being mindful and compassionate in a way that is meaningful to you. Whether it's five minutes a day or five hours doesn't matter. I'm going to call you so we can talk. I'm not abandoning you."

Daizon accepted the card and Dr. Wolf's two-handed politician's handshake. Should he tell her about the negative association he had with the gesture? After weeks of interacting with her, knowing she meant well, knowing what she wanted to convey by the gesture, he accepted she had a different intent. Then he had another thought. Was he giving up on a relationship with Amia too soon? Was he doing the same thing he did with all his previous relationships? Leaving when they were about to find out he was less than they believed? Did it matter? She would be better off without him in her life.

Outside, Amia plodded around the lush, freshly manicured lawn. A vast landscape of flowers surrounded her. Landscapers buzzed around like their own little swarm. The scent of freshly cut grass blended with the floral and ocean scents. The sun climbed toward the center of a white-blue sky. White wisps of clouds stretched out thin, ready to burst into nothing.

The clouds inside her mind stirred as pressure built. Energy crawled about her skin and mind. It was as if systems inside her mind were preparing for a system reboot.

Seagulls squawked and cawed. They flew in massive circles. Beyond the cliffside overlook, tumbling waves thumped somewhere beneath, along the white sands of the beach. That low rumbling surf raged inside her chest.

Amia traced the coastline with her eyes. The beach was a thin line that became more visible as it swung around the opposite side of the cove. Her eyes returned to their spot on the beach. She could not see it, but like her memory, she knew it was there. Then she found the trail that clung to the coastline. She smiled and tensed at the thought of walking it with Daizon.

What am I going to say to him? I think they matched us on a dating site, and oh, by the way, did you leave me for dead before coming back to save my life? Yeah, that's a trust builder. Maybe I could phrase it something like, what do you think of dating sites? Because I know Psyche and Eros matched us. Did you do this to me?

Amia watched others move about the grounds as if in their own little bubbles. This place was about alternate perspectives and finding new ways, healthy ways to see yourself and communicate. It was about understanding truth as a malleable concept based on infinite perspectives built through individual experiences. This was a core concept of clinical psychology. Truth was what we viewed through a lens. The more lenses we viewed, the broader the sense of truth. *But what about the lies we continually tell ourselves? Is Daizon my lie?*

She had to ask him about what Detective Johnson said. Daizon was always kind. Amia smirked and had chills thinking about his soft touch. He made her feel safe. It was like he was trying to help her regain her own strength and sense of self-confidence. He made sure she felt in control, even if the truth may have been otherwise.

His foresight seemed incredible as to her wants and needs. He never pushed or took advantage of a situation, although she sometimes wished he would. She wanted him to lean a fraction closer when they were millimeters apart. Surely the heated magnetism pulled at both of them and she was not the only one feeling the sparks. Dr. Wolf did not outright tell them not to engage with each other romantically. She urged them to be aware of the dangers of building a relationship while they were in the program. Instead of acting on base feelings and emotions, she encouraged them to build dialogue and friendships. Amia wanted to give in to the magnetism tugging her and Daizon together, not give up on it.

Amia could not believe Detective Johnson's assertion that Daizon might be the one who did those things to her. She would not believe those assertions. But what Beth had said and Psyche and Eros played on her mind. There was something there. Her stomach churned, as if trying to tell her there was more.

Daizon approached with a soft smile, and her thoughts fled with the gentle breeze that brushed her skin. It was as if everyone and every care vanished into a cloud that surrounded the two of them. Heat flooded her body and face. Her cheeks and eyes tightened with a smile that danced in greeting. It was the way he held her in his eyes. There was a depth of compassion, respect, and animal magnetism. Then his smile faltered with subtle downturn tics. The movement acted like a gust of wind, clearing the way to the sight of Daryll a short distance behind Daizon. Daryll nodded a greeting in recognition of her lingering stare.

Amia brought her focus back to Daizon, who now stood at the edge of her comfort bubble. She tensed. Sadness filled Daizon's eyes as he smiled and said, "Sorry." He took a step backward.

What was she doing? Amia reached out and stopped Daizon. "No, it's okay. I'm sorry. I don't know why I did that." She knew exactly why she'd done it. Detective Johnson had planted ideas in her head.

Daizon said, "I'm making you uncomfortable. It's not okay." He paused, searching for how to express the discomfort he tried to hide. He smiled again. It was a caring smile that tried to tell her everything would be okay, but it was the lie we always tell to make others feel better. "I talked with Dr. Wolf. We decided it would be best if I left the program."

"No," Amia interjected. "I told her no. You are not leaving."

He flashed a consoling smile. His lips twitched, and he took in a slow breath.

Realizing her reasoning was absent, Amia continued before he could speak. "I'll talk with her and tell her you're not leaving. You can't. It was Detective Johnson. She told you to leave. She said things to me."

It was true, but it did not mean the detective was wrong. Daizon offered a thin smile. "It's not her fault. She's just doing her job and trying to keep you safe. She's trying to find the person responsible for what happened to you. I can respect and appreciate her efforts, even if I don't like when they're directed at me."

Amia snapped, "And it doesn't matter what I think? Do you think I'm some porcelain princess without my own free will? I assure you, I am not made of porcelain. Oh, no, what I'm made of is much stronger. If you ever cared about me, if you ever wanted to know me, you will walk with me and we'll talk about this decision, because it affects both of us, not just you. Yes, I am scared, dammit, but that doesn't mean we give up."

Hesitantly, Daizon nodded his assent.

←🕊

Walking beside Amia had the feel of being inside a lucid dream he did not want to end. She was attractive, honest, intelligent, non-judging, and just happy to be alive. She loved life. Warm light filled her eyes. *God, how I wish I could see things the way she does. What happens when she remembers who she is? Will she be the same person? Will it be as though she's waking from a dream only to realize she's with this guy who was riding the sharp edge of a self-hating knife? Will she still think I'm some catch? Could she actually see herself with me, thinking about the things she does? Would I do that to her? She's been through enough pain.* Daizon smiled back at Amia as she squeezed his hand.

"It's okay. I'm here," she said after somehow peeking into his forbidden places.

Amia, even after everything that happened to her, or maybe because of everything that happened to her, was a blank slate. She could use multiple senses, perhaps developed a sixth sense, to see beyond his words and actions to understand some of the background noise. She cared. There was also a longing in her eyes, in the depth of them. Those emotions bled into her micro-expressions. The pain was there—Daizon could see it—but she pushed through her own pain to feel for others. She cared more for others than herself. This was her base personality. *How could I ever be worthy of a person like this?* He said, "I'm fine. I was just thinking that you are incredible. Everything that has happened to you, and I've never seen anyone with such a giving heart. I see the pain, too."

Amia withdrew her hand slightly before Daizon gently grasped it. He said, "I understand that pain. You've buried it a long way down, but it won't go away. It gnaws at your soul. If you ignore it and push it back down into the darkness, it will grow. It keeps growing until it becomes a hateful voice inside your head. The voice spreads seeds of doubt and hate throughout your mind. If I can help you in some small way, I think my advice would be to find that small dark voice and listen to what it has to say. Listen, before it grows into a monster you can't control. You deserve better." Stopping their walk, Daizon faced Amia. He held Amia's shoulders with outstretched arms. She embraced him, and wetness filled his eyes.

Of course Amia teared up in response. Even in trying to do something for her, he made it about himself. Amia kissed Daizon for a long, melting moment. And for a moment, all was right with the world. She was soft and everything he ever imagined as the best life had to offer. He smiled, wiped her tears, and said, "I'm sorry."

Before he slipped from her grasp, Amia clutched hold of him. She said, *"In un mondo pieno di oscurita, sei il posto luminoso e ti amero per sempre."* Her hand flashed over her mouth, and her eyes widened. She smiled widely, but her happiness stirred with confusion. "Nonna?"

Daizon watched the wonder, joy, and horror wash over Amia as the memory must have flashed before her eyes.

She stared at Daizon with a broken smile while collecting and processing her thoughts. She said, "My grandmother, my Nonna, would always tell me, *'In un mondo pieno di oscurita, sei il posto luminoso e ti amero per sempre.'* It means, in a world filled with darkness, you are the bright place, and I will always love you." Amia caressed delicate fingers over his cheek and cupped the side of his face. She pulled herself into him with a tight embrace. Voice breaking, she said, "They're all dead." Amia wept on Daizon's shoulder. "*Sono solo*. I'm alone. But I'm not. And you're not."

All at once, the energy changed. Amia's face morphed into that of a mouse being held by a hungry cat. She clearly flashed through another memory. It was as if she saw him for the first time all over again. Her breath caught, jaw slackened, eyebrows rose, and her eyes widened with a terrified focus as she backed away. A major tectonic shift rattled her world. "What's wrong?"

"I have to go." Amia slowly backed farther away.

He could tell she measured the space between them. Terror gripped hold of her. She was terrified of him. Daizon held up open palms in the most nonthreatening manner he could think of. "I'm not going to hurt you. You know me. You know that's the last thing in this world I want. I want to help you. What do you remember?"

"Don't." Amia thrust out her hand and stopped Daizon from advancing.

He paused, unsure. "Amia, please. I'm not a monster." The belief in her face and body language was clear as she continued creating space between them. They were in a secluded part of the trail system. Her face twisted with sadness and confusion.

Her voice trembled. "Oh God, no. We met through Psyche and Eros. We spoke over the phone. I came to Maine to see you."

Daryll placed an oversize hand on Daizon's shoulder. A firm grip meant to hold him in place, but it seemed unnecessary, as his legs felt rooted. Dumbfounded, Daizon watched as Amia ran away. She ran faster than she should be running. If he chased after her to make sure she was okay, she would only run faster and risk injuring herself. She ran from the monster she thought he was.

He tried the grounded breathing technique to settle himself. Air tickled his nose, rushed through his throat, and into his lungs. His diaphragm pushed out, and his chest heaved. Tingling vibrations attacked a numbness attached to his extremities. A new tingling numbness spread throughout him. Daizon wanted it to take him. She was right to run. He let out a hushed breath. "Run as fast as you can, Amia."

It was at that moment he noticed Daryll's pitying expression. It was too much, but Daizon could not think of anything to say to the big man. He turned back to the now empty trail, longing to chase after Amia, but knew better. He glanced at Daryll, "It's time to go."

CHAPTER THIRTY-FOUR

GAIN AND LOSS (PT. 11)

A mia ran on the twisted, uneven part of the path. Her muscles, joints, and tendons struggled to stay in unison. The strain on them was too much, and she stumbled, falling to the ground, crying. She looked back, half expecting, half wanting to see Daizon chasing after her. He was not. Memories assaulted her and mixed with recent ones, trying to find their place. "Nonna." Nonna was gone now, just like her parents. Amia was alone.

She slid her fingers over her silver earrings. Through the pain she was in, it was as if Nonna was with her, comforting her. *Non sarai mai sola.* You will never be alone. That's what Nonna told her when she gave her the earrings. That was before Amia went off to college. Amia did not want to leave her Nonna behind. She was everything.

Amia slipped into a memory. Eighteen, long black hair, and in her bedroom, she opened the box and withdrew the earrings. Nonna set the silver earrings on Amia's palm, cupped her hands over Amia's, and smiled rays of sunshine as she spoke. *"In un mondo pieno di oscurita, sei il posto luminoso e ti amero per sempre. Non sarai mai sola."* In a world filled with darkness, you are the bright place and I will always love you. You will never be alone.

It was the encouragement she needed before heading off to pursue her dream of becoming a therapist and helping children who did not have a Nonna to help them get through the tough times. She wanted to play with those kids and show them it was okay to laugh, play Scrabble, or cat's cradle, or simply be there for them. Then, as college went on, she remembered not being sure that was exactly what she wanted to do, but that was the path she'd chosen.

Another memory flashed into Amia's mind. Freshman year of college, when Nonna passed on, it made breathing hard. It was hard to put one foot in front of the other. Studying was a nightmare. Instead of living in the dorms and dealing with partying she really did not want to take part in, Amia purchased a home in Raleigh. Nonna told her before she died it would be an excellent investment, even if she moved after college. Amia huddled in her room, curled into a ball on her bed.

Whenever those lowest of moments would come, Amia would reach for her Nonna through her silver earrings. She would sense a warmth and know her Nonna was with her. Slowly, Amia opened herself to the idea of college again. Even though she focused more on college and her studies, she made a few friends. Slowly, she regained her ability to walk without thinking. Slowly, with the warmth from her silver earrings and time, she dreamed again.

She wanted to help those same kids, but that dream blended with helping people in a general sense. She had time to change her focus if she wanted. There was a new want seeding her mind. She wanted a family of her own, someone special, to share the wonders and hardships of life.

Her experience told her most of the men she met at college did not seem interested in anything long-term. Amia was not willing to pretend she was short-term. She decided she would finish college and focus on her career.

Late freshman year, Beth became her roommate. Over the next several years, Beth had insisted that was the time to explore and tried frequently to set Amia up with her boyfriend's friends. They were all different, but they seemed to have one characteristic in common: none of them wanted to know her; they wanted to have sex with her.

Eventually Amia met Baxter. He was intelligent, handsome, had plans for the future, was confident, and treated people with kindness—most of the time. She would have to learn the hard way that it was all a convoluted front. He was not her first lover, but he was the first one able to break down her walls.

Part of being in a relationship was being open to differences. She told herself Baxter was a good person. Then there was the dinner date with friends. He pleaded with her to put off her work for the night. "You'll have plenty of time over the weekend, babe. All you ever do is work. If you're not working at schoolwork, you're working at tai chi. If you're not working at tai chi, you're working with the kids at the youth center. It's not healthy staying in all the time or working all the time. You need to get out."

As much as she wanted to see the world, she feared it in equal measure. "I won't be able to relax." She was not keen on some things he wanted to do, but she kept quiet and let things pass. There was nothing wrong with prioritizing her career over partying.

When she finished her work early that night, Amia surprised him. It turned out to be a dinner party all right. Amia walked in on Baxter having dinner between the hostess's legs.

After Baxter, for the next couple of years, Amia focused on college, tai chi, and volunteer work with the kids. It was not until Beth brought up the idea of a reputable dating site focused on long-term relationships that Amia finally agreed. She created the profile on Psyche and Eros because they verified every account and their process appealed to her.

Then she thought people could probably circumvent the profile system. But after answering all the questions and verifying all her identity information, she decided there were easier ways to get laid if that was somebody's singular motivation. Scam artists would probably be less likely to go through all the verification processes, but she figured she could weed those profiles out.

When the highest-rated match came back as Daizon May, she knew it couldn't be him. She told Beth as much after they had a few laughs. "Online dating is not for me," she told Beth.

Curiosity itched, and without Beth knowing, Amia fact-checked Daizon's profile. He lived in Maine, served in the military, and worked construction before becoming an actor. He liked the woods, sports, fishing, hunting, and could be a bit of an introvert. He was averse to social websites and let his manager handle most of those kinds of interactions. He also enjoyed low-tech activities like being outdoors, playing golf, bowling, pool, darts, movies, the arts, and learning. His manager was a woman named Tonya. His phone number was private, so he used his manager's number for the account. Amia verified it was her number.

It made sense he would have a private number. Even though she knew the manager's number was authentic, she was not about to call his manager to set up a date with him. Amia wanted to find out more, but she did not have time for dreams leading nowhere.

Then he messaged her through their match on the site. "I enjoyed reading your profile and can't imagine how somebody like you is available and using a dating site. "

He basically stated her own feelings.

He continued in his letter:

> I wanted to let you know I am interested in getting to know you but want to verify you are actually who you say you are. I'm not looking for some internet hookup site to waste my time and effort on. I'm looking for an actual relationship. You know, a genuine person I can get to know and see where things go from there. I'm not looking for a fling. I look forward to hearing from you.

—Daizon

Amia's heart fluttered.

All the brief interactions through the site and on the phone seemed okay. She began wondering if his manager wrote the answers in his profile. He was amiable and made her laugh, even if he could never talk long. Being extra cautious, Amia refused his offer of a plane ticket, and she rented a car for the trip. Things might not work out, and she did not want to be stuck with a man she barely knew in an unfamiliar place. She would meet him at a tavern called Shady Jay's. It was north of Bar Harbor and Acadia National Park, just outside East Coast Harbor, Maine. If nothing else, she could visit the park. Pictures of the park she found online gave her ideas of places she wanted to visit.

Amia liked the idea of traveling to Maine. Well, if she was honest with herself, she was terrified of traveling to Maine or anywhere else, but she would not let her fear rule her any longer. The adventurer buried somewhere inside her really wanted to go.

Not wanting Beth to find out what she was up to, she told her she was just going for a visit. She told Beth she was going to stay at Matilda's but said nothing about meeting Daizon across the parking lot at Shady Jay's Tavern.

Before she left for Maine, Amia looked at herself in her full-size bedroom mirror. She could not remember the last time she truly looked at herself. Crystal-blue eyes stared back at her. They were her favorite attribute. "*Stelle per illuminare il cielo*. Stars to light the sky," Nonna would say.

Before her in the mirror was a young woman wearing no makeup, a gray sweatshirt hung like a miniskirt, and black capris leggings clung comfortably to her form. They were just the right snugness. And then farther down, gray cat slippers from L.L.Bean, the left slipper had the front half, and the right had the tail half. Amia smiled hesitantly at herself in the mirror before tossing off the slippers and clothes.

Her closet offered much of the same, but she also had professional attire, suits, and dresses. She slid through the rack and found her favorite, which she never dared wear. It was her figure-hugging *I'm in control, but possibly dangerous to the right man who dared tempt fate* kind of dress. Did she dare tempt fate for the right man? Was Daizon the right man?

Standing again in front of the mirror, this was an intelligent woman who carried herself professionally and with a sense of self-respect. Amia would step out of her comfort zone and be bold. She was a woman with curves and toned muscles. She was a woman who didn't use makeup often, but when she did it was to accentuate. It was the amount of makeup that said she preferred to enhance, not hide. After finishing the last few strokes of black mascara to her long lashes, her blue stars dazzled. She pulled her long black hair over her left shoulder, then her right. Then she flipped it in back of her. This was a woman who looked her future in the face and knew she was worth admiration and love from her future partner.

⚜

Amia remembered being inside Shady Jay's, sitting at the corner of the bar waiting for Daizon. The bar seemed the most hectic area of the whole place. People kept bumping into her and then apologizing or asking if they could buy her a drink. She smiled and repeated, "No thanks," many times. A large group danced to a country rock band, others surrounded the dance floor, and still others hung out in the game room or around the bar.

After being bumped into again and spilling a small amount of her drink, a guy in camouflage hunting garb apologized and placed a twenty on the bar after he steadied her. Luckily, none got on her dress. She nursed the drink and ordered another. A wave of nausea churned her stomach and flooded her head. She was probably sick from too much driving. Amia stared at her three-quarter-full glass on the bar. Was it her second? Maybe she'd had more? To top it off,

Daizon had not shown or called. Her head spun. She needed fresh air before she got sick. Where was he?

Amia made it to the parking lot. The ground shifted under her feet, and the hotel seemed miles away as the parking lot stretched out. Everything went black as somebody grabbed her. Loons hollered?

Amia blinked away from her memories to focus on her current surroundings. Her head swung quickly from rustling noises on the forest floor to birds whistling in the branches. An ocean breeze blew over her and through the woods. She lay on the trail she had been running on. Her heart was moments from bursting out of her chest. She breathed slow, controlled breaths. Amia thought back to that night at the bar. "Daizon?"

"Breathe, Amia, focus." She regained her feet and brushed herself off. The awful hurt in his eyes at the way she reacted to him. She watched him struggle with pain. He treated her with kindness and encouragement. He treated her with respect and a deep sense of humility. He treated her with love. Could he be the same man that drugged and left her for dead? "I have to remember. The Old Port was where I had lunch. I checked into Matilda's across from Shady Jay's. I know I went. He was? He wasn't there. Was he? No. God, the loons."

Flashing before her eyes, she imagined the Angel of Death pouring liquid fire on her naked form as she traveled through the clouds.

Back on the trail, her body tightened. Heart racing again, she darted glances toward a red squirrel who rattled his call of danger. A moment before, all she wanted was to remember who she was. She wanted to share that person with Daizon. Now all she wanted was to forget. How could she?

Amia reached for her silver earrings. She would never want to forget. Resolve washed over her. Posture strengthening, she ground herself to what was real. She breathed. The earth slowly solidified. She remembered the voice of the man she spoke with on the phone and played it in her mind. She played the voice she'd gotten to know over the last month. They had different speech patterns and tones. Daizon had a more defined Maine accent. Even if it was not heavily pronounced, it was there. The other man, his speech, seemed polished. Daizon had a rawness that drew you in. The person she'd spoken with over the phone made her laugh, but he'd lacked Daizon's rawness. The person on the phone was too polished. When they spoke by video chat, Daizon's face and lips never matched up. He excused it as a bad internet connection. A realization formed in Amia's mind. "Their voices didn't match. Daizon didn't show because it wasn't him."

A smile crept onto her face. It grew and spread throughout her body. "It wasn't him."

Amia glanced back from where she came. She moved by instinct. Her feet and legs picked up speed. Her lungs held a steadier rhythm. She followed the trail back to where she'd left Daizon. He was gone. She ran farther, but the trail was empty. How much time did she lose while her memories were coming flooding back? The sun—where was the sun? There was no way it could have traveled that far. A few members of the security staff jogged toward her.

Inside Dr. Wolf's office, she raised her eyes from a naughty escape to find a disheveled Amia about to knock. "Come in," she said. Dr. Wolf set her marker inside the pages and set the book down with the erotic cover faceup.

Again without thinking, Amia smiled at Dr. Wolf's choice of escape. Light returned to Amia's eyes, and she closed the door behind her. "My name is Amia Viardo. I'm a doctoral student at Raleigh, Massachusetts School of Psychology. I was supposed to start my practicum with Dr. Rorke weeks ago. Recent events before I arrived are still a little blurred, but they're there. My parents died in a car accident when I was a toddler. I survived the accident but don't remember them. My Nonna raised me."

Amia swallowed back the emotions threatening her voice. "She passed away early in my freshman year of college. She was my everything." Amia stole a breath, hoping to maintain control. "I came to Maine to meet Daizon May and . . . and . . . I ended up here. I—" Amia's stomach threatened to heave. "I remember Shady Jay's and loons screaming into the night. A black shadow poured liquid fire over my soul. He does it in my dreams. But I don't remember what happened to me."

Shaking her head, Amia said, "For the last month, I've been falling for the man I was supposed to meet. But I didn't see him at Shady Jay's. He wasn't there. He didn't do this to me. Whoever I spoke with—the person who did this to me—had a different voice. Daizon has a very slight Maine accent. The person I spoke with on the phone seemed polished and dry. I'm pretty sure it wasn't him. Who could have? I feel sick."

"Oh, Amia. It's going to be okay." Dr. Wolf stood and held out her arms. Amia rushed into Dr. Wolf's embrace. Dr. Wolf stroked

Amia's back and arm with slow circles. She said, "You're safe. It's okay to hurt. It's okay to be confused."

Dr. Wolf guided Amia to the couch. She poured a cup of water from the pitcher of ice water beside the couch on the end table. She sat with Amia on the couch and held her.

CHAPTER THIRTY-FIVE

AMIA VIARDO

Amia spent several minutes on the couch in Dr. Wolf's office with Dr. Wolf holding her. The rush of emotions, thoughts, and memories eventually settled. It was like waking from a dream within a dream only to realize some of what she dreamed was reality.

Dr. Wolf assumed a position on the other side of the couch. Amia said, "I don't know what I'm supposed to do. I have to call Dr. Rorke. I have to tell Daizon I'm sorry for the way I reacted. I know it wasn't him who did this to me. He trusted me and helped me. He saved my life." Amia tried shaking the confusion from her mind. She spoke faster than she could make sense of her thoughts.

Ever calm, Dr. Wolf emoted an acknowledgment of Amia's confusion. "I've already spoken with Dr. Rorke. You should know that our first concern is your health. Let's focus on this moment before we do anything else. Is that okay?"

"I understand. I've been reminding myself that those are memories and emotions and I have control of how I react."

"How would you react if our roles were reversed, and I came to you and said that?"

"I—" Amia attempted to slow down the tumbling thoughts inside her mind. *If our roles were reversed, what would I say?* Amia imagined herself as Dr. Wolf might see her. She closed her eyes and thought for several seconds. "I wouldn't expect you to have total control over your emotions. You would be experiencing a lot of confusion. I would want to provide you with a sense of comfort and security."

Amia knew she had been through a traumatic experience even if she couldn't remember the actual trauma. She knew her imagination was trying to make sense of what happened to her and fill in blanks. The pain wouldn't just go away. "If you said you had to control your emotions, I might think you were attempting to avoid them. Emotions sometimes get the best of us, and that's okay."

Dr. Wolf nodded with a thoughtful, consoling smile.

"I'm trying to speed through the healing process when I've only just begun." Amia wanted her normal back, but knew she would need to develop a new normal. Her thoughts drifted.

A diffuse afternoon sunlight filled the room with warmth. Amia smiled at the erotic book Dr. Wolf had set down when she first entered the room. The cover showed a glossed-over faded head shot of a woman at the moment of climax. It was titled *Release*. Amia inhaled a deep breath, and her body relaxed as she slowly exhaled.

Dr. Wolf glanced at her book and smiled. "How do you feel?"

Amia flexed her body. "Not as good as her. I feel like I need a good stretch after exhausting every muscle. I'm scared but hopeful. My recent memories seem almost déjà vu as they blend with my old ones. It's like I'm waking from a lucid dream and wondering how much of it was real." Amia smiled. "The fog is gone. I don't feel like an impostor controlling somebody else's body." Amia ran her hands over her skin. "I'm me."

"It's nice to meet you, Amia."

Amia crossed the couch and hugged Dr. Wolf. "Thank you."

Dr. Wolf replied, "You're welcome." Amia returned to her original spot on the couch. Dr. Wolf added, "Don't forget to thank yourself as well." Dr. Wolf placed a hand over her own heart, held it there for a moment, and then hugged herself.

Following the example, Amia placed a hand over her own heart. She said to herself, *Thank you for being strong, and kind, and caring. Thank you for understanding.* Amia crossed her arms and hugged herself. The action seemed warm and strange but comforting. It was like the warmth she received from her silver earrings. Amia glanced out the window at the sky. *Thank you, Nonna.*

Clarity grew inside Amia. She didn't have control of everything going on. She had choices in the way she led her life. Her happiness was not dependent on somebody else. "I have to know more about what happened to me. I don't think the person I talked to on the phone or through Psyche and Eros was Daizon, but I have to know. I also feel like I've been given an opportunity to work on myself here. I'm so grateful to you. I've worked hard at school for a long time to get to where I am, and I don't want to fall behind. How do we move forward?"

Dr. Wolf nodded. "One step, then another, and another." She paused. "How would you feel about completing your practicum here? I know with Dr. Rorke, you would have worked with children and young adults."

Amia enjoyed her volunteer work with the kids. Working with the kids felt safe. They were what she knew. Being at the Whole Me program over the last four weeks and working with Dr. Wolf felt right. The Whole Me program helped people grow. The program helped her grow. It challenged her to see herself with a fresh perspective, an empowering perspective. "I love working with kids. I think working with them helped fill a gap I felt from the loss of my Nonna and parents. What you do here, you help people on a whole different level. I would love the opportunity to learn more from you. How would a practicum here work?"

"Our intention is to help people who are suffering to feel a sense of being heard and understood. Imparting a notion of empowerment and connection, we help them find their own way, and every way is unique. We help them develop tools and exercises to use once the program ends. As we know, life doesn't always go the way we want."

Amia laughed and nodded.

"Your practicum has already begun. You've been helping the others through your tai chi instructions and in the way you've modeled yourself during a trying situation. You conducted yourself with courage and strength but also allowed yourself to be vulnerable and available. They want what you want. They want to be whole."

Dr. Wolf went through some internal thoughts. "Part of your practicum moving forward will include additional conversations between us after the meditations and exercises. I don't expect you to begin immediately. I'm sure you need some more time for your mind to settle. When you are ready, we'll introduce you and your new position as part of the Whole Me team."

Dr. Wolf glanced at her watch. "Detective Johnson and Beth should be here in about an hour."

Amia tensed at the mention of Detective Johnson. Seeing Beth would be good. How would she explain why she didn't tell Beth about her supposed date with Daizon? How would she explain the secrets?

Dr. Wolf topped off their ice waters. She said, "Your memory came back while you were on your walk with Daizon. Would you like to share that experience with me?"

Sipping her water, Amia explained.

Dr. Wolf listened. "You're doing great. I can imagine this must be extremely difficult for you. Having to relive losing your Nonna all over again and then reliving the trauma. It's a lot to have come back all at once. I can imagine your confused emotions regarding Daizon. I'm curious. What led you to feel you had to hide your budding relationship from Beth? You mentioned before that she is the best kind of tenacious."

Amia smiled and thought. Where did she start? She knew the question was not as straightforward as it seemed. The question was more about helping guide Amia to her own revelations. This was about Amia's search for love and her mindset. Amia nodded and told Dr. Wolf about her past failed relationships. She told her about Baxter. Amia said, "Beth and I didn't agree with each other all the time. I actually think we annoy each other sometimes. She would pester me for days and weeks in the early years of college to go out on dates, but after Baxter, she didn't push as much."

Dr. Wolf sipped some of her water.

Amia knew she hadn't answered the question. "I think the point about Baxter and the other boyfriends or acquaintances was that I gave up on believing love would ever happen for me. Even on the trip to meet who I thought was Daizon, I didn't really think anything would materialize out of the meeting."

Dr. Wolf nodded her acknowledgment. "Thank you for sharing. I'm looking forward to meeting Beth. Why don't we use the spare time we have to freshen up? We have another three and a half weeks of the program, so there will be plenty of opportunity for us to grow and learn more about each other."

Amia wondered how the conversation with Beth and the detective would go. She wondered about Daizon.

Chapter Thirty-Six

ACCUSATIONS

Daizon approached the sleek white double doors. They had long black accents and etched windows. Two thin accent windows framed either side of the doors. A matching sleek window with the same etching capped the entryway. Defined architectural lines of the massive modern home led out to points on the ocean horizon, an architectural drawing brought to life. The home sat back from a wide-open ocean bluff. It had long white walls with solar windows running the length. Black solar shingles capped the roof.

He glanced over to an extended wing of the house, which was the entertainment and exercise section of the home. He knew the inside housed a heated, in-ground saltwater swimming pool for laps. There was an eight-person jetted hot tub, a bar, and a pool table. A few fitness machines lined one small section, and workout accessories hung on the wall. The back of the room had a matted area for activities like yoga or meditation. A wall of folding glass doors opened the entire space up to a patio, which ran the length of the back of the house.

Daizon remembered hanging and taping the drywall inside the home. This was a home people dreamed of living in if they only had the money. Tonya answered the door wearing one of her usual flowing outfits. She flinched a few surprised glances at Daizon and over her shoulder. Then, as if pretending everything was normal, she greeted Daizon with a hug. She glanced to the sides, behind him, and finally asked, "What are you doing here? What happened? Are you okay?" She glanced again at his vehicle in the driveway and then around the property.

"I'm fine," Daizon said. "Where's the laptop? I know I should have called, but my phone was dead when I left the Whole Me program. Did I catch you at a bad time?" He was not fine, and they both knew it. He wanted answers. Driving along, he decided he had to find out exactly what Tonya knew. She was nervous as hell and hadn't invited him in.

She asked, "What laptop?"

"The one you used to sign me up for that damn account on Psyche and Eros."

With a tilt of her head and sad eyes, she said, "I'm sorry."

Daizon shook his head and shrugged. "You don't need to be sorry, Tonya. You tried to help me in your own way. I understand. I need to access the account, and I can't remember any of the account information. I know you saved it." Tonya held the door from opening wide, but movement behind her gained Daizon's attention. Daizon glanced over her shoulder. "What's going on?"

"Nothing is going on," she pleaded.

Kyle smiled at Tonya as he nudged past her to greet Daizon. They gripped hands. Tonya's actions made more sense. As Kyle greeted Daizon, Tonya gave Kyle a frustrated, *you arrogant idiot* look.

Kyle said, "Hey, bud. I've got some good news. We'll be working together on the next project."

Dumbfounded, Daizon shook his head. Tonya flashed a smile when Kyle glanced back at her. The smile faltered when Kyle turned back to Daizon.

"*Prime Suspect*." He slapped Daizon on the shoulder. "Is that fucking insane or what? You know they're going to forget all about you when they see me on the screen." Kyle puffed himself out.

"I'm sure they will." Daizon studied Tonya. "Where's Dave?"

"He's attending clients in California. You know how it is. Come in."

Tonya led Daizon through the grand, open space. The layout naturally drew eyes to the massive wall of windowed doors at the back of the home. Outside, a stone patio bled into a green long-grassed bluff with an assortment of wildflowers. Beyond the bluff, a long, thin beach extended to the left, while rocks lined the right. The blue ocean churned with small waves. Everything about this home provoked a powerful, breezy feeling.

Early tempest winds stirred inside Daizon as he felt out the situation between Tonya and Kyle. Deciphering Kyle's current disposition and intentions meant stepping into the churning cement truck inside the man's head.

Using her high hostess voice, Tonya said, "Can I get you a drink?" They arrived at the kitchen island, a long and thick white marble slab with black veins.

Kyle already had a Jack on the rocks, about a quarter full. Tonya fed more Jack into Kyle's glass. She motioned the bottle at Daizon.

"No thanks. Maybe some ice water."

Tonya dipped his glass and another glass into an ice bucket. She filled his with water and made herself a sombrero. Awkward smiles and glances danced between the three of them. Daizon's growing instinct told him they were having an affair, but he was sure she wouldn't do that to Dave. Kyle wore his usual brash smirk as he tipped back his glass and stared at Daizon. The knock of Tonya setting Daizon's water in front of him barely broke the two men's stares.

Tonya drank and smiled awkwardly again.

Daizon said, "Whatever you need to tell me, Tonya, just say it."

She fumbled with her fingers. "Somebody deleted your account."

"What?"

"The detective came by earlier today and took my laptop. Before she did, while she was here, I went to sign into your account, but it wasn't there. It's like you were never on it."

Kyle chuckled. "There's a small favor. Now they don't have anything on you."

"Screw you."

Kyle shrugged. "I'm just stating the obvious. Do you think they care about guilt or innocence? You've been around and know better. Don't worry. I've got your back."

"Did you delete the account?"

Kyle's smirk slid into a grin. "I didn't touch your fucking account, lover boy."

Clenching his fist and tightening his expression, Daizon eyed the big man—his friend. Kyle nonchalantly flexed his forearm, biceps, pecs, and then rolled his puffed-up neck and shoulders.

Tonya shook her head. "You are both in my home, and I expect civility."

"He's just fucking jealous of my masculinity. He's like one of those little puppy dogs attracting all the women but never having a clue of what to do with 'em."

"You think sleeping with my girlfriend was knowing what to do with 'em?" Daizon wanted to say more, but he narrowed his eyes at Tonya. "You know what kind of man he is." Kyle wore a smug smile in response. Daizon set his glass down, turned, and left the home.

Tonya chased after him. "Daizon. Daizon. You don't know everything. Daizon."

Daizon kept walking.

CHAPTER THIRTY-SEVEN

TANGLED

Detective Johnson, Beth, Dr. Wolf, and Amia squared off in Dr. Wolf's office. Beth held Amia's hand snugly beside her on the couch. Dr. Wolf sat in a chair in front of her desk, and Detective Johnson kind of hovered around her own chair. Her pacing amped up the anxiety in the room. Amia was grateful for the time Dr. Wolf gave her to collect herself before the meeting. They had discussed her conversations with Daizon before their scheduled date at Shady Jay's and contrasted them with her conversations with him while inside the Whole Me program. Beth squeezed Amia's trembling hand and smiled.

Far from appeased, Detective Johnson explained, "Both accounts on the Psyche and Eros dating site are no longer in the system. Somebody canceled the accounts. Representatives from Psyche and Eros explained it was common practice after people made successful matches. The representatives also informed me they have a policy of not keeping clients' personal information or communications on file. Apparently, this is one of the major attractions for professionals using their services." After a pause, Detective Johnson said, "The curious detail that stuck out for me—somebody wiped them clean while you were in the hospital, before the Whole Me program started. We have a team working on retrieving those accounts."

Amia said, "I had my laptop with me. I think it was in the rental car, but maybe I brought it into the hotel. I definitely brought clothes into the hotel across from Shady Jay's. You said before you didn't find my laptop. He must have hacked into my account. He might still have it. And what about other belongings?"

The detective shook her head. "They returned the rental car the same night of the incident. The hotel had your hotel key returned in the overnight box, and your room was clean. The tavern and hotel had their differences in opinion on who was responsible for the monthly fee associated with the security cameras owned by a third party. Basically, they agreed nothing big ever happened there, and they figured the appearance of security cameras would deter people enough. Forensics did not find your laptop or purse when they found the pieces of your phone and some of your clothes."

Detective Johnson held the top of her chair in a death grip. "I spoke with Mrs. Avendale after speaking with Mr. May. She verified his story about creating the account on Psyche and Eros and not using it. When I asked her if she could open the account for me to see, she tried signing in, only to find out the account no longer existed. Now, I already knew somebody had deleted it, but I wanted to see her reaction. She seemed genuinely surprised. The person who did this is as intelligent as they are wicked."

"Daizon is not wicked," Amia challenged. Beth squeezed Amia's hand in support and mirrored Amia's harsh stare at Detective Johnson. Amia continued in the same angry tone. "Do you know what the first thing he said to me was, after you planted those ideas in my head and told him he should leave? He said you were doing your job. No excuses. He stood up for you when I was angry. Does that sound like a wicked man? If it does, I think we need more of them."

Detective Johnson held out her placating hands. "No, he doesn't sound like a wicked man. All your experiences you've told me about don't paint the picture of a wicked man. But I've been alone with him. I've seen his movies. Did you know he has a Special Forces background? Trust me, he is both intelligent and capable of wicked things. I don't know if it's him, but given all the information, he's at the heart of everything."

Amia argued. "It could be somebody close to him." The detective nodded placatingly. Dr. Wolf and Beth remained quiet and still. Amia thought about her recent conversations with Daizon. She cracked the silence. "Daizon told me he had a friend." Amia paused, thinking twice if she should share. Would this betray his confidence? Amia also wanted control of her life and to find the individual responsible. She said, "Daizon told me about a friend who he caught with his last girlfriend. He said it was a friend he knew from his time in the military."

The detective perked up. "Do you remember his name?"

Amia tossed her head and searched her rebooted mind. "I think he said his name was Kyle." Detective Johnson flashed her best cat smile in response. Amia wondered what the detective already knew about Kyle. She wondered why this felt like a hollow victory.

Chapter Thirty-Eight

UNTANGLING

Detective Johnson had asked her questions and left Dr. Wolf's office with a few new leads. Dr. Wolf said to Amia, "Why don't you give Beth a tour of the grounds? I'm sure it will give the two of you a chance to talk."

Outside, Amia guided Beth over the lush landscape to Tarah and others from the group. Amia gave brief introductions, and they continued to the cliffside benches. Others milled about, chatting, walking, staring out at the ocean, or they did other various activities.

Beth soaked in the area and the goings-on. She glanced back at the facility before leaning against Amia. "How are you really?"

Amia smiled. This was the Beth she knew and loved, the one she remembered. "I met the man of my dreams. I hope he's not the man of my nightmares as well. Besides that, I'm gaining my strength back. I don't feel like a stranger in my own body." Fluffing her hair with an exaggerated pat, Amia rolled her eyes up and smiled. "I always wanted to try a pixie cut."

"Cute. It really is. Not quite long enough to call it a pixie cut yet, but it's getting there. Can I see?" Beth held out a tentative hand toward the back of Amia's head.

Amia nodded her agreement.

Beth's gentle fingertips explored over the raised parts on the back of Amia's head. "How does it look?"

After a brief inspection and some thought, Beth said, "It looks like you shaved your head, removed a bad tattoo, and now your hair is growing back in."

"So, people will think I made some questionable life choices?"

Beth swayed back and forth, scrunching her face. "It's more like a story magnet pulling you in for some deeper conversation."

Amia widened her eyes and tilted her head. "Or, it could be a lighthearted conversation to mask what we really want to know?" Amia provided the opening she knew her friend was looking for.

Beth took it. "Why didn't you tell me you were talking with him? Or, at least, that you were going on a date with him? I mean, that's dating safety one-oh-one."

"You know why. I didn't want you making a big deal out of something that was probably going to be nothing. They all lie and cheat. Why should I get my hopes up only to be let down again? Besides, come to find out, my first instinct was correct. It wasn't even him I was talking with."

Beth cycled through anger, sadness, and pity; her facial contortions were obvious. "You're making my point. Besides, not every man is a Baxter. Your actions showed you want to hope love exists, Amia. Why are you fighting it? Everybody makes mistakes. You were with Daizon here for like, what, a month? Almost five weeks? What does your gut tell you?"

"My gut tells me he's a good person. He's kindhearted, intelligent, and he wanted to help me be comfortable with who I am. None of that means he was falling in love with me." Was she lying to herself? She wanted to believe the things she said. Well, most of it. Maybe some of it. She wanted him to be falling in love with her. Her eyes wandered out to the ocean. "I'm a logical person. Besides, after our last experience in the woods—it didn't end well. I'm so confused."

Beth shook her head. "You know what I think?"

Amia raised her brows and sighed. She didn't want relationship advice right now.

"Figure out what you really want. You're going to finish your practicum here at this place, and look at it." Beth smiled and swept her arms wide, as if introducing the grandness of the place. "You already made one decision I never thought you would make. You look good. I mean, you look like a buzz-cut pixie with mended wings who's stronger but afraid to fly. Seriously, you look fit. I need your workout program."

Amia smiled. Beth probably was not too far off in her assessment. This facility, the Whole Me program, oozed a sense of welcomed calm, but it also challenged a person to open to the pain and suffering of life, to breathe it in, observe it for what it was, and breathe it out. This was her moment, her opportunity for growth. However difficult the circumstances leading to her opportunity, she had a choice of whether to seize the moment. Beth was right, she had taken steps toward what she wanted. Dr. Wolf pointed it out, and it was in the program's name, The Whole Me.

Amia wanted what everyone there wanted in some form, to feel comfortable with who she was. She could keep running. But where would that get her? "I think I am getting stronger." Amia gripped Beth's hand. "Thank you for coming."

Unsure of Amia's growing, determined smile, Beth went along with it, and maybe a tad further. "It's what friends do. Well, some friends. I am definitely better than others."

"Yes, you are." Staring at her friend for a moment, Amia saw mischief. "Don't track him down and grill him." The last thing Amia wanted right then was for her bullheaded friend to charge after Daizon.

"I don't know what you're talking about. Who?"

"Don't play dumb."

"How else would I get to know what his intentions are toward my best friend?"

"He doesn't have any intentions."

"How do you know? Did you ask? Did you call him and ask?"

"His phone number!" The number popped into Amia's head. "If it's actually him? I remember it. We can compare it to his actual phone number and see if they match. Come on."

Amia rushed Beth away.

⤙⚶

Back inside Dr. Wolf's office, Dr. Wolf compared the phone number Amia remembered with the one in Daizon's file. Amia and Beth fidgeted, anticipation getting the better of them. "It's not the same as the one I have on file."

Could she really dare to hope? Excited, Amia thrummed with nervous energy.

Beth smirked. "You're welcome."

Amia's smile grew and slid. "It's a California area code. Do you think it might be his friend Kyle?" If not his friend, then who was it? Who would do those things to her? Why? He knew too much about her. "What if it's somebody random, and they find out I have my memory back? They deleted our Psyche and Eros accounts, and they had access to all my personal information."

Dr. Wolf said, "Let's not get ahead of ourselves. Let's take care of what we have control over." Dr. Wolf retrieved her cell phone from her desk and dialed out. "Detective Johnson, I have a phone number for you. Amia remembered the number of the person she was communicating with before she came to Maine." She gave Detective Johnson the number after a moment and waited on the line, listening and nodding.

Amia's mind pulled in several directions. *Breathe, Amia. Slow down. I don't need to have everything under control. It's okay and normal to be anxious. I'm not a machine. Breathe. I don't have to be perfect. What is the most important thing for me to focus on while I'm here? Why did I choose to stay? I'm not staying here for Daizon. I want to see him and talk with him, and there might be something there, but that's not why I'm staying here. It's not the main reason. God, I need to see him.*

Beth whispered to Amia, "I've seen that look."

"I don't know what you're talking about."

"Really? I'd say you're trying to talk yourself into or out of something. Knowing you, I'd say out of something."

Amia smiled. Is that what she was doing, trying to talk herself out of attempting to pursue a potential relationship with Daizon? Isn't that what she always did? No, she was thinking, as any reasonable being would. She had to get herself together before she involved anybody else in her life. Besides, Amia was well aware she might have developed tunnel vision. They had developed a sense of closeness while sharing parts of their lives. Outside the facility, Amia knew things would be different. She could be inferring feelings not reciprocated.

At a place like the Whole Me, it was okay to be vulnerable and open in ways that might not be normal in the outside world. The outside world was different. "I use reason. That's who I am."

Beth's expression saddened. "Sweetheart, I know that's who you are and I think it's fantastic that you know that about yourself, but is it an excuse? I'm gonna tell you, and I hate to be the one, but love is messy and reason doesn't always take the lead."

Amia asked, "Would you say that if I fell for somebody else here? One of the other members of the program?"

"Maybe. You and I both know that's not the same thing. Think about it this way. Daizon was the one who actually answered all those questions on Psyche and Eros. He told you he answered them. They matched the two of you based on hundreds of questions you both answered. If nothing else, you could start from there. Don't let somebody ruin what could be a good thing. You fought for your identity and sense of self here. Are you willing to fight for more? Are you willing to fight for your happiness?"

Dumbstruck, Amia searched herself for answers. She was trying to figure things out in her own way. She was fighting for her happiness, wasn't she? Amia didn't need Daizon to make her happy.

During their conversation, Dr. Wolf finished her call. She stood patiently. Amia wondered how much she'd heard.

"Detective Johnson knows about the phone number. She said they linked it to a burner phone bought in California." She studied Amia and Beth. "Beth, thank you so much for coming. I wonder if you might come back tomorrow at the same time?"

Beth swept a glance at a disheveled Amia and nodded. "I will. Thank you." Beth squeezed Amia's hand. "I'm here for you. I'll be back."

After hugging Beth and saying goodbye, Amia stood before Dr. Wolf. A brief silence separated the moments. Dr. Wolf smiled. "It's good to have friends."

"It is. Beth means well. I mean, she cares a lot about me and wants me to be happy. She can be a little headlong and eager, but she has a good heart. She might not be tactful all the time. And her opinions might not always be wanted." Amia stopped herself, realizing she was going on a bit too long.

"It sounds like she has some admirable traits."

"Some of them, yes. I'm not a headlong person. That's not who I am. I like to think things through." Amia paused. "I like that she's not afraid of making poor decisions. To her, they are not poor decisions. They're growing pains."

"Do you think she doesn't feel the hurt from those pains like you or I do?"

Amia thought of her friend. She wanted to say no, but she knew Dr. Wolf wanted her to see through Beth's perspective. Beth had left her own practicum to come and see Amia. It was a selfless act in contrast with her outward tough persona. Amia knew Beth was softer than what she let on. Beth had her share of breakups with guys and the occasional gal. Amia saw the moments when Beth let her mask down, when she thought nobody was watching. She coped by hiding the hurt behind dark humor or getting involved in other people's lives. She felt better about herself by helping other people. "She feels the pain, maybe not as you or I do, but everyone deals with pain in their own way."

Amia slipped into her thoughts. *We all deal with suffering in our unique ways. Depression is a common aspect of life we all share at one point or another. It's a normal state of being for somebody who suffered for any length of time. Building walls to protect ourselves is another way we are similar. The walls may be different, but the sense of vulnerability is the same. We want to protect ourselves. We need to open ourselves to that pain and hurt with small doses, using mindfulness and compassion.* She said, "I need time to think."

"You're at the right place."

CHAPTER THIRTY-NINE

FRIENDS

A few dark clouds hung in the sky as dusk approached. Daizon wore his camouflage pants, black boots, and a black T-shirt. The lake below his boat had the look of warped blue glass as he slipped over it. The swaying grass had grown over a foot since he'd found Amia almost dead. If it had been that high before, he never would have found her. The grass parted and bent as he beached his boat. After he was out, he tugged it well onto shore, securing it.

Apparently he was one of the primary suspects, and he understood why. Whoever attacked Amia had cleaned after themselves and let him implicate himself by saving Amia. Was it Kyle?

Maybe Kyle was sick of feeling beholden to him? Daizon told Kyle multiple times he didn't owe him anything. Daizon wanted to forget what happened, and Kyle was a constant reminder. His military past was not like his childhood memories he had somehow buried. Seeing Amia that first time opened those military wounds. He relived the memories of saving Kyle's life and ending another.

Daizon forced a tight smile. This time he had saved a life.

Kyle was a womanizer, but was he capable of doing those things to Amia? *Would he set me up like that?* Did Kyle hate him enough to do those things? He remembered catching Kyle with Brittney.

There was no doubt in Daizon's mind Kyle had tried seducing the others as well. *But how does he go from seducing girlfriends, to pretending to be me, to attacking and leaving Amia for dead?*

Kyle was a prick, but he was a prick out in the open where everyone could see. He wore the badge with pride. Kyle said he slept with Brittney to challenge her loyalty. Daizon would want to know before they got married, if it ever got that far. They both knew Kyle was full of crap and it was a low act.

Head in some weird place, Daizon knew his mind had traveled down a familiar road. Self-blame was easier. His time in the Whole Me program had helped him resolve some of his issues. Maybe resolved overstated his progress. He started believing in and not hating himself. He did not want to lose those gains.

Inspecting the location, he found recent evidence of activity in the area. Bent grass was trying to stand back up again. Gravel areas maintained slight indentations. Daizon went to the rock where Amia hit her head. It wore stains from where blood dripped down. A few of the smaller rocks had bloodstains as well. He imagined the terror she must have felt at that moment. She probably thought she was going to die, and this was how it was going to happen. Daizon imagined the struggle. He remembered her pale blue look of death when he found her. He remembered the bruises and wheelchair a few weeks later when he saw her again. Besides not remembering anything about who she was, she'd also endured temporary paralysis. It must have been hell, waking and feeling like an alien in her own body.

When did her attacker notice the blood at the back of her head? Was that why he beat her? Daizon remembered the smell of bleach when he found her. The rain must have helped wash it away, but when the guy finished, he must have dumped it over her. He took everything she owned and left her for dead. Why didn't he take her silver earrings? An oversight? It was a cloudy night and about to rain. Did he not mean to kill her? Was that a mistake? Maybe the guy hadn't planned on killing her? Maybe once he saw what happened to her head after she'd hit the rock, he panicked, thinking she would die? Daizon glanced around. A month later, and he never would have found her. The guy who attacked her, he did those things and left her there like some leftover food for the insects and animals. Daizon's blood heated. *Breathe.*

Anger was easy. It was too easy. He honed it while in the military, used it like some inexhaustible well to draw from, and became a killer. It would be easy to say the things he did were not his fault. It would be easy to say those actions were not him. That monster was a part of him, and Daizon would live with the things he'd done.

Thinking back to his childhood, the things done to him, he would live with those, too. Daizon placed a hand to his heart. "May I treat myself with the kindness and compassion I would show others. May I and others feel peace. Along with the pain, may we also feel the goodness. We will not be perfect, and that's okay. We are imperfect beings. I can be my best at this moment."

Daizon looked up to the vastness of the sky with a few dark patches of clouds threatening to disturb an otherwise blue sky. He thought of the sky and imagined it stretching out to Amia at the Whole Me facility. "May you find your way to peace and happiness."

Leaving the investigation alone was not an option for Daizon. The way Amia pulled away from him like he was something vile. The memory running through his mind felt like a knife that repeatedly plunged into his heart, pulled out, and plunged in again.

Energy and focus flooded his body. Daizon scanned the area. *Where did the guy bring Amia in from?* What direction made sense? His house was up on the side of the mountain, out of sight. From there, it was easier for him to use his boat at the bottom.

Where would somebody else come from? Daizon thought of the boat launch on the other side of the pond, then he heard a car travel past his house down the mountain road. Daizon followed the road with a mental map and imagined the nearest point from where he was to the road. Sure enough, he heard the car go down the hill and around the corner he imagined in his mind. He locked in the direction and walked.

Several steps in, Daizon found a game trail that went in the same general direction. Following it for a while, Daizon realized he was familiar with that particular game trail. He had a hunting blind farther out, where it came to a small clearing. Kyle knew the trail too. Before he reached the clearing and his blind, he noticed a few broken branch tips. Too much time had passed for any kind of track, but fluttering on one of the broken branch tips was a piece of frayed fabric. Shiny purple, maybe an inch and a half of soft stretchy material with torn threads. Cashmere? It had to be torn from Amia's clothing. Confidence in his insights growing, Daizon pushed on.

Past his hunting blind, the game trail led all the way to a turnaround spot for plow trucks in the winter. A few people parked their vehicles there once in a while to go hunting on his property without permission. He had posted signs plainly visible. Some people parked there to walk a nearby trout stream that led to the pond. Daizon scanned the area for more clues, wondering if Detective Johnson and her department had found the turnaround spot.

Moving way too fast for the road, a yellow Toyota Prius with Massachusetts plates zipped past Daizon and around the corner to go up the hill before it screeched to a halt. It was a short-haired peacock of a woman. She cranked her head around, zipped the car in reverse to him, and unrolled the passenger's side window. Daizon approached cautiously from a diagonal. Her hand slipped inside her purse. She smiled like a cat acting innocent after stealing some treats. In the back seat, he noticed a large black duffel bag, probably filled with clothes. Standing slightly back from the window, he asked, "Can I help you?"

Her eyes widened. "It is you. I was just heading up to talk with you."

"I'm sorry. Who are you?"

"My name is Beth. I'm Amia's friend from Massachusetts. She told me not to come, but I've never been good at cowing to societal pressures. It's nice to meet you, Daizon. I loved you in *Into the Dragon's Den*."

Daizon glanced at Beth's hand, still in her purse. She smiled and raised her brows like she was harmless. "Is that a gun or a Taser?"

Her smile widened. "Amia said you were perceptive. She also doesn't think it was you." Beth tried scooting forward in her seat to get a better look at Daizon. "I can wait up at your place if you're busy?" She glanced behind her and at the corner in front of her. "I should probably move. This doesn't look like the best place to talk. I'll see you there." She smiled, rolled her window up, and bolted up the road. Daizon smirked and shook his head.

Beth had parked in his driveway between his basketball hoop and the six-car garage. Three garage doors remained closed the way he'd left them. Instead of waiting in her car, Beth had made herself at home on the rear deck. Her posture puffed as she sat at his deck table with a Taser in front of her on the table. She made a playful show of casually bouncing it between her fingers. She wore a grin as he strode past the ramp entry to the wraparound deck and entered from the back stairs.

"I'm glad to see you made yourself comfortable. Can I get you something to drink? Tea, coffee, beer?" Daizon walked past her and into his home, leaving the door open.

"A beer sounds good."

Daizon returned with two beers. He set one bottle in front of her and brought the other with him to the opposite side of the table. After setting down his bottle and before sitting, he slowly held out his hands, reached into his shoulder holster, and withdrew his Beretta. He placed it on the table in front of him with the barrel pointing off to the side. Smiling as her eyes bugged wide, he twisted the cap off his beer bottle. "I can open yours if you like? I figured you would want to know that I wasn't trying to drug you."

Beth's grin grew. "I see why she likes you so much." Beth cranked the cap off and chugged a deep drink. She looked down at the lake. "Is that where it happened?"

Without glancing behind him, Daizon replied, "It is."

"You saved her life?"

"I found her, used some first aid knowledge, and called for help."

"Amia said you told her you were preparing for a role, doing research. Why were you really there?"

Daizon studied Beth. He imagined Amia and Beth together, their friendship. Beth would be the more aggressive and talkative type, while Amia would balance the relationship with the qualities of a listener who was less aggressive. They were both perceptive and intelligent. Beth had more of a street-smart intelligence about her, while Amia had more of a practiced, hard study type of intelligence. Beth was loyal, coming all this way to Maine for Amia and here to see him. How many friends would do that? Daizon naturally thought of Kyle. Perhaps they had a codependency between them? "I was there to prepare for a role. I was also there for my own reasons. Those reasons did not include bringing Amia any type of harm. I didn't know she was going to be there."

"Amia said you sent her flower arrangements while she was in the hospital and that you treated her with kindness and respect while at the Whole Me program."

It was a statement, but Beth hung on it like it was a question. Daizon was not sure how to answer. He'd wanted Amia to have a sense at the hospital that somebody cared. As far as the Whole Me program, he probably received more from that relationship than he ever gave. His lip twitched up at the thought of Amia's spirit.

"Thank you for being there for my friend." Beth inhaled deeply and produced a wicked smirk. "Now, why the hell did you leave?"

"If you saw the way she looked and acted toward me when her memory came back, you wouldn't ask me that question. She needed time without me there."

"Do you know anything about women? Fucking men."

Daizon shook his head, wondering what he'd done wrong. He thought about that moment on the trail. He thought about the detective. Daizon would have made the same decision again.

"After she had her moment and gave you that ugly stare you both have now told me about, she said she ran off and all her memories flooded back. She was scared, and rightfully so. After the flood of memories, she went looking for you to apologize. She needed a bit of time and space." Beth exaggerated her sweep of his home and the surroundings. "Not this much."

A grin tugged at his lip. Running it through his mind, Daizon figured Amia must have digested the memories and worked out that he was not the man who attacked her. But could she really be sure? Amia had to have some questions. Again, he circled back to his decision to leave being the correct one.

Daizon gazed down at the lake as the setting sun cast long shadows. He pulled the purple fabric from his pocket and slid it over the table to Beth. "I'm going to find the person who did this."

Beth rubbed her fingers over the smooth fabric. "Is it your friend?"

Apparently, Beth and Amia had quite a long conversation. "I don't know for sure it's him. I know a few things, and I'm learning more. Whoever attacked Amia was trying to implicate me. They deleted the account my manager and I set up on that dating site. They left Amia for dead right down there." Daizon pointed toward the part of the lake where it happened. "I don't think they thought I would find her the next morning. I don't think they planned on her living. They've tried covering their tracks with everything they left pointing at me. I'm convinced I was meant to take the fall. Amia's the only one who could vouch for me, and I'm not sure how good her word would be in court. The detective investigating the case has it out for me as well."

Beth perked up. "Amia remembered the phone number she called for you. She gave it to Dr. Wolf and confirmed it didn't match the phone number you had on file. Dr. Wolf then gave that information to Detective Johnson."

"Do you have it? The phone number she remembered?"

Beth frowned and shook her head. She retrieved a business card from her purse. "I have Detective Johnson's phone number."

CHAPTER FORTY

YIN AND YANG

The sun settled on the western horizon while the full moon danced above the ocean in the east. Excused from the current mindfulness and compassion session, Amia found herself out on the lawn in as secluded a spot as she could find, flowing with the tai chi movements. The movements were based on yin and yang, the balance of energy. What she learned focused on the flow of motion, breathing, and balance. She'd picked it up for the health benefits, and it helped settle her mind. She knew what she practiced focused mainly on the yin positive aspects, the flow state, and not the more aggressive nature associated with the yang aspects.

Amia sped up her forms. Daizon had taught her how she could use many of those same techniques in self-defense. He saw the strengths and weaknesses of what she did. He taught her to use the same or similar flowing movements with intent and force.

Force flowed from a solid core and generated power and momentum from the feet through point of impact, which could be a hand, foot, elbow, or knee. He smiled when he'd told her, "We use the head as a blunt weapon sometimes—not the best use of it." Hands, mind, and body were to remain loose until the moment before impact. Fingers folded in, thumb wrapped over fingers, forming a tight ball, and the strike ended behind the target, not at the target. He admitted he did not know if tai chi instructors taught striking the way he instructed, but it was the most effective method he knew.

Amia alternated between slow and fast, focusing on the different energy as she expressed her intent. It was like venting anger in controlled doses. A realization dawned on her. It felt good to let loose. She was always in control. She focused too much on the control aspect. Amia had a right to be angry. She was attacked and could remember none of it other than the parking lot going dark, loons hollering, and an Angel of Death figure she knew had to represent her assailant.

Amia thought of her Nonna holding her when she was sixteen. It was after she had cried herself into a ball on her bed, tears for a boy who'd made her feel less than. He'd dumped her for Rebecca, her high school friend. Rebecca was pretty and so developed. Her parents doted on her and gave her everything she ever wanted.

Moving forward in her mind, Amia thought of the first guy Beth set her up with in college, Tom. Tom was handsome and knew he was handsome. He kept in shape and had a nice, confident smile. When they went bowling, his hands were all over her. It was a first date. She smiled it off for most of the night. He had done nothing horribly wrong. He did not grope her aggressively; it was more of a multiple slaps on the ass kind of thing. Given the right moment, a slap on the ass would have been fine, maybe even welcomed, but that first date was not the right moment.

Tom's idea of talking was him asking questions and then talking over her and moving on to another topic. When he'd attempted to steal third base after she'd already swatted him out at second, Amia called a cab.

Amia realized as she went through her tai chi movements, it was not that she didn't want to be touched; it was the fact Tom felt doing so was his right. He did whatever the hell he wanted. Her happiness didn't matter. He did what he did to make himself happy.

Then there were others over the years. It was almost like every man took the same course, Womanizing One-Oh-One. Some guys were more advanced, up in the four hundred and graduate level classes. These were the guys like Baxter.

The nightmare, as she told Dr. Wolf, was not far off from the truth. She remembered the night.

The memories had Amia speeding through the aggressively altered tai chi movements at a reckless pace. She had watched Daizon move at a dizzying pace and slide smoothly into a slow, methodical pace. He made it look so easy. She pushed her boundaries.

Amia imagined the creature who'd assaulted her. It was a cross between the Angel of Death and the silhouette of a man. She used quick defensive movements combined with aggressive kicks, punches, and she kept flowing faster. She had to move faster. She sped up even more. The next sweep of her leg threw her off-balance, and the next thing she knew, she was staring up at the sky.

A few moments passed like that, and her breathing slowed. Stroking the ground, she let the grass slip through her fingers. She felt how the grass held her body like a bumpy air cushion. Amia relaxed her muscles into her newfound bed, knowing full well where she was.

Thinking back to those past relationships, then to Baxter, and now Daizon, Amia wondered again how much of her relationship issues manifested out of her fear of not being enough. She kept boyfriends at a distance, especially after Baxter. She'd planned to give the man she thought was Daizon a chance at Shady Jay's. Inside the Whole Me program, Amia let herself get to know him.

She let him into her private world. She let him into her life, and he allowed her into his. The only expectations were that they would treat each other with kindness, respect, and honesty. They did not share every little thought. They shared in ways that pushed their comfort boundaries. This place of trust they had negotiated would be where they would build their foundation.

Amia imagined being held by Daizon's longing and attentive eyes. Amia slid her fingers over her lips ever so gently with her fingertips. She remembered melting into him as he held her. Her memory had to choose that moment to return. She smiled and laughed, close to tears. Then she remembered the beaten look on his face when she thought he could be the monster who attacked her. He might have been somebody's monster at some point, but at that moment, he stood as a man with a broken heart. There were so many opportunities for him to take advantage of her growing desire for him while he was there, but he hadn't.

She'd held his broken heart and tossed it back to him after she ripped it out. Could he forgive something like that? Either way, it was not fair to leave him thinking she thought he was a monster when she didn't.

What was fair to her? The onset of night began with a few stars peeking past dark clouds, and as the night grew, more stars lit. Amia thought of each point of light as a memory shining beside its neighbor. They would greet each other like old acquaintances.

Amia realized that even before she'd come to this place, she'd lived a good life, but she was not whole. It felt good to yell and get angry. It felt good to tap into her aggressive nature even if it was not her go-to way of expressing herself. She thought of what she wanted.

CHAPTER FORTY-ONE

NO MORE MAYBES

Morning shower complete, Amia observed her reflection in the mirror again. The day and night before had both exhausted and exhilarated Amia. The experience was too much and not enough. She made phone calls the previous day to her bank, credit card companies, and the Boys and Girls Club where she volunteered. Nothing erroneous had happened with her accounts, and she let the kids know she had not abandoned them. She called Beth as well. Apparently, she and Beth had stories to tell each other. Beth had probably gone to see Daizon even after being told not to go.

The person in the mirror was no longer a stranger. She looked a lot different with her short hair. "A pixie with a buzz cut." She smiled and shook her head.

She drew her fingers lightly around the sides of her face, from forehead to cheek, to chin, and then the base of her neck. Then she rubbed her silver earrings again, found her blue stars in the mirror, and smiled. Warmth filled her. She rubbed her arms and squeezed herself. Her body was her own. She placed a hand over her heart. "Thank you."

Amia knew how lucky she was. She thought of the people who did not survive the things she survived. She thought of the people with memory loss and knew every one of them had a different story of their own recovery. Amia knew some of them never recovered their memories. With her hand still over her heart, she said aloud, "May we find peace and happiness."

Amia shared breakfast with Caitlyn and Tarah. They knew something was up from the previous day, and since Daizon was no longer there, their guesses revolved around something happening between the two of them. Amia smiled and laughed at some of their guesses. "No, he didn't try to ravish me in the woods. And no, he wasn't running away because things were getting complicated. He didn't touch me inappropriately."

Caitlyn chimed in, "He could touch me inappropriately." She smiled at their stunned looks. "Too soon?"

They laughed.

Caitlyn's expression drew more serious. She took a few breaths. "I see what he sees in you. Stop it. You can close your flytraps. I am capable of compliments. Anyway, you have a sense of realness and authenticity to you. That, and you're strong-willed as well as kind. I don't know how I would have handled your situation. You inspire us to all be better people, not for the sake of somebody else, but for ourselves. That means a lot." Caitlyn's eyes had glazed over by the end, and that got the three of them into a little group cry and hug. "Don't tell everyone that I'm actually soft."

They laughed again.

Amia said, "Thank you. I think you are just as beautiful on the inside."

Caitlyn smiled. "No, I'm not, but I want to be."

"A chrysalis to a butterfly," Tarah added.

Then Amia noticed Dr. Avendale in a suit, returning a badge to the front desk. His short, dark brown curly hair was slicked back and styled. His expensive suit shimmered and clung to his form. He was muscular, not like Daizon, but he was fit. Then he made direct eye contact for what seemed an extra heartbeat with his dark brown eyes. Realizing she had her fists clenched tight, she loosened her fingers and flexed them a few times. She flashed a smile and waved, wanting to thank him, remembering what Daizon told her.

He smiled at everyone at the table and nodded hello before striding out. Dr. Avendale walked tall with a long casual strut that seemed exaggerated, as if for show.

Caitlyn said, "Hello, Mr. Mysterious."

Tarah asked, "Do you know him?"

Amia watched as he exited. "That was Dr. Avendale. I wanted to thank him for helping me." He never once glanced back. He kept strutting along. "Dr. Avendale helped me in the early part of my recovery. Him and his wife donated the money to the program that made it possible for me to be here."

Tarah said, "He was one of your doctors at the hospital?"

"Dr. Hemp was my doctor, but he consulted with Dr. Avendale. Dr. Avendale filled in here once for Dr. Hemp. He's the one I have to thank for the pink crash helmet."

They laughed.

Amia glanced at the reception desk. "Excuse me." Amia went to the desk.

Sherri pushed up her oversized red glasses. "Hi, Amia. How can I help you?"

Amia glanced at Dr. Avendale's badge, which was lying just out of view on the desk. Amia glanced back at the exit for a moment. "You probably can't tell me why Dr. Avendale was here?"

"Sorry. You're welcome to ask Dr. Wolf. She might know."

"I will. Thank you, Sherri."

⤝

Amia walked along the outer edges of the meditation room. She read some of the inspirational quotes and words on the wall. Once everyone learned she regained her memory, Amia had to answer a barrage of questions. There were congratulations, cheers, smiles, hugs, and laughter.

Dr. Wolf explained the loss of Daizon from the program as a personal matter and she would keep in contact with him. She assured everyone he had his journey, and they had theirs.

The others showed Amia a warmth she did not expect. She allowed their happiness and concern instead of holding them at arm's length. "Thank you," she said. "Thank you. I appreciate your kindness."

Dr. Wolf addressed the group. "Amia, we learned, is a doctoral psychology student and was due to start her practicum this summer. As you all know, everything doesn't always go as we plan. She has accepted an offer to stay on here, working as my assistant until her classes start back up in the fall. We'll work out the details as we go. She will be another resource for all of us to access while we are here, if you choose."

There were smiles, claps, and whistles.

"Before Amia begins, she has some business to attend to away from the facility. I think, as you can all imagine with her memory back, she has some catching up to do as well."

Amia did not think Dr. Wolf would allow her to leave. Amia explained in Dr. Wolf's office, "They're rushing a new bank card to the bank up here. Speaking with everyone on the phone yesterday, most of my finances seem secure." The only account messed with was her Psyche and Eros account.

"I would like to purchase some of those personal items he stole. You know, phone, purse, wallet, makeup, clothes . . . " Amia paused. "There were other things he stole. Things I can't purchase. I want to go to where it all began. I want to see Daizon." It was not a brilliant argument, but it was the truth.

"Do you believe what you want to do is in line with the core of this program?"

Without hesitation, Amia nodded. "I've never been more sure in my life. I have a long way to go, but I know what I want. This program and everyone's help here have led me to where I am. Part of how I want to move forward is out of my control and scary. I've always shied away from those scary parts, not saying and doing things for fear of what might happen or to avoid conflict. I want that to end."

"The compassionate thing to do isn't always the easy thing to do. Good for you. I'll be here if you need me."

Further on in their conversation, Amia remembered her other question. "Do you know why Dr. Avendale donated money to the program?"

"Dr. Avendale and his wife do a lot of philanthropic activities. He heard about the program and wanted to learn more about it. He thought some of his patients might benefit from a program like the Whole Me. I told him I would give him a tour of the facilities and introduce him to the group in a couple more weeks, when we're closer to completion."

Amia tried pairing the new information with his strut and slicked-back hair. Some surgeons could be cockier and more self-assured than others. It was one way they coped with what they did for a living. Amia nodded.

⁓

Beth held her car door open for Amia in the parking lot. She wore a massive smile that spoke of mischief. Riding as a passenger in Beth's car was an experience Amia was not looking forward to repeating. The thought of riding as a passenger with her for an entire day was unimaginable. Before Amia sat, she briefly wondered if she would live long enough to face some of the scary things inside her mind. She smiled hesitantly at Beth.

Beth cocked her head sideways. "Get in, sweetheart. Time's wasting. Put your big-girl pants on."

Amia imagined this was how she would actually die. She smiled and buckled up. At least it would be with a friend.

As they drove along, they were surrounded by so many trees. Calling Maine the Pine Tree State misled visitors into thinking that's all they would see. There was a fantastic variety of oak, pine, birch, cedar, ash, maple, and who knew what else. She unrolled her window and breathed it in. Amia finally asked about the mischievous grin Beth could not wipe away. "What did you do?"

Beth tried her innocent look, but her smirk corrupted it. She had said nothing, and Beth was not one to hold her thoughts to herself. "I'm excited to spend some quality time together. That's all."

Amia already had a pretty good idea. She knew her friend. "You called him?"

Her smirk widened. "I did not call him."

"Tell me you didn't do what I think."

It was a full-on display of smugness. "I didn't do what you think."

"Liar."

"Sometimes."

"You know you're not my only friend? I can make more."

"Yeah, but there's a break-in period of getting to know each other, and that's so exhausting. Plus, do you know how far I came to see you? I dropped everything. How many friends do you have like that?"

Amia slid out a grin. "Enough."

Beth raised an eyebrow and slapped Amia's arm.

Amia laughed. "Thank you."

"That's better. You're welcome. Now I know I'm appreciated."

"Cream for a rash is appreciated, too."

"Don't ruin the moment."

"Okay already, tell me about what happened. You know I love you."

Beth bobbed a contented wiggle. "He is even more stunning in real life. You know he's fallen madly for you?"

Amia blushed, even though she knew Beth was teasing her. "He barely knows who I am. I'm sure that's not quite what he said."

"You get too caught up in words. Semantics really. I'm a believer in action and intent, and his speak volumes."

Amia thought of her time with him, and she smiled. "He has a way of making you feel at ease and on your toes at the same time. He's been unexpected, humble, and kind toward me."

Tossing her eyes and head about, Beth said, "I'd say that about sums up my experience with him as well. Of course, I had my Taser with me, just in case he was, well, you know, something other than polite." Beth shared her encounter with Daizon.

Where to start with her questions? "He put his gun on the table, and that made you feel more comfortable?"

"Hell no, but I had my Taser on the table in front of me. I realized it was a gesture, kind of like putting our cards on the table. He was trying to make me feel comfortable and off-balance at the same time. I mean, to be fair, I was sitting on his back porch, and he barely knew who I was."

There was a lot Amia did not know about Daizon. Beth seemed completely satisfied with how he handled the encounter. Amia thought of the lake and the mountains from the pictures where he found her. He would wake up there every day. Did she really want to go there? "What was his place like?"

"It's like something out of a magazine. Really, the views." Beth must have glimpsed the tightness in Amia. She gripped Amia's hand. "We don't have to go."

Amia breathed out some of the tension. "Yes, I do."

Collecting some more thoughts, Amia asked, "Does he really think it was his friend?"

"He doesn't know. I don't think he wanted to go there, but he did not deny it could be him. I convinced him to talk with Detective Johnson about what he found and his suspicions."

Amia thought for a couple of seconds. "What happens if Daizon's friend is there when we show up? We really should call." Amia shook her head. *Stop trying to talk your way out of going. Don't push him away because you're scared.*

CHAPTER FORTY-TWO

NO GOOD DEED

I t was a pleasant afternoon, except for Detective Johnson at his back. Daizon led her along the game trail through the woods. He showed her his hunting blind and then the broken branch tip where he'd found the torn piece of fabric. She wanted him to remain in front of her at all times. Part of their deal was that he would not bring a firearm along. Each step seemed like some kind of mistake. She had a hair trigger and wanted him for what happened to Amia.

You're overthinking it, Daizon, he said to himself. *She has to consider you. You want her to find the person who attacked Amia, right? Helping the detective helps Amia.*

When they stopped, the detective scanned the woods. Birds and squirrels mirrored the detective's nerves and called out their warnings. They fluttered around or scurried about and nattered. The detective tried hiding her emotions behind a scowl. He knew she was searching for other information she was not telling him about. She said, "You know you shouldn't have removed the evidence from the scene."

Daizon aimed a blank face at the detective.

"Everything we have leads more and more to you. You know that, right?"

"And yet I'm helping you anyway. It's good one of us is doing your job."

She tried to show the jab did not connect, that she did not care what he thought, but a quick roll of her eyes and tightening of her jaw let him know he'd landed a blow. She asked, "How often do you travel to California?"

"It depends on where a project is being filmed."

"How about last November, around the sixteenth?" The detective inspected some branches, still focusing on him and his reactions.

Daizon thought back. He was doing a reprisal in the role of *The Dragon*. Detective Johnson tried hiding an ever-so-slight grin. "I was out there."

She teased a high-pitched tone. "Was there a visit to Long Beach, by chance?"

"No. I'm guessing the phone number Amia gave you is associated with an address out there?"

The detective studied him. He figured she was working on catching him in a lie. What did she find out? Kyle had gone out to visit him. He'd really gone out there to take advantage of Daizon's connections, leveraging some of them for himself. Daizon was unaware Kyle had already taken care of Brittney. Kyle had helped a few actors and actresses out with their fighting techniques. He used his brash charm, and now he had a role.

Detective Johnson's demeanor softened, as if questioning what she believed. Daizon sensed a trap. She glanced around the area again. "You said Kyle knew this area well. Was he out in California around that same time in November?"

Daizon nodded. "He was." Daizon's gut tightened. It did not seem to matter that Kyle had betrayed him. Daizon felt low. The stakes of what happened meant Daizon had to place his personal feelings aside. It could have been Kyle. Was seducing his girlfriends not enough anymore? Did he want to take over his life? "I don't think he did it. Kyle can be an ass, but he's like that to your face. He doesn't hide it. You said it's a California number Amia gave you? Is it possible it's, like, some random person who's obsessed with me? I'm sure not everyone likes me. I've seen how some of those same people who complain about violence in the movies carry it out in real life. They have a hard time distinguishing between the entertainment aspect of the illusion and reality."

"I doubt it's somebody random. I'm not ruling it out, but I doubt it. None of the letters you gave me turned out to be anything significant. Amia told me Kyle and your last girlfriend had relations. That alone triggers some questions. I think the first question that comes to mind is, why would you still be friends with him?"

"I've asked myself a version of that question thousands of times."

Detective Johnson waited for him to expound.

He did not want to go into some long story where his answer would most likely trigger more questions. He stayed quiet.

Detective Johnson shook her head. "You say you want to help, but you refuse to answer my simple questions."

"I answered it. You didn't like the answer. Do you want the truth or for me to make up something you want to hear?"

The detective remained unimpressed.

"Let me rephrase my answer. I don't know why we are still friends. I've given him the cold shoulder, and it has strained our friendship for a long time. I don't know. I don't even know if you can call what we have a friendship. He's more like an annoying family member you try to distance yourself from. That said, we've been through a lot together, relied on each other. I guess the bond we have is hard to break."

"He was banging the headboards of your bed with your girlfriend."

"Have you met Kyle?"

"Not yet. Soon."

"Don't underestimate his charm. You know how you have some friends that are full of shit and you know they're full of shit?"

She nodded.

"He's not one of those people. He has a way with women. They know going in that he's not looking for a relationship, or at least not a long one. I've tried to figure it out. I don't know. He has a dry sense of brutally honest humor. He projects a sense of self-confidence that doesn't border on cocky—it's full-out cocky. I'm sure there's a lot going on that he doesn't share, and I don't push. He doesn't push me for that type of information, either. A lot happened while we were serving, and we don't talk about it. We already know what we went through without rehashing it. That's probably why we are still friends."

"I'll do my best to resist his charms. You said you've been through a lot together and you don't believe it's him, but everything I hear and see tells me something different. I'm curious, do you think it was him or not? Who else should I be looking at?"

Daizon knew damn well Kyle was capable. Why couldn't he fully commit to saying it was him? Did he not want to believe it was true? "I don't know. I don't want to believe it was him, that he would go that far. But I'd be lying if I didn't think it could be him. I don't know who else it might be."

Daizon scanned the area. He glanced back toward the road. "There's a snowmobile–ATV trail that sweeps past to the east side of the lake. But the south side where I found Amia—" Daizon shook his head. "Nobody goes there. I went back there yesterday. The lakeside grass is a foot and a half taller. I never would have found her if what happened to her happened now. Nobody would have found her, not alive."

"Who else knew about the game trail?"

"I posted the property, but like I said, a few hunters and anglers will occasionally try their luck. Kyle knows about it. He helped me build the hunting blind. I told Dave I would set him up down here for the coming hunting season. He's not much of an outdoorsman, but he likes to pretend."

"Dave?"

"Avendale. Tonya's husband. He's a brain surgeon out in California. We were supposed to go fishing that morning, but he traveled back to California for an emergency the day before. I called him after I called emergency services to make sure I was doing everything I could to help save Amia's life."

"In your previous statement, you said you were visiting the Avendales the night before."

"I was. Dave got a phone call and had to fly out. He has clients from all over the world. His trips to Maine are always either getting cut short or canceled. I guess there are advantages and disadvantages to being one of the world's top brain surgeons. I told him he should open a practice on the East Coast so he wouldn't have to waste so much of his time flying coast to coast. He told me he was working on it, but I think he enjoys using the time to unwind."

The detective's bullshit reader was on high. "What time did he leave, and how long did you stay with Mrs. Avendale after he left?"

Shit. Daizon swore at himself. *Christ.* Daizon knew she'd caught him in a lie. It was his first lie when he found Amia and called for help. He'd told the detective he was over at Tonya and Dave's until late at night and then went home because he planned to go fishing in the morning. He had left much earlier to bury Holly, his cat.

Daizon realized after he used his clothes to help Amia he might become a suspect. He hadn't given it a second thought; he'd acted.

His whole credibility was shot because of one small lie. *Fuck.* He tried seeing the situation from the detective's point of view. Daizon had lied about the timing of his whereabouts the night before. He'd found a body on his property in a location nobody visited. He'd saved Amia's life by covering her in his clothes. Then he'd admitted himself into a program where Amia was so he could prepare for a role of an amnesiac killer. That was the story. Daizon hadn't known Amia would be there. The detective would think his motive was to make sure she couldn't identify him. Then he threw his best friend, who he has a grudge against, under the bus. *Fuck.*

Daizon took a breath, knowing he had to look guilty. "I left Tonya and Dave's not long after Dave left. So, if Dave left around ten thirty or eleven, I left maybe around eleven thirty or noon."

Detective Johnson's hand eased to her holster, probably as some function of fear. Their eyes locked. "Both you and Tonya told me you were over there late. Now you're telling me eleven thirty or noon. Why the lie if there's nothing to hide? Both of you lied. Why?"

"I came back early to bury my cat. She was hit by a car and had managed to crawl home and die at my front door. She was healthy and only eight years old. She died alone." Daizon didn't believe anything he said would matter. He closed his eyes and took a few deep breaths. An accusatory image flashed before his eyes. "I killed a woman on one of my missions. She was a terrorist, and maybe I shouldn't feel the way I do, but when I saw Amia, she looked like a fallen angel or something, giving me a chance to save a life. I could have just called for help, but I knew she would have died. I did what I did to save her life. She had fought as long as she could alone. She needed my help."

Pressure built inside Daizon's head as he fought his watering eyes. He breathed slow and steady to control himself. He allowed the air to enter and fill him.

Detective Johnson withdrew her weapon. She spoke in an authoritative voice, and some distant part of him recognized her terror. "Lie down on the ground with your arms away from your body facedown. I don't want to see any sudden movements. Spread your legs and arms. Palms up. I have my gun to your head, and I think you know I won't hesitate. Fold one hand at a time to the small of your back. Keep your palms up."

She put a knee to the small of his back as she was about to apply the handcuffs. He thought, *Tighten the stomach, whip around, weapon in the right hand, elbow to the armpit*. It would have been so easy to escape. She believed him cowed. His father's words came back to him as they always did. *People see what they want. The truth never matters.*

Numbness filled him. He remembered spattered brains everywhere, trying to stuff them back in her head. Detective Johnson read him his rights. He had the right to remain silent. He had the right to suffer, the right to die. Did he understand these rights? Daizon shook his head.

"You have everyone fooled. Evidence doesn't lie. I know you purchased the burner phone in California. You screwed up using your credit card. You almost had me believing you. You're sick."

Why the hell would he buy a burner phone with his own credit card? He would have used cash. He thought of Amia, glad she was at the Whole Me program, safe. She was safe because he'd helped save her life. Maybe he had some kind of hero complex? He wanted to be her hero.

CHAPTER FORTY-THREE

ASSEMBLING AMIA

Anxiety and excitement ebbed and flowed as the day progressed. Amia opened and closed herself off to difficult emotions as Beth drove. Whether it was the fear of Beth's driving, the thought of seeing Daizon away from the Whole Me program, or the thought of claiming and reshaping her identity, Amia knew parts of the day would be difficult. She also knew letting things happen was not a choice. That was avoidance. Before Beth and Amia traveled to Daizon's, they had a few errands to run.

Detective Johnson had provided a copy of the police report and helped get a temporary identification. Amia verified her information with her bank and credit card companies already over the phone, and she would have new cards forwarded to a local branch. The bank had Amia's picture on file. Dressed in her pink scrubs with short hair, Amia understood the clerk's glances between the photo and her new self. Amia smiled and handed over the paperwork. The clerk's eyes filled with sadness and empathy. It was a brief conversation and well wishes as Amia headed out with her new debit and credit cards in hand. It was time to address her phone and attire.

Her phone represented her connection to the world, and the scrubs were nice and all, but she wanted to feel like herself again, or maybe like her new self.

⟍⟋

Back in the car, Beth wore her smirk. "Don't tell me you're not thinking about the impression you want to make later on."

"He's seen me and knows who I am, kind of . . . well, not the real me, but he's seen me. What are you trying to do to me? If you're trying to get me to second-guess myself, it's working."

"I visited him yesterday. Do you really think I would bring you to him if I thought you weren't doing what was right for you? I'm just teasing, and honestly, I think you need it."

"I need to be teased?"

"Yes. You have so much going on in that little brain, you need to be reminded to ease up on overthinking."

"He's in my thoughts, but your driving helps keep me in the moment."

Beth grinned as she sped out of a corner. The wheels and metal frame of her yellow Prius sang in a hissing, groaning chorus.

Amia screamed. "Stop it! Please, just drive slower for now. I don't want to die. I've spent enough time in the hospital. When I'm completely better, you can drive like your normal self, but please." Anger and fear shook Amia. She breathed. Part of her felt good speaking her mind, but Beth was her friend.

Beth was about to say something, stopped herself, and slowed down at the sight of Amia struggling. "I'm sorry."

It was silent in the car for a bit. Beth, not known for holding her tongue long, said, "I pushed you into opening that account on

Psyche and Eros. None of this would have happened if it weren't for me. It hurts me knowing that I caused you all this pain. You're my best friend, and you've always been there for me through all my relationships, never judging, just being there. Through all my mistakes and crazy emotions, you were there for me. I know you don't have a lot of friends, that you keep people at a distance, so you make me feel special by allowing me into your life. It means a lot. I always meant well when I tried setting you up. I did. You know that, right?"

"I know. What happened to me is not your fault. It's not my fault either. Besides, if I didn't go on those other dates and meet those other guys, how on earth would I know what I wasn't looking for in a guy? They weren't all unpleasant experiences. Did I ever tell you about Baxter and the queen?"

"He was a tool and didn't know what he had. For what he offered, all you needed to do was charge Mr. Tingles."

Amia smirked. "Have you been looking through my bed table drawers?"

They laughed.

⚜

Amia picked up a new phone with the same number from the carrier. It was a pleasant surprise when she found almost all her information had been saved to the cloud.

It seemed strange to Amia that whoever attacked her did not steal any of her assets. They took her belongings, but they did that to cover their tracks. They returned her rental car, cleaned out her room, and returned her hotel key. Police had found her phone in pieces. From what she'd found, the only tampering done was regarding her and Daizon's Psyche and Eros accounts.

She thought about Shady Jay's Tavern, and as much as she wanted to see Daizon, being attacked and left for dead on the edge of his property twisted her stomach. One of her goals for the day was to open herself to at least one of those places and events. She wanted to view them as separate from what happened to her. She needed to face those demons as part of her healing. Going to those places had everything to do with not wanting to be held captive by them. Amia wanted to move forward, but to do that, she had to revisit her past.

She might move forward with Daizon, and she might not. She hoped their relationship would work out more than she would admit. She understood he knew her only from the Whole Me program. There was a lot he had not shared about his life. He had demons of his own.

Amia smiled at the next thought. She knew he was at that facility for more than her. He gave himself to the program wholeheartedly. *Good for him.*

⤙

Amia and Beth tried on new clothes and modeled them for each other at the mall they'd found. Beth enjoyed her flashy and tight outfits, while Amia went with soft tones and fluid fabrics. She found a new satchel-style, cross-body white purse that appealed to her growing new sense of self. The purse spoke of flow and professionalism. Or maybe it just went well with the lilac blouse and high-rise trousers that held snugly through the waist and hips while flowing down the rest of the way to her calves.

A few twists in the mirror and she knew this was her. She was not flashy, but she flashed with her own sense of style. This person in the mirror did not have to pretend to be comfortable with who she was. She was far from perfect, but that was okay.

Watching her, Beth grew a smile. "You are stunning. I love it."

⚜

Amia wore the new outfit as they traveled to Daizon's home. She itched with wanting to call before they arrived, but Beth convinced her a surprise was in order. Amia remembered how her surprise visit with Baxter went. Her anxiety grew again as they approached the mountain he lived on.

Forest pushed in on either side of the road. It was wide enough, she supposed. The tight sensation could have been her anxiety. The higher they climbed, the more it seemed like an amusement park ride. When the road leveled off for a moment, the pit in her stomach anticipated the fall to come.

Instead, all her muscles slowly relaxed. Nestled on the side of the mountain was a beautiful home. The architecture had the home shaped to the side of the mountain, a part of the mountain and forest.

They knocked on the front door. Shades were drawn, and the lights were on inside, but Daizon didn't answer. Beth said, "Maybe he's out back. Wait until you see the view from his deck."

Amia's muscles tightened again as she followed Beth past the top entrance of the deck, over the freshly cut lawn, around the house, and up the stairs to his massive deck. The craftsmanship gave off a sense of warmth and welcome. The whole place seemed an oasis overlooking something picturesque. Her muscles relaxed. Whoever had built this place took pride in what they did for a living. The view went beyond the mountain bowl they were in to the far reaches, where the eye could no longer pick out detail. There were ancient mountains all around settling into the earth. Valleys, ponds, and lakes nestled in little pockets everywhere.

Below was Daizon's small lake. *Breathe*, she told herself when she searched for the place in the pictures. The small lake was picturesque, but she could not identify where she almost died. Amia knew she would want Daizon to show her where he found her. She needed to see it. Beth's knocking finally got her attention.

Standing on the deck, Amia glimpsed a black SUV as it growled and climbed the mountain road. Beth said, "Maybe that's him."

The man wore a shiny suit and had slicked-back curly hair. His dark eyes met hers. He smiled as he rounded the corner of the house. "Daizon, I heard you were back home. I didn't know you had company already." Dr. Avendale's smile broadened as he turned the corner of the ramp and stepped onto the main part of the deck. He offered a surprised smile to Amia and Beth.

Amia instinctively stepped back a few steps, bringing herself closer to Beth. Seeing Amia's reaction, Beth reached into her purse and held her hand there.

"Relax," he said, holding his hands out wide and high. "Amia, are you okay? I'm here to visit Daizon. He left the Whole Me program early. I thought I'd come out to visit, see how he was doing, and get his opinion on how effective he thought the program was. Wow, I rarely get this reaction from people. How is your head? Are you two okay?"

His voice sank into Amia's mind. She kept staring at his slicked-back curls. She said, "Hello, Dr. Avendale. My head is feeling much better. Thank you."

Maintaining his smile, he cocked his head and nodded. "I heard you regained your memory and wanted to talk with you yesterday, but Dr. Wolf insisted I wait another week or two. You're looking well." Dr. Avendale slowly dropped his hands and offered one of them to Amia. "It's a pleasure to meet the real you, Amia."

Amia allowed her tension level to decrease a bit. She offered a smile instead of her hand in greeting. "I'm sorry. We're not trying to be rude. It's a safety thing, you know—two women and a man we don't really know."

He stepped back and kept his smile affable. "I understand completely. No offense taken or need to apologize. I get it. It's good to see two young women such as yourselves so self-aware. Where's Daizon?"

Beth said, "We don't know. We were going to surprise him, but apparently he has other things going on."

His smile faltered at the news. "Are you sure?"

Beth waved a hand at the empty house. "It looks like he thought he'd be right back. I saw a coffee cup out and a few lights were on, but the cat's water bowl and food dish are full. I haven't seen his cat, either. The place is empty, and he locked the door."

Amia asked, "You tried the handle?"

"Well, yeah," Beth said, as if it were a given.

Dr. Avendale strode to the door and shook the handle. "His cat died almost two months ago. Did you see a brandy glass?" He peeked inside, using his hands to block out the sun.

Amia and Beth gave each other dumbfounded looks. Beth said, "No, just a coffee cup."

"He's probably at my place. I'm not supposed to be back for a few more days." He stewed.

Amia and Beth waited for him to expand. Instead, he gave them a dismissive glance and strode off with a purpose. "He's been having an affair with my wife."

His words struck Amia like a hammer pounding a stubborn nail. Beth gripped Amia's hand and called to Dr. Avendale, "We're going to follow you."

Keeping his stride, he gave the both of them a disgusted glance. "I thought you were more intelligent."

Beth shook her head. "What the hell was that? Talk about Dr. Jekyll and Mr. Hyde."

Amia shook off the hammering blows. It was not true. The Daizon she knew would not do that. Then she realized, "It's not Daizon having an affair with Dr. Avendale's wife. It's his friend Kyle. What if Kyle did something to Daizon? Is that why Daizon's home was left like this? We have to call Daizon and Detective Johnson."

CHAPTER FORTY-FOUR

FRIENDS YOU KEEP

Day progressed to night as Daizon sat in the holding cell. Detective Johnson tucked him away with plain white walls, no furniture, and a toilet hole in the corner. There was a small sliver of a window near the ceiling. Sitting with his back against the wall, he watched the room grow dark. He sat with his thoughts.

He did some side straddle hops, crunches, and push-ups. Detective Johnson came by several times and asked if he was ready to talk. He stared her in the eyes and went about his business in the cell. She wasn't ready to listen.

She put him in the cell, thinking it would break him. In the detective's imaginings, she had enough to lock him away for life, or so she wanted him to believe. She wasn't interested in hearing the truth. She wanted him to share in her fabrication. He'd told her what had happened, and this was his reward.

Meanwhile, whoever had attacked Amia would probably get away with it. Daizon knew he would probably take the fall. Besides the fabricated evidence, Detective Johnson had something against him from the very beginning. Maybe she really believed he did those things to Amia. Daizon never should have told the detective about the woman he killed while serving in the military. Apparently he hadn't punished himself enough for her death.

Sitting against the back wall, Daizon thought about the exercises he'd done before he left the program. He had nothing but time. Controlling the rhythm of his breath, he closed his eyes and brought himself back to the moment, right before he saved Kyle. He paused the moment in his mind to see her whole.

In his imagining, it was the moment before he pulled the trigger of his assault rifle. He put a hole in her head as he was trained to do. The back of her head burst apart, and her life was over. It was later that he found out she was a terrorist. At the time, she was a woman with mush sprayed out from the back of her head, and her dead eyes stared at him with blank accusation. The light had gone out. He pushed Kyle away as he tried applying first aid. He wrapped her head with a bandage, ignoring the brain matter splattered everywhere.

Daizon sped himself forward and imagined himself sitting on the rock he went to that night on the mountain. This time he brought Mindful Compassionate Daizon. There were so many stars in this place with few lights. The moon was bright over the mountains and a cool, dry breeze seemed to always blow.

He had washed a few times, but could not rid himself of the smell of her. Mindful Compassionate Daizon sat beside him with a consoling smile. Daizon said to him, "I think I know part of the reason it hurts so much. She was me those times I was assaulted. Part of me wishes I could be her now. The thing is, I know Kyle wasn't doing anything wrong. She was hiding in a false wall and jumped Kyle from behind, stabbing him. Everything happened in a few seconds. Just as he gained control, I walked in, and well, you know the end. Maybe I saw what I wanted to see? Maybe I expected Kyle to be capable of those things, so it wasn't a stretch?"

Mindful Compassionate Daizon nodded. "That's a lot of maybes."

"I think it's because I want the truth to be something different."

"Is it because we want the truth to be different, or is it because we don't know what the truth is?"

Daizon said, "I only have my view. I think I had a blind spot at that moment because of the things that happened to me. Part of me feels like I killed the victim to save the assailant, even though I know better."

"The things that happened to us caused a lot of pain. We know she killed others and would have killed more. She was a verified terrorist. She may have even killed many of those kids we saw. If we had it to do all over again, would we save Kyle's life?"

Daizon nodded. "It's what they trained me to do. I wouldn't like it, but I wouldn't hesitate."

Mindful Compassionate Daizon mirrored the nod. "If we would do the same thing in the end, maybe it's time to forgive?"

Daizon could not change what had happened. He knew the scenario revealed his weakness. He wanted to die and wanted to hope. It was his constant conundrum.

In his cell, Daizon imagined Amia's soft expression and dazzling blue eyes. Her eyes and what was behind them lit his world. His smile grew in the cell's darkness. Thoughts of the way Amia fought to see into those dark places of her mind helped him as he traveled to his. The Whole Me program helped as well, but how far he traveled was up to him.

Everyone there was on their own journey, getting familiar with their own dark places. They were getting familiar with the light places as well. He was not alone and did not have to pretend to be anything he was not. He was good at pretending and made a decent living from those abilities. The key seemed a broadening of his perspective of himself as well as his general view. Everybody suffered in their own way.

Detective Johnson pulled the metal slat window open on the door with a screech and clang. "Is Kyle having an affair with Tonya?"

Daizon kept quiet and listened.

The detective sighed. "Amia is on her way over there, and she says Dr. Avendale is looking to catch them in the act. She said Dr. Avendale thinks it's you having the affair with his wife. I told Amia not to go, but she thought you might be there because you were not at home. We lost the connection, and I couldn't reach her back."

"Why the hell didn't you tell her I was here at the beginning of the phone call? She can't get in the middle of that. Get over there and help her. What are you still doing here? Knowing Kyle, he probably is having an affair with Tonya. When I saw the two of them yesterday, that would have been my guess. Detective, I know you don't want to hear this, but I think one of them lured and left Amia for dead. I don't think they meant for her to be found that soon or that she would survive the night. They set everything up to look like I did it. I think somewhere inside, you know what I'm saying rings true. Please listen to me. Go now."

He wondered briefly if Tonya and Kyle were setting him up. *No.* Silence overtook the cell. Then the tiny door screeched shut.

CHAPTER FORTY-FIVE

DARK PLACES

Amia's focus slogged as they wound through the rural roads at a frightening speed. She'd told Detective Johnson what was going on, but her phone had slipped out of her hand as they went around a corner. She rocked back and forth, barely able to hold herself in position. Amia was not about to reach for the phone, which banged and slid about. She stayed silent as Beth displayed her driving skills. Beth was beautiful and frightening. She grinned at Amia. "I can slow down?"

Amia shook her head. "Maybe don't follow so close."

Dr. Avendale drove madly. From the way Daizon described Kyle to her, it would be like a hornet meeting an electrified swatter. If Dr. Avendale knew Daizon, he would know he couldn't win in a fair fight. Intelligent, Dr. Avendale would not go unprepared for that altercation. *No.* "He has a gun."

Beth's eyes widened.

"Think about it. He wouldn't go after somebody like Daizon without a weapon. He probably keeps it in his glove compartment, or center console, or somewhere in his truck." Amia paused as more thoughts rushed into her mind. "Dr. Avendale acted like Daizon was his friend, even though he believed Daizon was having an affair with his wife. You saw how he dressed and his polished look. He's a brain surgeon. Imagine his suave ego trying to handle that situation. He values the way people perceive him and would not want that image tarnished. His wife having an affair. He knows about it but says nothing for months, maybe longer?"

Amia flashed into a memory. It was that night at Shady Jay's waiting at the bar. Men bumped into her quite a few times already, and Daizon had not shown or answered his phone. She didn't want to get too upset. Something might have happened to him. At that point, she thought it had better be an accident that sent him to the hospital, nothing life-threatening, of course.

The smell of alcohol, perfume, and sweat wafted throughout the crowded tavern. She was sure an abundance of hormones wafted in the air as well, with all the grinding and playful sexual teasing.

At that point, she was fine. She was not drunk. She nursed her drink. A man wearing hunting garb bumped into her. With one hand he deftly steadied the hand she held her drink with; the other hand gripped her opposite shoulder near her neck, gaining her attention. He had a confident smile and slicked-back curly hair poking out from under his hat. Dr. Avendale said, "Sorry, let me buy you another." He smiled even wider, and it reached those dark eyes. He put twenty dollars on the counter, glanced at her drink, smiled, and quickly left.

Back in the car, Amia must have paled a few shades during the memory. She was light and dizzy. She told herself, *Breathe, Amia. Breathe.*

Beth asked, "What's wrong?"

"He's the one who assaulted me and left me for dead. I remember him from Shady Jay's. It was him. He was dressed in hunting clothes, but I remember his slicked-back curly hair poking out from under his hat. And those eyes have haunted my nightmares for too long. Slow down. We need help. If Daizon or Kyle went over there, they are in more danger than I thought."

A hundred yards ahead of them, Dr. Avendale pulled into his oceanside driveway. His SUV door shut. He flipped the tail of his suit over the pistol after tucking it into his pants at the small of his back. Beth screeched to a halt maybe thirty yards away. His attention swung back and forth between his home and them. He walked toward Amia and Beth.

"Drive, Beth. Honk your horn and drive." They sped past Dr. Avendale with Beth tapping the tiny horn as if it were some Morse code message saying, *Get the hell out. There's danger.* Amia turned around and watched as he rushed to his SUV. The lights flashed on, and it whipped backward. "He's coming after us."

Amia turned back around and slid herself out of the top part of the seat belt. Her hand hopped around for her phone on the floor. Finally, she gripped it as Beth skidded to a halt. Her forehead bounced off the dash.

Reaching over, Beth said, "Sorry. Are you all right? We have a problem." The road ended at a large, almost empty parking area. A big white sign with black letters read, PRIVATE BEACH, ACCESS BY PERMISSION ONLY.

Gaining fast behind them down the middle of the tight road was the SUV. Beth said, "He's not going to let us get past him, and the banks on either side of the road are too steep." The road acted as an aisle that split two sides of a saltwater marsh.

Searching the parking lot area, they found what looked like the main trail to the private beach on the far-left side. Lined with heavy tree growth on the edges, the parking lot stretched a good hundred yards or more to the right. An empty, full-size pickup truck sat tucked in the corner at the far end of the parking lot.

Beth grabbed her Taser and phone. Head tingling and throbbing, Amia realized she had her phone in her hand. A second realization hit; she had her wits. She hoped. They locked the doors and ran toward the darkness of the trail. Music played in the distance, somewhere between the beach and the house they'd fled from. Electricity in the air charged her skin. Glancing up, she saw a storm front approaching.

Amia said, "You call nine-one-one, and I'll call Daizon."

Chapter Forty-Six

Vanishing Lights

One set of lights and then another vanished in the distance toward the beach as Detective Johnson and Daizon arrived at Tonya and Dave's home. Storm clouds rolled and writhed as they approached from a short distance away. Electricity bounced over the humid air and danced on the skin. Hair rose.

⚓

Detective Johnson had surprised Daizon when, after sliding the metal window shut on his door, she opened the holding cell door. "To be clear, I'm not asking you to do anything besides try to de-escalate the situation we might encounter. Dr. Avendale has some serious explaining to do. He didn't fly out to California on the day of Amia's assault. He flew out the next day. When I spoke with Mrs. Avendale, she said he was due back later this week, but he arrived back in Maine yesterday. I checked, and he owns a nine-millimeter."

Daizon shook his head in disbelief. He thought of taking Dave hunting and fishing. Dave had an arrogance to him, but he seemed affable. Then Daizon thought of the way he'd found Amia and what Dave had done to her. He thought of Dave's text back to him after he'd sent the picture of his catch that morning. His gut tightened. He told Detective Johnson about the interaction before adding, "He wished me good luck, surprised I still went fishing without him."

⤟

At Dave and Tonya's, Daizon glanced at the bare driveway and around the area. He said, "I don't see Beth's yellow Prius." He stepped toward where the lights faded down the street. The only thing down there was a private beach. Tonya and Dave's place was the closest to the beach. The other homes led off the opposite way because of zoning restrictions. It was like having a corner lot on a private beach.

Detective Johnson said, "Let's talk with Mrs. Avendale and see if she has company."

Nobody answered the door, but classic rock music played in the distance somewhere down on the beach. Daizon glanced at the detective, who also noticed the music. They rounded the house to the beach. A fire burned on the beach in the distance toward the point. Two people, a man and a woman, were already on the beach. Approaching them, sure enough, Daizon recognized Tonya wearing white shorts and a darker-colored bikini top. A thin white mesh draped over her torso. Remaining with the fire was a large man wearing dark shorts and a tank top. Daizon figured it was probably Kyle. The music stopped playing as droplets of rain fell.

Sure enough, it was a surprised Tonya who met Daizon and the detective several hundred yards away from the fire. Tonya asked,

"Daizon? What are you doing? Why were you honking your horn like that?" Tonya had a caught-but-not-ready-to-admit-anything posture. The posture said he was the one in the wrong because it was none of his business.

Not impressed, Daizon said, "Dave knows you're having an affair. He thought it was with me. He's the one who left Amia for dead at my place and tried to set everything up to look like it was me. Amia followed him here with her friend. He went to my place and found them instead. Now he thinks I'm here with you." Daizon glanced at Kyle down by the fire. Then, as if some hearing delay finally sounded in his mind, Daizon shot his head back at Tonya. "How long ago did you hear the horn?"

Tonya glanced at the detective, as if finally noticing who it was. "Maybe five minutes ago." Tonya shook her head, absorbing everything. Her eyes widened. "He keeps his gun in his glove compartment."

Daizon's phone vibrated. He did not recognize the out-of-area phone number, but somehow knew it was Amia. "Hello, Amia?" He looked up at the fire and within a few steps quickly built up speed. "Run toward the fire, Amia. I'm on the other side with Detective Johnson."

Detective Johnson, at about the same time, received her own call. She was not far behind to start, but that fire was probably a few hundred yards away or more. Distances were deceptive in open spaces like the ocean and beach.

CHAPTER FORTY-SEVEN

SINNERS AND HEROES

E ventually the trail twisted around a half loop to a long beach. To the left, the beach seemed to end with a bunch of large black boulders; to the right, the boulders hung toward the tree line for a distance until rock fingers reached out to the ocean, not quite making it. A sliver of beach passed by the fingers.

Amia took her phone from her ear and tucked it into her pocket. She led Beth closer to the powerful rolling ocean surf to see past the rock fingers. There was a fire on the other side of them in the distance. She smiled at Beth. "Daizon and Detective Johnson are on the other side of that bonfire."

Rain fell in small droplets at first and built into a steady pelt. Lightning flashed over the ocean. A grumble of thunder followed. They glanced back to the path they came from, expecting Dr. Avendale at any moment, but there was nothing. He couldn't be too far behind. They ran.

Glances back showed a dark, windy, empty beach behind them. They scanned the blackness of the jagged tree line. A glance at each other, and they both suspected there had to be another trail from the parking lot. The lightning in the distance flashed them quick glimpses of an empty shoreline and jagged tree line.

Another flash of lightning highlighted a man walking toward them. He walked around the edges of the rock fingers they headed toward. With his muscular, wide upper body trimmed to a narrow waist, loose shorts, and muscular legs, he cast the shadow of a werewolf. He paused at the sight of them running toward him.

They slowed to a tentative walk. The tree line remained void of Dr. Avendale. The man before them was not Daizon or Dr. Avendale. Amia said, "It must be the owner of the truck we saw in the parking area." Hesitantly, they increased their speed again toward the man and the dimming fire behind him.

The rain's intensity increased with a cold gust of wind. Everything beyond twenty yards became a blur. Having noticed them, the man, more of a blurred shadow now, stayed where he was.

Thumping waves got louder and pushed farther up the shore. The crustacean smell faded into more of a wet earthiness. A suited shadow slid down the edge of the rock fingers from above. The big man did not see or hear the other man coming. Amia and Beth pointed and gave muffled shouts. "Watch out. He has a gun. Run."

Like something in slow motion, Dr. Avendale raised his gun and walked toward the big man. The big man ducked and charged at his assailant. Snap. Snap. Snap. There were three flashes and the big man did not move. He lay there on the rock finger. Dr. Avendale turned toward Amia and Beth as lightning cracked and thunder shook the earth.

⚓

Daizon passed the rain-dwindled fire toward the shadows of what he knew were rock fingers reaching out from the tree line. Kyle ignored Daizon's calls before he rounded the fingers. The wind and rain gave him plausible deniability as to whether he heard Daizon or not. Daizon knew the prick was probably laughing at his perceived situation. Kyle disappeared on the other side of the fingers.

Kyle would see Amia and Beth coming toward him on the other side and wonder what was going on. He'd probably parked at the private beach to avoid the obvious connection with Tonya. Kyle could have thought Daizon was Dave. A firearm produced muffled pops and flashes on the other side of the rocks. Then the storm showed what a real flash of lightning and crack of thunder was. Daizon glanced back at the detective. He knew Amia was over there, and he rushed to the other side of the rock fingers.

He approached the last slick rock finger with hurried caution. On the other side of the last finger, he saw Kyle lying still at the base of the rock. Amia and Beth ran toward Kyle and him. A greedy sense of relief spread through Daizon at the sight of Amia safe. She leaped into his arms and kissed him. Joy filled him as he held and kissed her. His sense of joy just as quickly dashed at the sight of Kyle. As he approached Kyle, Daizon searched the area for Dave, who was nowhere to be seen.

Amia said, "It was Dr. Avendale. He shot him. He glanced at us, turned, and just jogged off." Amia pointed to where the finger jetted out from above.

Daizon kneeled beside Kyle, who was facedown. "Kyle. Kyle." Daizon rolled Kyle over. His pulse was weak. Scanning his body, Daizon found Kyle shot in the chest up by the shoulder, twice maybe, and once more near his left hip.

Kyle opened his eyes. "Fuck." He coughed and found Daizon mixed with the rain pelting him. He squinted through the pain.

Daizon held Kyle down with minimal effort when he tried to get up. "Hold on, asshole. Help is coming."

Kyle coughed as he laughed. Kyle observed Amia and Beth, how Amia stood beside Daizon. Then Detective Johnson ran up with her pistol out and scanned the area. Kyle's grin grew.

Daizon tore his shirt into strips and wrapped them around Kyle's wounds. There was no hesitation about helping the man who had an affair with his girlfriend. He was selfless when it came right down to it. This was the man she knew. He was complex, but at his core he was a good and kind man who cared about others more than himself.

Kyle eyed Detective Johnson as she kept a vigilant watch. He could have been suffering delusions from his injuries, but she probably suspected this was his normal, from what Daizon had told her about him. Kyle told the detective, "Nice cuffs."

The corner of Detective Johnson's lips quirked up. Then she shook her head as she noticed Daizon watching. She called for an ambulance and advised the police. Seeing Amia and Beth okay, the detective asked, "Where'd he go?"

Amia pointed to the base of the rock finger again. "I think there's a trail up there."

Daizon added, "It's a path to the private beach parking area."

Amia shared a look with Beth. They knew they'd taken the long way around. Amia said to the detective, "Dr. Avendale is not thinking clearly right now. He had a blank gaze as he looked at Beth and me. It was almost to say if he wanted to kill me, he would have. He just jogged off. Where's Mrs. Avendale?"

Their attention swung in the house's direction. After a few quick minutes, several gunshots cut through the storm as muffled pops. Then there was silence, followed by wailing sirens. Sirens went to the home and the private parking area.

Daizon held on to Amia, and she held Beth's hand. Detective Johnson stayed beside Kyle.

⤜

They arrived at the Avendale residence minus Kyle, who left in an ambulance. Police led Mrs. Avendale to a squad car in handcuffs. With blood spatter on her face and clothes, she glanced at them in a trancelike state of shock.

Another ambulance showed. The lights from emergency vehicles flashed everywhere. A police officer exiting the home shook her head at the paramedics. Daizon gripped Amia's hand and forced a smile and nod. It was a bittersweet smile, filled with sadness and hope. He said as he held her, "Everything will be okay."

CHAPTER FORTY-EIGHT

HAPPY BEGINNINGS

It was the last day of the Whole Me program. Amia, dressed in her professional attire, led the final group exercise at the Zen Garden. She breathed with a hand held over her heart and a soft, warm smile. "May we be free from suffering. May we show kindness and compassion to others and ourselves. May we be well."

With a sense of accomplishment and euphoria, they all repeated her words. The only one not there was Daizon. Amia smiled both inwardly and outwardly as Tarah neared. Everyone approached one another with smiles, handshakes, and hugs. There were well wishes and numbers exchanged from friendships made.

These people were not alone in their own little worlds anymore. A warmth grew inside Amia; she knew she'd helped guide some of them on their journey. This was what she wanted to do with her life. It felt right.

Tarah said, "Girl, you've come a long way. You look like a confident beast warrior right now. You were inspiring before, but now, baby, you're damn well hot. Are you going to be there tonight?"

"I wouldn't miss tonight for the world. And trying your own material for the first time, I'm excited for you." They hugged.

A few more handshakes. Faith approached Amia with her generous smile and jovial nature. She carried herself straighter while maintaining an easy way about her. She opened her arms to Amia, and Amia accepted the offer. Faith said, "I'm stronger with your help, Dr. Wolf, and the help of the others. Y'all helped this mama feel worthy of some self-love. I love my babies more than anything, and I miss them so much. I can be stronger now for them and me. I can be weak, too. You and Dr. Wolf, you're blessings from the Lord."

"I feel blessed to have met you, Faith. How fortunate your babies are to have a mama like you. You've got this. You have my information if you need a friendly voice. I fully expect to see some of those pictures you promised me."

Faith grinned wide. "I'll do my best to not send too many at a time. Thank you, sweetie."

They broke apart, and Caitlyn stood there with her best nonchalant posture. Then she slid a grin at Amia's offer of a handshake, walked past, and embraced her for a hug. "You know I have to have a thick skin in what I do for work? Now I'm working on being soft-skinned sometimes too. It's difficult letting my guard down and letting people in, but I'm working on it. I need to surround myself with friends like you. You know, the ones that care about what's really going on. Who knows, maybe I can find my special somebody one day and share."

Releasing her from the hug, Amia said, "It feels good to open up to a friend, and I know those special somebodies are out there for all of us." She thought about her past relationships and then about Daizon. "It's hard opening that part of ourselves up because we know it leaves us open and vulnerable to the greatest pain. The thing is, if we don't open up, we never gain what we want in full.

I think it's a conundrum we all face when we begin a relationship. It's good to know we all go through those same struggles. I think anybody you let into your private bubble will feel as lucky as I do in knowing you. Thank you for allowing me in."

"You bitch. I'm supposed to be making you the teary-eyed one. You're making me rethink this bubble thing." Caitlyn winked.

Amia asked, "Are you going tonight?"

"And hear the mighty Nitrous perform her own music? You know I have to see what the fuss is about."

Amia smiled. "I'll see you there."

Rachael shook hands with Amia. She maintained a firm handshake. Inside her rugged demeanor, there was softness. Even now, it seemed difficult for her to let people see her soft side. She had a deep empathy for people but was very self-conscious of how they perceived her. Her way of coping with anger issues was by presenting a rugged profile and letting her emotions out in angry bursts. She learned how to create a sheath for her sharp edge so she would not cut the people she cared about most. She offered Amia a smile. "I'm not like everybody else. My coarse personality helps me cope with the assholes. I need that. The biggest difference is I know it's okay to be an asshole when I need to be, so I don't aim that anger at the people I love. I came here for Tina, my girlfriend, but being here and allowing myself to receive this care, that's something I'll always be grateful for. I did this. We did this." Rachael motioned to the large, jovial group.

"We did." Amia smirked. "We all have to let that inner asshole out every once in a while. It feels good to vent and share those feelings. We also need to remember too much stink and nobody wants to be around us."

"Roses need their thorns, right?"

Amia replied, "Yes, they do." They laughed, and Rachael patted Amia on the shoulder before she joined another group conversation.

Dr. Wolf graciously shook hands and conversed with Travis, Conner, Bill, Judy, Monica, and Maxie. They all had little side conversations going on as well. They basked in the positive energy flowing through the room. Dr. Wolf found Amia's gaze and nodded with a soft smile. Knowing she had Amia's attention, she cast her eyes around the room and nodded again at Amia as if to ask, Can you imagine a greater reward?

Dr. Wolf portrayed what was sometimes the hardest thing anyone could ever be—she was herself. She was her unapologetic, caring, and intuitive self. She was much more, but would also be the first to tell you she did not know everything and made her fair share of mistakes. She owned them in a way to show it was okay to be imperfect. Dr. Wolf was the epitome of what it meant to be your best self, not your perfect self.

CHAPTER FORTY-NINE

BLOOMING STARS

The parking lot at Shady Jay's Tavern overflowed with vehicles. Many of them parked on the hotel side of the parking lot and made reservations ahead of time, like she had done almost three months before. She'd never made it to her room that night. A three-quarter moon stood bright in the clear sky. Stars bloomed like flowers.

Most of the group was already inside. Beth had left the state and come back for this occasion. She wanted to know Tarah better as well. She sat with Amia until Daizon pulled up beside them. He pulled in on the same side as Beth. Beth said, "I'll be inside." She gripped Amia's hand and smirked. "I'll see you inside. Remember, he's just a guy." She winked, opened the door, and stood for a moment, looking at Daizon inside his metallic, midnight-blue Tacoma truck.

Beth held the passenger door open of Amia's rented hybrid SUV. She roamed her eyes over his choice of black slacks and a silky lavender short-sleeve shirt, the top few buttons undone. He had every bit of the heartthrob look everyone expected to see. Beth ducked her head back into the car. "Don't do what I would do. You might not make it inside." She pulled her head out and smirked at Daizon. She pointed two fingers at her eyes and then at his. "Don't forget, I have a Taser." She walked off.

"It's good to see you too, Beth."

Amia exited the safety of her driver's seat. It was a different kind of fear that had its grip on her. She stood, her muscles lacking coordination. She inhaled some anxiety-reducing breaths. Daizon stepped around the vehicle and slightly into her personal space. He said, "You look amazing."

She wore the same outfit from the night of the storm. "Thank you. It probably looks better dry."

His tiny smile grew into a big smirk, and he shook his head as if she had misunderstood. "Wet or dry doesn't matter. It's the way you wear it. You look amazing."

Amia smiled wide and found her legs worked as she pressed herself into him, her lips to his. Daizon swallowed her into his embrace. He pulled her into him with a firm, wanting grip. He didn't hold himself back the way he had at the Whole Me. Her skin danced with lightning wherever he touched her. It thrummed through her body. She matched his want with her own. A car door slammed shut somewhere in the parking lot. They smiled at each other as they glanced around the bustling parking lot, people pretending not to notice. They made a silent agreement—to be continued.

Amia gazed into his intense eyes. "How did it go with Tonya? How is she?"

"She's a mess. I let her know we didn't blame her for Dave's actions, that I'm still her friend. She told me that she didn't know you would be there. She meant well. Everything that happened to you . . . she was having a hard time accepting Dave would do those things. I let her know if it weren't for her insistence on me trying to find happiness, we never would have met. I told her I accepted the role after having a conversation with the producers about our expectations from each other and visions for the project."

Amia threaded her fingers with his and squeezed. She could tell it was difficult for him to see his friend suffering. She kissed his hand and smiled.

Daizon squeezed her hand back, acknowledging her invitation that it was all right to continue, that she would not betray his trust. "Tonya loved Dave, and she killed him. She told me the police found more evidence at one of their rental properties. She'll be wearing an ankle bracelet and confined to her home under the plea agreement. Knowing he would have killed her, along with what he did to you and Kyle, plus trying to frame me, that only dulls the pain she is in. It might even make her feel more responsible. I understand that kind of pain."

Amia hugged and kissed him again. She held him tight.

Inside Shady Jay's, they met the rest of the group. They had secured seats at the far corner of the dance area. Daizon noticed Kyle and Detective Johnson playing pool in the other room. Kyle had his arm in a loose sling. She rubbed against him in a teasing fashion, while occasionally tapping the handcuffs dangling at her side. She pushed him away and invited him in. Daizon wondered who might win as they jockeyed for control of their budding relationship. Then he wondered whether it was a relationship or relations.

Daizon introduced Amia to Nick and Ellie as they tended the bar. Amia seemed to recognize Ellie. They smiled at each other and shook hands as they exchanged greetings. Ellie winked at Amia and said, "I love your outfit. Have I seen you in here before?"

"Thank you, Ellie." Amia gave Daizon a subtle smirk. "My date showed up this time."

Ellie adopted a playful smirk of her own as she studied the two of them. She said to Amia, "Well, if this one gives you any trouble, I'm available."

Through her laugh, Amia said, "I'll let you know."

Seeing Amia relax in a playful, honest way helped Daizon relax. He worried how being at the place where her nightmare started would affect her. He wanted to be there for her and allow her space to enjoy her new friendships. What he was finding out was that they were there for each other.

Receiving their tavern special, strawberry lemonades, they headed toward the group of tables where the recently graduated participants of the Whole Me program congregated for their celebration. Daizon saw Conner at the bar and told Amia, "I'll be a minute."

She glanced at where he wanted to go and nodded her encouragement. She seemed to know there was something about Conner that affected him.

Nerves fluttering, Daizon stepped beside Conner. "Hi, Conner, can I talk with you for a minute?"

Conner seemed more comfortable than when they'd first met. The Whole Me program had obviously helped him. Still, Conner tensed as he said, "Sure."

Facing each other, Daizon inhaled deeply and tried relaxing. That simple gesture helped Conner ease his own posture. Daizon said, "I'm sorry. I haven't given you a fair shake. I tried not to let my feelings show, but obviously I failed. I wanted to let you know why."

Daizon inhaled another deep breath as Conner remained quiet, most likely not sure what to say. "When I was in fifth grade, I had a man attempt to rape me in a cemetery. I'm sure you don't want to hear the details, but the important part, why I acted the way I did toward you. He could be your doppelgänger. Obviously, he was a lot younger, but when I look at you, I see him."

Conner's expression softened. He said, "I'm sorry, Daizon. I don't know the right words. Are there right words?" He shook his head as he absorbed the information. "Really, you treated me pretty well. And now, knowing this? I'm amazed you were able to treat me the way you did. I've been bullied my whole life. Within my online games, in those skins, that's where I feel safe. Here, this is hard for me." Conner smiled and motioned to all the people mingling about Shady Jay's.

Daizon glanced around, nodding his understanding. "I pretend. I've never been comfortable around large groups of people either. My father used to tell me, 'People will see what they want to see.' Basically, if you act a certain way, that's what they will see. That advice got me to where I could cope, but I took it way too far."

Daizon reached out his hand, and Conner's spirits seemed to lift as he accepted the olive branch. Daizon patted Conner on the shoulder as they parted. "I'll see you over there."

He felt lighter as he approached the group and Amia at their booth. Amia leaned into him. "Anything you want to share?"

Daizon glanced at Conner and gave him an easy nod. "I owed him an apology." He opened his heart to Amia and shared the rest of his story.

More hugs and kisses followed. His respect for Amia grew, and somehow, from the way she leaned into him and said, "You're amazing," he knew she meant what she said. He knew her respect for him grew as well.

Sitting on the other side of the table, talking with Tarah, Beth seemed oblivious until their kisses gained her attention. She raised her eyebrows and cast her eyes between them. Beth and Amia shared some silent communications.

Amia joked with Beth, "Stop your gloating. It's not becoming."
Beth smiled wider, and the group laughed louder.

After the group had shared stories for a while, it was time for
Tarah to perform. Laughing beside him, with him, Amia leaned
in to Daizon's ear and breathed, "Have I told you what you do to
me?"

He hardened at the insinuation and adjusted himself with a
slight wiggle. He shook his head.

Amia grazed his inner thigh with a finger. She drew slow circles
and nipped his ear before assuming an innocent posture. She
watched him writhe with a grin.

Not having to feel guilty about playing along, not having to hold
himself back any longer, Daizon stroked a finger at the base of
Amia's neck. First, he worked a massage from her earlobes down
a V to the base of her neck and back again. Then he slid his hand
down her spine and back up. He varied the pressure from intense
to barely touching. When she shivered, he leaned into her ear and
breathed, "Tell me."

They paused their game as Tarah, or as she was better known,
Nitrous, stepped up to the microphone on the stage. Wearing a
cheeky smile, she stared straight at Amia, Daizon, Beth, and the
rest of the group. She had told Amia beforehand this would be her
first performance without hiding behind the drugs and makeup
she thought made the show possible. Sometimes the next steps
took place on old ground. This was her time. She wanted more
than singing in taverns, pubs, and bars. She wanted the world to
hear her voice.

Always too scared to take the next step, Tarah worried about
all the what-ifs, fears, and excuses. She'd gone to the Whole Me
program hoping she would find the strength and self-confidence
she only pretended to have. She went because she could not
pretend any longer.

Tarah gripped the microphone, and her presence demanded attention. She had shaved the side of her head, allowing her rose tattoo a clean stage. Her hair formed the shape of smooth flower petals that climbed and then wrapped around her head. She reached out with a glass of strawberry lemonade. She held it out in a toast. "Before I begin tonight, I want to thank some special friends. They helped make this world bearable." She saluted and drank. Then she aimed the glass at everyone else in the tavern. "Now, to all you lovely strangers, you're in for a treat. You can get out on the dance floor and move your feet. Or you can sit at your table and pound your meat. I have a brand-new story to start the night. Listen close as I share my plight. Grab your partner, grab your friend. This is the story about a heart on the mend."

Tarah stepped back as the drums conjured a quickening beat. One of the electric guitars sprang to life, and then the other. With clear and cunning eyes, Tarah scanned the audience and her friends. Her voice filled the room with glory, and the crowd erupted.

Chapter Fifty

Live and Love

Amia sat beside Daizon in his small aluminum boat. The twin electric motors reminded Amia of dragonflies as they hummed. A few wispy white clouds floated across the blue sky at eight in the morning. Glassy water split behind them in small waves as they headed toward the cove. A couple more weeks had passed since her class at the Whole Me program ended. Her practicum with Dr. Wolf had one more week. Graduate school and Daizon's new acting role started the week after. They worked on the details of how they would make their relationship work for both of them.

She grinned at the thought of spending more time with Daizon than was probably proper. Amia said no at first to Daizon's offer of staying with him while she finished her practicum. Technically, she still had a hotel room. She had paid for the entirety of her stay up front. Daizon offered his services to help her feel she was getting the most out of the single-bedroom suite. Before long, she took him up on both offers. Amia worried she was becoming an addict. The more Daizon gave of himself, the more she desired. Trying to understand her feelings for him, she knew it was much deeper than the sex. He filled her being with a sense of completeness. With him, she felt whole. Maybe that was why she had opened so completely to him.

Approaching the tall grass, she didn't recognize the area within the cove. Daizon set his hand over a fist she hadn't realized she'd made. His voice had a calmness to it that resonated within her. "I'm here and you're safe. Are you ready?"

Not realizing her throat had tightened and dried, she cleared it. "I'm ready."

Tall grass parted and opened to a gravel shore that seemed a tiny oasis. Daizon hopped out and tugged the boat farther onto the rocky beach. He held the boat steady as she climbed out. Lush green surrounded them. Their path through the tall grass opened a channel to view the lake. It was beautiful. As she turned to the rocky place where Daizon must have found her, she couldn't understand why her view seemed to narrow. Maybe it had something to do with the faded bloodstains where her head must have landed.

Black crept in from the corners of her world, and Daizon appeared in front of her. He was saying something, but she couldn't hear him. Holding her by the waist to steady her, he exaggerated a slow breath. He tried again. She couldn't understand what he wanted. Wanting to please him, she smiled as her eyes fluttered. A deep sense of calm washed over her.

Glowing with glittering skin, Daizon was with Amia in a field of flowers, holding her hand. His fingertips stroked her face ever so gently before sifting back through her hair. He said, "I love you, Amia. Breathe. You need to breathe. I won't let anyone hurt you. You're safe."

Amia pressed her own glittering hand to his beautiful face. She took his hand and said, "Come fly with me."

She stood, spread her wonderful wings, and he spread his. They leaped toward the bluest of skies and flew. They soared, and it was wonderful.

⤜

Amia woke in Daizon's room to find something at her feet, a small orange fluff ball attempting to get at her feet through the sheets. Her sense of time and place was off. She reached down and petted Jerry. She laughed, remembering her conversation with Daizon as he named him. He said, "I know Tom was the cat and Jerry the mouse. Doesn't he look more like a Jerry than a Tom, though?"

"He's going to develop a complex if he ever sees the cartoon."

Amia scratched Jerry's head and shook off the dizziness. *What time is it?* The clock beside the bed read 12:30. It was light outside, and she heard voices. She remembered— "The cookout!"

The water, boat, long grass, and Daizon telling her to breathe flashed in her mind. She gathered herself and freshened up in the master bathroom.

About to go searching for Daizon to apologize, she found him at the bedroom doorway as she left the bathroom. "I'm so sorry. I can't believe I fainted. Are you okay?"

Laughing, Daizon wrapped her in his arms. "I think that's my line. Are you okay?"

"I am. It took me a moment. I don't have any issues up here, at the house, or even on the lake, but it would seem my mind raced as we beached at the spot where it happened. We'll try again later."

Daizon bent down and gathered her eyes. He brushed her face with his feathery touch. Then he kissed her. "When you're comfortable." He kissed her again. "There's no rush." He glanced and nodded with a smirk toward the backyard. "Kyle, on the other hand, is testing how far Daryll will let him tease. Kyle thinks he can take Daryll even with his one arm hobbled."

Shaking her head, Amia laughed. "Go. Daryll has a lot of patience, but Kyle . . . How are the ladies holding up?"

Daizon grinned a devilish smirk and shook his head, trying not to laugh. She playfully slapped his shoulder and followed him out of the bedroom and to their group of friends, who were waiting with noisemakers and party hats. They sang "Happy Birthday." They were all out of tune. Tarah and Beth laughed. Kyle and Daryll cranked their noisemakers around in a circle.

Sherri nudged Detective Johnson, who seemed not so interested in showing off her singing voice. Then, carrying a large cake, Dr. Wolf beamed with a mischievous smile. Amia followed her to the coffee table, where she set it down.

Amia realized they were correct. It was her twenty-fifth birthday, and she had totally forgotten. She remembered her Nonna and the cakes she'd made over the years. On the verge of tears, she blew out the two and five candles. "Thank you! Thank you so much!"

Approaching with a large square package, Daizon said, "Happy Birthday. Detective Johnson helped me with this."

Amia tore off the pink wrapping. A chestnut frame had an image of Amia wearing her cap and gown, along with her brand-new silver earrings. She had her arms wrapped around her Nonna in front of the high school. She remembered the day. There was no wiping her tears away. Stunned, she wrapped her arms around Daizon and asked, "How?"

"The doctor's office she worked at had a box of her belongings in storage. They shared stories with me about how proud she was of you. They all signed the back and send their love."

Sure enough, the back contained several personalized messages. Daizon kissed her cheek and turned the frame back to the front.

He pointed out the engraving at the bottom, *Stelle per illuminare il cielo*. Amia translated aloud, "Stars to light the sky."

FROM THE AUTHOR

Thank you for reading or listening to *Stars to Light the Sky*. In the end, everyone who worked on this project did so intending to create the best possible product for the reader or listener. Any shortcomings are most likely mine. If you would like to leave an honest review, I would appreciate it. If you would rather not, that's okay too. Thank you either way.

I need to thank my wife for her support. She knows how much I would one day like to be a full-time author and allows me room to dream.

I've thanked the people I've worked with along the way to the completion of this book. Thank you again.

This book deals with difficult subject matter. I've tried my best at balancing entertainment and reality. I've read and studied a lot, as well as having my own experiences with seeking help. It's okay to seek help. There are hotlines, friends, family, and professionals that want to help you get better. If one doesn't work for you, try another, and another until you find what works for you.

"Neurons that fire together, wire together." Donald Hebb, 1949

ABOUT THE AUTHOR

Dennis is the author of *Stars to Light the Sky*, a romantic-suspense novel.

He writes about love, hope, pain, and healing, among other subjects, as he explores aspects of what makes us, us.

Dennis lives in Maine with his wife, Janet, and their three cats, Milo, Lui, and Ozzie. You'll find pictures and videos on his website and social media accounts.

You can find more information about the author and his book, along with news, special offers, and ways to stay in contact, on his website: https://dennisrcrocker.com.